ON LAND

Books

OTHER BOOKS

*Published by Forg

# DARK LIGHT DAWN

## JON LAND

### Created by Fabrizio Boccardi

A TOM DOHERTY ASSOCIATES BOOK

NEW YORK

DARK LIGHT: DAWN

A Forge Book
Published by Tom Doherty Associates
175 Fifth Avenue
New York, NY 10010

www.tor-forge.com

Forge® is a registered trademark of Macmillan Publishing Group, LLC.

The Library of Congress Cataloging-in-Publication Data
is available upon request.

ISBN 978-0-7653-2872-4 (hardcover)
ISBN 978-0-7653-9778-2 (ebook)

Our books may be purchased in bulk for promotional, educational, or business use. Please contact your local bookseller or the Macmillan Corporate and Premium Sales Department at 1-800-221-7945, extension 5442, or by email at MacmillanSpecialMarkets@macmillan.com.

First Edition: August 2017

Printed in the United States of America

0  9  8  7  6  5  4  3  2  1

## DEDICATION AND ACKNOWLEDGMENTS

Two for the price of one on this page, and a little story to boot. In 2006, my terrific publisher and friend, Tom Doherty, brought me together with Fabrizio Boccardi, a visionary entrepreneur who had an idea for a dark, modern antihero named Michael Tiranno, aka "The Tyrant." I hadn't written a book in a few years, but that didn't diminish Tom's faith in me in the slightest. He thought I was the right man for the job of helping Fabrizio realize his vision.

And, man, was he right.

While that kind of forethought still defines what makes a great publisher, I don't think even Tom could foresee how well received *The Seven Sins: The Tyrant Ascending* and *Black Scorpion: The Tyrant Returns* would ultimately become.

So when Fabrizio came up with the concept for a potential second series, he and Tom reached out to me again. Even though the notion of a horror-thriller was a bit out of my wheelhouse, they still had faith I could get it done.

Faith.

Not a word you see tossed around a lot these days about the publishing industry, and the story you're about to plunge into is a direct result of that faith. I've learned to place my faith in Fabrizio as well, because I know his pushing to make me better is what makes this book, in my (not so) humble opinion, the blast it is to read. That's the greatest compliment I can give a collaborator and, in this case, the creator of and creative force behind *Dark Light: Dawn*.

So thank you, Tom, and thank you, Fabrizio. This book is dedicated to both of you for giving me the opportunity to do what I love the most.

In the beginning,

when God created the heavens and the earth,

The earth was a formless wasteland,

And darkness covered the abyss.

# DARK
# LIGHT

# PROLOGUE

## 65 Million Years Ago

The asteroid hurtled through space at sixty thousand miles per hour. Unburdened by gravity, unnoticed by the primitive planet to which it was headed, it was little more than a speck set against a black galactic vacuum, until it turned into a fireball upon entering the planet's atmosphere.

Just as the asteroid had encountered nothing in its path along the journey that had covered billions of years, so it encountered nothing to slow the force of its impact now. When it struck the planet that would eventually be called Earth, the asteroid unleashed energy a billion times that of the nuclear bombs that would be unleashed to end a war sixty-five million years later.

Impact instantly created a massive crater nearly twenty miles in diameter, emitting a massive pulse of infrared radiation that killed all life within a radius the size of half the United States today. So too the incredible wash of heat, stretching into the thousands of degrees, ignited firestorms that dotted the globe like thousands of giant bonfires lit simultaneously that burned until there was nothing left to ingest.

Compared to the effects that followed, though, all that was nothing.

The impact inhibited photosynthesis by creating a blanket of dust that blocked sunlight for up to a year. Further, the asteroid vaporized tons of sulfur-rich carbonate rock, creating a massive cloud of sulfuric acid that turned day to virtual night. And the ensuing lack of sunlight over a prolonged stretch of time caused a chain reaction that turned ocean waters acidic, all marine life left to join the plants and land-based animals on a path toward certain death.

Viewed from space, where the asteroid had entered the atmosphere, the struggle of the sun's rays to penetrate the dust cloud created an eerie halo effect, a strange glow that reached all the way to the Earth's surface.

A dark light.

# ONE

### Yucatán Peninsula, Mexico; 1990

Perhaps, *señor*, your findings were wrong," José Herrera of Mexico's Ministry of Interior told Dale Denton.

"Bullshit," Denton shot back, "I'm not paying this surtax, as you call it, and then have you still shut us down."

Herrera ran his gaze along the bevy of pumping apparatus erected over the rocky, uneven terrain. "It would seem at this point there is nothing to shut down."

Nearby, a fleet of mobile storage tanks sat idle in a neat row, their shiny finishes coated by a thin layer of dust whipped about by the wind. Across the side of the nearest, someone had drawn a message in the dust:

*Las Tierra del Diablo* . . .

"What's that mean exactly?" Denton asked Herrera.

"It means 'the Land of the Devil,' *señor.*"

"More bullshit," groused Denton. "How much more of a payoff to the local bosses do I have to make to end the vandalism?"

Herrera's expression remained flat, still fixed on the message scrawled across the truck's side. "In these parts, such things are inevitable."

"Really? You want to know what else is inevitable, José? Losing every dollar my partner and I have sank into the project because our equipment keeps getting sabotaged."

"There's no evidence of that at all, *señor.*"

"Maybe not, but it's the best explanation I can come up with for why our pumps stopped working before they pulled an ounce of oil out of the ground. Somebody doesn't want us here, *amigo*, probably the same people who like defacing our trucks. I thought I paid off every official in the phone book to make sure shit like this didn't happen. Isn't that right, Professor?" Denton asked, turning to the older man just behind him.

Though it was early in the morning, Professor Orson Beekman was already sweating up a storm, dabbing constantly at his brow and swabbing his face with an already moist rag he carried, hanging out his back pocket. He offered up a nod, but nothing more.

"In any event, I cannot control all of the locals," Herrera insisted defensively. "And we advised you to invest in the local economy."

"You mean another bribe."

Herrera shrugged, his lips flirting with a smile. "The price of doing business."

"Except we're flat busted, everything tied up in all the iron, steel, and rubber you see before you. Why don't you get the boss, or mayor, or whatever here so I can have a one-on-one with him?"

"Chief," Herrera corrected. "The locals here are Indians."

"Running around with blow guns and wearing grass skirts, something like that?"

Herrera looked offended, expression wrinkling in displeasure. "They are a civilized people, *señor*. Grateful for the work your presence here brings them."

Denton's gaze strayed to the side of the defaced mobile storage tanker again. "They don't act like it, *amigo*. I need to get with my partner on this to figure out where we go from here. Tell you one thing, though: it won't be to the bank."


Just after Herrera departed, Ben Younger jogged up over the ridge from the gulley. He and Dale Denton were the same age, but Younger looked ten years less than his thirty-five years while Denton looked ten years more. They'd been business partners almost since the day they'd graduated college together, encountering reasonable success at a trio of energy and technology start-ups until both realized their ambitions stretched far beyond their current means. So they pooled every dollar they could scrounge up to buy mineral rights to oil and gas reserves here in the Yucatán that had continually frustrated the much larger energy interests, only to encounter those same frustrations. Almost from the beginning, the site had been riddled by a continual series of odd, often inexplicable circumstances that involved broken equipment, work crews growing violently ill, and pumps failing to pull up oil that maybe wasn't there after all.

All those big conglomerates that had preceded them here had all given up, having concluded that whatever oil might've been as much as five miles underground wasn't worth the resources they were expending and constant setbacks they were experiencing. Rumors that the land was actually cursed or haunted had made retaining local work crews a challenge and further opened the door for Denton and Younger. Either they'd strike it rich in the blink of an eye, or go broke almost as fast. A matter of risk versus reward, and so far there'd been no reward for all the risk they'd assumed in staking their claim here.

The first challenge was finding the elusive oil reserves, and for this they turned to the mercurial geophysicist Orson Beekman, who'd been fired from every job in the industry he'd ever held. Beekman, though, claimed to have developed a new means of detecting oil deep below ground level without the expense or bother of drilling exploratory wells. The team of Younger and Denton brought him in as a partner with a twenty percent stake in the company's equity, which currently amounted to considerably less than zero.

Professor Beekman's work had begun with an exhaustive analysis of the potential oil reserves this area might well contain. In 1978, geophysicists Antonio Camargo and Glen Penfield were working for the Mexican state-owned oil company Petróleos Mexicanos, or Pemex, as part of an airborne magnetic survey of the Gulf of Mexico north of the Yucatán peninsula. Penfield's job was to use geophysical data to scout possible locations for oil drilling. In the data, Penfield found a huge underwater ring forty miles across. He then obtained a gravity map of the Yucatán made in the 1960s that suggested an impact feature. Penfield found another arc on the peninsula itself, the ends of which pointed northward. Comparing the two maps, he found the separate arcs formed a circle, over a hundred miles wide, centered near the Yucatán village of Chicxulub. Penfield felt certain the shape had been created by a cataclysmic event in geologic history, and not just any event either:

He was convinced he'd found the crater left by the asteroid that struck the Earth sixty-five million years ago, causing the Ice Age.

As a footnote to that, Penfield's report indicated no evidence of the oil reserves he'd expected to find and that the larger oil companies had previously believed had been there as well. What it failed to note, and what Beekman had learned firsthand from Penfield himself, was that he'd stopped looking before actually completing his fieldwork. Beekman had taken Penfield's original research, applied some new algorithms and his own geothermal research and determined that the oil reserves others had

dismissed as echoes were actually miles beneath what the older technologies were capable of mining. But new deep bore and slant drilling had
changed that paradigm, though to what level, nobody really knew, any
more than they knew whether the quantity of reserves justified the inor-
dinate expense of pulling them up.

Of course, none of that had helped the energy giants who'd previously
staked their claim here, only to have their efforts waylaid and ultimately
upended by a series of mind-numbing misfortunes that kept occurring
no matter how many precautions were put into place. So Dale Denton
and Ben Younger had stepped into that vacated chasm, willing to risk the
whole of their collective assets, and more, on the area's untapped potential. Their work had essentially picked up where Penfield's had left off,
cutting a deal with the latest incarnation of Petróleos Mexicanos to share
any revenue on a sliding scale in return for the mineral exploration rights.
For their part, Mexican officials thought their new American partners
were crazy for even trying, after others had cut their losses and pulled out.
They were clearly out on a limb here, the officials going along because the
work padded their pockets and kept their families well fed, even if Denton's and Younger's were about to go hungry.

Simply stated, Ben Younger and Dale Denton wanted to be tycoons,
multi-millionaires whose families would want for nothing. They'd married their wives within a month of each other eight years ago, but both
couples remained childless. Ben and his wife Melissa had failed to conceive at every turn and, having exhausted virtually every medical option,
were now considering adoption. Dale and his wife Danielle had encountered only marginally better results in the form of two pregnancies that
had both ended in miscarriages. Since he'd been down here, Ben missed
Melissa terribly, while Dale Denton managed a single call to Danielle
every week, keeping it as short as possible.

And right now, both men were wondering if they'd ever see their wives
again.

"I think maybe we're gonna need to disappear for a while," Dale Denton
said, trailing Ben Younger across the field.

Younger stopped in an area marked by cones where Orson Beekman's
seismological studies had identified potentially vast reserves of oil the exploratory drilling rigs had theoretically tapped into. They'd been re-

placed by massive extraction pump apparatus connected to feed lines going down between three and five miles, deeper maybe than anyone had ever drilled before. So far, despite all indications to the contrary, the massive pumpjack machines hadn't produced a single barrel of oil, much less a reservoir. And then, just yesterday, all work ceased after pressure readings rose into the red, in the wake of an underground tremor that had likely caused a snare in the line feeding air and oil-mud downward.

"Disappear for a while," Ben repeated. "Meaning what?"

"Meaning where do you think I got the money to fund the pumping part of the job, partner? Sure thing, right, so I did what I had to do."

"I cosigned the damn loan documents for the bank," Younger said, the Mexican sun roasting his skin.

"Yeah," Denton smirked, trying for a wink, "had you fooled good there, didn't I? Next time, I'd recommend reading the fine print."

"I trusted you to take care of the financing."

"And I did. Only what the bank lent us ran out faster than expected. I got the rest from the kind of people who don't rewrite their notes. We don't pay up in a timely fashion, we're not just fucked, we're dead."

"And you didn't think to ask me first?" Ben shook his head. "You give a whole new meaning to the word *asshole*."

"Yeah, partner, spelled R-I-C-H. Because that's what we're gonna be. Just gotta be patient."

"If we don't end up dead first, you mean." Younger paused. "I don't know how I let anything you do surprise me anymore. Maybe I'll just go home. Pretend we never met and start over."

"But you won't, will you, partner? You won't because deep down you want this as bad as I do and are willing do whatever it takes, just like I am."

"You better hope so, because that's the only thing that can save both our asses. And, as it turns out, I've got an idea," Ben said.

"It better be a good one."

Ben lifted his gaze back up out of the hole. "Well, let me put it this way, Dale. If I can pull this off, we're saved, and if I can't, I'll just be dead a bit quicker than you."


Ben led Denton into the center of their array of drilling rigs to a jagged fissure in the ground caused by the underground tremor that had put their efforts even further behind. The two stood over it, gazing down into a shaft-sized abyss, where the snarl in the primary feeder line had been identified nine hundred feet down.

"We should have used brine, instead of oil-rich mud," Ben said, "like the engineers told us."

"I don't remember you complaining when you saw the difference in expense. But, sure, whatever you say, partner. So we pay the freight and switch to the brine formula," Denton agreed. "Problem is that won't cure the clog that's about to bankrupt us. What we need is industrial strength Drano."

"Or the next best thing: me," Ben said, casting his gaze into the abyss once more. "I'm going down there to fix the damn thing."

Denton shook his head. "Sounds like the water down here has finally softened your brain."

Ben pointed down into the darkness. "You're looking at a fresh opening carved into one of the deepest cave systems in the world. Geological sonar readings indicate there's plenty of room to maneuver down there, so I should be able to reach the snarl in the line."

"Exactly how much do you want to die in that fucking hole?" Denton asked, looking up from the chasm.

Ben stared Denton right in the eye. "You should have thought of that before you signed our lives away. So, hey, what have I got to lose?"

# TWO

## Yucatán Peninsula, Mexico; 1990

A portion of the team of workers idled by the stoppage drilled a series of stakes through the ground face and into the layers of rock and shale below. Then heavy-duty climbing rope was strung around them for maximum support. The seven-sixteenths diameter rope came in two-hundred-foot lengths. They had five on site that, once fastened together, would give Younger a thousand feet.

"So what's the record for an underground descent?" Denton wondered.

Ben was testing the array of carabiners clipped to his belt. "Two thousand feet into the Huautla cave right here in Mexico I believe, part of the same system as this one, carved out in prehistory. I'll only need to manage half of that."

"Well," Denton said, shaking his head, "that's a relief."

In the trees around them, families of spider monkeys suddenly appeared and began cackling and hooting louder, as if to laugh at them. A few angry ones, Ben noticed, were throwing shit at each other, an apt metaphor for what he felt his world was going to.

"I hate the word *should*. Never heard it used in any way that was even remotely reassuring."

Ben might have been a veteran mountain and rock climber, but the challenge here dwarfed any he'd experienced before. No matter how arduous, or even impossible, the task, at least when climbing he had a route to follow, the terrain ahead mapped in advance. Here he was descending blind with no idea whatsoever what awaited him, with forty pounds of gear—in the form of tools and materials he needed to repair the snare in the line—on his back. A thousand feet might not have been a relatively great distance outside with his eyes to guide him, but underground, amid utter darkness, Ben wasn't sure how much his experience really helped.

First time for everything, he supposed.

"You and that adventure streak of yours aside, you've never done anything in conditions like this," Denton said, pretty much summing up Ben's own thoughts.

"The only condition that matters at this point, Dale," Ben told him, "is that of our bank account. Now, get the men ready to lower me into the chasm."

The first stretch into the fissure opened by the underground tremor came easily, Ben holding the rope with both gloved hands, as it slowly lowered him through the expanse that resembled the width of a submarine corridor, barely big enough for two. He reached the end of the first of the five ropes with nary an issue, starting in on the second in identical fashion until the cave widened and sloped to the left toward the actual location of the stuck feeder line.

Big oil companies, Ben reflected, maintained huge exploration budgets for potential underground reserves in previously untapped locations like the Yucatán. The cutting edge technology to first determine the location of such reserves and then drill down to reach them had changed the face of oil exploration forever, while still leaving it in the hands of a few mega-conglomerates like Texaco, Exxon, and Royal Dutch Shell. They could afford a misfire and the tens of millions in losses that came with it, while a start-up like the one founded by him and Dale Denton had no such luxury. The few borrowed millions they had tied up in this venture, first in the geophysical surveys that had identified the reserves and then the much greater expense to construct the drilling and pumping apparatus, had maxed out everything they could leverage on their limited assets. So, even before dwindling funds forced Dale Denton to borrow money off the street, they were essentially betting their futures on what was essentially a fifty-fifty proposition at best. Driving stakes literal and figurative into land abandoned by local and foreign interests alike, scared off by an area soured by bad luck and riddled by rumors and superstition.

In that moment, as he threaded his way through the increasingly narrow channel, Ben Younger was glad his wife Melissa couldn't have kids. What would have happened to them, after all, growing up broke and fatherless on the chance he died down here?

He plucked the walkie-talkie from his belt and pressed the TALK button. "How's the weather up there, Dale?"

"Hot as hell, partner."

"Then you'd love it down here. Thirty degrees cooler and sinking. How far down am I?"

"Looks like you've gone through maybe three-quarters of the second rope. You should be at the source of the snarl in the line before you know it."

"Can't wait."

"Say the word and we'll pull you out of there."

"Just make sure you pull hard."

Ben clipped the walkie-talkie back to his belt and continued working his way down, the shifting angle of the fissure resembling more of a corkscrew, until it widened appreciably to allow for a comfortable descent. Ben fell into an easy rhythm not unlike the sensation of rappelling down a sheer mountain face with few handholds. The dark complicated matters, much different than night he'd grown accustomed to and even comfortable within. This was more utter blackness with nothing to break it other than his dome light that shined weakly in whatever direction he turned, barely making a dent in the nothingness before him.

*Las Tierra del Diablo* . . .

That message flashed through his mind again, not so much for the words themselves as the empty, idled tanker across which they were scrawled. It made him think of the long line of vehicles that, should they all remain empty, meant bankruptcy. Great motivation to keep himself going.

The rope continued to spiral out as he continued along the cave's winding shape. The easy descent allowed Ben to recover his bearings, knowing he'd be level with the snag in the line just before the thousand-foot mark. That meant he'd be cutting things very close, no rope to spare and the odds of success getting lower the deeper into the cave he dropped.

Ben felt himself struck by the rapid, panicked breathing consistent with claustrophobia. He might have scaled some of the highest peaks in the world, but that said nothing for his ability to negotiate much tighter spaces like this so far beneath the ground instead of towering over it. He used his watch to check the depth of his descent and found, thankfully, he was closing on the snarl in the line that pumped oil-mud downward to force the contents of the crude back up. And, sure enough, another hundred feet found him drawing even with the point where the dark gray shape of Kevlar tubing that formed the feeder line had been snared by a jagged rock formation resettled by the tremor.

Ben again snatched the walkie-talkie from his belt, stopping briefly when the walls around him seemed to shift and move. Ben waited for the illusion to subside, continued anyway when it didn't.

"Dale, do you read me?"

Nothing but static answered his call.

"Dale, this is Ben, come in."

Still nothing.

"Dale, do you copy?"

When his call still garnered no response, Ben turned his attention to the task before him. There was no way to unsnare the line without tearing the fabric. So he used a small, battery-operated cutting tool to open the feed line on both sides of the snarl, careful to hold fast to the lower portion so it didn't fall. With that process complete, he fished a bypass device Beekman had rigged for him from his pack and threaded it. Then he worked an epoxy, impervious to heat or pressure, around the bypass joints, to make sure the line was airtight, assuring an unobstructed flow of oil-mud downward.

*I did it!*

Ben had never felt more triumphant, until a gust of wind rattled him, shaking him in his dangling perch above nothing but black empty air. Air neither hot nor cold surging more through, than past him. The feeling, like none he'd ever experienced, dappled his arms with gooseflesh. It was as if he'd been sucked into the canister of a vacuum cleaner in the ON position. Even after the brush of air passed, he continued to feel something swirl around inside him, making him feel woozy and forcing him to blink the life back into his blurring eyes.

Suddenly, Ben felt a surge of heat emanating from nowhere and everywhere at the same time. Then it turned cold, frightfully cold, pushing a chill through Ben that left a pulsing throb in his head like some kind of whole-body brain freeze.

*I'm down too deep.*

The instant he formed that thought, something jerked the line from above. Ben passed it off to a miscommunication at the other end of the line above the surface and snatched the walkie-talkie from his belt. He fumbled it upward precariously in the same hand grasping the heat gun.

"What the hell, boys?"

No response.

"Dale, you there? I'm all done down here. Mission accomplished."

No response again.

"Dale, this is Ben, come in!"

Nothing greeted his call, not even static this time. Just dead air, the same air that seemed to be everywhere around and inside him, the world starting to spin, stealing his sense of balance as the wooziness returned.

*What's happening to me?*

He'd done some scuba diving, too, deeper than he should have at times, and knew what it was like to be trapped in a black, endless void. The surreal sense of surrender that sets in when you have to listen to your heartbeat to know you're alive.

This far underground, just over the point where he would've needed oxygen to survive, survival could be precarious indeed. Such depths could also cause dizziness and delirium; Ben was struck by that very sensation as the entire chasm seemed to quake and bounce, stealing his sense of equilibrium. Then he realized it wasn't a product of the depth at all, rather of yet another seismic tremor that shook the walls, now seeming to extend outward around him. It felt as though he was dropping through the emptiness, falling into the void.

And then he was, watching the severed rope shrink in shape and then disappear altogether as he fell.


Dale Denton felt the tremor too, felt it in his core, as well as in the maddening vibrations of the rope in the work crew's collective grasp.

"Pull him up! Pull him up!" Denton ordered, not bothering to disguise the panic in his voice.

There was more, he realized: the monkeys. They were screeching and shrieking even louder, the group that had been throwing shit at each other going at it with claws and teeth. Fur and blood flew, no quarter given by either side.

The unrestrained fury spread, from animal to animal and tree to tree, until the shrieking made Denton cringe. Then a few of the monkeys jumped out of the trees and lurched about aggressively, scampering uncomfortably close to him and his workers with teeth bared and snapping.

Those workers were pulling up on the rope in a desperate fury. Hands lashed across each other in a virtual blur, drawing the rope from the abyss and leaving it to collect in a pile that looked like giant strands of spaghetti.

Denton tossed handfuls of rocks at the monkeys to chase them back, but they held their ground, seeming to grow bolder, while their brethren in the trees continued to tear each other apart. He turned his attention from them to lend his efforts to his workers struggling to pull Ben Younger back to the surface.

By then, though, the rope was coming too fast, too easy. And too much, too much rope. Ben Younger had been down just over nine hundred feet of the thousand feet when the unspooling started.

"Ben! Ben!" Denton cried out into his walkie-talkie.

But only white noise greeted him, whistling wind sounds that reminded him of a banshee's screams.

"Ben!" he yelled into the mouthpiece again, as the end of the rope emerged through the entrance to the underground cave, shredded as if something had bitten through it.

# THREE

## Yucatán Peninsula, Mexico; 1990

A ledge in the widening shaft had broken his fall. Ben moved his upper body first; neck, then shoulders, then arms, finding everything intact and in working order. He must've instinctively tried to grab at the shaft face for a handhold, leaving both his palms scraped raw, even through his gloves. His chin and forehead were bleeding, likely from banging up against the face as he dropped. He touched the wounds and felt his fingers come away wet and warm. He'd lost his helmet and its dome light in the fall, so he couldn't be sure of anything around him, his world utterly black.

He'd taken the brunt of the impact on his left leg, currently curled under him. He moved it gingerly in manual fashion, recalling the lessons of what to do when sustaining a fall while rock climbing. He catalogued the injury as best he could, checking to make sure at the very least no bone had penetrated the skin. There was numbness and swelling, but not a lot of pain yet. And he found he could move his toes and turn his foot from left to right inside his boot. He felt for his walkie-talkie but it was gone, shed somehow during the fall or, perhaps, on impact, leaving Ben to resist the absurd temptation to shout up the length of the shaft at the top of his lungs.

*Is this how it ends?*

Ben had barely formed that thought when he caught a flicker of light just off to his right. It was there and then gone, then flickered again like a weak, stubborn strobe. He groped his hand out toward the source, careful not to put any pressure at all on his broken or badly sprained leg. His bloodied palm scraped metal and then his hand closed on the hard hat with dome light affixed to its front, pulling it toward him.

The bulb had loosened and the fitting bent, but he was able to maneuver the bulb to find the contact points well enough to make it stay on beyond a flicker, so long as he didn't jar it. Instead of redonning the hard hat, Ben rotated it slowly about the ledge he'd landed upon.

The shaft continued spiraling downward before him, fortune the only thing that had spared him the full drop. The opposite wall face featured scaled impressions more like the hand and foot holds he was used to when rock climbing. If he could reach it, he might be able to pull his way upward even with a useless leg.

Ben aimed his dome light forward and up from the ledge, forming a plan. But the bulb was flickering again, rebelling against him, until he stilled the hard hat and it caught. He again worked the fittings the best he could to stabilize it, careful not to snap the whole housing off, the bulb angling sharply to the right in the process and catching something he first took to be his lost rope. Only it wasn't a rope at all.

It was the Kevlar feed line, continuing its descent through the void toward the oil-rich pockets of magma he and Dale Denton were betting their lives lay below.

The world wobbled in and out of the half-light cast by his hard hat's flickering bulb. Ben eased it back into place over his skull gingerly, hoping for the best. Then he rose all the way on his good leg and started, ever so slowly, to put pressure on his bad one. This as he extended his hand toward the feed line to use as a brace.

When his leg gave out.

Ben flailed desperately, groping at air, hand finding hold upon the line when a burst of agony surged through him, the fractured bone separating against the weight asked of it. He screamed, but squeezed harder instead of letting go. Fingers tight around the line, starting to pull himself upward.

*Could he make it back to the surface this way, could he actually scale a thousand feet of feeder line?* Ben had no choice, kept shifting hand over hand, shimmying with his working leg while his shattered one dangled numb and useless.

He rocked sideways and slammed into the jagged face, planting his good leg on a second ledge barely wide enough to hold him. He clung fast to the Kevlar with his stronger right hand and probed the face for a hold with his left. There was another ledge just over his head and he flailed for it, rocking on the Kevlar tubing until his left hand closed on the ledge and he prepared to add his right as well.

Until the ledge came apart with a tumble of black rubble behind it. Ben barely managed to grab firm hold of the feed line again, the momentum slamming him into the face and bouncing him backward into a precarious sway over the dark emptiness below. He smacked the face again, less hard this time, and recoiled away.

His dome light caught something in its flickering glow resting inside a chasm revealed by the tumbling rubble. As his vision cleared, though, Ben realized the object he spotted was glowing all on its own. An eerie, translucent sheen from what looked like some kind of lava-coated rock bored through with equidistant holes from which the glow emanated.

*Impossible* . . .

Ben closed his eyes, opened them again. The rock was still there, still glowing just outside his reach. Something made him reach out toward it, but the feed line jerked downward, leaving Ben desperately flailing for something, *anything*, to grab on to. He was trying for the ledge, to save himself from falling, when his outstretched gloved hand slid into the chasm instead.

And closed on the glowing rock.

Back on the surface, amid the swirling panic, the four generators powering the exploratory drilling rigs exploded one after the other in sequence, starting from the one closest to the hole to the farthest away.

Dale Denton had been around his share of explosions and knew his way around dynamite. But these were different. He felt them in the pit of his stomach, his very core, as if they were sucking the oxygen out of the air. He passed it off to his imagination until a glance toward Beekman showed the scientist looking as if the air had been drained from his lungs.

"Professor!" he cried out, taking the older man by the arms. "Professor!"

Shaking him now, trying to force the life back into his eyes.

The generators continued to spark, then flame. Field workers rushed toward them wielding fire extinguishers like M16s. Denton heard secondary popping sounds, followed by something fizzling.

"What's happening?" Beekman gasped in a high-pitched wail that carried his voice over the shrieks of the monkeys.

Amid all the ear-wrenching screeching, Denton realized the monkeys were tearing each other apart. Not just blood and fur flying anymore, but also tufts of flesh and limbs torn from their joints. He thought he glimpsed one monkey triumphantly jerking the severed head of a fallen one into the air, jumping up and down on a tree limb until a trio of the animals dropped upon him; the victorious squeals morphed into a blistering anguish as one severed head and then another hit the ground. All this while the animals that had already dropped to the ground were hooting and cackling; attention swung from the workers back to what was unfolding in the trees.

"What's happening?" Beekman gasped again.

Denton was still holding him by the shoulders. "You tell me, Professor."

Only slightly bigger in diameter than his palm, the rock Ben had inadvertently grasped seemed to pulsate with raw energy, while radiating the strangest light he'd ever seen.

*A dark light*, Ben thought.

Suddenly, he felt a pleasant soothing warmth surging through him that made everything seem just fine in spite of his plight. He jerked the rock toward him from its resting place, just clearing the chamber the tumbling rocks had revealed, when a sensation that was blistering hot and icy cold at the same time seared his palm through his glove. His fingers jerked open involuntarily and before he could close them again, the rock was falling, that strange dark light emanating from its very core swallowed by the darkness.

Ben felt a rumbling in the pit of his stomach, realized it was everywhere around him, the entire cave rattling as if ready to break apart, hard enough to threaten his grip on the feed line. His fingertips felt warm, then felt like nothing at all. He was struck by the illusion that he was holding nothing at all, just hanging free in the air. Falling.

*Am I dying?*

He must have landed on another ledge, but was afraid to feel for the edge. The eerie dark light of the rock that had fallen with him carved fissures through the darkness, and Ben stretched a hand out for it, when something brushed past it. Then he felt the same sensation against his face, the back of his head, felt it all around him.

*Bats*, Ben realized, *waves and waves of bats* . . .

They were everywhere, a vast black curtain closing over his world, wings passing close enough to hear their flutter. In their panicked rage, some of the bats flew right into him, seeming to bounce off before they could snare on his equipment. Ben made himself as small as he could, turned one way and then another with no effect.

His light-headedness remained when the bats flew en masse upward and disappeared into the blackness above him. And then Ben was struck by the odd sensation that he was falling again, when he really wasn't. Flailing for something to grasp, when there was nothing but darkness to claim him.

Back on the surface, Dale Denton felt the rumbling too. The ground, the brush and trees that bordered the field all seemed to be shaking, accompanied by a scorching hot blast of air that singed the hairs on the forearms beneath his rolled-up sleeves. Everything, the entire world, seemed to be shaking. Something like static electricity raised gooseflesh to his arms and set the hairs on the back of his neck standing on edge. He realized the surviving, still-shrieking monkeys were fleeing now, scampering away in all directions and leaving their dead behind.

Then a black wave burst out of the hole down which Ben Younger had vanished. It made Denton think of an oil slick, until he discerned flapping wings and realized it was bats, unleashed from their underground lair with relentless ferocity. Their path taking them over the fleeing hordes of monkeys, whipping the animals into a renewed frenzy, with the sky's light suddenly stolen from them.

The air grew even more prickly, as if an electrical storm had seized the area without a cloud in sight. Denton had the sense something impossible was happening, the world coming apart from its very core like a frigid window cracking when exposed to a sudden blast of heat. The bats seeming to dive bomb the fleeing monkeys, swarming and swallowing them in an endless black blanket of rage, as a second wave attacked the workers who swatted at them desperately with bare hands or whatever tools they could find. A few brave ones raced to help their fellow workers whose faces were being ravaged by the concentrated attack, the bats fleeing with bloody pieces of flesh still stuck to their teeth.

The world seemed to bob and weave in rhythm with the crazed gyrations of the bats, as if they were dragging the planet behind them. Gazing off into the distance, Denton saw ribbons of darkness seeming to soak the air, the screeching of the monkeys ebbing now to a mere flutter before dissipating altogether.

"Oh God, oh God, oh God," Beekman mumbled, before sinking to his knees in terror.

Denton couldn't chase all the screaming and wailing from his ears, until another sound drowned them out. The familiar *whoosh-whoosh* of the drills driving downward, slicing through earth, shale, and limestone for the oil that had drawn him here. Working again, even though the generators powering them had exploded.

Moments later, the ground ruptured in all the places well lines had been run, ruptured to allow torrents of tarry oil sands to burst out of the ground in fountains of black. They burst from all the drills at once, tearing the big derricks from their moorings and opening uncapped holes in the earth from which the fountains were free to flow in constant geysers that climbed for the sky. Denton was able to reason quite coherently that too much feed pressure had blown each and every one of those lines. But no rational explanation existed for how it could happen simultaneously with this degree of force. Just as rational thought couldn't explain how oil rigs lacking a power source could have switched themselves back on.

The windblown gushers of black ooze seemed to mesh higher in the sky, a curtain of darkness raining downward to coat Dale Denton with the means to secure his future.

Ben Younger awakened to the feeling he was glued to the ground, groggy and light-headed with no clue where he was or how he'd gotten there. He looked up to see he was partially submerged in an oozing swamp of mud and muck. He sat up, realizing his clothes and skin were sticky with a black sheen of unrefined oil, tar black and thick as oatmeal in patches. He tried to get his bearings, push his memory for how he'd gotten wherever he was exactly, but there was nothing after the darkness had seemed to claim him down in the cave.

*I must've passed out*, Ben reasoned.

And, somehow, he'd managed to climb out a different shaft of the underground cave that had left him here.

*Unless I'm dead.*

But the soak and smell of the crude oil with which he was covered told him he wasn't. They must've been on the verge of hitting, when the feed line was snared. Bypassing the snare was all it took to unearth reserves so vast, the initial flow came too fast to get the well caps in place.

In other words, he and Dale Denton had done it.

In the distance, an ink blotch seemed to have leaked over a world turned rich and black with oil hurdling into the air, the blowout preventers woefully ill-equipped to handle such pressure. Ben pictured the secondary capping procedures being put into effect, imagined Dale Denton supervising the process, drenched in oil that flew off him like sweat and spittle as he raced about.

Ben literally pinched himself to make sure he was awake, to make sure this wasn't some near-death vision to soothe his entry into the afterlife. Satisfied he was very much alive, he tried to push himself up from the swamp, but his hands slipped from the muck coating them. He dipped them in the nearby pooling water and wiped them off as best he could, enough to get the leverage he needed. He realized one of his gloves had been shredded by what looked like scorch marks, and tugged it off to reveal what he first took to be a burn. Then Ben realized it was more like an unfinished tattoo carved into his palm.

The same palm that had tightened around the glowing rock down in the cave he'd somehow managed to escape.

*"Señor,"* his Mexican foreman called out, pointing into the distance, "you must see this."

At first, Dale Denton didn't think the figure in the distance was real, more a trick of the eye or illusion he somehow shared with his foreman. He grabbed a pair of binoculars from a nearby kit and pressed them against his eyes, getting a closer view of a black-soaked specter wobbling its way straight for him.

His mind was still racked by losing Ben Younger in the ancient cave, the terrible feeling in the pit of his stomach that had followed the rope being jerked from the ground with Ben nowhere to be found. Maybe it was the pain of that moment making him think the approaching figure was his business partner and oldest friend, wanting something to be true so much that his mind conjured the sight for him.

As the figure drew closer, though, Denton realized it wasn't a conjuring or an illusion at all.

It was Ben Younger.


Next thing Ben knew, he was walking, pushing himself in the general direction of the oil field that was still gushing black ooze into the air. Only then did Ben remember how he'd shattered his leg in the fall. Yet, somehow, that leg didn't hurt anymore, just a dull ache left where agony from what felt like a fractured bone had dominated after his fall inside the cave.

He didn't know how far he walked through the oil-rich haze, or how long it took him to reach the outskirts of the field in which they'd drilled a dozen wells. By the look of things in the narrowing distance, all twelve had sprouted oil in a manner unseen since the early heyday of the wildcatters, the well caps not yet in place.

He spotted Dale Denton standing in the center of it all, lowering his binoculars in shock over Ben's reappearance. It was still day, but the black-tinted air made it feel like night. Ben continued on, staggering stiff-legged up to Denton.

"What's the matter, old buddy?" Ben said, managing a bright smile that cut through his grime-infested face. "You look like you just saw a ghost?"

And then he collapsed in Denton's arms.

# PART 2

# THE DEAD ZONE

## The Present

The battle line between good and evil
runs through the heart of every man.

—Alexander Solzhenitsyn

# FOUR

### Atlantic Rainforest, Brazil

The private jet is coming into Rio de Janeiro now, Your Eminence," Father Pascal Jimenez told Cardinal Martenko over the satellite phone aboard the Falcon 50, emblazoned with the Vatican crest.

"I'm glad you decided to put off your retirement for this final assignment, Father. There was simply no one more qualified or better equipped to deal with such a situation. Hence, my intervention in areas no longer in my purview."

Cardinal Josef Martenko was now head of the Vatican Bank. But for years prior to ascending to that lofty position, he'd served the Curia as the head of its so-called Miracle Commission, devoted to investigating phenomena not explicable through traditional means. Jimenez's background as a scientist, together with his own unique experience, provided just the credentials to join the commission's ranks. And he'd served as one of the commission's investigators for more than a decade before announcing his sudden retirement without providing an explanation.

"It feels good to be able to do a favor for a man who has done so much for me, Your Eminence," Jimenez lied, wishing he'd never answered Martenko's call.

"Still, I must apologize, especially in view of what happened in the course of your last assignment."

Jimenez shuddered. "How is the boy?"

"Improving every day, and with no memory of what transpired."

"I wish I could say the same."

"He was suffering from a serious psychosis, Father."

"You weren't there, Your Eminence. And this was no psychosis."

"I read your report, Father," Martenko said, after a pause. "You were sent to disprove possession, not involve yourself in an exorcism."

"My report only detailed what I witnessed."

"I pray that you encounter nothing similar in Brazil."

The flight path into Rio de Janeiro had taken the Falcon 50 over the massive statue of Christ the Redeemer, *Cristo Redentor* in Portuguese, at the summit of Mount Corcovado. From that angle, the statue seemed ready to take flight, its massive arms looking like wings. And Jimenez imagined the statue's blank eyes trailing him as he passed over it, the sun's angle casting shadows that made it appear tears were rolling down its soapstone-tiled cheeks.

Jimenez imagined those tears were for him, the Lord expressing His disappointment over his decision to leave the church. So many years, so many investigations . . . People wanted to believe so badly, *needed* to believe in something, just as he had ever since the day that had changed his life. Jimenez desperately wanted to give it to them, but never could. Not once, save for the recent apparent exorcism, had his investigations yielded anything other than a scientific explanation for the apparent miracle that had occurred. That was, after all, what the Vatican wanted every time the Curia dispatched him to the site of a potential miracle. For his part, though, Jimenez had wanted to unlock the mysterious link between God and man, to find His message and His word in phenomena that suggested a divine hand. But he'd failed in that task for a decade and saw no reason to believe anything was going to change.

"I'd appreciate you keeping me in the loop on this investigation," Cardinal Martenko told him. "Even though our paths have veered in different directions, what's happened in Brazil may take us both back to where we started."

"Given the circumstances," Jimenez started, resting his elbows atop the reports from the scene he'd read during the long flight from Rome, "do you believe there's some connection to Nigeria, Your Eminence?"

"I believe, Pascal, that's what you're going to find out."


"You don't belong here, Padre."

"But I am here, Colonel," Father Pascal Jimenez told the man wearing the Brazilian military uniform, who'd met him on the airport tarmac minutes before. "And we both need to make the best of that."

Colonel Rene Arocha cocked his gaze toward Jimenez in the Humvee's backseat. "My concern lies over why a man of your reputation would be dispatched over a matter involving a Catholic mission."

"You mean the fact that everyone in that mission somehow vanished from the face of the Earth?"

The vehicle thumped over the uneven, unpaved road, further worsened by the sudden torrents that poured from the sky during the rainy season. Those torrents both widened the ruts and turned them into miniature black-bottom lakes, threatening to swallow the Humvee's huge tires at every turn. Right now the day was gray but dry, the clouds above spiraling and darkening to near black with the portent of a coming deluge later. Somewhere in the distance, Jimenez thought he heard the rumble of thunder.

Next to him in the Humvee's backseat, Arocha had stiffened visibly. "All the same, after my government alerted the church, we were not expecting a visit from the Vatican's so-called Miracle Commission."

Jimenez smiled ever so thinly. "And I was told I'd be met by someone from the Brazilian military," he said, leaving things there and drawing a shrug from Arocha.

The colonel was a broad-shouldered man, his face pitted with acne scars and a complexion that seemed two-toned from the way the jungle canopy allowed light to filter into the Humvee's cab. His eyes were steely and cold, focused with an intensity that unnerved Jimenez every time he met them. Certainly not the eyes of an officer from something as mundane as the Ministry of the Environment. More like *Agência Brasileira de Inteligência*, the Brazilian intelligence service and the kind of agency with which Jimenez had become all too familiar over the years.

Jimenez knew little of their ultimate location, other than it was a sprawling valley nearly a hundred kilometers from the airport that had, until very recently, been teaming with plant and animal species found nowhere else in the world.

"So, perhaps," the priest picked up, "it lies in our mutual best interests to accept the fact that both of us are here because others wanted us to be."

"In your case, Padre, that's because the church wants an explanation for an event science can't explain."

"That remains to be seen, Colonel. And, speaking of which, your government was supposed to transmit pictures and on-scene reporting to me while I was in transit, but I've yet to receive either."

"That is because my department never sent them," Colonel Arocha said gravely. "We did not want to risk starting a panic or permitting fact to dissolve into rumor. The Internet is not a very good caretaker of secrets."

Jimenez tried not to look as uneasy and suspicious as he felt. "What exactly is your role in the Brazilian military, Colonel?"

Arocha forced a shrug. "I'm kind of a jack of all trades, Padre. Today it's the Ministry of the Environment, since they're responsible for oversight of the rainforest where the . . . incident occurred."

"Incident?"

This time Arocha's shrug was real. "We don't know what else to call it."

"That's why I'm here, to help you in that process and determine the fates of those assigned to our mission."

Arocha forced a grin. "If that was all your assignment was about, I very much doubt the Vatican would have arranged for a private jet."

"Just as you would seem to have your own experience in such matters."

"Miracles, Padre?"

"Secrets," Jimenez said.

Much to his surprise, Arocha grinned broadly. "It would seem we're kindred spirits of a sort, then."

"I suppose we are," the priest conceded.

The grin washed off Arocha's face, his expression going blank and stopping just short of fear. "Then be warned, Padre: What you're about to see is no miracle."


The drive lapsed into silence, Jimenez left to study the scenery out the windows, until the Humvee was waved through one checkpoint and then another, just before the ground leveled out enough to allow for a command and control center. The post came complete with a bevy of armed soldiers, heavy armored vehicles, and several Brazilian military helicopters, one of which sat already warming on a makeshift pad.

"That's our taxi the rest of the way, Padre," Arocha explained, opening the door on his side of the backseat to let in a flood of humid air so thick with moisture that Jimenez thought he'd stepped into a steam room. "There are no decent roads where we're going and we can't afford to be stranded, believe me."

Jimenez didn't bother to ask why, just climbed out after the colonel and followed him to the helicopter, pinning the safari hat that was a souvenir from another assignment to his head. If his sense of direction hadn't betrayed him, they were somewhere close to a massive nature preserve carved out of the Guapiaçu Valley that was home to all manner of plant and animal life known nowhere else on the planet, along with several indigenous tribes seldom exposed to the outside world.

The chopper lifted off before Father Jimenez had gotten his shoulder harness snapped home, soaring into the air and rapidly climbing over the tree line.

"I'm told this commission of yours exists to debunk these so-called miracles," Arocha said, after signaling Jimenez to don his headset.

"There must be a hundred percent certainty when it comes to such things," Jimenez explained to him. "Otherwise, the church would fall prey to all manner of hoaxes and concoctions. There can be absolutely no doubt for a true miracle to be proclaimed."

Such was Jimenez's mandate. He held two doctorates, in astrobiology and astrogeology, providing him the knowledge he needed to debunk phenomena that could be explained away on a scientifically rational basis. A memory flared of another investigation with a governmental and military presence of comparable magnitude, suggesting he was once again about to encounter something destined to challenge even his sensibilities. *Just as he had in Nigeria, twenty-seven years ago, before he'd entered the priesthood.*

"Can you provide some hint, some indication of what happened to this Catholic mission?" Jimenez asked suddenly, to spare himself from pondering that further.

"I know the missionaries were here to preach Christianity to the natives."

"That's not what I asked you, Colonel."

"It's my answer, all the same."

Arocha looked away, and Father Jimenez refocused his gaze forward as their chopper flitted over a rise in the tree line. Instantly what felt like wind shear shook the craft, the sensation hitting Jimenez like a punch to the stomach that sucked out his wind. He realized he suddenly felt cold and clammy, the ambient temperature beyond seeming to drop like a stone. The air looked ash gray, the blackening clouds swallowing the light as if determined to swap night for day. Thunder rumbled again, closer and louder, leaving a hollow pang in the center of Jimenez's stomach. He thought it might be a panic attack, until a glance toward Arocha showed him gritting his teeth and breathing rapidly to ward off the very same effects.

"Colonel?"

"I should have warned you about that, Padre."

The chopper hit a thick wall of air that felt more like mud, pushing through it to soar directly over the Guapiaçu Valley.

Jimenez focused his gazed downward, blinking rapidly to clear his eyes as he felt his breath catch in his throat. He stopped just short of making the sign of the Holy Trinity, reminding himself he was here more as a scientist than a priest.

"What in God's name . . ."

Arocha didn't break his stare from what lay beneath them. "God, Padre, had nothing to do with this."

# FIVE

## Sana'a, Yemen

The sky over the city of Sana'a was on fire, a shifting kaleidoscope beyond the lead assault chopper that continually dissolved into flame.

"Now this," Commander Max Borgia said to his lead SEAL team, strapped in tight against the bulkhead, "is a clusterfuck."

"Then it's a good thing we got the Pope himself leading us," smiled Griffon, holding a Solo cup turned makeshift spittoon. "I forgot, is it Max the First?"

"Know what else you forgot?" said Chief Petty Officer Nathan Hobbs, now in his umpteenth deployment after accepting an honorable discharge, only to re-up a mere month later. "Fact that a griffon is a goddamn dog."

"You got a problem with that?"

"An especially dumb dog."

"Bullshit!"

"Woof, woof!"

Small arms fire strafed the chopper, none of the SEALS on board riled much by it.

"How much farther to the LZ, Pope?" Hobbs asked Max.

"Less than two klicks if we don't get shot to hell."

His fellow SEALs had started calling Max "Pope" because his last name mirrored that of the infamous Rodrigo Borgia who became Pope Alexander VI. But the nickname had stuck because of Max's uncanny ability to work, or shoot, himself out of impossible situations time and time again.

Petty Officer Second Class Townsend, the greenest of the group, looked up from a Stephen King paperback, peering out from behind glasses disguised as sports goggles. "This is Yemen. I'd say we're already there."

"How can you read in all this shit?" Griffon asked him, his carrot-colored hair peeking out from beneath his helmet.

"It settles the mind."

Griffon checked what remained of the cover. "What, vampires, were-wolves, and other assorted monsters?"

Townsend closed the book. "No worse than the ones we're about to come face-to-face with."

The chopper wavered in the air, bucking wildly as the pilot dipped and darted to avoid making them an even riper target for RPG fire.

"One klick now," Max announced. He squeezed his neoprene glove over his left hand and then started in on the right, studying the silver dollar–sized birthmark as if its impressionistic design might hold some message. "We'll be coming in hot."

Their mission, he reviewed in his mind, was to evacuate the U.S. Embassy in the Yemeni capital of Sana'a's new city of al-Jadid, a sprawling urban center in contrast to the Old City District better known as al-Qadeemah. All-out civil war had broken out between government forces and rebels who now had the capital surrounded, thanks to Iran's backing of the extremist Huthie faction, supplying the rebel fighters with a seemingly inexhaustible supply of heavy weapons. The State Department had ordered the embassy evacuated, save for a small support staff to pack up vitals and shred the incredible volume of documents accumulated since its reopening.

Then word was passed along that Ambassador Clare Travis had elected to stay behind, unwilling to order others to do a job she wasn't willing to do herself. Ambassador Travis and her support staff were protected by a small contingent of marines working in tandem with a local warlord who'd been paid more money than he'd seen in his entire life for the effort. The last report they'd gotten from the compound indicated they'd holed themselves up in a protective bunker that had likely been breached, given the lack of any further communication.

The warlord they'd hired, along with his fighters, had fled the city when faced with the magnitude and ferocity of the attacking rebel force. That left only the marines to face off against hundreds of armed fighters, separated from them by a perimeter security wall that, according to reports, was crumbling at this very moment. That stranded the embassy support staff trapped inside the compound bunker with no route of escape available and no options save for one:

The SEALs.

Specifically this particular SEAL Team 6, better known as the Pope and his Disciples. Beyond the chopper, there was only fire and smoke, the embassy's location seeming to be right in the epicenter of it all.

"Coming up on the LZ now, boys," Max told his men in the lead chopper, fitting an old ring that looked like something he'd plucked from a Cracker Jack box onto his finger.

"That again?" Griffon said, trying for lightness.

Max regarded the scratched-up dark plastic jewel, held in place with superglue that had dried over the base, and squeezed a neoprene glove over his hand. "It's my good-luck charm."

"How's that?"

"One true love of my life gave it to me."

"Bullshit," Griffon chided. "No offense, Pope, but you and love in the same sentence don't make for a good fit."

"Then shut the fuck up and get ready to do some fast roping."

"The Pope has spoken!" Hobbs exclaimed.

The mission parameters were unambiguous. The two SEAL teams would fight back the enemy through all means necessary to create enough space for the third chopper to land to evacuate the ambassador, support staff, and marines who'd remained to guard them.

As the embassy drew within view, though, Max saw the mission was going to be anything but routine.

Rebel fighters had breached the walls, firing with their rifles pointed toward the sky, hooting and hollering over the gunfire of their own making. A few had spotted the marines clustered in an armored forward guard post and opened fire, the marines returning it through slats in the bulletproof glass. They'd positioned themselves for extraction there as ordered. But the timing of the breach had conspired against them, one clusterfuck piled atop another.

"Donald, this is Mickey," Max heard the mission's commanding officer, Admiral Keene Darby from the aircraft carrier *George H. W. Bush*, bark in his earpiece. "Do you copy?"

"Roger that, Mickey," Max said into his throat mic. "Approaching hot zone now."

As if to accentuate that statement, a fresh series of explosions flared within the embassy walls, creating a shock wave sufficient to buckle Max's chopper. The primary buildings were being hit by a torrent of RPG fire.

Target practice for the fighters forming the lawless mob laying siege to the compound.

"Negative, Donald, we have an abort."

"And we still have Americans, including Snow White, in the Magic Kingdom, Mickey, alive and breathing at last check."

"Negative. I repeat, negative. We have eyes on your sit and the view's all wrong for a drop. Do you copy? Please confirm."

Max could feel all his muscles tensing. "We do what we do, Mickey."

"Say again, Donald, say again."

"I have garble from this end, Mickey," Max said, buying himself time to think. "Please repeat all after bullshit."

"Mickey, be advised that this order comes from Walt himself at Disney World."

Meaning the president. At the White House.

"You're breaking up, Donald." Max thumbed the throat mic's extension to muddle his own words. "We are taking fire. Will reconnect when hostages are in tow."

"Negative, Mickey. Repeat, negative. You are to abandon all—"

Max clicked off his com unit, meeting the gazes of eleven of the men under his command who didn't need to be told what had just transpired. Their expressions told him they were up on the facts and good to go regardless.

"Hey," Griffon said, winking, "we could get our asses court-martialed for this."

"What?" Max responded, making himself look puzzled. "I can't hear you."

"I said, let's fry us some cockroaches."

"Now that I heard," Max said.

As another RPG took out the chopper's tail section.

# SIX

## Sana'a, Yemen

Max smelled smoke and fried wires, bells chiming and lights flashing everywhere in the cockpit before him. Through the haze, he glimpsed the pilot frantically trying to maintain a measure of control, enough to set down to avoid a crash certain to ignite the fuel tank with the flame burst already sprouting through the remnants of the tail. He watched the pilot working the throttle and steering mechanism, turning the craft into the oversteer to keep it from twisting onto its side from the spin. At the same time, he somehow managed to angle it for the embassy grounds, coming in fast, hot, and fiery.

"Brace yourself, boys!" Max cried out, his words mostly lost to a wild splatter of fire coming from the other two Black Hawk UH-60s that had moved up to flanking positions.

He heard the clamor of the M60D machine guns both were packing, glimpsed their fire strafing the embassy grounds and eviscerating anyone in its path. The gunners were clearing the field, training fire from the opposite pods toward the street mobs to hold them at bay. Buying time with enemy lives as currency. The LZ being cleared, the fire burning the air and leaving Max's own ears scorched.

*Get Ambassador Travis, the marines, and embassy support staff, and get the fuck out of Dodge. . . .*

The original mission anyway, before Walt himself had tried to pull the plug on Donald and the other ducks. There'd be hell to pay for this, for sure. But Max could live in a cell; what he couldn't live with was the haunting vision of trapped Americans being roasted to death by enemy fire.

The sudden wash of air through his stomach told Max they were about to hit. The landing was hard, jarring, but left the chopper intact and upright.

The windshield had cracked into spiderweb patterns on impact with the ground, fissures of flame visible everywhere in splintered fashion beyond. The ratcheting click-clack of gunfire was constant, as half of Max's team emerged into the bullet-scorched night. The remaining SEALs from the trailing chopper, fast-roped down, while the evac craft hovered overhead unleashing a torrent of machine-gun fire from pods on both sides. That fire scattered the bulk of the fighters gathered outside the embassy gates, buying the SEALs the time they'd need to advance through the embassy grounds to retrieve the ambassador and her staff.

Two of the SEALs fast-roping fell to enemy fire. One in Max's chopper had been lost to shrapnel and another to a broken leg that left him immobilized. That one, Boone, named after Daniel for his Tennessee heritage and ability to track, was the best shot in the outfit and closeted himself within the smoking wreckage to pick off any baddie who crossed his path.

In all, twenty-seven seconds had passed since impact with the ground, plenty of time for Max to assess the situation from all angles. The embassy grounds within the walled courtyard were laid out in a circle with the fortified guard post, in which the marines were clustered defensively, sitting dead center. Concrete and reinforced tungsten steel with eight-inch-thick space-age polymer a hundred times harder than glass that was built as a first line of defense in the event of an incursion, as opposed to a setting from which to wage a final stand. And, true to that assessment, the post was currently being battered by a barrage of small and heavy arms fire.

Muzzle flashes illuminated the night from assault rifle bores protruding through the fire slots. For a time, the fighters remained so focused on breaching the grounds that they failed to notice twenty SEALs converging on their position, caught now in virtual crossfire, chewing them up from both flanks. A pair of fighters readying grenades to toss at the post hurled them at the SEALs instead.

The SEALs scattered and rolled from the grenades' path, but that exposed three of them to enemy fire they were powerless to fend off. Max was opening up on their killers even as bullets whipsawed their bodies, each hitting with a *thump* loud enough to hear, even through the maelstrom. He knew other SEALs had added their fire to his, but couldn't say which ones or from where they were firing. The world had slowed to a crawl, almost preternaturally slow until . . .

*Until . . .*

. . . the birthmark that looked like a crisscrossing grid carved into his palm, currently squeezed inside a neoprene glove, began to hurt. Not just hurt, but also *burn*, burn enough to make it bleed.

Max shoved the thought aside, pushed past the pain in his gloved hand now sticky with blood, and kept firing, shifting to move into defensive position around the armored shed. Secure it as best he could and keep it secure during evac of those trapped inside. The focus of it all intensified his senses. Max couldn't explain why he turned, swung, dropped, fired this way or that. Enemy fighters kept pouring over the walls, cut down in waves by a combination of fire from the SEALs on the ground and heavy machine-gun fire from the chopper above. Meanwhile, Griffon led three other SEALs through the incessant hail of fire toward the armored shack to begin the evacuation process.

For now those inside were holding out, but holding out wouldn't do them much good much longer. So Max kept firing to change that, three-shot bursts now to conserve as much ammo as he could. He glimpsed five SEALs now shepherding the wounded marines, and a few members of the embassy's support staff, out from the armored guard post. He became conscious of the trailing chopper adding its heavy machine-gun fire to that of the evac craft. In order to get out of here, both would have to land amid the mess and clutter into which the courtyard had dissolved. Max's mental count had fourteen SEALs still standing to go with six wounded and four dead now. That hadn't hit him yet, but it would once they were airborne with hostages in tow, the time when everything settled in.

Bullets continued to whiz past him in a stream interrupted by brief flutters of silence that left Max wondering if he was still alive. His answer came in the next enemies he downed, death reminding him of life. The wave attacking now was wielding machetes and long-bladed knives, interspersed with Kalashnikov AK-47 assault rifles.

Two medics were tending to the wounded and had already readied the dead for transport too, when both surviving choppers angled noses down for landing behind streams of fire blaring from their heavy machine guns. Through it all, the clanging of the expended shells banging up against each other on the ground claimed his hearing. Max was backpedaling now, herding the rescued marines and staff members toward the choppers just settling down with their powerful rotor wash kicking stray debris into the air that rained back down like confetti.

That final marine, limping with blood soaking through a thigh of his fatigues, veered Max's way suddenly out of the smoke and vapor cloud, enemy fire lighting up the air around him.

"Where's the bunker?" Max yelled over the constant din of fire.

"Basement in the office compound, set back from the guard post," the marine said, thrusting a shaky finger to the complex's most modern structure. "The ambassador ordered us to hold the bitches back while she finished the job there, like she's got a death wish."

"Then it's my job to make sure it doesn't come true," Max said, swinging away from the marine and eyeing the main compound.

# SEVEN

## Sana'a, Yemen

RPGs, fired from the neighboring rooftops of similarly charred buildings, took out more walls and windows from the embassy's surviving structures. The high ground belonged to the enemy, the logistics of the mission offering no opportunity to get one of their own snipers into position to rule the air, not tonight. Max snapped a fresh magazine home, Griffon and Bates flanking him on either side charting the clearest path to the main complex.

The main embassy building might as well have been a mile away instead of a hundred feet through a landscape congested with smoke, fire, char, and rubble. With no clear path, Max led the other two SEALs on a zigzagging route that used the smoke and rubble for cover. The fragments of the mob that had managed to penetrate the complex rushed about with no discernible purpose other than wanton destruction. The constant din of gunfire mixed with explosions had dimmed Max's hearing to the point where the scene felt surreal and dreamlike, oddly beautiful and horrible at the same time. The smoke and flame lent the night a visceral clarity, sharply intense in focus. Enter that, embrace it, and the night was his; try to skirt its edges and he'd risk succumbing to the chaos.

Max ducked against a building to reload, reaching for a fresh magazine when a pair of hands burst from a shrapnel-ravaged window and grabbed hold of his shoulders, trying to jerk him backward. Max slammed the M4's butt backward, hammering a soft midsection, then jerked forward again. The fighter flew out the window with knife in hand. Going for Max's machine gun, instead of trying for him with the knife. He never even got close to wrenching the weapon free, before Max twisted the knife around and jammed it under the fighter's thorax, digging deep, feeling the warm gush of the fighter's blood spilling onto him.

"Take that, you fucker!"

Did he say that or only think it? Impossible to discern amid the fire-storm raging around him. But he did know he felt buoyant, even joyful, strangely at home in this conflagration of violence he found himself embracing. The blood soaking him smelled sweet and coppery, suddenly not altogether unpleasant, even welcome, as he twisted away from the fighter's still convulsing form, finally slamming another fresh magazine home.

He watched the fighter die. He never should've remained stationary for even those few seconds, but he wanted, needed, to watch the man wheeze and twitch toward death.

And when he finally did, the M4 began dancing in Max's grasp again, bringing more death with it and leaving him only wishing he could watch more fighters die similarly up close and personal. Reveling in their agony and the terror stretched over their faces, as death came to claim them.

*What's happening to me?*

"You all right, Pope?" Grif asked him, suddenly by his side.

Max wanted to say he wasn't, not at all.

"Never better," he said instead, the pain in his hand feeling like his skin was peeling off. So he shed his glove, the blood leaking from the mark on his palm spraying outward when he tossed it aside. "Snow White's trapped in the bunker. Cover me."

A cluster of fighters had just breeched the entrance to the main building, when Max and Griffon poured fire into them, leaving their bodies in a clump Max leaped over en route to a heavy steel door that had been blasted open. Max felt the heat of fresh enemy fire blistering the air around him, digging chunks from the walls as his men dove for cover to return it.

Max continued steering for the breached entrance to and then down the winding, catwalk-like stairs to the bunker. He felt he was gliding, floating more than running. He should've been heaving for breath, but he felt no burning in his lungs or sledgehammering of his heart against his chest wall.

He drained his magazine on two fighters who spun out at the foot of the stairs, was snapping a fresh one home when two more lunged at him when he leaped the final stretch to the floor. No way he could complete the process in time to fire at them, so he hammered the butt of his M4 into the forehead of the nearest with one hand, while yanking his knife from its sheath with the other. His original intention had been to stab the second fighter with the blade, but the man's boots ground to a halt as his rifle steadied, so Max sent the knife whizzing through the air with a flick of his wrist instead. It lodged in the man's throat, a fountain of blood erupting, while Max split the rest of the first fighter's skull with two more thrusts of the butt of his M4, enjoying the sound and feel of it cracking so much he struck the man a third time, square in the face.

*What am I . . .*

Max was in motion again before he could complete the thought, gliding forward with his final magazine rammed home and ready. His next clear sight through an open doorway, in crystal-sharp focus, was of four uniformed fighters stamping at a dead marine's body, while two more hovered over a pair of kneeling hostages. Max shot the stampers first, his peripheral vision following the other two fighters jerking the hostages to their feet, knives held at their throats.

He recognized the female hostage as Ambassador Clare Travis. Her face was bloodied and bruised, her blouse torn to reveal her bra beneath it. She looked as if she were fighting to stay strong and resilient, in the grasp of a fighter with an eye socket crusted over with scar tissue. That fighter struggled to steady a pistol on Max in a trembling hand, while his other held the knife's edge against the ambassador's throat.

*"Drop the gun!"* he wailed in Arabic. *"Drop the gun!"*

The moment froze, as Max held his ground and his M4, no clear shot through the smoke and flame glow lighting the scene.

*"Drop the gun!"*

Max felt a strange, eerie, almost preternatural calm grip him.

*"Drop the gun!"* the fighter wailed again.

And Max did, because it was his only move. Standing there weaponless now with no fear, regret, or even concern, his heart rate slowing to a soft tick in his chest.

The fighter holding the ambassador at knifepoint extended his pistol further forward, his finger starting to curl round the trigger.

*"Khalass!"* Max called out in Arabic, holding up his bare right hand, with blood still leaking from the birthmark burned into his palm. "Stop!"

The fighter's eyes locked on that hand, then with Max's gaze. The fighter tried to break the stare but couldn't. Fear filled his eyes, and he jerked his pistol to the right. Aimed now for the second fighter, even as he struggled desperately, and futilely, to stop his own motion, as if he was no longer in control of his motor functions.

*"What, what are you doing?"* the second man, holding a young man who looked like a college-age intern, at knifepoint as well, screeched.

*"Aasef! Aasef!"* the first fighter wailed. "I'm sorry, I'm sorry!"

Then he fired twice into the other fighter's face, the young embassy worker left to stumble aside.

The fighter still holding Ambassador Travis at knifepoint finally dropped the pistol and jerked his knife from the ambassador's throat toward his own.

*"Allah Asharim! Allah Asharim!"*

And then he drew the blade sideways, a geyser of blood bursting from his slit throat, spraying Ambassador Travis as Max moved to grab hold of her.

"Come on!" he cried out, helping the intern to his feet and then scooping up his M4. "Time to get you home, Ambassador."

The ambassador's knees buckled, Max catching her just before she hit the floor. He scooped her up over his shoulder, her weight slowing him not in the slightest as he mounted the stairs and burst outside, the intern shielded behind him, amid a courtyard swarming with fighters.

"Want me to take her, Pope?" Griffon said, rushing to his side.

"I got this," Max told him, barely breaking stride to level his M4 in his other hand.

Griffon and Bates fell into step behind him, skirting their way back to the choppers. The trip home would be a tight squeeze, weight more a problem than numbers. But, as one of Max's commanding officers had once said, *Sometimes you just have to go the fuck with it.*

Tonight was going to be one of those times. And not all the SEALs would be making the trip, not alive anyway. Max had lost men before, but this was different. This was all on him because he was the one who'd violated orders by refusing to shit-can the mission and dropped straight into a firestorm instead.

Max didn't have time to doubt or question himself, his final magazine almost drained, when he hoisted Ambassador Travis into the evac chopper. A final wave of fighters had just breached the gate in an insect-like swarm, when Max felt his trigger click empty. Then the smoke and haze vanished in a curtain of fire that was everywhere and nowhere at once. Max knew something was wrong, because he felt no heat, the blistering radiance not even making him squint, as if the flames that weren't there had frozen the world around him. He felt nothing at all, not even any pain.

Except the pain radiating from his silver dollar–sized birthmark again. But it was different now, more biting than hot, as if razor-sharp teeth were tearing into his palm, shredding the skin.

That pain was the only thing he could feel, when the next moment found Max a spectator shielded by the fanning flames. Watching an endless flood of fighters converge on his men and the embassy person-nel they'd rescued, seeming to swallow them before the bodies started falling to an endless ribbon of gunfire Max followed in slow motion, his own team being slaughtered before his eyes. He tried to move, do some-thing, *anything*, but the cold-hot flames held him captive, time slow-ing to a crawl before starting to move like the picture was skipping. Then the world picked up speed again in time to capture one of the remaining choppers bursting into flames under the torrent of enemy fire, a moment before a trio of rebels wielding grenade launchers took out the other with RPGs. He saw fighters reduced to charred, smoking skeletons, seeming to grin as they advanced, their bones clacking with each step.

Max squeezed his eyes closed, his face still stained with the blood of the fallen enemy fighters. Opened them again to find the battle exactly where he'd left it without flames or skeletons, the last of his men squeez-ing aboard the two choppers.

*What the fuck, what the fuck was—*

A *vision*, Max realized, that's what it must've been, a vision. Or a pre-monition maybe, something like that.

Either way, the fighters flooded through the toppled gate wielding a combination of ancient carbines and AK-47s, while a trio of them mounted the retaining wall steadying grenade launchers.

Max knew what was going to happen. He knew what was coming.

Because he'd seen it. In his vision.

Max thought he heard Grif screaming his name, as he shed his empty M4 assault rifle and stooped over the M60D heavy machine gun still fixed to the pod of the downed Black Hawk. In what felt like an extension of his vision, he saw himself reaching for an M60D and tearing it from its mounts—loosened by the crash, of course, because how else could he have torn steel from steel?

In the back of his mind somewhere, Max registered how much the thing weighed, with still half an ammo belt, no less. But that didn't matter because it felt featherlight in his grasp, as he opened up on the fighters surging through the embassy gates with the choppers in their sights. He fired and kept firing, wave after wave of the bloodthirsty horde downed by a barrage he swept from left to right and back again. Never easing up on the trigger, even as the heat blowing from the barrel blew back into him like a desert wind.

The horde kept coming in an endless stream, mirroring almost precisely what he'd seen in the crazed vision that had seized him. The spacing and weapons were the same, right down to the heavy machine guns and grenade launchers being steadied atop the embassy's perimeter security wall, laid waste to by his M60D's armor-piercing shells before they could begin firing.

Otherwise . . .

Max could only hope he had enough bullets to provide cover for the choppers' liftoff and escape, expecting the hollow click to sound any moment in all its finality. But the belt kept feeding and the bullets kept coming, as if this particular ammo pack was rigged to infinity. His hands cried out from the weight and the heat that felt as if it were peeling back his flesh. But this was no vision; it was undeniably, and terrifyingly, real, cast in the sharp focus combat always left in its aftermath.

Through the smoky haze before him, Max saw the onslaught ending, the attack wave receding as the fighters turned and fled back out through the gate, before they joined the wave of fallen bodies.

"*Pope,*" Max thought he heard, his finger cramping on a trigger producing only hollow clacks now. "*Pope . . .*"

Then a hand jarred his shoulder, Max swinging to find Griffon painted in blood and sweat yanking him away. Max felt the heat rising off the M60D's barrel, bleeding smoke-like steam that stained the air between them.

"Let's get the fuck out of here, man," Griffon said in a scratchy voice laced with disbelief over what he'd just seen. "Let's go home."

# EIGHT

### Atlanta, Georgia

The last thing Victoria Tanoury remembered before the crash was fitting the Apple Watch her fiancé had just given her around her wrist.

"So wherever the World Health Organization sends you, I'll always be as close as your wrist," Thomas had told her, smiling.

He watched Vicky pawing over his gift to her.

"What are you doing?"

"Looking for the OFF switch," she said, smiling back at him.

She watched Thomas return his attention to the road, saw his eyes bulge in the same moment his forearms tensed wildly on the wheel.

*"Jesus Christ! What's she doing there?"*

Vicky felt him slam on the brakes, swinging back to the front in time to glimpse a little girl standing in the middle of the road, before Thomas veered sharply to avoid her. Their car spun out of control, careening across the roadway, slammed in one direction and then another until it was launched airborne. It seemed to hover for a very long time before crashing down in a sloped patch of ground beneath the overpass. It landed on its roof with a crunching impact that stole what little was left of Vicky's breath, then rolled back upright.

Her disorientation was instantly deepened by the smell of gasoline flooding the SUV's cab. She turned to Thomas to see blood frothing from his mouth, a look of terror and puzzlement frozen on his features.

"Did I hit her?" he managed, gagging at the end.

Vicky tried to sound reassuring. "Don't try to talk."

But he latched a shuddering hand onto her wrist. "The little girl in the middle of the road . . . Please tell me I didn't hit her."

Vicky eased his hand off her. "You didn't hit her," she said, wondering how the little girl had strayed into the middle of the freeway and what happened to her, after Thomas just managed to avoid her.

She felt suddenly hot, the stench of gasoline replaced by oil smoke. And then she was retching, the hot tongues of sprouting flames reaching for her, even as Thomas's eyes locked open and blood oozed from his mouth in thick wads.

She didn't want to leave him, but instinct drove her to reach for the release on her shoulder harness.

*Click.*

But nothing happened, the harness didn't release, keeping her pinned in place, trapped in the car.

"Help! Help!"

Her screams hurt her own ears. It hurt to breathe now too, her throat feeling as if she'd swallowed acid, and she tried not to inhale. Then the next time she let herself, there was no air left, only heat, until something that felt like ice crystals showered her.

Air flooded her lungs and Vicky felt herself being carried away, toward the next life, Vicky thought, until she glimpsed the sun-drenched silhouette of a uniformed policeman dragging her away. The stench of gasoline dissipated, and she was vaguely conscious of the rock-laden shoulder of the access road that ran beneath the freeway.

"Ma'am, can you hear me? Ma'am, look at me!"

An explosion sent flames climbing toward the sun over his shoulder, Vicky recovering enough of her senses to think about Thomas stolen from her a second time, all trace of him lost, along with the love they'd shared.

"Let me sit you up, ma'am."

Vicky realized she was retching horribly, as if to cough all the accumulated smoke from her lungs. Sirens were wailing by the time she could breathe again, as the officer continued to comfort her.

"I was on my way home," he told her. "Funny how I never take this route, never. But there was a detour. That's what saved your life. I only wish I could have saved . . ."

"My fiancé," Vicky completed, when the officer's voice tailed off. "He swerved to avoid a little girl in the middle of the road. Please tell me she's all right. Please tell me she wasn't hurt."

The officer scratched at his scalp, looking puzzled. "I can't, ma'am, because I didn't notice any little girl. And I didn't see the angel who set up that detour either, but I know you must have one watching over you."

•   •   •

Vicky had spent the funeral reliving the accident in her mind, trying to fill in the empty spaces that began with the sickening crunch of metal and ended with her strapped to a headboard. The whole morning had passed in a fog of empty gestures and solemn condolences that left her feeling numb. Numb to the cold hands pressed into hers, the tight embraces that left her soaking in the scents of stale cigarettes, dry-cleaning chemicals, hairspray, and too much perfume or cologne. She'd always been sensitive to smells; her first paper in a biochemical medicine class was a study in how to use scents to help diagnose disease. Back then, she'd never imagined the career path that would end up taking her into virology and epidemiology where stints with the Centers for Disease Control and, more recently, the World Health Organization had branded her a prodigy.

But Vicky didn't care much about that now; she didn't care much about anything beyond burying the fiancé she truly loved on the very day they were supposed to be married.

*So you won't ever be able to hide from me . . .*

It was Thomas, though, who would now be hiding from her. Forever. Somewhere no Apple Watch could reach him, Vicky thought, watching the minute change on it. The reception was in full swing, the house they'd shared in the year since they'd gotten engaged packed to the brim with milling, somber souls searching for the right words to say when none existed. It would've been easier for all, herself included, if they didn't bother. If they just remained silent. But none did, and each genuine show of condolence left Vicky gazing at her watch to keep Thomas alive in her mind, at the very least.

She felt a lot of things, but mostly she felt alone. Her mother had died in childbirth and she hadn't spoken to her father in years now, their estrangement dating back even beyond that. Vicky searched her mind for a time she felt different, anything other than hatred for her father, but was denied it save for snippets of memory so long in the past, she couldn't even be sure they were real.

She'd met Thomas, a noted cancer researcher, at a conference on the role of genetics in epidemiology through history and couldn't believe her luck. How many times had she woken in the morning expecting to find him gone, their love blessed with a fairy tale–like feeling to the point she always feared it would end, or she'd wake up to the realization it had all been a dream. Now that dream really had ended, and the pain left her throat clogged and mouth desert dry no matter how many glasses of water people kept handing her at the house in which she and Thomas had planned to start their family.

Vicky tried to settle herself with some deep breaths, but felt her muscles seizing, the breath bottlenecking in her throat, as if she were in the midst of some panic attack. She fled to an upstairs bathroom and locked the door behind her. Closed the toilet seat and sat down upon it, breathing deeply again.

She heard a scant buzzing sound, remembering her cell phone from the handbag that now seemed to be vibrating slightly, snapping her alert again. Vicky fished it out because it was her work phone, to be carried on her person at all times, since she was on the first-line response team to alerts called by the World Health Organization.

HEADQUARTERS lit up in the Caller ID box and she answered it.

"Vicky?"

"Who is this?" she asked, voice short and scratchy.

"I'm so sorry to be bothering you at a time like this, so terribly sorry," said Neal Van Royce, an assistant director at the WHO. "But it's an emergency, a true one."

"I'm kind of dealing with my own emergency here, Neal."

"I know that, and you have my deepest condolences, as well as my apology. I have no right to be disturbing you in a time like this, no right at all. But it's a potential Level One. That's the only reason why I'm calling."

"Where?"

"A remote village in Jordan. We need someone who speaks the language, someone with your qualifications."

"I'm not the only one on staff fluent in Arabic."

"Vicky, the dire nature of what's happening over there falls under your precise area of expertise."

She shifted atop the closed toilet seat. "Care to give me some notion of what we're facing?"

"I can't, not over the phone without a secure line. But I can tell you it's something you've never seen before."

"I've seen quite a lot."

"Nothing like this, Doctor," Van Royce told her.

# NINE

## Az-Zubayr, Iraq

I see almost all the men of your village are gone," the dark figure said from the cargo bed of a pickup truck between two black-clad figures wielding assault rifles, addressing those who'd been herded into the village square. "I suppose they've joined the local militias corrupted by the West into seeking to wage war on those who serve the one true God as He wills. Because they are infidels, no doubt. But my presence here today does not come from hatred of such infidels; it comes from hatred of those who oppose me and the word of the one true God."

The figure cast his gaze over the people of Az-Zubayr, a small desert village located at the foot of the Sinjār Mountains in western Iraq. The buildings were a loose amalgam of sand-shaded brick and mortar with not a single doorway carved out in uniform fashion. Angled this way and that, as if the world was slanted and nobody cared.

"I am Mohammed al-Qadir, chosen by God himself to lead the New Islamic Front. And had your men chose to fight alongside, instead of against, me, they would have known an entirely different destiny than the one that will greet their return."

Al-Qadir leaped agilely down from the bed of the pickup truck. His flowing black cleric's robes billowed outward in the stiff desert wind, creating the illusion he was floating. He stood silhouetted by the truck's frame, the tawny color of his ruddy complexion a fine match for the rust beginning to overtake its frame. His motions were smooth and agile, befitting a man much younger than his fifty-odd years. His eyes held all those years and more, piercing but tired somehow, as they blinked lazily and seemed to focus on something no one else could see. He was tall and broad with a long black beard and black hair flowing untamed from the confines of his *keffiyeh*. His black robes concealed the chiseled frame born of a past to which not even his closest advisers were privy. He wore a

pistol holstered under his left arm so it seemed to hang in the air. A
sheathed sword hung from the right side of his belt.

Enclosed by a bevy of his hooded gunmen, al-Qadir clasped his hands
behind his back and moved closer to the villagers, his sandaled feet
scratching against the desert floor that passed for a square dominated by
interconnected market stalls featuring carts of dust-coated vegetables. No
guards accompanied al-Qadir in his stroll; no warrior of his reputed acumen needed escort to walk through a crowd of women, children, the in-
firm, and the elderly.

"Most of your men will never see their homes again," he said, starting
in again suddenly. "They will fall to the misplaced ideals that have claimed
them and those who escape deaths at the hands of my holy warriors will
return home to an even worse fate. They will return home to find that
the Front has taken their daughters as the slaves God willed them to be.
They will serve me as they were put onto God's Earth to serve, and they
will do so without protest lest they see the side of me that lacks all com-
passion."

Al-Qadir stopped before the stooped figure of an old woman with wrin-
kles dug so deep into her face they seemed more the work of a hammer and
chisel than the years. He smiled and stroked her cheek tenderly, respect-
fully. The old woman cowered and turned away so fast, she stumbled and
felt her knobby legs almost give out.

"The mothers and grandmothers gathered here," the leader of the New
Islamic Front resumed, "will be spared to tell the tale of my coming to
those who come in my wake. You will tell them of how I took only what
the one true God willed to be mine."

Now al-Qadir stopped before a long-haired teenage boy doing his best
to look defiant, refusing to show any fear or deference or to break al-
Qadir's stare. He smiled at the boy, impressed by his bravery and bravado, then turned his gaze on the woman the boy had positioned himself
protectively before.

"You are this one's mother?"

She nodded.

"And your husband has left to wage war on the holy mission of my
forces?"

The woman said nothing, swallowed hard.

"I'll take that as a yes. In the spirit of our righteous God, I'm going to
give you a choice." Then al-Qadir turned to address the whole of the

square. "I am going to give all the mothers here a choice. I'm going to spare your sons the kind of deaths I am reputed to bring to those who would oppose me. You may have heard the tales of how I've cut the limbs off of the sons of those who stand against the word of our God, and made their parents watch while they died bleeding, screaming from the agony I wrought.

"But that is not my intention here," al-Qadir continued, steering back for the pickup truck, "because, as I said, I wish to show you my mercy imposed by the one true God. Because He has bestowed a great gift upon me, a gift that once released into the world will punish all infidels who would besmirch or ignore His Word. Those days, the End of Days, are coming and only those who give their allegiance and prove their loyalty to me as His vessel will be spared."

He climbed gracefully back into its cargo bed and rotated his gaze among the faces aimed his way, beginning to show a glimmer of hope al-Qadir relished in quashing. He smiled thinly before he resumed, tugging at the long beard so thick it threatened to swallow his hand.

"So I am going to give all of the mothers a choice: Kill your firstborn sons, or force me to do so in your stead, but not before I torture them until they beg for death, their tears mixing with blood spilled on your cursed sand." Then, over the desperate shrieks and cries of protest, "Take a knife to their throat or their heart, so they may die quickly at your feet without suffering. Those who comply may comfort them in their dying moments. Those who don't will witness my warriors cut off one limb at a time to prolong their agony. Then watch them burned alive by my hand."

The shrieks and pleas grew louder, echoing off the face of the towering Sinjār Mountains to the west of the village.

"This is what your men who survive will find upon their return," al-Qadir said over the women, many of whom had sunk to their knees, now crying hysterically. "They have brought this upon you. They have left me no choice. You bow and pray to me as if I am the one true God, when I am merely His servant, follower of His word on Earth. I serve His will, and when your men left to make war with me, they also made war against God. And when they return you can tell them had they turned toward instead of against Him, then their firstborn sons would still be alive to greet them."

As al-Qadir finished, a portion of his men dispersed through the crowd, handing knives to the women who let them fall at their feet while they hugged their children close. Those same men yanked the girls and young women away, leering at them as if to choose which they would take for themselves. The ripe and fertile would serve them well, al-Qadir thought, the younger well suited to more menial chores until they came of age.

Al-Qadir watched the process unfold through a surreal fog that left him euphoric, reveling in the power that was his to dispense as he pleased. He knew the mothers would try defiance, leaving the blades glinting in the naked sunlight until his warriors made an example of one or two of the boys, starting with the teenage boy who'd refused to show fear of him.

Al-Qadir drew his sword from its sheath and again eased himself down from the truck bed, starting toward the boy once so full of bravado and now with a urine stain spreading down the front of his Punjabi trousers. Al-Qadir envisioned his screams, envisioned his blood painting the air with the prophecies of things to come. Blood sinking into the sand, as the modern world would sink into the oblivion of history.

Then the burning, those who did not heed the word of God reduced to nothing more than embers drifting off to dissipate in the air as if they had never been born at all.

But first the screams, al-Qadir thought, as he brought the sword over-head and sliced downward, lopping one of the boy's arms off at the shoulder.

"Now," he said, through the screams and cries, "I take the other one."

# TEN

## Yucatán Peninsula, Mexico

I t might've helped if I'd had a better idea of what we were dealing with here, Professor."

Orson Beekman swabbed the sweat from his face with an already soaked handkerchief and looked across the Jeep's front seat at Eric Racine. "You were informed of everything you needed to know to get the job done. And this object you found . . ."

"The rock."

"The *object* you found—you're certain no one touched it, moved it?"

"Those were my instructions."

"That doesn't answer my question."

Beekman felt hot air surging through the open-air Jeep. No roof, windows, or sides. Utterly exposed to the elements that right now included wind dappled with the dusty grit kicked up by the vehicle's oversized tires and then blown against him, sandblasting his skin. The road cutting through the back edge of the Yucatán was unpaved, branches whipping past him, just missing his skin.

"My orders to the security team before I left for the airstrip two hours ago were explicit," Racine explained, as the Jeep's headlights cut through night's first fall.

The setting sun had burned the sky a beautiful shade of orange that made Beekman think of an autumn scene set against falling leaves. So too this landscape seemed almost preternaturally beautiful, in stark contrast to what he recalled from his previous visits to the area, and the barren wasteland that had yielded a fortune in black gold way back in 1990.

Along with something else, as it turned out.

"They secured the area around the find and I personally told the members of my team to stand clear," Racine continued. "Not that I needed to with the stories floating around from the Mexicans we've come into contact with."

Beekman knew those stories all too well, having heard them himself for nearly thirty years now. How the area was cursed. How the rational explanations for a wasteland forming amid the rich ground flora of the Yucatán didn't hold. How years before bigger oil companies had abandoned drilling efforts when inexplicable, bizarre, and often tragic circumstances befell them.

How his own journeys here were made always with a level of fear and foreboding.

*Las Tierra del Diablo* . . .

The Land of the Devil.

Beekman recalled the first time he saw those words painted across the side of a tanker. He, Dale Denton, and Ben Younger had passed it off as nothing more than graffiti, dismissing the rumors and folktales that hung over the area like the clouds of oil that had darkened the sky the day they'd struck oil and struck it rich. Beekman had been there when Younger had staggered through the black rain that seemed to tumble in sheets from the sky, having somehow ended up over a mile away with no memory of how he'd gotten there, or how he'd managed to escape the chasm down which he'd disappeared.

Younger might not even have remembered his encounter with the object, or rock as Racine called it, deep underground had it not been for the strange mark it had left on his palm after he'd grasped it. His mind had gone dark in that moment and didn't switch on again until he awoke in a dried-out riverbed.

The company that grew into Western Energy Technologies, WET, had been looking for the object ever since, sparing no expense, without success. Any number of archaeological and geological teams had failed to recover it either within the chasm or greater cave systems themselves. Dale Denton still refused to accept defeat and redoubled his efforts. But none had paid any dividends until he'd hired Eric Racine, an expert in planetary science and geophysics who'd cut his teeth on NASA's Mars Rover program. The cost to retain Racine's team, along with acquiring the required equipment, dwarfed the costs of all previous efforts combined.

"Could you explain how you located the object?" Beekman asked him.

"I treated the site as I would a foreign planet, asteroid, or moon I was studying," Racine explained. "Life, or anything organic, is distinguishable by a unique thermal signature that sets it apart from the surrounding landscape. That's one of the things the Mars Rover keyed on. So I applied those same principles here by chilling small grids with a combination of gaseous dry ice and liquefied Freon, and then using thermal imagery to scan for outstanding heat signatures. Based on what little you told me about the . . . object, I was proceeding on the assumption that it radiated significant, heat-producing energy that would, without question, stand out. We were ninety days and three square miles into the process when we finally located it."

Beekman nodded, trying to appear casual.

"You haven't asked the most obvious question," Racine continued, when Beekman remained silent.

"What's that?"

"How a rock can give off so much heat, so much energy, without any indicators or evidence as to how. I believe you haven't asked because you've already formed some conclusions, probably years ago. I believe that's why you finally gave up on all your archaeologists and geologists from this world and turned to someone with experience dealing with foreign ones."

Beekman noticed the flora was starting to thin, the Jeep encountering less brush as the green world around him began to brown. He recalled the same impression the first time he, Denton, and Younger had driven out here, the world dimming from a paradise to a wasteland, even as their Mexican partners assured them the rumors that had chased off the big oil companies were exaggerated and unfounded. Everything seemed the same today, no regrowth he could see, the hold a once lavish landscape had relinquished never regained.

Beekman glimpsed the clearing ahead through the barren branches and corpse-like trees, the sooty smell of oil that had never left the air scraping at his nostrils.

"I have my theories," he said finally.

"Involving the object's origins, no doubt." Racine's gaze darted from the narrowing roadbed to the titanium, vacuum-sealed container resting on the Jeep's passenger-side floor between Beekman's feet. "Based on the need for that."

"Precautions, that's all."

It was the same type of container in which astronauts stored samples collected from space to warrant against contamination from a foreign body or microbe prior to returning to Earth. Pressurized to maintain proper oxygen and pH levels to ensure no degradation would befall the object in transit. It hummed slightly, powered by an advanced lithium battery with a life measured in years and capable of withstanding the rigors of space.

The clearing drew closer, the smell stronger. Beekman felt his insides nudged by excitement, his heart rate picking up. A long quest about to be fulfilled at last, his nervous energy rooted in the vast potential of the object Eric Racine had managed to locate twenty-seven years after Ben Younger had likely been the first human being to ever encounter it.

The tools required to complete that effort were stored in a guitar case–sized kit laid across the Jeep's backseat. Distance from the stone needed to be kept, and the proper precautions observed, at all times.

"Those strange occurrences all those years ago, the way you struck oil," Racine chimed suddenly, as they rumbled into the scrub and stone layered over the clearing, "you think the object was somehow to blame."

"I never said that."

"You didn't have to."

"And you don't sound like a scientist."

"I like to keep an open mind, Professor. You said none of my team members were to get any closer to this object than absolutely necessary, you said not to touch it under any circumstances, even while wearing gloves designed for work in outer space. That tells me you must like to keep an open mind too." Racine glanced across the seat again. "It also tells me NASA should be informed of our findings. Immediately."

"Only NASA isn't who's paying a small fortune for your services," Beekman said sternly. "And I'd also remind you about the confidentiality and exclusivity agreements you signed with Western Energy Technologies, specifically the penalty clauses, if anything is disclosed in any way, shape, or form."

Racine swallowed hard and stiffened behind the wheel, gaze fixed forward, when he suddenly jammed on the brakes.

"Something's not right."

Racine parked the Jeep there and climbed out, not waiting for Beekman before moving through the last of the trees, toward the camp they'd set up in the general area of the find. At first glance, there seemed to be no sign whatsoever of Racine's team or their guards. Moving further into the clearing, though, Beekman saw the bodies lying askew amid the depression in the ground they'd cleared in order to dig down. The thick coppery stench of blood rose over the sooty oil stench riding the air like a cloud.

Beekman felt his insides wobble, processing the scene the way he might upon just waking from a dream unsure of the line between what was real and what wasn't. But the bodies were real and so was the blood. Everywhere, the awful carnage looking as if it had bubbled out of the barren landscape.

He spotted the two armed security guards next, Mexican special ops veterans who'd freelanced for the drug cartels at one point. They were recognizable from their longer sleeves and tactical trousers lined with ammo-filled cargo pockets. But something looked utterly wrong about the assault rifles lying near their corpses. Drawing closer, Beekman saw the barrel had broken off one, and the barrel of the other was, literally, bent in half.

*I warned them, I goddamn warned them. . . .*

"One of them's alive. Over there. Against that tree."

It was Racine's voice, reaching Beekman like a flutter at the edge of his consciousness. He turned to follow Racine's gaze toward the rotting stump of a long-dead tree where the figure of a woman sat slumped, shoulders sagging, positioned to the side so they couldn't see her face.

Beekman watched the pistol flash in Racine's hand, a squat snub-nosed with a two-inch barrel. They approached the figure together slowly, side-by-side, the revolver poking the air ahead of them.

"It's Lindsay," Beekman heard Racine say, in the moment he discerned the figure's long hair, matted and tangled with blood.

Swinging around to approach the young woman from the front, Beekman saw still more blood covered her face, obscuring her features except for a few blank smears where she'd swiped it from her skin. Her lips were trembling in an eerie rhythm that matched the quivering throes of her slumped frame.

"Lindsay," Racine said, stooping before her, the revolver forgotten in his hand. "What happened here, Lindsay?"

The young woman's eyes widened to marble-like spheres, seeming to extend forward out of her head. Her right hand was obscured by ground brush, the machete she was holding so darkened by blood, Beekman glimpsed only a dark blur snapping up and out. Heard the swish of it entering Racine's belly and the plop of his insides spilling out as it withdrew.

He fell over on his side, still clutching the gun. Beekman, breathless now, saw the agony and terror in his eyes. Lindsay's shadow drenched him in darkness, as she rose with her back scraping the stump the whole way. Her eyes, empty spheres shining through the mottled blackness of dried blood, found Beekman.

"He was here," the woman named Lindsay said, confusion and fear painting her features.

And the machete started upward in her grasp.

"He was here."

Beekman backpedaled, stumbled over a nest of rocks and fell backward. Back crawling as Lindsay shuffled toward him. Beekman noticed her other hand was clenched into a fist that sprayed blood with every maddening pulse.

"*Las Tierra del Diablo*," Lindsay said, still coming. "The devil was here, he was here!"

Beekman continued to claw backward, unable to get his feet under him to rise. The blood-soaked figure seemed to pick up speed before him, gliding or even floating now more than walking. She steadied the machete, blood still dripping from its blade, in line with him.

Beekman closed his eyes, shutting out the world. Barely heard the three roars, more like blasts, that pierced the air, their echoes lingering.

Beekman opened his eyes to find Lindsay staggering on, chunks of her skull missing, her face unrecognizable except for the lifeless, bulging eyes that stayed locked on him as her feet dragged across the ground.

The still stirring Racine shot her two more times, then a third. The final bullet took her dead center in the head, blowing out the rest of her brains. She froze in mid-step, empty eyes still fixed on Beekman before she keeled over at his feet.

Beekman watched the last of the life fade from Racine's eyes behind her, the fat revolver smoking in his grasp, before he let it go. Beekman looked back toward Lindsay, her hand spasming open in death to reveal a perfectly spherical, blood-soaked rock that she'd been holding. It had embedded itself in her palm, pushing out the back of her hand through gristle and bone.

So his warnings had gone unheeded and now, and now . . .

And now *what* exactly?

As the last strands of light darkened in the young woman's eyes, the rock-thing popped free and plopped to the ground, just out of Beekman's reach.

"He'll be coming back," he heard Lindsay say, even though her lips never moved and she was still clearly dead.

# ELEVEN

### Atlantic Rainforest, Brazil

**W**ell, Padre, is this what you expected?"

Father Jimenez had no answer for Colonel Arocha now, any more than he'd had six hours before when their chopper had first crossed over the area he'd been sent to investigate.

A huge swatch of the Guapiaçu Valley he had first viewed overhead from the chopper was . . . gone. Looked to have been ravaged by a mammoth fire capable of leaving nothing but scorched, barren earth dotted by dead trees in its wake. But there was no char scent carried on the air, no smoldering refuse of the kind known to linger for weeks or months after such a calamity.

The helicopter had landed on a flat stretch of earth among six others that had arrived ahead of it. The makeshift command center was awash with assembled tents and prefabricated structures. Entering it alongside Arocha, Jimenez recognized a bevy of American personnel, uniformed and otherwise, whose ID badges identified them as NASA, the National Science Foundation, the National Oceanic and Atmospheric Administration, and the CIA's Directorate of Science and Technology. So many of them cluttered about that they could barely move, or position their various equipment, without bumping into each other or the complement of U.S. soldiers there to protect them.

*From what?* Jimenez found himself wondering.

To a man, and woman, their clothes were literally dripping with perspiration. He'd never felt anything like it, not in all his experience and travels. The air so thick it actually felt difficult to breathe.

Arocha had led the priest through the chaos to the perimeter of what they'd viewed from the air, guarded by soldiers stationed at ten-yard intervals and set before hastily erected fencing. The guards waved Arocha through a break in the fencing blocked by a large armored vehicle.

Jimenez had brought his forensics case along to take samples and conduct rudimentary field tests, but he began his investigation with observation.

"Padre?" Arocha prodded, finally losing patience with the process.

A pair of soldiers had accompanied him into the field from the command center. Neither had spoken a word, riding his shadow and tensing when any of the other personnel cleared to enter the area ventured too close. Jimenez took them to be *Agência Brasileira de Inteligência* personnel as well, junior officers in all likelihood who were part of whatever division to which Arocha was attached.

"We're running out of daylight," the colonel persisted.

Spoken as if he had no desire to be on these dead grounds after dark, and Jimenez didn't blame him. In his role with the Vatican's investigative branch, the so-called Miracle Commission, he had visited the sites of numerous blights and burns he was ultimately able to explain off as some form of natural disaster or phenomena, but nothing like this either in terms of scale or effect.

Jimenez stooped and scooped up a handful of dirt in his gloved hand that felt like ground glass. Normally among nature's most fertile, now dead for all intents and purposes. Drooping petrified tree branches looked like gnarled arthritic fingers knotted in the air. There was no brush, no flora, no foliage for as far as his gaze could stretch amid the valley's parched, rolling land. Nor did he glimpse a single animal, bird, or insect.

"When did this happen?" Jimenez heard himself ask Arocha, as if it were someone else posing the question.

Arocha stood a few feet from the priest, hands clasped behind his back. "We can't say. What we can say is that satellite views show everything normal as of seventy-two hours ago. Forty-eight hours ago, contact was lost with your Catholic mission nearby and a military team was sent to investigate." He stopped to take a deep breath he quickly abandoned. "This is what they found. By then we were fielding calls from the department in the church responsible for the mission's oversight. I imagine that explains why you were dispatched so quickly."

*So did I initially,* Jimenez thought, thinking back to his phone call with Cardinal Martenko. *But now I realize I was dispatched for another reason as well, because I've investigated something similar before. . . .*

"Approximately two days ago, then," he put forth. "Any way of narrowing the time frame down further?"

Arocha took a deep breath, brought his hands from behind his back and let them dangle stiffly by his sides, his gaze sweeping about the various personnel busy inspecting the site and collecting samples. "As you can see for yourself, we've requested help from the top experts we could assemble and more are already en route. I've arranged for you to speak to some scientific personnel who've been examining the site, but so far they're being very tight-lipped."

Jimenez crouched and sifted more dirt the color of ash through his hand. Its touch singed his palm through his plastic gloves with what first felt searing hot and, just as quickly, turned icy cold, the odd sensation seeming to spread up his arm until he dropped the ash back down and yanked the glove off, as if it were on fire. The stifling, airless heat claimed him again, except for his now exposed hand that remained numb and icy.

Jimenez spotted a woman working with highly sophisticated equipment nearby. She wore black cargo pants with overstuffed pockets and a baseball cap with the initials NIS, for the National Institute of Science. Jimenez rose and approached her, Arocha clinging to his shadow the whole way.

"Father Pascal Jimenez," he said, without extending the numb hand now tucked into his pocket. "Vatican investigative branch."

"Professor Susan Baron," she said, rising from the ground. "NASA investigative branch."

"I assume you've checked the area for radiation, Professor."

"Of course. Not a trace. Can I show you something, Father?" Baron said, and proceeded to lead Jimenez and Arocha to the nearest tree. "Touch it and tell me what you feel."

Jimenez obliged. "Cold and hard as concrete."

Baron nodded. "At first glance, this level of destruction appears to be the product of fire. But there's no searing or scorch marks. If I had to speculate . . ."

"Please do."

". . . I'd say this is closer to the opposite. Exposure to temperatures approaching absolute zero."

"I don't imagine you've experienced anything like that before, Professor."

"I don't believe anyone ever has, Father."

"So do you have an explanation?"

"Scientific or supernatural?"

"Take your pick."

"None, on either count."

Arocha eased himself closer, as if to remind them he was there. "Isn't blight normally a sign of God's judgment?"

"You know your Bible, Colonel," Jimenez told him.

"Only since yesterday, Padre."

Jimenez ran his hand over the tree bark again, realized it had fused to the texture of something like porcelain. "This wasn't a blight," he said, gaze tilting toward Baron who nodded in agreement.

"Then what was it?"

"Best guess, Colonel?"

"That will have to do for now."

Jimenez gazed about, recalling his study of the geophysical characteristics of the area over the course of the long flight aboard the Vatican's jet that had brought him here from Rome. "There's no volcanic plane in the area or any fault lines suggesting a venting of superheated gases. That leaves something meteorological," Jimenez said, sounding even more uncertain than he felt. "An unprecedented collision of pressure systems that created some kind of environmental vortex."

Baron nodded. "My thinking is proceeding along similar lines."

"And what effect would such a phenomenon have on human beings?" Arocha asked them both.

"Well, it's difficult to say," Jimenez told him, touching the bark again to the realization that it felt colder in the areas reached by sunlight. "Depending on where they were in relation to the center of the vortex, petrified or mummified would be a possibility."

"To that point," Baron added, "you'll note again the absence of any remaining flora. And my preliminary field tests have detected refuse layered into the dried soil bed, indicative of severe erosion and blight consistent with the effects of a devastating drought. I've been dispatched to the sites of several such occurrences, but in each instance the process had unfolded over weeks, even months, as opposed to a single day. Again, the near-petrified condition of the soil on its own suggests the effects of some massive blast or burn, maybe both, but there remains no other evidence or indication to suggest anything of the kind, nor is there any evidence of rapid or instantaneous decomposition."

"How large is the total affected area, Professor?"

"Approximately seven miles in all directions," Arocha said skeptically.

"A circle," Jimenez heard himself mutter.

"Is that important?"

The priest remained silent and turned back toward the woman from NASA instead of responding. He eased his hand from his pocket. The warmth and feeling were returning, though not fast enough. Meanwhile, he realized suddenly that the sky was darkening, blackened clouds swirling about ominously in a pattern unlike anything Jimenez had ever seen. An illusion, or a trick of his imagination, he hoped.

"Any preliminary analysis on the composition of the ash refuse?" he asked, as thunder rumbled and the ground seemed to tremble as if to echo that cadence.

Baron shook her head. "Nothing definitive yet, though that might well provide the best indication of whatever it is we're facing here."

More thunder rumbled and Jimenez felt the first dollops of rain strike him. It felt warm, almost hot, as if shed by the superheated moist air.

"Interesting choice of words, Professor," he noted to Baron.

"What?"

"Facing," Jimenez followed, leaving it there.

"I didn't mean to imply or suggest anything by it."

"Too bad there are no witnesses to make our job easier," the priest told her.

Arocha eased Jimenez aside and lowered his voice to a whisper. "Actually, Padre, that's not entirely true. . . ."

# TWELVE

## USS *George H. W. Bush*, the Mediterranean Sea

Right now, son, you're staring down the barrel of a court-martial, I shit you not."

Admiral Keene Darby faced Max from the other side of his desk in the bowels of the aircraft carrier off which the mission to Sana'a, Yemen, had been staged.

"I'm waiting for an explanation here, Commander."

Max remained standing at attention. "I don't have one, sir."

Darby jerked a phone receiver from its cradle. "Maybe you'd like to tell that to the families of the SEALs whose bodies you hauled back. Maybe you'd like to pay the medical bills for the ones who were wounded. Uncle Sam is generous with his dime, son, when his orders are followed. But he is one pissed off, angry relative when he's ignored."

"I could say the transmission aborting the mission was garbled, sir."

"Is that what you're saying?"

"No, sir, it's not, because that wouldn't be the truth."

"And what is the truth, son?"

"That I felt I had to do something and that we saved a lot of lives last night, sir."

"You taking the credit for that?"

"No, sir!"

"How about the blame for disregarding a direct order?"

Max remained at attention. "Yes, sir!"

"Personal initiative?"

"Yes, sir!"

"Bullshit. The United States Navy isn't a democracy, son. I need to inform you and your team of that fact?"

"No, sir, because the decision to proceed was mine and mine alone."

"Not reluctant to assume responsibility, are you, son?"

"No, sir, I am not."

"Well, normally you could be looking at a court-martial, dishonorable discharge or something damn close, if Ambassador Clare Travis hadn't intervened. Woman's got powerful friends in Washington and says she'll unleash the wrath of God if you're punished the way you deserve to be for disobeying a direct order. Hell, she's even threatening to nominate you for a Medal of Honor." Darby leaned back in his chair, drawing a squeak as he reclined slightly. "Son, you're good, but you're also the luckiest goddamn son of a bitch I've ever seen."

Darby pulled a cigar from the top drawer of his desk and lit it lovingly.

"A Cuban," Max noted. "I'm impressed, sir."

Darby puffed away. "Maybe I'll share one with you, when we got cause to celebrate something, other than the bullshit I'm not buying one little bit. I look into your eyes, you know what I see? A fuckload you're not telling me. I'd like to kick your ass into the Mediterranean and dangle a life preserver on a fishing line over you until you smarten up. But I can't afford to see you drown, not with the world catching fire and us needing every man who can wield a hose. And the fact is nobody in J-SOC," he continued, referring to the Joint Special Operations Command, "can wield one as well as you. I don't know how you pull your ass out of the shit you do, but I do know I can't afford to lose a man I trust to get the job done more than I've ever trusted anyone in combat before. The whole Middle East is soaked in gasoline and this maniac Mohammed al-Qadir, together with his New Islamic Front cutthroats and psychopaths, is holding the match." Darby regarded Max from as far back as his chair would allow. "How much you know about the fuckwad?"

"I know he's a fuckwad, sir."

"Stop playing with me, son."

"I've seen the intel, Admiral."

"How much?"

"All of it. Man makes bin Laden look like a choir boy and the head of ISIS al-Baghdadi like the man playing the piano."

Darby's eyes flashed like LED lights, as if he was determining how to proceed. "You listen up good to me, son, because I'm going to tell you only once how we're going to play this. All communications are recorded, but funny thing, Commander. We had tech issues around the time you were in the air. Recording equipment went down for exactly three minutes. You hearing me here?"

"I am, sir."

"So there's no record of any mission abort or recall, no record of anything other than your original go order from stage point Charlie when your Black Hawks took to the air. We got nothing but radio silence, followed by marines, embassy personnel, and the ambassador herself, who would've otherwise been turned into terrorist bumper stickers coming home safe and sound. That's the way it will be from this point forward. You copy?"

"Yes, sir."

Darby rose stiffly. "Then stay frosty and be ready for the next call to arms, which you can expect soon," he said and blew cigar smoke in Max's face. "Close as you'll come to smoking one today, son."

Max stepped back and saluted.

Darby noticed the red, raw impressionistic design etched across his palm. "Looks like your hand got nicked in that firefight," he said, after returning the salute.

Max tucked the hand away, as if embarrassed. "Just a birthmark, sir."

"Glad to hear that, 'cause I can't imagine getting a tattoo there. But right now you got the word *trouble* tattooed on your forehead. That means you're going to take some forced leave."

"For how long, sir?" Max asked.

"Indefinitely, son. Until the dust settles."

Max stiffened, but remained silent. His hand with the strange birthmark was starting to ache now. It had always bothered him occasionally, when the adrenaline was pumping, but never anything like this.

"At least, that's what we'll call it, so Washington can pull its collective thumb out of its collective ass. We'll call it indefinite 'cause that way I can recall you anytime I want. Like next week, tomorrow, or twenty minutes from now. We clear?"

Max stood before him, hoping the admiral wouldn't notice the grimace of pain stretched across his features, even as the hand suddenly felt wet. He glanced down and saw the smear of blood coating his palm, thickening as he watched, and tightened his hand into a fist, hoping the admiral wouldn't notice that either.

"Is that clear, son?"

"Clear, sir," Max said.

"Then get your ass out of here before I change my mind and chew it off."

Max saluted, droplets of blood trailing him all the way to the door.

. . .

Once in the hall he sopped up the blood in his handkerchief, then watched a fresh pool of red originating from the outlines of his birthmark's impression. He remembered now how it had happened at times when he was a boy, how his father had wrapped it in silence while his mother looked on with fear filling her eyes, muttering quiet prayers and crossing herself over and over again. He'd never asked her why she was scared, and then the hand had stopped bleeding.

But now the bleeding was back, worse than ever, the pain stronger than ever, and he needed to finally pay a visit to the only person who might be able to tell him why.

# THIRTEEN

## *George H. W. Bush*

oments after Max closed the door to Darby's office behind him, the door leading into the admiral's conference room opened and a man dressed in a dark suit and dress shirt without a tie glided through it, as if he were floating. The thin lighting was murky at best, well suited to his features that seemed to shift each time a different tone of light struck him, like he was liquid instead of solid. His skin was baby smooth and shiny, his face a translucent mask that glowed when the light struck him directly. Snug and form-fitting to account for why the man never smiled, or flashed anything but a blank expression at all.

"I don't like you, son," the admiral told him, shaking the illusion off, "and I don't like the way you operate."

The figure stopped far enough away from Darby's desk to remain cloaked in formlessness, more like a holographic version of himself that might switch off at any time. "You watch the same drone footage of what went down on those embassy grounds as I did?"

"Combat does strange things to a man."

The man looked down, then up again. "How many men you figure your boy killed inside the embassy compound?"

"I lost count."

"And how much does that gun he stripped off its mount on the Black Hawk weigh?"

"Couldn't say."

"Take a guess, Admiral."

"Heavy."

"And with the ammo pack?"

"Heavier. How's that?"

Darby thought he saw the man smirk. "How's this, Admiral? Max Borgia was seventeen when he enlisted."

"Bullshit."

"That's also not his real name."

"And just how do you know that?"

"Let's say I've been following this SEAL they call the Pope for a while now. Let's say the fact that he scored the highest of any SEAL in BUD/S training history put him on my radar, and plenty that's happened since has kept him there. Let's say there are some oddities in his background that drew my attention." The man studied the droplets of blood drying on the floor. "What he calls his birthmark, for example."

"What else could it be?"

"What's your security clearance, Admiral?"

"As high as yours, I imagine."

"Don't bet on that," the man said. "And you're not cleared to hear my theories on Max Borgia's background and plenty more about him. Suffice it to say, I deemed him worthy of my department's attention."

"Want to give me some more details into that department?"

The man smirked. "Ask Langley."

"I did. They said they'd get back to me." Darby leaned forward. "You're on this ship because of Max Borgia, aren't you?"

"And you should be thanking me for that," the man said, half winking. "After all, Max Borgia's only serving in this man's Navy today, because I allowed him to stay in it."

"Then let me make something as absolutely clear as I can: This shit stops now. So whatever it is you're slinging about Max Borgia won't stick to these walls." The admiral leaned forward, his chair creaking again. "You're a ghost, Agent Man, about as CIA as my left nut. Max Borgia is under my command. That makes me his daddy, his granddaddy, and his mama all rolled into one. Know what, Agent Man? I don't know who you are or what house you're really haunting, but whatever you got on your mind, maybe you should take it up with J-SOC directly. They got an eight hundred number I can give you."

The man started toward the door through which Max had just left. Then he stopped, looking back one last time at Darby and smirking again like a man hiding a winning lottery ticket in his wallet.

"You saw what he did at the embassy, Admiral, you saw the look in his eyes."

"I saw what he did, and that's all I needed to see."

Darby thought the man might've flirted with a smile. "Then you missed the best part."

"And what's that, Casper?"

This time the smile broke through. "He enjoyed it."

Darby pressed his cigar out in an ashtray. "Right now I'm thinking seriously of kicking you off my ship."

"No need, Admiral, because I'm heading out now," the man said.

"Anywhere special?"

"The Brazilian rainforest. And if I'm headed there, you can count on it being special indeed."

# FOURTEEN

## London, England

I know how difficult this must be for you," Dr. Neal Van Royce, assistant director of the World Health Organization for Field Operations, said to Vicky, after the plane he'd dispatched to Atlanta had landed in London.

Vicky shrugged off his comment. "What can you tell me about what we're facing?"

"Let's just say the reported symptoms defy explanation."

"That would explain the radio silence," Vicky told him, brushing her long hair from her face only to have the warm breeze blow it right back. "Why no one's uttering a word through the normal channels I checked en route."

Van Royce, a short portly man with more mustache hair than the thin strands riding his scalp, stopped and regarded her closer. "Speaking of words, you're so good to have come all this way. After all you've been through . . ." He shook his head. "What a horrible experience. I just can't imagine."

"Neither can I, sometimes. Still. Likely forever."

She started to grope for more words, then gave up the effort. Thomas's funeral had been the worst day of her life for a myriad of reasons. As a virologist specializing in epidemiology, her training and experience had taught her that life itself was something that lay within her control. Helping to resolve a potential epidemic or pandemic, at least stopping it in its tracks, was among the most vital and worthy acts any person could perform. But the tragedy had left her feeling powerless, nothing at all within her control after watching the man she wanted to spend the rest of her life with die right in front of her.

The call from Van Royce at the reception following the funeral, she supposed, had saved her. The mission and mystery he'd alluded to instantly restored her purpose and, more, sense of self that the tragedy had torn away. The accident had stolen two lives, not one: her fiancé's actual one and hers, at least figuratively. The pain became a great sucking wound vacuuming up her life and hope. How ironic that a person charged with saving the lives of millions felt helpless to preserve her own.

Today, though, found her back in the field, the only place she could at least try to leave her own tragedy behind. Vicky had risen to become one of the World Health Organization's most promising experts in potential pandemics, specializing in the Middle East. The choice, and assignment, had been a natural outgrowth of her fluency in Arabic, thanks to being raised by a Lebanese nanny after her mother's death in childbirth. A woman whose last name she'd ultimately taken as an adult to avoid any connection with the father she so despised. She had been fully bilingual for as long as she could remember, holding tightly to her adopted language until she went away to college. Even in the WHO, experts in her field who spoke Arabic were rare and that helped speed her ascent through the ranks there after a stint with the CDC. It also meant being dispatched to the Middle East on multiple occasions, often to war zones with little or no security to protect her and her mobile team.

The WHO had arranged for a car, a large SUV, to be waiting for them with a driver when they landed in Amman, prepacked with all the equipment they may, or may not, need. Remote villages tended to have very little in terms of modern diagnostic capabilities. They had caught a break, though, with the fact that this particular village boasted a working clinic operated by Doctors Without Borders. Still, better to be safe than sorry, and the SUV contained blood and DNA analyzers, along with a collapsible X-ray machine and portable MRI that was almost as accurate as the full-scale model.

The Jordanian village of Amalla, set against the foot of the Abarim mountain range, was, typically, steeped in poverty. Dominated by cheap clapboard shacks squeezed up against each other, nestled about a patchwork of ruddy streets and parched land. More shacks had been added in scattershot fashion to accommodate any number of Iraqi and Syrian refugees, and that kind of overcrowding was a recipe for disaster, providing the easiest route for a potential pathogen to spread.

"I expected a formal briefing from headquarters, while we were in the air from London," she told Van Royce.

"That would've meant using the Internet and we're dark on this. I told you that."

"Yes, you did. But not why. Still."

Van Royce's expression was flat and grim. "That you need to see for yourself."

# FIFTEEN

## Amalla, Jordan

Only a single doctor, Van Royce explained, remained at the Amalla clinic, the other personnel from the Doctors Without Borders organization having fled when it became clear they might be dealing with something far beyond both their capabilities and intentions when they volunteered to serve the organization. That doctor's reporting had become increasingly cryptic and scattershot, and then, perhaps half a day before, had stopped entirely.

"So we can't even be sure that the one doctor is still there," Van Royce told her.

"Or," Vicky offered, the grimness of her tone completing the thought for her.

Van Royce chose to ignore her insinuation. "Fortunately," he said instead, "the doctor who remained on site has some experience in the field of potential pathogens. That means he should be familiar with the proper procedures to follow, enacting a protocol intended to lessen the ability of the potential pathogen to spread outside this limited, isolated area."

That was the one positive here, since the WHO was normally not cast in the role of first responders. That task was normally left to local authorities, even in the African subcontinent where disease so flourished. So many potential pathogens owed their origins to issues of sanitation. Unclean water, raw sewage, insect-riddled crops. Ebola, for example, owed the vast bulk of its spread to the primitive way corpses were handled and readied for burial.

The regional clinic erected by Doctors Without Borders in Amalla was a simple one-story concrete slab with horizontal windows mounted high to avoid injury to patients in the event the glass was shattered by a bomb blast nearby. Dr. Pierre Robelais was smoking a cigarette outside when Vicky and Van Royce pulled up in the SUV, the sight of a medical professional in full scrubs greeted by both of them with great relief, since they'd both feared the worst.

"Forgoing protective gear?" Van Royce asked Robelais, shifting about in his own bulky suit, after introductions had been exchanged.

Robelais, a tall, gaunt man with a thick black beard, shrugged. "I had close contact with the first six patients well before we began to suspect the involvement of a pathogen. In this part of the world, we're used to rolling the dice."

"You said the first six patients," Vicky noted.

"We've had eight more cases, fourteen in all now." He flicked his cigarette aside. "Let me show you."

The first thing Vicky noticed upon entering the bunker-like clinic in full biohazard gear alongside Van Royce were beds squeezed into makeshift cubicles divided by what looked like bedsheets strung across clotheslines in what had been a waiting room.

"These are the most recent eight patients," Robelais explained. "We've divided the other six among the four examination rooms and kept only the lab free."

"What about support personnel?" Van Royce wondered.

"They left with the other two doctors rotating in and out of here. Not what they signed up for, I believe is how they put it. Right now I've got three volunteers, a trio of women who live in the village. Three's all I can handle because that's all the hazmat suits I had on hand."

"We have an extra one we can give you," Vicky told him.

"Too late for that."

"Procedure, Doctor. I'll go out to the car and get it for you."

While Robelais donned his biohazard suit, Vicky absorbed more of the scene, struck by what she heard:

Coughing, sneezing, retching, moaning, vomiting . . .

The most dangerous pandemics threatening the world were remarkably similar from a symptomatic standpoint. Distinctions, of course, were always present but almost invariably the most lethal pathogens produced the same response in the body.

"I'd like to start with the first recorded patient," Vicky told Robelais, when he reappeared wearing the protective suit. "Establish a symptomatic baseline for what we're looking at."

"Right this way, then," he said in French-accented English, leading her down the hall to the first room on the right. "The first patient we treated is in here."

Vicky had examined almost as many cadavers as she had infected living victims, and her first impression of what greeted her in the exam room was that the victim was a combination of the two. Her initial, visual examination, something she relied on intuitively far more than most in her field, was of a corpse with the first signs of rigor mortis beginning to set in.

Before she proceeded any further, Vicky jogged her phone to the audio record function and tested the levels to make sure no observation, no matter how casual, was lost. Then she checked the Apple Watch Thomas had given her that she'd barely taken off since the accident, in order to note the time for the record. Sometimes in her field, the simplest clue proved the most important, and if that clue were to be casually discarded, both valuable time and more lives could be lost.

"The victim's flesh is pale and languid, uniform in color along his face, neck, and parts of his arms," she narrated. "It appears dried out, chapped and ready to crack. His hair is dry and listless, and several clumps of strands have been shed to the pillow or floor."

Vicky noticed that even though the patient was breathing on his own and in no distress, the sheet covering him up to his neck didn't flutter or billow at all, his breaths clearly too shallow and short to ruffle his chest enough to rustle it.

The victim was a veritable corpse to the naked eye, a fact that seemed to be confirmed by touch as well.

Vicky found examining a corpse or living subject through hazmat gloves to be a distinctly frustrating experience. In her mind an examination needed to make the fullest use of sensory input to reach a successful and satisfactory conclusion. This was especially true given, first, that she was often encountering an infection never seen before in its current form and, second, that her fieldwork potentially involved a threat to millions of lives as opposed to that of a single patient. Science and training might've formed the body of her work, but making preliminary assessments based simply on what her eyes detected came from a part of her mind she neither understood fully nor tried to.

Before continuing her examination, Vicky consulted a small, old-fashioned chalkboard hanging from the same pole supporting a section of the plastic sheeting.

"Strangely," she resumed, repositioning her phone to make sure the recording missed nothing, "the patient's vitals are reasonably normal. Heart rate, blood pressure, pulse all indicate anything but what his appearance otherwise suggests should be drastically anomalous vital signs. Doctor," she called to Robelais, "what else can you tell us about this patient?"

"Nothing," he responded. "I saw him for the first time when his family carried him inside; weak, short of breath, and bleeding from the eyes, nose, and ears. They haven't been back since."

Vicky felt something tug at her spine. "Has anyone checked on them?"

"That was two days ago. It's been just me here alone practically ever since. That's why I stopped issuing reports. No time, especially with fourteen patients total now, but this man was the first."

Vicky inspected the patient's hands, wishing she could better feel them through her gloves. There was so much to be gleaned from an examination through touch, to the point where she resisted the temptation to break protocol and risk flesh-to-flesh contact. She could tell the man's hands were rough and callused. There might have been some bruising, but it was hard to determine given the rigidity in the patient's dermal layers. The calluses seemed ridged in a pattern that indicated work with manual tools, shovels and rakes perhaps. And although the skin's rigid condition made it harder for her to discern tone, Vicky thought she could detect the kind of variances that suggested a man exposed frequently to the sun in patterns she took to mean the man's work kept him in a single direction for a prolonged period.

A farmer, then, most likely.

"A neighbor of this patient was brought in this morning," Robelais reported, after consulting a chipped wooden clipboard he'd been holding. "I'm sorry I neglected to mention that."

"Understandable under the circumstances, Doctor. What was the time lag between admissions?"

Robelais checked his clipboard again. "Thirty-six hours, according to this, but that may not be precise. The other dozen patients arrived in between."

"So this contagion, whatever it is, we can safely assume, is now thirty-six hours old," Vicky noted, judging that to be the contagion's approximate incubation period. And the fact that Robelais showed no signs of the initial symptoms led her to conclude, on a preliminary basis, that the pathogen wasn't spread through the air.

She began a general, physical examination of the man. She started in the throat area, checking the glands there, along the jawline, and then at the armpit area. There was swelling, but nothing grossly apparent. What was apparent was a general rigidity of the skin and overall musculature, as if the patient were holding his muscles tight, flexing them. His stomach and torso area were similarly rigid and her initial examination of his liver, kidneys, bladder, and intestinal fabric felt hardened.

*Rigor mortis indeed*, Vicky thought. If this were some kind of test, and they'd brought her in here to examine the man blindfolded, she would've guessed he was already dead and suffering from the first stages of that.

On the contrary, though, he was still alive.

And that made whatever had struck this village something she'd never encountered before, either directly or via case study. The patient showed no response to stimulus, had no reflex capacity. An examination of his eyes revealed them to be utterly lifeless, the pupils fixed and dilated, and the whites stained by what looked like ink blotches of red where blood must've leaked. She noted his eye color as blue, but closer examination revealed an ash-gray hue seemed to be overtaking it, strongest at the perimeter and spreading toward the center—something else Vicky had never encountered before, either in study or the field.

The beam of her penlight shined through them revealed no swelling of the brain, though she suspected it too would have exhibited an increased rigidity had she been able to examine it. The patient's heartbeat should've been more pronounced than it sounded through the stethoscope, a fact Vicky first passed off to the cumbersome nature of the biohazard suit and then wondered if perhaps it was more due to general rigidity plaguing his chest cavity as well.

*Starting from the inside and moving outward*, she thought, making another mental note.

As Vicky pried open the patient's mouth, a frothy stream of blood drained out from swollen gums. Swabbing away the blood revealed that most of his teeth had fallen out, some still in his mouth under his tongue, while the rest were loose and on the verge of following. She traced a finger along the gum line, feeling a pinch and pulling the finger away before her glove could tear. She first thought it was the broken base of a tooth still lodged beneath the gum. Closer inspection, though, revealed it to be something else entirely: a new tooth, the tip pointy and sharp.

Vicky inspected his gums again, using a probe this time, and not believing what she uncovered.

The patient was growing a fresh set of teeth to replace the ones that had fallen out, perhaps even forcing them from the gums the way his second set of teeth had pushed out the first.

"Can you step outside with me for a moment, Doctor?" Van Royce asked her, looking up from a text message or e-mail he'd received on his phone.

"Wait, I want to try one more thing." She looked toward Robelais through her helmet's plastic antifog plate. "Have you been drawing blood?"

"Yes, several times," he told her. "The last time I tried was one hour ago."

"What do you mean tried?"

"I encountered . . . difficulties."

"Difficulties?"

"A new symptom," Robelais said, as if embarrassed by his lack of understanding. "Or, perhaps, a gradation of what was already present. Here," he said, handing her a syringe from a tray poised atop a nearby cart.

Vicky took the syringe and peeled back the sterile wrapping. She found a vein just beneath the crook in the patient's elbow. She tried to pinch the skin to make the vein protrude a bit more, but couldn't even budge it. Then she patted the skin in the general area around the vein to flush some blood to the area, also with no effect at all.

Ultimately, she held the arm steady and slipped the needle into place over the blue of the vein, easing the plunger down.

It didn't move.

She pressed harder.

The needle still didn't budge, not even piercing the skin, the vein remaining untouched beneath it.

"What the . . ." she heard Van Royce start, before his voice trailed off.

Vicky pressed her thumb with as much force as she could muster, until her knuckle started to throb.

*Crack!*

*Ping!*

The two sounds made her lurch back reflexively, rocking the gurney on which the patient lay. She looked down at the plunger still clutched in her grasp. The needle had broken off at the stem and dropped to the building's tile floor.

"Doctor," Van Royce was saying, his voice sterner. "A moment outside, please."

Vicky followed him back into the hallway, glad to be able to strip off her hazmat mask and breathe freely again. Even more glad when they slid through a curtain formed of the same plastic sheeting into an empty cubicle.

"Before you ask," she started, catching up to her own breathing, "the answer's no, I've never seen or studied anything like this before."

"That's not what I was going to say," Van Royce told her, his tone as grim and somber as his expression. "While you were examining the patient, I received word of another possible outbreak, considerably more advanced."

"Where?"

"Egypt, the Sinai Peninsula. Another team from the WHO is already en route."

"But they won't get there before we can, Neal," Vicky told him.

# SIXTEEN

## Alberta, Canada

Dale Denton watched Orson Beekman approaching him across the frozen patch of wasteland. Nothing but scrub and light snow cover with a smattering of rolling hills and mountains in the distance that looked as if they'd been painted onto the scene beneath the blazing sunlight that belied the actual temperature.

"Doesn't look like much, does it, Professor?" Denton greeted, with a wide grin showcasing the deep furrows and lines the sun had carved into his face through all his years working the fields. "But the oil sands situated beneath this land have helped make Alberta responsible for around ninety-five percent of oil reserves in this country. Know how much of those our company owns the mineral rights to?"

"No," Beekman said, exhausted from coming straight here from Houston. He'd stopped there only long enough to secure the rock, or whatever it was, in the safest environment possible after returning from the Yucatán. "I don't."

"Neither do I, to tell you the truth, not exactly. But I know there weren't a lot of other bidders when I got involved a whole bunch of years ago. Plenty of others knew the oil sands were here, but only a very few saw the profit in that someday. Everybody knows you've got to risk a fortune to make a fortune, and I'm hardly a stranger to risk. Show me a man who's afraid of taking risks, and I'll show you a failure. I've been walking a tightrope with a blindfold on my whole goddamn life. Familiar territory now, my own backyard." Denton paused and looked Beekman over, as if seeing him for the first time. "Congratulations on a successful trip, by the way."

Beekman shivered and wrapped his arms tighter around himself. Denton had had cold-weather gear waiting for him to change into at the airfield, but so far it wasn't doing much good. He'd felt cold ever since leaving

Mexico, unable to chase the experience at the site of the find in the Yucatán from his mind.

"Successful?" he managed to repeat, incredulous at Denton's use of the word.

"In spite of the collateral damage, of course," Denton said matter-of-factly, as if the deaths of Racine and his team meant nothing to him. "Those people knew the risks and were paid handsomely for it."

Beekman shuddered. "You weren't there. The damage was a lot more than collateral."

Denton seemed unmoved. "You gave explicit orders Racine's team violated. I hope you don't feel either of us bears any responsibility for this."

"You don't understand."

"I think I do."

"I'm not talking about the deaths; I'm talking about what caused them and how. I'm talking about the object. And no amount of sanitization or cover-up can change the fact that it was directly to blame for what happened."

"A rock?"

"I don't need to tell you that this is no ordinary rock."

Denton scowled, his breath misting before him. In point of fact, he had gone into damage control mode as soon as Beekman provided his initial, stumbling report over the satellite phone. Bribes were prepared for the proper Mexican officials, and by the time Beekman reached the airport after cursory questioning, blame for the massacre had been laid with the Sinaloa drug cartel. He didn't have to clear Customs and no one questioned the contents of the vacuum-sealed container that hadn't left his sight, and didn't until he secured it at Western Energy Technologies headquarters in Houston.

"Please don't insult me with your mumbo jumbo, Professor," Denton scoffed. "I'm a businessman and, last time I checked, you were a geophysicist. Let's stay on subject and on point here."

"I imagine that's what Pandora was doing just before she opened the infamous box."

"There's no room for myths or spook stories in our line of work. We knew the rock, stone, object, or whatever you want to call it was potentially dangerous and you warned Racine to that effect. Please don't expect me to base my decisions on the actions of a single unstable and unbalanced individual. That's right, Professor, I've reviewed the personnel files. This woman responsible for this mess suffered from bipolar disorder, and I'm betting the autopsy on her shows she'd stopped taking her meds."

"Have you even read my report?"

"You look around here and see oil fields," Denton said, instead of responding. "Know what I see, Professor? I see the past, soon to be the distant past. I see a finite resource that's bleeding away as we stand here. Imagine a world that no longer has oil to fuel it. Now, imagine a world that no longer *needs* oil to fuel it. And whoever comes up with a new energy source to replace fossil fuels will be the next Google, Apple, Microsoft, or Intel. All indications point to the fact our long-lost rock possesses that kind of potential. But we can't determine that unless we put aside likening it to Pandora's box, the Holy Grail, the Golden Fleece, or the goddamn pot of gold at the end of the rainbow. Because you just might have brought back a real pot of gold from the Yucatán. So let's focus on the bigger picture, the fact that something we've been searching for ever since Ben Younger happened upon it in that underground cave twenty-seven years ago is now in our possession."

"It was burning through the young woman's hand," Beekman told him, something he had left out of his report.

"Burning?"

"That's what I thought at first, except upon inspection the surrounding skin showed no signs of heat scoring, bubbling, puckering, or burn marks."

"All the better it's tucked away safely in our lab, then."

"I'm not sure how safely anymore."

Denton's eyes bore into Beekman the same way the drill was slicing through the rock, shale, and limestone of Alberta. "What about its origins and actual composition?"

"Once I'm sure it's safe, we'll run X-ray, spectrographic, and magnetic resonance core testing toward that end."

"I trust my gut over all of them, Professor. We were standing side-by-side in Mexico when Ben Younger appeared out of nowhere. The answers to everything that happened to him afterward, including his death, lies with this rock."

"All I'm saying is that we need to go slow here, exercise all measure of caution. If we're right about the potential the rock's energy has to change the world, we must also accept the fact that it has the power to—"

"Spare me the lecture, Professor," Denton interrupted. "We've been over this before. A million times. And if I let myself get spooked as easily as you do, there wouldn't have been a Mexico or the hundred-million-dollar lab where potentially the greatest scientific discovery ever known to man is waiting for us." Denton swept his gaze about the wasteland so rich with oil sands that it might as well have been a paradise. "Look around you," he prompted to Beekman, wearing no jacket and only a sweater rolled up at the sleeves. "When others were shutting down or reducing their operations, I was expanding those of Western Energy Technologies. And I've purchased tens of thousands of additional acres *since* prices sank. Time and time again, I should've lost, but I never did, because I always win. It's all about the future, and we're going to own that future, Professor, lock, stock, and fucking barrel."

Thanks to an object no bigger than a baseball, Denton thought, WET was poised to make another fortune from pioneering a new source of energy, but only if his gut feeling was correct. Ben Younger, likely the first person to ever encounter the rock's power, was dead and buried, what was left of him anyway, after plunging from a sixtieth-floor office window in a Manhattan skyscraper. He might well have been the first man to ever lay eyes upon it, carrying its mark with him from that day forward without realizing its true power and origins.

Energy Is Power.

Another of Denton's catchphrases that had become the motto of Western Energy Technologies. As a boy he'd watched his parents die in a cotton field, barely avoiding the tornado that gobbled them up after the work foreman had refused to heed the advance warnings. He ended up being raised in an old-fashioned Jesuit orphanage where the rest of his rearing was done in misery by no one in particular. That's how Dale Denton had learned to rely only on himself.

He'd never gotten the sight of that funnel cloud sucking his parents up into its vortex out of his mind. He'd watched breathless, horrified, but also fascinated. And, if the theories Professor Beekman had developed about the object now held in WET's Houston labs were correct, Denton was about to harness a completely new energy source, a game changer in the world of energy that would hopefully justify the fortune he'd spent over the years to recover it.

"I'm going to say this one more time," Beekman told him, shivering anew. "We should delay the experimentation phase a bit longer, at least until we have a clearer notion of what we're dealing with."

"And I believe we shouldn't. Enough said," Denton finished, leaving it there. "You have your instructions, Professor. Utilize any precautions you wish to make sure we don't destroy the world before we get the chance to own it, but I want you to be ready to go ahead by the time I return to Houston."

His phone rang and Denton excused himself to take the call, walking far enough away to keep Beekman from overhearing any of the conversation. He listened briefly to the speaker's words, ending the call with, "Keep me informed," while nodding, before starting back toward Beekman.

"A day for loose ends, Professor," Denton said, his phone pocketed again. "Time to tie them up once and for all, before they can strangle us."

# SEVENTEEN

## Atlantic Rainforest, Brazil

T oo bad there are no witnesses to make our job easier."

"Actually, Padre, that's not entirely true. . . ."

But the skies had opened and the storm's deluge began before Arocha could explain further and escort Father Jimenez to wherever these witnesses might be. He'd remained coy and evasive, elaborating no further while Jimenez resigned himself to spending the night in a tented base camp well back from the site, under guard by both Brazilian and now American soldiers.

His tent was sturdily erected, made of heavy waterproof canvas that kept the interior dry from the torrents slapping at its pitched roof that buckled but never gave under the onslaught of gale-force winds. The storm seemed to wash the heat from the air, drawing in a cold dankness behind it that chilled Jimenez to the bone. Left him shaking in clothes still moist and clammy from the sweat bred by the oppressive humidity earlier in the day.

But this was a different chill than he was accustomed to, a chill that seemed to spread outward from the hand that had sifted through the ash earlier in the day. Jimenez bundled up in his sleeping bag and slept fitfully, intermittently, his slumber disrupted by a combination of the rampaging winds testing the bonds of his tent and dark dreams bred by memories of a day long ago that still haunted him.

A cold knife against his throat, a dark figure poised over Jimenez, taunting him.

"Your God is not here."

Words Jimenez would never forget. But he had managed to survive that day, as he would survive this night that seemed to grow colder each time he was awoken by the chattering of his own teeth. The shrill, howling wind pushed right through the canvas of his tent as if it were made of mesh. His work for the Vatican had taken him to the Andes once in the dead of winter. He'd never known such cold before, certain he never would again.

Until now.

He could never remember a time where he welcomed the sunrise more. But it was several more hours into the morning light before Colonel Arocha had come to collect him for their trip up the river.

"Interesting storm last night, Colonel."

"Padre?"

"Such a sudden drop in temperature, all that wind. I thought my tent might be blown away like Dorothy's house in *The Wizard of Oz*."

The perplexed look on Arocha's face made Jimenez think the analogy had escaped him, until the colonel spoke. "I don't know what you are speaking of. There was no storm last night."


They trucked to the shoreline where a Brazilian military launch was waiting for them, something growing very clear to the priest from the trip's outset.

"The fish," he started.

"You won't see a single one, Padre," Arocha nodded. "But if you check out the shore, you won't see any washed up there either. Could be they got away."

"Could be? Is there another alternative?"

Jimenez thought he saw trepidation, even fear, suddenly brimming in the colonel's eyes, but then it was gone. "Whatever happened back there at the site, what you saw, tends to spawn much speculation."

"With good reason."

"I was thinking of past natural disasters where animals and birds had the foresight to flee the area in time. Maybe that was true of the fish here."

"But you don't think so."

"I don't know what to think, Padre. This isn't a confessional. We need to stick to what we know."

Which, Jimenez almost said, still amounted to practically nothing. He'd donned his scientist's hat for the past twenty-four hours, examining areas of the Dead Zone he was allowed to access with an eye toward forming a logical sequence of cause and effect. Even the strangest and most inexplicable occurrences tended to have logical explanations, once properly analyzed. While Jimenez lacked both the equipment and a measure of the expertise required to perform such an analysis here, a scientist formed his initial hypothesis often from the barest data.

The past twenty-four hours, though, had only compounded his confusion. And he could only hope that the survivors who awaited him down river would be able to shed some light where he could see only darkness now.

Father Jimenez stood next to Colonel Arocha in the military launch's stern, gazing intently at the water in the hope of spotting a fish, any fish. But there was nothing, not even any insects buzzing around a stagnant pool of water. The scene was placid and serene on the one hand, terrifying in what it suggested on the other. Even the currents had stilled, as if they too had fled the scene with the birds and fish.

"How much do you know about this particular Catholic mission, about where we're going?" Arocha asked.

"The Vatican approved its formation to help indoctrinate one of the oldest living indigenous peoples in civilization today about the life and teachings of Christ," Jimenez told him. "What with their way of life all but wiped out by encroachment onto their native lands."

"You're speaking of the conglomerates that see this region as a vast piggy bank. Those companies are the lifeblood of Brazil's economy, Padre."

"I'm an investigator, not an economist, Colonel."

Arocha took a deep breath. "Then be warned that those in my government beholden to such economists are adverse to disruption."

"You didn't mention how many survivors there were," Jimenez said, uncomfortable with the digression.

"Only one."

"I'd like to hear more about him. What did he see? What has he said?"

"It's a *she*, a young child, in fact, and I'm afraid the answers to your questions are a bit complicated. Better you see, and hear, for yourself. What I can tell you is no trace was found of her family, the rest of the tribe, or any of the missionaries. The mission itself was reduced to rubble, no trace of the remains of the missionaries and other natives found anywhere. Just this little girl." Arocha looked as if he'd swallowed something bitter. "It makes no sense"

"What else should I know?"

"Like I said, it's better that you see for yourself," Arocha said, sounding unsure for the first time.


As chief investigator of the Vatican's so-called Miracle Commission, Jimenez had found himself on a hundred scenes of purported miracles and inexplicable events. Though it was his duty to be objective, he'd managed to disprove each and every one to the satisfaction of the Curia.

Jimenez's extensive training in science had made him question whether that discipline could coexist with faith, whether the two could even be made part of the same conversation. And, yet, as the years passed, and circumstances conspired to erode his own faith, he found himself wanting to find at least one true miracle, one act that science couldn't explain under any circumstances. Well, maybe, just maybe, he'd gotten his wish. Only it wasn't a miracle at all.

"We're almost there," Arocha said suddenly.

The colonel's words snapped him out of some kind of trance. Jimenez checked his watch, ten minutes lost to his thoughts.

The launch glided up against a dock, and Arocha extended a hand down to Jimenez to help him, after climbing up himself. More soldiers were waiting to guide them the rest of the way on foot through the dense reaches of the jungle the men at the head of the procession cleared with machetes, working in tandem. But the thick leaf structure had browned. It felt dried-out and coarse to the touch, the individual leaves breaking when bent and leaving a grayish, powdery residue on Jimenez's fingertips. Here too there were no bird or animal sounds, nothing to suggest anything other than death.

The walk ended at a checkpoint and camp that reminded Jimenez of a smaller version of the one set up just outside the Dead Zone. Soldiers from both the Brazilian and United States armies stood watch over a hastily erected perimeter, but the priest found himself studying the government officials gathered inside the security perimeter instead. They seemed to recognize Arocha on sight and showed immediate deference to him, altering Jimenez's assessment of the weight the man may have carried. Clearly he was more important than he'd let on, and the priest even began to wonder if his rank and very uniform might cloak his true position and importance. Little more than a costume.

"We brought the survivor here," Arocha explained, as men dressed in civilian garb gathering evidence and snapping off pictures of the area acknowledged his presence. "She's been under guard ever since. Questioning has been kept to a minimum and only by those directly cleared by me."

Jimenez spotted a pile of stray items that had been salvaged from the Dead Zone. There were wooden plates and utensils heaped amid chunks of wood and stone, gray with ash that looked burned into them. Jimenez noted the frayed bindings of books, missing all their pages, along with tattered clumps of cloth he took to be the remnants of clothes and thick round discs he assumed were wheels for a cart or wagon.

Near the top of the pile, the arms and face of a stuffed animal toy protruded.

"Would you mind, Colonel?" Jimenez asked as he approached.

"Not at all, Padre. We'll be bagging all this up shortly for transport and further analysis."

Jimenez plucked the stuffed animal from the pile. It was a bear that carried the same burnt odor he recalled from the Dead Zone, the ash coating that darkened its once white fur identical as well.

"Has this little girl been able to describe what she saw?" he wondered, tucking the toy under his arm.

"Not exactly," Arocha said, stopping just before a folding table where two soldiers stood protectively over her.

She must have heard or sensed their approach and looked up, seeming to focus on Father Jimenez. He noticed her eyes looked like milky, opaque marbles wedged into her head.

The little girl was blind.


"When she does speak," Jimenez heard Arocha say from alongside him, "her language is a local variant of Tupi. Are you familiar with that?"

"Somewhat." Jimenez found himself studying the little girl, as if she were a lab experiment. "I may need an interpreter."

Arocha nodded. "We have one on site. Come, let me introduce you."


When they reached the table, Jimenez realized the little girl was speaking to herself in a muted tone, the words barely intelligible.

"Oré r-ub, ybak-y-pe t-ekó-ar, I moeté-pyr-amo nde r-era t'o-îkó. T'o-ur nde Reino! Tó-ñe-moñang nde r-emi-motara yby-pe."

"Her name is Belinha," Arocha offered. "I'll fetch the translator, Padre."

"No need yet. The language is much closer to Brazilian Portuguese. She's reciting the Lord's Prayer in Tupi."

*"Ybak-y-pe i ñe-moñanga îabé! Oré r-emi-'u, 'ara-îabi'õ-nduara, e-î-me'eng kori orébe,"* the blind girl continued.

Belinha stopped when Jimenez's shadow fell over her. *"Morubixaba,"* she said, using the Tupi word for "chief," focusing on him so intensely that Jimenez swore she could see.

"No," he told her, adding, *"Karaíba."* The word technically meant "prophet" but was also Tupi vernacular for priest or man of God. *"I have something for you,"* Jimenez continued, as well as he could in Tupi, and eased the stuffed animal into the girl's grasp.

She held the toy at arm's distance, her sightless eyes even glassier as she seemed to regard it. *"Pûera,"* the little girl followed.

*Pûera* was Tupi for "dead."

Jimenez asked her what had happened, what she remembered.

*"Pûera,"* Belinha repeated, all of her attention back on the doll. And, as Jimenez watched, she plucked the stuffed animal's tiny, marble-like eyes from its head and tossed them aside.

*"What happened?"* he posed in Tupi.

The little girl started flopping the toy's stuffed, worn arms, stretching it at the seams. Jimenez thought he heard a ripping sound.

*"What in God's name did this, Belinha?"* Father Jimenez asked this time, hoping the different phrasing might spur something in the little girl.

Belinha looked up, seeming to look at him—no, not so much *at* as *through*. He thought he heard her whisper something and leaned in closer so he might hear better.

"Your God is not here," she said in English, a mischievous grin stretching across her face.

The breath froze in Jimenez's throat, chilled not just by the blind girl's words, but also her placid expression that suggested she somehow knew the importance of those words to him, the pain and memories they inspired.

From Nigeria years and years ago, before he'd entered the priesthood, and the source of the dream that had haunted his sleep the night before.

*Your God is not here.*

"Say that again, please," Jimenez implored the little girl.

But the little girl was no longer listening, no longer paying attention.
"Please. Repeat what you just said."

Her tiny fingers were squeezing the bear's stuffed arms now, behaving as if he wasn't even there. Jimenez wanted to reach out and shake her, make her repeat her words. Then he swallowed hard, certain in that moment the girl could see him. He watched one of the bear's arms come free in her grasp. The other stuffed arm followed, leaving Belinha holding both of them, and what was left of the bear fell to the ground.

*"My name is not Belinha,"* she said, reverting back to her native language, *"it's Bituah."*

Something about that name sounded familiar to Jimenez, but he was too unsettled to give the matter further thought. He moved away, trying to settle himself, when Arocha drew even.

"What did she just say, Padre?"

"It was nothing," Jimenez lied. "Just gibberish."

*Your God is not here. . . .*

In that moment, a strange-looking helicopter like none Jimenez had ever seen before in all his travels settled over the modest clearing, seeming impervious to the whims of the wind. They'd taken the launch here because no pilot would ever dare chancing such dense and dangerous foliage, much less with the winds and weather having turned so unpredictable. But this chopper set down undeterred through a space barely wide enough to accommodate the reach of its rotor that seemed to spin in slow motion.

Jimenez watched as a well-built man with otherwise the most nondescript features he'd ever seen leap out before the pod had even settled on the ground. The man approached Arocha, his face aglow in the sunlight that had suddenly broken through, his skin boasting the sheen of flesh-colored porcelain.

Like a mask.

Arocha met the man halfway to the chopper, listened briefly, and then retraced his steps to Jimenez.

"He'd like to speak with you."

Jimenez realized the stranger was staring straight at him, his entire face seeming to change at the whims of the trees and brush around him. The man approached in the shadow of a half dozen men wearing military tactical gear with thigh holsters fastened tight and carrying assault rifles, their eyes unnerving in their steely sureness.

"We need to go, Father Jimenez," the man said, his voice so flat his lips didn't even seem to move. "The United States government appreciates your cooperation."

"How did you know my name?"

The man gestured for Jimenez to follow him. "I told the pilot to keep the engine warm. Come on, I've got a plane waiting."

Jimenez dug his heels, literally, into the ground. "I don't even know who you are, what you're doing here; who sent you. My orders come from the Vatican."

"I know, Father," the man said, unclipping a satellite phone from his belt and handing it to Jimenez.

The phone began to ring just as he took it in his grasp, and he answered it, pressed against his ear. "Yes? . . . Yes, Your Eminence," he said, holding his eyes on the man standing before him. "I understand, Your Eminence. Whatever you say."

Jimenez ended the call and, stupefied, handed the phone back over.

"Where are we going?" he asked the man.

"The aircraft carrier *George H. W. Bush*, currently on station in the Mediterranean. I'll explain everything once we're in the air."

"In the name of all that's holy, what's this about?"

"Nigeria, Father, twenty-seven years ago," the man told him. "That's why you're coming with me."

# EIGHTEEN

### Syrian Desert, Iraq-Syria Border

Y ou can take off your blindfolds now."

The five men kneeling before Mohammed al-Qadir removed the bundled, tightly wrapped *keffiyehs* that had been fastened in place through the duration of the trip here, sweeping their squinted eyes about and showing clear surprise at their surroundings. Even more surprise flashed when they regarded each other for the first time, unable to hide their shock over having been brought here in the company of life-long enemies with whom they shared nothing in common.

"Yes," al-Qadir told them, "you find yourself in the good graces of he who speaks in the voice of the one true God. You should not be surprised that, as the four most powerful tribal leaders in this entire region, and one of the senior remaining leaders of ISIS, He has deemed you worthy of an audience before his earthly vessel."

Al-Qadir rotated his gaze among his five visitors, smug in his satisfaction of how his fighters had managed to penetrate their defenses and snatch them from their roosts in the middle of the night. These men who saw themselves as invincible reduced to cowering, desperate men.

"Two Sunni and two Shia," al-Qadir continued, addressing the tribal leaders and ignoring the ISIS commander for now. "Unthinkable that you would actually put aside your centuries of hostility and hatred to join forces against a common enemy—at least that's what the hated West would have us believe. Tell me, is it true? Is the infidel West right?"

None of the men spoke, keeping their stares focused straight ahead as if the world extended no further than that. The confines around them were primitive at best, an underground cave structure made habitable by generators providing light and ventilation. Al-Qadir had reinforced the walls and ceiling, and used the cave's natural design to erect separate living and meeting facilities.

"By the grace of God, you are fortunate enough to not just still be alive, but to find yourselves with an audience inside one of the many underground compounds the New Islamic Front calls home," al-Qadir told them placidly, standing over the men as a cleric might before administering a blessing, including the ISIS commander again in his address. "You find yourselves somewhere beneath a vast desert floor. More than sixty million years ago a vast sea rolled where this desert lies today. In that sea, with each cycle of birth and death, the shells and bones of countless creatures slowly sank to the ocean floor, as if Allah Himself has insulated our holy mission from the prying eyes of our enemies' spy planes, drones, and satellites. I brought you here as my guests so you may have the opportunity to choose between life and death, mediocrity and greatness, defeat and victory, staid tradition and a fated future. I have amassed more resources, more finances and weapons, than any movement in the history of this or any land. That is why I am winning, that is why the New Islamic Front *will* win. Now, rise before me."

The five men, among the most powerful leaders in the desolate lands of western Iraq and Syria, obliged, a gesture utterly foreign to all of them.

"Now, a token of my hospitality," al-Qadir said to them, as a member of his elite guard shed his assault rifle long enough to move about the guests with a tray holding six servings of cool mint tea in opaque, frosted glasses. "Something to refresh with after your long journey."

The men took the glasses but stopped short of drinking.

"You have nothing to fear from me, at least not yet," al-Qadir told them. "If I wanted you dead, you'd be with your ancestors now. Instead, I wanted you to know I could get to you at anytime and anywhere, that the men you command and all your power cannot protect you from me. You wouldn't listen to my more diplomatic overtures, so you forced my hand. Now, drink your tea. Sample my hospitality."

The ISIS commander tossed his cup against a stone wall, where it shattered on impact and sprayed the auburn-colored liquid into the air.

"I will have nothing of this," he raged. "I will not lie with dogs who can't smell their own shit."

The ISIS commander stiffened defiantly, refusing to break al-Qadir's stare. Al-Qadir approached him slowly, his expression calm, diplomatic, placating.

"I will not," the ISIS commander started, feeling further emboldened.

The rest of his words were lost to a gasp and a gurgle, blood pouring through his hands that had risen reflexively to his slit throat. Al-Qadir had drawn his curved, ceremonial *janbīyah* knife and sliced upward in such a blur that the other four men had never even recorded the motion. But they watched now as the ISIS commander crumpled to his knees and then keeled over facedown, twitching toward death.

Al-Qadir then handed his knife to a fighter to wipe it clean, and took his own glass of tea from the tray before him.

"I brought you here today to share the wondrous faith I feel, because such faith allows us to overcome any enemy and win any battle. Everything I do, I do *Bismillah Arrahman Arraheem*, in the name of Allah; so I have and so I will, and I now ask you to join me. *Enna lillah wa enna elaihe Rajioun* . . . To God we belong and to Him we will return. But before we do we will take back our destiny with a great weapon Allah has provided us to do His bidding. Your only chance to survive is to join my crusade and reap the riches fighters in my service enjoy in pursuit, not of a mere Caliphate, but the entire world. A plan whose scope matches the great vision of Allah. And your presence here allows you to set aside your differences to share that vision and join me in this holiest of crusades. Now, let us drink," al-Qadir finished, raising his glass of tea in the semblance of a toast. "*Inshallah*, as Allah wills."

# NINETEEN

## New York City

**M**ax sat behind the wheel of his rental car, slowly peeling off the gauze wrapped over his palm. His birthmark had been bleeding off and on ever since Yemen, the throbbing almost constant. And from the moment the bleeding had started in Admiral Darby's office on board the *George H. W. Bush*, Max knew he needed to see his mother. She was the last person alive who knew the truth behind the birthmark's origins, how he could have been born with one identical in all respects to his father's to the point that it had grown in proportion with him.

As a young boy, Max had never much questioned its presence, seeing it as nothing more than a bond between father and son. They'd raise their hands and touch palms, sharing something only they could, a unique demonstration of endearing love that left Max so proud of the mark, no matter how much the other kids chided him. Only well into his teenage years had the anomaly struck him. A parent passing a birthmark to a child was utterly unprecedented, as far as he could tell, and that had led to questions his father had always dodged and his mother ignored.

Max had left things at that, choosing not to dwell on the mark, until it was no more than an afterthought that left him fondly recalling the good times he'd shared with his father. But then the fiery pain had come during the raid in Yemen, an agony that cut to the bone and beyond, like nothing that he'd ever experienced, and rekindled the questions he thought buried as a boy. And there was something else beyond that, something that had been plaguing him ever since the raid in Yemen.

Killing was a function of combat, a necessary evil when the mission called upon it. Max was hardly a stranger to the act, but he'd always been impassive about it, seeing his victims as faceless, formless entities more than willing to do the same to him. Yemen, though, had been different. In Yemen, the more he killed, the more he wanted to kill. He remembered the gleeful feeling of watching blood spray into the air as he dropped fighter after fighter. He remembered the joy he felt, the utter ecstasy, as he stood in the courtyard with M60 hoisted, obliterating waves of the enemy and actually feeling a letdown when the big gun clacked empty, and it was time to evacuate the scene.

Max hated the memory of that, the reality of it. Maybe he'd been at this too long already, was becoming desensitized as a result. But that didn't explain the strange visions he'd been having or his suddenly prescient view of the future.

Something was happening to him, and Max believed it had something to do with his birthmark and his family history. His mother was the only person who knew the truth of its origins, but that didn't mean she could tell him much more than that. It would depend on what kind of day she was having, the state of her mind varying by the hour or even minute.

Being placed on indefinite leave by Admiral Darby had afforded him this opportunity. He'd hitched a ride on a U.S. military chopper to Athens, where he boarded a military transport for the trip back stateside. But he was taking a great risk by coming here, the risk of being recognized by someone, anyone, as Max Younger here in the city of his birth very, very real. The vast resources that had been expended toward building his new identity might not cushion him from the determined pursuit of someone like his father's business partner, Dale Denton, who'd like nothing better than to see Max arrested for what he'd done in his former life.

There should've been more happy memories sprinkled in amid the sad from that period, but he could seldom conjure even one, other than boyhood trips made with his father, before the demands of business claimed him for good. Grand adventures to far-flung places that dotted his otherwise miserable adolescence with moments of supreme happiness and contentment, where anything could happen and sometimes did.

Max's mother had shown increasing signs of the madness for as long as Max could remember, dating back, his father had hinted, to his very birth. In the wake of his father's death and subsequent disgrace, she'd been institutionalized at Creedmoor Psychiatric Center, a state-sponsored facility located in Queens.

Max had come here straight from the airport the night before, only to learn at the front desk that visiting hours had ended and he'd have to come back today. So twelve hours later, he'd pulled into the sprawling parking lot that adjoined the building to find it strangely abandoned, save for a trio of the facility's vans laid waste to by locals, wheel spokes sitting on cinder blocks and all the glass shattered. There was also a trio of burned-out car husks that hadn't been there last night when he'd parked in virtually the same spot.

*What had happened?* Max thought, reaching into his pocket for the re-assuring touch of his old mood ring. *Where are all the vehicles belonging to staff and visitors?*

He felt about his pocket to no avail. His ever-present good-luck charm was gone.

Max climbed out of his rental car, on edge and wanting for the weapon he wasn't permitted to carry outside of deployments, especially here in New York City. He took his cell phone from his pocket and absurdly flirted with the notion of calling Creedmoor, even as he approached the main entrance, its glass doors boarded over and sprinkled with graffiti.

It was as if the facility had been abandoned and shuttered in the twelve hours since he'd been here last; impossible, of course, in stark contrast to what he saw to the contrary. Inside, he could hear a phone ringing and ringing. It stopped and then started right up again, continuing to go un-answered. The double doors weren't locked, which Max took as a good sign. Except the security cameras were nowhere in evidence and a small garden that adorned a sitting area was marred by overgrowth and clumps of dead flowers. The benches were gone too, torn from their chain moor-ings that remained oddly in place, affixed to red-stamped concrete brick adorning the area.

"Hello," Max called out, after entering.

The doors rattling closed with an echo had left the reception and lobby area in silence. A normally bustling greeting area, shrouded today in shad-ows broken only by several flickering overhead lights. The reception sta-tion was abandoned and reams of paper that looked to have sprayed from it fluttered to the floor after being whipped up by the flood of air that had preceded Max inside.

"Hello?" he called again, his voice echoing in tinny fashion.

Some of the stray pages were streaked with red, finger paint Max had thought at first glance, while second and closer glance made him think it could be blood. The same was true of the walls, red-smeared designs he tried to tell himself were impressionistic designs meant to add color to the lifelessness of the facility. But the coppery smell told him that was blood too, adding something else entirely.

He continued on, through stuffy, overheated air that grew steamier the further he advanced. A smell clung to that stale air, a rancid mix of rot, waste, and death. He headed toward the elevators, but found neither of the pair to be operational, and took the stairs to the third floor instead where the air felt even staler.

Turning the corner onto his mother's wing brought him onto floors slick as ice with more of what he'd first thought to be red finger paint streaking the walls on both sides. Max continued on, the stench no less intense even as the steam-baked air gave way to a chill icy enough to leave his breath misting lightly before him. He drew closer to the end of the hall and saw the red streaks traced into a pattern that formed a message in Latin:

*Ecce venit cum nubibus, et videbit eum omnis oculus, et qui eum pupugerunt. Et plangent se super eum omnes tribus terræ: Etiam.*

Max had never studied Latin but, somehow, when he read the words, he saw the English translation:

*Behold, He arrives with the clouds, and every eye shall see Him, even those who pierced Him. And all the tribes of the Earth shall lament for themselves over Him.*

He turned away from the wall briefly, and when he turned back, the Latin version of the words was back.

Max started on again. Turning the corner, he spotted a tall, white figure with a shock of flowing gray hair standing at the end of the hall facing an electronic door that kept opening and closing before her, opening and closing. She stood board stiff, elongated skeletal fingers extending toward the floor from her sides, finished in absurdly long nails stained with more of the red finger paint, looking more like nail polish now.

"Excuse me," Max called to her, picking up his pace, as his heart too picked up. "Ma'am?"

She didn't turn, didn't acknowledge him.

"What happened here, ma'am?" he asked, stopping far enough away from her based on his instinct for proximity.

The woman turned slowly, her attention roused, Max recognizing her immediately:

His mother, her eyes empty and lifeless—someone else's eyes forced into her skull, gashes down both sides of her face, explaining the blood on her nails. She looked ghostly pale, sickly white. A corpse, it seemed, dressed in a white gown-like smock, its front blotched with blood from where she'd wiped her nails. Her spine held so stiff and straight she seemed to be floating weightlessly over the floor and her face quivering in what looked like a constant spasm.

"Mom," Max heard himself say. "It's me, Mom."

The woman's eyes widened, the slightest of grins edging across her expression. Her voice, when she finally opened her lips, sounded vaguely masculine, gravelly in tone as if it had been strained through a cheese grater, spoken with a grin.

*"Your mother's not here."*

# TWENTY

**New York City**

M ax's eyes snapped open, roused from the nightmare by the sound of a siren screeching close by. His hands were gripping the steering wheel so tight, he'd squeezed the blood from them. He was still inside his rental car, only the parking lot was half full with no sign anywhere of the burned-out husks of other vehicles. So too the entrance of Creedmoor was as it had been the night before, fronted by a sitting area and well-kept garden. And the glass doors were still intact, as opposed to being covered in plywood and graffiti.

Max pushed a hand into his pocket to find the old mood ring just where it always was, breathing a sigh of relief, even as he recognized the same odd feeling that had taken hold of him in Yemen. Just before he'd opened fire with the M60D machine gun, to hold back the last of the fighters breaching the embassy compound.

*Your mother's not here.*

Max slipped the ring over his finger, before climbing out of the car. He entered the building with his heart hammering against his chest and beating so fast it left him light-headed. But the lobby was just as he recalled, as well. So he checked in at the reception desk, was given a visitor's badge, and waited briefly for an aide to escort him to his mother, using an elevator that had been shut down in his vision.

Max had no idea what to expect from this point. His mother's condition had robbed her of the ability to retain anything for very long, her sense of time and memory skewed to the point that reality had become whatever she chose to make it. An aide escorted him to a third-floor rec room and directed Max toward a solitary figure standing before a window covered in a thick grate that barely allowed any light in. From behind the figure looked exactly like the one from his vision, his mother as a walking corpse.

Max approached her stiffly, fearing the sight that would greet him when she turned around.

"Mom?" he uttered, forcing the word past the clog in his throat.

The figure turned slowly, just as it had in the vision, Max holding his breath in the last moment before they were face-to-face.

"Max!" his mother beamed, hugging him tight.

Max hugged her back, smelling harsh disinfectant soap and feeling his mother's long, limp white hair. It had been beautiful once and perfectly kept. At least, though, her eyes were the same, as she pulled away to regard him. A bit laggard, due to the medication, but full of life and love.

"Come, we'll sit."

She interlaced her arm with his and led Max to a table set against the far wall, treating him as if he'd visited the day or week before. She shuffled more than walked, her slippers curled up on the underside and dragging.

Max eased her chair out from the table and she sat down before a game of solitaire she'd left unfinished. She gathered the cards up, fingernails well manicured as opposed to dagger-long and polished in blood. The rec room beyond them was plain and casual enough, save for the heavy security grates bolted over the windows looking out over Queens Village to discourage the more unruly residents from attempting an ill-fated flight from three stories up.

"I knew you'd come on my birthday," she said, smiling. "I knew you'd surprise me!"

*Is it her birthday?*

Max searched his mind for the answer, but it had been banished from his memory as so many other parts of his life, and past, had, making him feel terribly guilty.

"You look tired, Max," his mother said, leaning across the table. She started to extend a hand to touch him, but changed her mind. "You're working too hard. That school's got you run down. You need to have more fun. You only get to live your high school years once."

*That was over ten years ago. You remember, Mom, not long before I had to disappear, and Dad jumped out of a sixtieth-floor office window.*

The thoughts formed, but never quite made their way into words. Max couldn't bear to do that to his mother and it wouldn't have stuck anyway. Better to just leave her to the delusions that dominated her life.

Melissa Younger was at the Creedmoor Psychiatric Center as a ward of the state. Destitute in all ways, without a dollar to her name that she wouldn't have known how to spend anymore anyway. There had been millions once, tens of millions, hundreds even. But it was gone now, every penny of it, lost to the scandal and disgrace that had followed Ben Younger's suicide.

His mother would likely live out the rest of her life here, among hundreds of other residents with varying degrees of mental illness, all of whom wore the same white, shapeless smock-like clothing. Beyond their corner table against a grated window, the rec room was a portrait of normalcy for Creedmoor. There was a Ping-Pong table where a man wearing sunglasses was playing an imaginary game against an invisible opponent, wielding a paddle absent a ball. Another man, meanwhile, was tapping the missing ball over and over again against a wall and never missing. He could've been at it for five minutes, five hours, or since yesterday for all Max knew. A number of residents were gathered around a television, either entranced by what was playing on the screen or paying no attention to it at all.

As a SEAL, Max could never recall a time when he *wasn't* on guard. But this was different, his defenses ill-equipped to deal with these surroundings. He felt himself tense, his muscles tightening into bonded steel bands beneath his skin, as he swept his gaze further about the room.

A woman had her ear pressed against the television set's front-firing speaker. Six other women were squeezed around a table playing a card game under the watchful eye of an attendant, there to mitigate disputes that seemed to occur every other minute. More residents clustered before the rec room's other windows, looking out as if they were watching a movie, reacting to things no one else was seeing. Max hated the fact that his mother lived among them, hated even more that this was where she belonged.

"Where's your father, Max?" his mother asked suddenly.

"Working."

"He's always working. Works too hard, pushes himself too hard. Who do you think you take after? The two of you are exactly alike. Sometimes I look at you and think I'm looking at him."

Max wanted to tell his mother that his father was gone and had been for almost ten years now. He wouldn't be coming to visit, and she was in here because of how it had all ended. Max was already gone when it had all transpired, out of necessity rather than choice. Had abandoned the family name and started a new life under a new identity, also out of necessity. He had buried the boy he had been to be reborn at the age of seventeen as a man, day one in that process after he'd killed for the first time.

*Maybe if I'd been there for her, this never would've happened. . . .*

"Your father doesn't come as much as he used to, Max."

Max felt a clog fill his throat, so thick he couldn't swallow. "He's been busy, like you said."

"Every day I wake up, you know my first thought? Maybe this is the day he's going to come and take me home. I warned him, you know."

"About what, Mom?"

"What was coming. All the tribulations. She told me all about them."

This was different, a new subject broached, Max thought, unsure whether that was a good thing or a bad.

"Who told you?" he asked, trying not to push too hard.

"The little girl," she repeated, lips starting to quiver. "You know—Lilith."

"What little girl?" Max asked her, a chill passing through him, accompanied by a distant memory shrouded in haze. "Who's Lilith?"

His mother scolded him with her eyes. "Come on, silly. You used to play with her when you were a little boy." His mother lowered her voice. "Nobody else knows about Lilith here. You're the first person I've told, because you used to play with her when you were very young. Sometimes she scares me; she's blind and yet she seems to see everything. Lilith's coming has to stay a secret. Promise me, you won't tell anyone, not a soul. Promise me!"

"I promise, Mom," Max said, starting to recall an imaginary friend from his childhood who'd indeed been a little girl. "Is she here now?"

His mother patted his forearm, grinning. "No, silly. If Lilith were here, you'd see her too. She only comes when I'm alone, loves to surprise me. But I'm not alone now; you're here." She leaned closer to him, lowered her voice. "Promise me, you won't tell anyone about her, not a soul. Promise me!"

"I promise, Mom."

"Because I'd miss Lilith so much if she stopped coming. She tells me things."

The way his mother said that made Max lean more forward, not able to leave things there. "Like what?"

"When people are going to die. She'll point someone out and shake her head. Then the next day . . ." Max's mother let that thought dangle. "Anyway, she's never wrong. She was even right about you coming today."

"Lilith told you I was coming to visit?"

Melissa Younger nodded. "This morning, right after she wished me happy birthday. She said you were coming. She told me some men were coming to hurt you."

"When?"

"Today."

# TWENTY-ONE

### New York City

*S*he told me some men were coming to hurt you. . . .

The words stuck in Max's head, but he didn't want to press the subject any further, didn't want to risk agitating his mother. He took her hand in his left, turning his right palm over to reveal the birthmark, dry of blood now, thankfully.

"How did I get this, Mom?"

His mother's smile vanished. "You, you were born with it, of course. It's, it's a birthmark. Good luck, many say."

A slight ooze of blood had once more begun to trace the impression's outline.

"Dad has one too, you know, Mom. Identical in all respects."

"Then you should ask him, Max," his mother said, turning away again. "You should ask your father."

"He told me to ask you."

"Lilith told me you'd ask that question, warned me not to tell you. She's going to be mad that I even mentioned her to you." His mother turned her head back toward him. "How can she see me, if she's blind? How can that be, Max, how can that be?" His mother leaned further across the table and snatched Max's right hand in a boney grip. "How's your girlfriend?"

"She's not my girlfriend, Mom," he said, knowing exactly to whom she was referring.

"Yes, she is, but she shouldn't be. She's bad for you, Max, she's bad for you," his mother continued. Her hand dug into his forearm, her eyes catching fire as her words speeded up, blurring into each other. "She's very bad for you—a whore, that's what she is!"

"Mom—"

"No good! Dangerous, just like her father. You got your father's mark; she got her father's nasty soul. That's the way it is with parents and children. Stay away from her, Max, promise me you'll stay away for your own good!"

"I'll stay away from her," Max soothed, trying to restore order to his mother's fractured mind.

"Promise!"

"I promise."

His mother's breathing started to slow, the episode over. "You have a great life ahead of you, Max. The sky's the limit. You're going to be a great leader, the kind of leader people would die for. And many are going to die for you—Lilith told me that too."

"I should talk to Lilith myself," Max said, having no idea why.

"She says you'll be seeing her again soon."

"I will?"

His mother nodded. "Uh-huh. She told me she misses you."

Something about the way his mother said that left Max cold, the madness receding from her tone in that brief instant.

*She misses you.*

He felt his breaths growing shorter and shallower, the rec room seeming to shrink around him. Everything was still in place, just more compacted, the other residents on this floor of Creedmoor pressing in so close he could smell the stale perspiration rising through their clothes. The card table occupied by a quartet of drooling fifty-year-olds was the size of a postage stamp and the players themselves elongated to the point they were as tall as the ceiling but pressed as thin as stick figures.

Max shook himself alert, the rec room back to what it should have been.

"Your real father's very proud of you, Max," his mother said, squeezing his hand even harder and looking like the version of her he'd met in his vision, all of a sudden.

"What do you mean my *real* father?"

"You're going to make him proud. Lilith told me."

"What else, Mom, what else did she tell you?"

Melissa Younger seemed to notice something awry with the other residents and turned away from him, looking distressed. Max watched the attendants on duty in the rec room shuffling about, tentatively at first, then with a bit more bounce in their measured steps. One had just raised a walkie-talkie to his lips to report and probably summon reinforcements. Another was trying to comfort a woman in a wheelchair who kept trying to roll away from him.

Max realized his mother was squeezing his hand so tight, her own gnarled fingers were quivering. "Your real father's very proud of you, Max," she repeated. "I know he is."

She got that way sometimes, stuck in a loop. But this was different, as if someone had hit REWIND and then PLAY again. Time skewed and running in random order.

Things seemed to be calming down in the rec room, the attendants managing to quell whatever collective angst had struck the residents and restore order.

"Tell me more about what you meant by my real father, Mom," Max said, hoping his mother didn't notice the discomfort in his voice.

Before she could respond, though, a cadence of voices singing in tune broke her train of thought.

*"Happy birthday to you, happy birthday to you. . . ."*

Max hadn't noticed the trio of nurses enter the rec room, the one in the center holding a lavish birthday cake that looked like coconut cream, his mother's favorite.

*"Happy birthday, dear Melissa, happy birthday to you!"*

The residents gathered in the rec room applauded, as the nurse set the cake down between Max and his mother, a single candle sparkling in its center amid a heart made of gooey red frosting and the distinct aroma of coconut reaching him.

"Come on, Mom," Max prodded, "blow out the candle, but don't forget to make a wish."

His mother, what was left of her anyway, squeezed her eyes closed and mumbled something under her breath. Then she opened them, smiled serenely, and blew out the lone candle.

The residents clapped, some of them approaching now.

"Would you like to know what I wished for, Max?" his mother asked him.

"You can't tell me, or it won't come true, Mom."

His mother ignored him. "I wished for things to go back to the way they used to be."

Max reached across the table and touched her hand. "A tough wish to come true."

Another of the nurses laid some paper plates down on the table. "Make for a nice dessert," she said to him. "If you don't mind, of course."

Max noticed a pair of orderlies in white scrubs had entered the rec room wheeling a cart that reminded him of the kind flight attendants once used, with the meals preloaded on trays sized to the multiple slots inside. The wheels squeaked and left a thin jagged scratch along the linoleum in their wake, like a car leaking fluid. The orderlies began passing the trays out to the rec room's occupants, trays containing a thin sandwich sealed in plastic wrap, a side of what looked like some kind of macaroni salad, and a truly sad-looking chocolate chip cookie.

His mother's birthday cake would make for quite the treat indeed, Max thought, as his eyes met one of the orderly's. Something was all wrong about them, as if they'd been looking his way the whole time.

"So, so," his mother was saying, caught in one of her mind loops where her brain seemed to seize up. "So . . ."

Before him, the nurse was slicing his mother's birthday cake into the thinnest slices he'd ever seen to make sure there was enough to go around for everyone. This as, across the room, one of the elderly residents of Creedmoor tossed his wrapped sandwich to the floor.

"Peddle this crap to someone else, Barney Fife," he snapped.

"Yeah, yeah," a woman seated near him chimed in, tossing her sandwich aside too. "You're not Bubba. Bubba wouldn't call this a lunch. Where's Bubba?"

The orderlies swung back to the game table, toward the cake, Max, or both.

Max couldn't see their hands, lost inside the cart with the squeaky wheels that had left scratches on the linoleum floor.

*She told me some men were coming to hurt you.*

Max was halfway out of his chair by the time he caught steel glinting in the rec room's fluorescent lighting, as the hands of the two orderlies emerged from the cart, matching glares focused intently on him. The nurse was cutting the cake, and then she wasn't because Max had stripped the knife from her grasp, his motion so fluid that she continued the slicing motion, as if she still held it.

The knife had barely found his grasp when he hurled it in the same moment the first man's pistol cleared the cart, glistening even more. The blade found the man's throat, digging in all the way to the hilt and twisting him backward into the second fake orderly.

Impact stole that man's grasp on the ugly, squat pistol from him and the gun went flying. He was seasoned enough to go for the now dead man's because it was closer, failing to anticipate the difficulties of prying an object free of a death grip. That gave Max enough time to close the gap between them in the length of a breath, upon the man just as his hand jerked the dead orderly's pistol level.

*BANG!*

Max felt the bullet whiz over the center of his scalp, close enough to register the heat even as he recorded, absurdly, a few Creedmoor residents never breaking their gazes from the television tuned to the golden oldies station—*Bonanza*, he thought.

By then he'd lashed a kick that caught the second gunman under the chin, surprised when the man maintained enough presence of mind to re-steady the pistol. Max caught the man's wrist in mid-motion and jerked it downward with one hand, while the other smashed into his windpipe with curled knuckles leading. He felt the cartilage crack, seeming to break away. Heard the man's breath catch in his throat with a wheeze that sounded like a clogged vacuum cleaner winding down.

Only when the man dropped to his knees, did Max realize he was holding the pistol now, while standing between the bodies of the two men he'd just killed.

"Happy birthday to meeeeeeeeee," his mother sang behind him, amid the chaos spreading through the rec room, "happy birthday to me!"

One of the residents watching *Bonanza* clutched the remote like it was his favorite toy and turned up the volume on the television.

"Change the channel, change the channel!" another implored.

His words aimed at Max, as an emergency alarm began to wail and more orderlies, a veritable army of them, burst into the rec room to restore order.

Max swung back to his mother to find her eating the cake with her hands, her face dribbled with specks of the red heart, which looked too much like blood.

# TWENTY-TWO

## Sinai Peninsula, Egypt

A re there any updates, anything new?" Vicky asked Neal Van Royce, as their Land Rover thumped over the uneven road that cut through Egypt's Sinai Peninsula.

"Before I lost cell service an hour ago, there was more confirmation of cases in Syria, Iraq, Lebanon, the Arab Emirates, and Saudi Arabia." His expression grew dour as he pocketed his Samsung phone. "It's spreading, Vicky."

Vicky checked her iPhone and found she had no service either. She hadn't said two words to either their driver or the other two heavily armed soldiers assigned as their escorts, all members of the Egyptian Special Forces.

Decades before, Egypt had divided the Sinai into two separate governorates. The more metropolitan south Sinai and the desolate north where they were headed now. Specifically a clinic in a remote village not far from this governorate's capital of Al Arish where all indications pointed to another outbreak that had begun prior to the one they'd viewed in Jordan the day before.

Their destination, the town of Ashkar, turned out to be located well out from Al Arish, twenty miles at least. The day was so clear and bright, they could see the structures of Al Arish in the distance as the only break in the ribbon of sand that stretched the entire distance to the city.

A modern professional clinic, courtesy of the United Nations, was located on the outskirts of Ashkar. As they drew closer, it stood out in its modernity compared to the buildings that rimmed as flat a stretch of land as Vicky had ever seen. There was a paved parking lot, ambulances, and signs in both English and Arabic directing patients and visitors to the proper entrance. But what was missing stood out more: traffic, both vehicular and pedestrian. No signs of life in view anywhere.

"That's strange," said Van Royce.

"What?"

"There were supposed to be representatives from the Egyptian government and army here to meet us," he told her, checking his phone again,
as if service had miraculously been restored.

Their vehicle was equipped with a military radio mounted on the dash.
The driver raised the mic to his mouth and tried again to raise someone
in Cairo, but got only static in response, before giving up and returning
the mic to its stand.

"Maybe they're waiting inside," Vicky said.

They parked next to an ambulance in the lot, the driver to remain with
the vehicle while the other two Egyptian soldiers accompanied them inside.

They entered the clinic to find no Egyptian government or military
officials there either; in fact, *nobody* was there. The front reception desk
had been abandoned, the waiting room empty and soundless. No visible
signs of life at all, save for an ancient wall-mounted television broadcast-
ing a silent picture that jumped in and out of focus.

"What the hell, Neal?"

"I don't know," Van Royce stammered. He started to reach for his phone
again, then stopped. "I don't know."

"How many patients?"

"A dozen at the last report, a few hours ago."

Vicky started toward the double doors that led to the examination
rooms and admittance area.

"I'm not sure that's a good idea," Van Royce said, trying to position himself before her.

Vicky kept right on going. "I do."


The exam and hospital-type rooms, which turned out to be more like
wards cut into cubicles with plastic curtains draped between beds, were
all empty. No patient, infected or otherwise, was present. But rumpled
bed linens remained in place, stained in patches by something the color
of mold.

Vicky took out her phone and snapped some pictures. The automatic
flash cut through the murky darkness, illuminating something on the
floor.

"Clearly, the clinic's been evacuated," Van Royce was saying. "By the Egyptian government or military."

Vicky crouched and activated the flashlight feature on her phone. "We need to know what happened here. We need to figure this out."

"Not if it means walking straight into a hot zone," he cautioned. "We shouldn't have ventured in this far, should never have risked exposure. Where the hell did they go; the patients, the doctors, the Egyptian government representatives we were supposed to meet? . . . What in God's name happened?"

"Look at this," Vicky said, aiming her iPhone's flashlight downward, so Van Royce could see what she'd just spotted.

She felt him crouch alongside her. "Are those . . ."

"Footprints," Vicky completed for him, using the focused beam to trace their shape, dried dark red. "Left in blood, leading from that bed with the rumpled linens."

Van Royce tugged her back upright with him. "We'll drive into the village, find the nearest military post," Van Royce said, leading the way outside as he checked his phone yet again. "Nothing," he reported.

"Then let's go find *something*."


They saw no other moving vehicles, as their driver wound about the hard-packed gravel streets strewn with mud ruts. The only signs of life they passed were squawking chickens, a few stray dogs, and a soccer ball blowing back and forth between a pair of buildings with battered roofs encased in plastic.

"It's been evacuated," Van Royce said, sweeping his gaze about.

"No," corrected Vicky, "abandoned, and fast. If it had been evacuated, a perimeter zone would've been established by the Egyptian military." She spotted a shape, a shadow ahead, just off to the right. "Did you see that?" she asked Van Royce.

"See what?"

"I don't know," Vicky told him, looking for it again.

They were edging toward what looked like an outdoor market perched in a covered alley that turned day into night. She saw another shape, then a third, seeming to move from the darkness to the light, as if stirred by their presence.

"Did you—"

"Yes," Van Royce interrupted, "this time, yes. There's something moving out there, I saw them moving. . . ."

Van Royce stopped when, incredibly, Vicky's phone buzzed, signaling an incoming call. She held his stare as she unclasped her iPhone from its holster and drew it upward.

Nothing, the screen dark, meaning no call had ever come in. She checked the watch Thomas had given her and found no CALL icon there either.

"Must be a glitch," she said to Van Royce, not at all convinced of that.

Then Vicky's Apple Watch chimed, signaling an incoming text message.

GET OUT! the watch display face read.

"Vicky!" Van Royce called to her.

Another chime.

GET OUT!GET OUT!GET OUT!GET OUT!GET OUT!GET OUT!GET OUT!GET OUT!GET OUT!GET OUT!GET OUT!GET OUT!GET OUT!GET OUT!GET OUT!GET OUT!

Filling out the entire face of the watch and then continuing to scroll downward without pause.

*"Vicky!"*

Vicky looked up from the watch face toward their Egyptian driver "We need to get out of here," she said, abruptly enough to startle him. *"Now!"*

"Vicky!" Van Royce wailed, his voice prickling with fear, eyes bulging.

"Drive!" she ordered the man behind the wheel whose name she suddenly couldn't remember. "Drive!"

He gave the Land Rover as much gas as it would take, the tires squealing against the gravel.

"Faster, faster, for the love of God!" Vicky urged.

The driver reversed wildly, spinning the car around to retrace their route from the village.

GET OUT!GET OUT!GET OUT!GET OUT!GET OUT!GET OUT!GET OUT!GET OUT!GET OUT!

The message scroll continued, as the Land Rover thumped and thudded over the rut-strewn street, the desert beyond the village in clear view now. It tore down the lone access road, both Vicky and Van Royce looking back at the village's shrinking form.

GET OUT!GET OUT!GET OUT!GET OUT!GET OUT!GET OUT!GET OUT!GET OUT!GET OU-

The scroll finally stopped there, just as the first two explosions sounded, igniting a flame burst that swallowed the town from sight. The next two blasts followed in rapid succession, pushing out a shock wave that lifted the Land Rover off the road and dropped it back down without missing a step. The driver struggled to maintain control, the vehicle bucking like a bronco, and Vicky realized the windows and sunroof had cracked into varying sizes of spiderweb patterns from the same shock wave that had lifted the vehicle up and dropped it back down.

Behind them the village had vanished in a thick gush of smoke still belching plumes of fire. Vicky wasn't sure whether the blast of heat she felt next was conjured by the continued ripple of secondary explosions or her imagination. But it didn't matter.

Because the town of Ashkar, and whatever secrets it held, had vanished into oblivion.

Her breathing steadied, Vicky finally looked back at her watch's face, the texts gone, seemingly sucked back into the ether of cyberspace, as if they'd never been there at all. But the number from which they'd come was embedded in her mind, frozen before her eyes.

404 . . . A Georgia exchange.

Her dead fiancé Thomas's phone number.

PART 3

BEFORE

The only thing necessary for the triumph of evil
is for good men to do nothing.

—Edmund Burke

# TWENTY-THREE

## London, England; 1990

The meteorite was the size of a football, though jagged at the edges, its ridged structure bright and shiny beneath the spill of the fluorescent work lights.

"It looks like quartz," a young man whose name tag identified him as NICK advanced, rising from a crouch over the ground depression in which the purported meteorite had landed.

"Is that a scientific conclusion?" his field partner BETH, according to her name tag, asked him.

Nick smirked. "I was only saying."

"We're not supposed to do that," she said, pad and pen in hand. "This is a scientific exploration, strictly."

"Then my hypothesis is that the space object's structure and appearance most closely resembles quartz deposits on our planet."

"That's better. . . ."

"Thank you."

"You didn't let me finish," Beth said acerbically, having jotted down the note Nick had recited. "I was going to say that's better but . . ."

"There's always a but, isn't there?"

". . . you should've said *potential* space object until we have gained confirmation."

"Fine," Nick relented. "*Potential* space object."

"What kind? We need to determine a classification," Beth told him.

Nick yanked the rock hammer from his tool belt. "Why don't we just take a sample; you know, to shave off and examine under a microscope? Get a real close look."

"Well," Beth said, weighing Nick's suggestion, "that would facilitate the carbon dating process."

Nick flashed the smile that had been winning him girls since he was fourteen. "See, I'm not as stupid as I look."

Beth gazed back into the depression in the ground shaped like a miniature crater. "Then how would you classify it?"

"We back to that again?"

"Come on, Nick: chondrite, iron, or carbonaceous?"

"Give me a hint."

"Chondrite means stony."

"Chondrite!"

Beth rolled her eyes. "But it's ridged, not smooth."

"Carbon-whatever then."

"Last guess."

"Okay, iron," Nick said, positioning the rock hammer over one of the ridged finger-like extensions jutting out from the football-sized rock, where it looked to have broken off from a larger body. "Now it's my turn."

With that, he tapped the rock hammer lightly against the largest extension. When the sample he sought refused to yield, he tapped harder, then followed that up with a third strike that dropped the jagged knob into his work glove, revealing a dark hole.

"Uh-oh," Nick managed, just before a thin cloud burst from inside the small meteorite, showering him in white drizzle that looked like powdered sugar.

The door to London's Science Museum teaching lab opened and Pascal Jimenez stepped through, followed by the rest of the sixth form students from the Reading School, the equivalent of high school seniors in America, who'd come to the museum for a hands-on field trip. For Jimenez, professor of astrobiology and planetary science at the University of Oxford, everything had to be hands-on.

"I believe we've all learned an important lesson," Jimenez announced, once all the students were squeezed into the lab. "Never assume an object is harmless. Never disrupt an object's integrity until you are certain of its composition and, even, origins."

Nick was still brushing the white powder Jimenez had rigged inside the faux-meteorite sample from his face and clothes. "How was I supposed to know it was dangerous?"

"You weren't," Jimenez told him, told them all. "That's the point. You must assume it's dangerous until proven otherwise." He rotated his gaze about the students clustered around him. "The crude belief is that meteorites are just space rocks, broken off splinters of debris floating through outer space. In fact, in some cases they may have traveled billions of miles from planetary systems entirely different from our own. And the mistake too many make is to regard even the smallest samples as safe, when they may, in fact, be quite dangerous."

Jimenez turned toward the sixth former with Johnson's Baby Powder stubbornly clinging to his clothes. "Can you tell me what ALH84001 is?"

"Er, no, sir," Nick said sheepishly.

"Of course you can't; I wouldn't expect you could. ALH84001 is a four-point-five-billion-year-old rock discovered in Antarctica that's believed to have been dislodged from Mars sixteen million years ago and fell to Earth thirteen thousand years ago. Some believe it contains fossil evidence that life on Mars actually existed at one point."

"And did it?" the girl, whose name tag read BETH in big black letters, asked.

"No one knows for sure, young woman," Jimenez told her, "and that is precisely my point." His gaze fell back on the sample rock he used for classroom demonstrations like this. "Mankind is under the mistaken impression that the worst damage meteorites can do would be something equivalent to the strike that brought on the Ice Age and wiped out the dinosaurs."

Nick chuckled. "You mean, there's something worse than that?"

"I do indeed, young man," Jimenez replied, taking a few steps toward him. "We have barely scratched the surface of the secrets our own universe and others may hold. That baby powder you're now wearing could just as easily have been a foreign germ, some virus or bacteria, released into a world where no natural immunity to its ravages exists and no medical means to treat it can be found in time before it wipes out all life on Earth."

"Wow," said the girl named Beth, "that's scary."

Jimenez nodded. "Quite so, young lady, quite so. It wouldn't take a meteorite of the size that wiped out the dinosaurs to end life on Earth again." His gaze drifted to his football-sized sample rock. "It wouldn't take something very big at all."

"But you've got no evidence of that," Nick argued halfheartedly. "It's not like it's ever happened."

"No," Jimenez acknowledged, pausing long enough to meet the gazes of the other students. "But what if the meteorite that caused the Ice Age was no larger than our demonstration model here? The theory of singularity postulates that objects no bigger than our model at all could have a mass equal to objects a trillion times larger. And they wouldn't even require such mass, if they were able to radiate a comparable level of energy minus it. Confounding prospects, I know; that's what makes me still as much a student of our planet as you."

With that, Beth fished a copy of Jimenez's book on just that subject from her backpack.

"Speaking of which, would you sign my book?" she asked, handing it over.

Jimenez readied his pen, took the book in hand. *"For Beth,"* Jimenez narrated, as he jotted an inscription onto the title page, *"some mysteries can never be solved."*

# TWENTY-FOUR

## New York City, 1990

'm pregnant."

At first, Ben Younger felt he must've heard his wife wrong, but the look on her face told him he hadn't.

"Are you screwing with me?" he asked, standing on the balcony of their tenth-floor penthouse that overlooked Central Park.

Melissa grinned. "No, we did that together."

Before the oil strike in Mexico, with the condition of the fledgling energy concern he'd started with Dale Denton truly dire, Ben would look down at the homeless people pushing their shopping carts along the concrete grid that cut through the park. He'd watch them scouring through trash cans, their life's possessions bulging out of black trash bags, in fear over how close he and Melissa were to the same fate. They were several months behind on the mortgage they'd fought to get based on expectations that hadn't come to pass and American Express seemed to have their numbers on speed dial. But they'd weathered that storm just long enough for luck to turn their way in the Yucatán.

A few nights after returning from Mexico, though, Ben had been awakened by horrible, guttural shrieks and rushed out onto the balcony. Gazing downward, he spotted two huge black dogs fighting madly. The animals seemed intent on tearing each other apart, neither giving an inch. Ben couldn't bear to watch, imagining he could see the spray of blood and froth into the air. The dogs were screaming so loud, he had trouble falling back to sleep, even once the night finally grew silent. The balcony was his first stop again when he gave up tossing and turning just after dawn. He gazed downward, half expecting to see the body of at least one of the dogs, but there was nothing.

The strange mark covered by a gauze bandage wrapped tightly around his palm was itching horribly. Ben didn't remember much of what had happened down in that cave he'd somehow managed to climb out of. But he remembered the rock he'd grasped and the mark it had left on his palm in a fiery red color that seemed to have drained all the blood from the rest of his hand. The first doctor he'd seen insisted it was a burn and treated it as such with salves and gauze, counseling patience. But the morning after watching the dogs fight, two weeks after his return from the Yucatán, it had begun itching horribly and hadn't stopped since, as if, as if . . .

As if *what?*

Ben tried not to think about the dogs anymore, but every time he lapsed, the itching grew worse again.


"Could you repeat that please?" he said to Melissa, standing in the very same spot. "I just want to make sure I heard it right."

"If I say it again, we might end up with twins," Melissa grinned, her eyes shiny with tears of joy.

"Missy" was all Ben could manage. "I . . ."

"Yeah, that was my first thought too." She noticed him scratching. "What's wrong with your hand?"

He pulled the wrapped palm behind him. "It's itchy. Healing process, that's all."

Melissa didn't look convinced. "Maybe you should get it checked again."

"It's fine," Ben said, a wave of happiness like none he'd ever experienced before catching him in its grasp.


Ben thought there was no news that could possibly trump what he'd learned from Dale Denton earlier that day about the potential size of the reserves their oil field was producing. Unprecedented didn't begin to describe it.

Nor did it even begin to describe the news Missy had just shared . . .

*I'm pregnant.*

. . . because it was impossible. They'd been trying to have a child for eight years now, ever since they'd been married. After five, they learned Missy was infertile, and all attempts at artificial insemination, leaving them no hope they'd ever be able to have a child.

Until now.

And, strangely, for Ben the impossible was nothing new, especially after going to an orthopedist to have the leg he thought he'd broken when he'd fallen inside the cave examined. The doctor had reviewed the X-rays, seemingly baffled by the fact that there was indeed a fracture, but it had healed entirely. The doctor could offer no explanation for the anomaly, other than to suggest it was actually an older break. So maybe the fall hadn't been as bad as Ben had thought, a trick played by the memory that continued to betray him. And now Melissa was pregnant. A month ago, Ben was broke with a mortgage he couldn't afford and a marriage he feared would crumble under the weight of the pressure. Now he was about to become a father and soon to be rich, beyond anything he'd ever imagined.

His hand had started itching even worse, after Missy had given him the miraculous news, and all the scratching had shredded the tape and frayed the gauze beneath it. Ben decided the wound he'd suffered upon grasping the rock just needed redressing, maybe an extra layer of antibiotic ointment.

He moved to the bathroom, leaving the door open so he'd be able to hear Missy if she called out to him. Not even five minutes after hearing the news, Ben couldn't imagine letting her too far out of his sight for the next nine months.

He peeled off the tape and unwrapped the gauze layered beneath it, exposure to fresh air seeming to effectively quell the itching then and there. Ben still plucked the Neosporin from the medicine cabinet behind the mirror and squeezed some onto his finger. Ready to smear it on and rebandage the wound as the doctor who'd first dressed it in Mexico advised when he spotted a pale shape amid the inflamed red patch of skin. A scratchy assemblage of lines crisscrossing each other like some random figure of calligraphy.

Ben remembered the rock that had seared his skin when he'd taken it in his grasp, the strange pattern emblazoned upon it amid an unnerving glow he remembered, inexplicably, as a dark light. That was the pattern he saw now, still embedded into his palm. Not fading away, as doctors indicated it would in the course of the normal healing process. If anything, the mark looked even more defined and pronounced.

"Is everything all right?" Missy called to him from down the hall.

"Never better," Ben said back to her, applying the ointment and then reaching for fresh gauze. "How could it not be?"

# TWENTY-FIVE

## New York City, 1990

Dale Denton's wife Danielle had greeted the reports of the staggering size of their oil strike in the Yucatán the way she greeted everything: by pouring herself a glass of wine in their brownstone's elegant great room, its furniture laid over a priceless Persian carpet dominated by burgundy that helped disguise the various red wine spills over the years.

"Want one?" she asked Denton.

"I don't drink. Or maybe you've forgotten."

"Come on, make an exception. Let's celebrate."

The brownstone had been in the Denton family for generations, mortgaged to the hilt and on the verge of being lost to foreclosure when he and Ben Younger struck black gold in the Yucatán. Strange how when Denton considered failure down there his first thought had been of losing the brownstone, not Danielle, along with its priceless furnishings in the form of antiques and heirlooms. Every piece of wood in the ornate, pre-war building was hand-carved, from the moldings to the banisters. It had belonged to his grandparents and then his parents before passing to him. Denton loved the hustle and pace of the city and looked at living in this enclave in Turtle Bay as a respite, a perfect complement to that. Quiet enough to make him want to return to his world beyond it.

"And I've got news to share too," she continued, "one that calls for a bottle, not a glass. You're sure you don't want any?" she asked, holding that bottle. And when he demurred, "Good. More for me. So we're gonna be rich, my credit cards reactivated. I can hardly wait."

"So what's your news?" Denton forced himself to ask her.

Danielle drained her first glass fast, in almost a single gulp. "I have a question for you first. I know you like having your ass kissed. So, tell me, the women you pay for, do you make them kiss your ass too, I mean *really* kiss your ass?"

"Have another wine."

Danielle poured herself one and started sipping. "There's something I want to tell you. Down there in Mexico, I was hoping that field was dry. I was hoping you'd thrown it all away, everything."

"In which case, we'd have nothing and I'd probably be dead."

"Well worth it, since *you'd* have nothing, my dear, and I wouldn't give a single shit if you were dead."

Denton watched her drain her second glass. "The only thing you hate more than me is yourself. You should get some help."

She stood there in the shadows of the pantry. Almost thirty-nine now, four years his senior and looking ten years older than that in the murky light with not enough makeup donned to disguise lines drawn by the booze and cigarettes. The rosy, vein-riddled blotches rose from her cheeks like lanterns, bright enough to read the paper by. She had smirk lines instead of those normally carved by smiles. Deeper somehow, as if she'd carved them into her face to be revealed when not filled in by makeup.

"Maybe it's time we ended this charade," Denton suggested. "Split up, go our separate ways, so you can drink yourself to death."

She smirked at him, like a poker player knowing they held the winning hand. "You know, maybe that's a good idea. And in the process I can kill another of your unborn kids."

Denton's eyes widened, couldn't find the breath to respond.

"That's my news, Dale," he heard Danielle tell him. "I'm pregnant. Again."

# TWENTY-SIX

### New York City, 1990

Ben emerged from the bathroom with hand freshly wrapped, the skin etched into what looked like a calligraphy figure already starting to itch again by the time he rejoined Melissa on the balcony.

"Where's the baby going to sleep?" she asked herself more than him, gripping the railing hard enough to squeeze the blood from her hands.

"A nice problem to have. A move is in order anyway."

"A move?"

"We got the geophysical estimates on the size of the reserves back. Unfortunately, they're only the second biggest the world," Ben said, no longer able to contain his smile.

Melissa's moist eyes widened. "Did you say . . ."

"I said we're rich, babe. Rich beyond our wildest imaginations, rich beyond anything we ever dreamed of, rich enough to afford a dozen bedrooms if we wanted."

"Nope," she smiled, hand lowering to her belly. "Just one more."


"Guess I owe you an apology," Melissa resumed, fidgeting a bit.

"For what?"

"Saying you were crazy to put everything we had into Mexico, and for thinking Dale Denton was leading you around by the tail. I told you as much, remember?"

"As I recall, it was a different part of the anatomy you referenced."

"Only because I thought that snake had cut them off."

"He's not a snake."

"Okay, an asshole then."

"Who happens to be my best friend."

Melissa rolled her eyes. "Whatever you say, Ben."

"What are *you* saying exactly?"

"Nothing."

"Too late to go back now."

"I'm pregnant, remember? Pregnant women say lots of things they don't mean. Must be all those hormones racing around."

"Don't do this," Ben said, feeling the familiar nervous flutter in his stomach.

"What?"

"Avoid the issue."

"What issue?"

Ben shook his head, started to turn back to view the world beyond their balcony. "That's what I'm talking about."

Melissa grabbed hold of his arm and pulled him back around. "I don't like Dale Denton."

"Then don't. But every bit of success I've achieved I owe to him. He put his entire inheritance into our venture, and if Mexico had gone bust, he'd be in an even deeper gutter. Hell, we'd all be sharing an apartment in Queens if we were lucky."

Denton came from real money. Serious money, the most serious because it was old. He insisted Ben tag along for holidays when Ben didn't have enough money to go home from the upscale, private high school from which he'd won a scholarship. Then Denton had encouraged him to apply to Princeton, where Ben had gotten in early decision, while Denton had to wait for his parents to pull strings to secure his admittance. They'd roomed together all four years, the last two in a glitzy two-bedroom apartment the Denton family had bought instead of paying rent.

"Dale Denton scares me, Ben."

"Why?"

Melissa shrugged. The way the sunlight danced in her hair, illuminating strands blown free by the breeze ten stories up, made her skin shine the way it had when they'd been in college. In that moment, she didn't look a day older, even though it often felt to Ben as if a hundred years had passed since graduation.

"It's just something about him, like . . ." Melissa stopped as if she was finished, but then started again. "When I was a little girl, we had this dog. I wanted to like it and whenever my parents were around, it couldn't have been nicer or more loving. But when it was just the two of us, the dog got this look in his eyes and snarled at me whenever I got too close. Like he was showing his true self, and the rest was just an act. That's the way Dale Denton makes me feel, and I think he knows that I—"

Melissa stopped when the phone rang, and Ben moved back inside to answer it.


"Are you kidding me?" Ben asked after Dale Denton shared the news about Danielle being pregnant again. "You're kidding me, right?"

"Now why would I do that, partner?"

"You're not going to believe this: Missy's pregnant too."

"You're right I don't believe it," Denton responded, after a pause. "Impossible."

"That's what I said."

"I just pinched myself. Now, I'm knocking wood."

"I'm knocking too." Ben hesitated, groping for his next words. "It'll be different for you and Dani this time, Dale, I can feel it."

"Sure, and to mark the occasion she celebrated with a glass of wine. A few of them, actually."

"You're kidding."

"Wish I was, partner, wish I was."

"She was abused as a child, Dale. It's a tough cycle to break. She's just scared. But if she keeps drinking during the pregnancy . . ."

"I know, I know."

"Then do something about it."

"Like what?"

"I could have Missy talk to her."

"Bad idea, partner. Danielle thinks Missy's crazy."

"It's called manic depression. It's a disease."

"That's good, because Danielle also thinks Missy's sick. Then again, Danielle thinks everyone is sick. Maybe that's why she hates everyone."

"Including you, Dale. I never saw a woman happier after miscarrying."

"That was because of the antidepressants the docs gave her."

"It's because she hates your guts, wants to cause you pain because she blames you for all of hers."

"I guess she's got to blame somebody. Hey, you care so much about me, maybe I should be having a kid with you, partner."

"Sorry, I'm taken. And if you can keep Dani away from the bottle, having a kid might be just what she needs."

"Fat chance. Our kid will be in boarding school by the third grade." Denton stopped, surprising himself when he picked up again. "Something I never told you, partner, about the ones we lost. I don't know if they were boys or girls. I never asked. I didn't want to know. This time, I'm going to be there from the first sonogram. Do things differently, starting now. Every bottle of booze is going in the trash as soon as I get off this call, Danielle's stash of pills too. I'll hire twenty-four security to watch her every move, if I have to."

"Well, you can certainly afford it."

"Money can't buy everything," Denton told him. "Speaking of which, what do the doctors have to say about how Missy ended up pregnant?"

"They don't, because they can't. Hey, when's Danielle's delivery date?"

"January twenty-eighth."

Ben almost dropped the phone. "Did you say the twenty-*eighth*? Man, you are not going to believe this."

"What?"

"Missy's delivery date. It's January twenty-eighth too."

# TWENTY-SEVEN

### London, England; 1991, nine months later

**W**hat do you know about Nigeria, Professor?"

Pascal Jimenez leaned forward in the chair set before the desk of England's Secretary of State for Defense, after being roused from his sleep by MI6 officials pounding on his door.

"With all due respect, Mr. Secretary, you could have asked me that question over the phone, or summoned me in the morning."

"Except the morning may be too late," Alan Neville said grimly. "We, as in the British government, need you in the air by sunrise. Your Special Air Service escorts are already en route and will be meeting you at our RAF base in Northolt."

"What's this have to do with Nigeria?"

"That's where you're going, Professor."

"With the SAS? I'm a planetary scientist," Jimenez told Neville, "a geophysicist, not a military specialist."

"And a planetary scientist, a geophysicist, is exactly what we need."

"Thirty-six hours ago, Western satellites detected a massive explosion in the southeast sector of Nigeria," Neville continued. "We believe it was caused by some kind of meteor strike, but satellites and geological observatory sites recorded no intrusion into our atmosphere or flame trail."

Jimenez remained silent, waiting for him to continue.

"Reports from the nation's government were sketchy at best, their response to our queries nonexistent. The explosion's source severely disrupted their communications, especially in the affected region." Neville rose, laying his palms down on the desk as he looked down at Jimenez. "Three hours ago, we finally received our first actual communiqués.

A delay resulted when we requested confirmation, believing the translations must be wrong."

"Why?" Jimenez asked, as if he were listening to someone else pose the question.

"Because the communiqués specified hordes of dead animal carcasses drifting along rivers, washing up on shorelines along with fish, and birds that seemed to have dropped out of the sky. And there were reports of entire indigenous tribes being wiped out, erased from existence in a time frame consistent with the period our satellites recorded the explosion."

"Wiped out by what?"

"That, Professor, is what we need you to find out."


"I'll need to put a team together," Jimenez told him. "In forty-eight hours, I can assemble the top experts in the world."

Neville shook his head. "We don't have forty-eight hours, nor can we afford widening the circle to that degree, not until we have at least a preliminary analysis of what we're facing." He stopped long enough to regard Jimenez closely. "So we've taken the liberty of assembling a team for you. The best geological minds the United Kingdom has to offer. You can review their dossiers on the flight."


Jimenez considered the rest of Neville's words, and what he'd been able to glean from the latest reports that were updated further via Telex while he was on board the C-130 Hercules that was the primary workhorse of the Royal Air Force's Tactical Air Transport fleet. By all accounts, the southeastern region of Nigeria had been struck by an asteroid he estimated to be the approximate size and weight of the American-made plane in which they were now flying. He couldn't be sure of that until he was able to study the area of the strike directly. And yet any near-Earth object responsible for such an incredible loss of life, along with the physical damage reported, could not possibly have averted the watchful eyes of planetary observatories all across the world.

Jimenez was at a loss to explain any of it.

Half the jump seats in the hold of the C-130 were occupied, divided almost evenly between an SAS A-team and the scientific team Secretary

Neville had told him was being assembled. The members of that team had all arrived minutes before Jimenez, having been told even less than he had. Jimenez knew all of them by reputation, and half the eight by sight, comforted no end by their degrees of experience and expertise. All the very best in their respective physics and geological fields. Amazing Neville had been able to gather such a prestigious group with barely any notice, another fact that spoke to the suspected enormity of whatever had happened in Nigeria.

Another half hour passed before the SAS team arrived via helicopter, led by a figure as much shadow as man in the blackness of the night who introduced himself only as "Cambridge," all his team members using cities in the U.K. for their names.

"I'm glad you're coming" was all Jimenez said to him.

"Save the platitudes until we get you back home safe" was all Cambridge said back, in a thick British accent. "And from all I'm hearing, we've got our work cut out for us."

The C-130 had set down at the nearest airfield to the decimated area in the southern-based jungle regions of Nigeria. They were met there by a dozen of the best soldiers the country had to offer, whose presence drew a smirk from Cambridge. The soldiers were no more than escorts, their sole assignment being to get Jimenez and his team to the part of civilization that had been spared nearest the strike.

That required a long and arduous drive, over roads often cut through dense swatches of forest, to a Catholic mission. The priest in charge there, Father Josef Martenko, had been advised to expect them. Martenko was a bright-eyed man a bit older than Jimenez. He wore a black, short-sleeved shirt with his priest's collar darkened at the edges by sweat. He had supplies that included food and water already boxed up for them and advised that they spend the night, and set out fresh come the morning.

"I'm going to give you my best guide," the priest told him. "Knows the jungle better than any other native I know who speaks English."

"What do the natives say about the strike?" Jimenez asked Martenko, having spotted enough shocked and terrified faces to know plenty had been driven to the mission by either rumors, or something actually worth fearing.

"Superstition among these indigenous tribes runs very deep. They believe it was the work of God, or the devil, or some combination of the two," the priest explained. "But that's not the real problem you face here, no."

"Then what is, Father?"

"You know about the Maitatsine rebels, Doctor?"

"It's professor, and, yes, I've heard of them. Read a few reports on the flight."

"I doubt those reports mentioned they've been massing in the jungles down here for some time, using them as a staging ground for their operations."

"So far from the center of the country?"

Martenko nodded, the motion looking pained. "The army would never follow the rebels down here, so the jungle's swimming with them. They've been spotted in villages not far from where we're standing now." The priest cast a gaze beyond Jimenez toward the SAS troops who'd taken the opportunity to check their ordnance and gear up for the long slog ahead. "The Nigerian soldiers who'll be accompanying you aren't worth much if it comes to a fight, so you better hope those men are."

Martenko went on to explain that the rebel group had been founded by Mohammed Marwa Maitatsine, a radical Islamist who'd rallied alienated elements of the urban poor by first launching attacks against traditional mosques, dividing the cities into armed camps with the goal toward igniting a full-scale Islamic revolution. His death in 1980 had done little to forestall the movement or its momentum. And now the efforts of the group, also known as Yan Tatsine, to foment civil war had reached a fevered, frenzied pitch that threatened to sweep across all of Nigeria.

"Maitatsine has seized upon your meteor strike for its own purposes," the priest told Jimenez, his dry voice sounding dire. "They're using the chaos and uncertainty to fan rumors that the strike was no more than a story concocted by the Nigerian government to cover their culpability in allowing Western industry to poison the land and water, resulting in the deaths of human and animals alike. Just an excuse to establish a firm base down here, since these forests offer the perfect staging ground to launch attacks all over the country." Martenko stopped, regarding Jimenez grimly, before he continued. "And if you end up crossing paths with them, whatever destroyed a large chunk of the jungle will be the least of your problems."

# TWENTY-EIGHT

## New York City, 1991

omething bad, partner?" Dale Denton asked, after Ben Younger entered his office unannounced, without knocking.

"You tell me," Ben said, stopping just short of Denton's desk and squeezing the back of one of the leather chairs set there.

The walls of Denton's office were decorated with souvenirs from various job sites they'd worked over the years, including several from projects begun after returning from the Yucatán nine months before. There were pipe fittings and the actual drill bit that had bored through the surface of their first exploratory site. There was a granite rock formation that had revealed their first find eight thousand feet below the surface and an oil-coated slab of petrified wood from the Yucatán strike itself. The only exception was a wall calendar flipped to the current month of January with the first twenty-seven days crossed out and the twenty-eighth circled in red.

"What are you up to in the Yucatán?" Ben resumed, holding his position directly in front of Dale Denton.

"What makes you think I'm up to anything, partner?"

"The books, specifically. Two million dollars expensed under 'Exploration' for fields we leased to Exxon."

Denton rose casually from his chair and popped a breath mint in his mouth. "Let it go, Ben."

"Let *what* go?" Ben asked, feeling his hand begin to throb, the red outline of the impression left by that strange rock nine months before seeming to darken.

"Tell me you're not the least bit curious about what happened down there."

"I'm the one who risked his life, Dale. Or maybe you're forgetting," Ben added, holding up his hand so Denton could see the mark the experience had left on his palm.

"I haven't forgotten at all. That's why I've got Beekman at the site supervising the team that's trying to retrace your steps, find the thing that left you with that nasty mark."

"The rock, you mean."

"It wasn't a rock, pal. You know that as well as I do, so stop fooling yourself." Denton shook his head, Ben unable to tell the source of whatever was eating him. "Don't you ever wonder how you managed to get out? How you managed a thousand-foot climb and ended up, what, a mile from our site?"

Ben pulled his hand back, turning the palm over so Denton couldn't see it.

"Every day," he told Denton finally. "All the time. Sometimes I think about it so much I can't even sleep. I lie in bed at night, wondering if this is the time I'll finally remember. But I never do. And at some point, I have to accept I never will."

"Follow my lead, partner: never give up."

"You should have asked me first, sought my approval."

Denton shook his head, scoffing. "And what would you have said?"

"Told you not to bother, that it was a waste of time and money, *our* money. A fool's errand."

"Won't know that until we find it, partner," Denton said, forcing a smile.

"You'll never find it."

"Why?"

"Because whatever it is, it's not meant to be found," Ben said, surprising himself with his own words.

Denton lowered his voice, sounding almost conciliatory. "Something happened down there, Ben, something nobody can explain. You want to deny that?"

"How can I deny something I don't even remember happening?"

"That's the point. You don't remember. But I do, starting with all life in the area going batshit crazy. You didn't experience that part of the story, did you? And I'm convinced that it all goes back to this rock. You take hold of it, and all of a sudden the world's going nuts, and oil's shooting up and out of the ground."

"And that's a bad thing?"

"You're telling me none of this makes you the least bit curious? That you don't think finding that rock is worth the expense we can easily spare?"

"No," he lied. "It's a rock, Dale. Superheated from gases escaping from the Earth's very core, but a rock all the same."

"I believe there might be more to it than that."

"Something worth two million bucks and climbing?"

"Beekman's got a couple thoughts, theories."

"Care to elaborate?"

"Nope, not until we're sure."

"Sure about what, Dale?"

Denton nodded, more to himself than Ben. "If I'd told you we were going to become oil tycoons overnight, would you have believed me?"

"Not a chance."

"So trust me, when it comes to your rock."

"*My* rock?"

"Finders keepers, partner." Denton leaned back and interlaced his hands behind his head. "Come on, you telling me you haven't thought about it, even considered the possibility?"

"What possibility would that be?"

Denton's eyes scolded him. "You can't lie to me, partner; we've known each other too long. Missy getting pregnant was supposed to be impossible. And I took every precaution to keep Danielle from getting pregnant again, short of getting my tubes tied," he said with a wink. "I even started grinding up her birth control pills and dissolving them in her coffee. Yet, hey, here we are. Two kids who never should've been conceived at all about to be born. You want to call that coincidence, go ahead."

"Because that's what it is."

"This coming from a man who has no idea how he climbed out of a cave without a rope and ended up over a mile from where he started without a single scratch on him."

Ben shook his head, frowning. "And that's your rationale for spending two million dollars and counting?"

Denton stared at him for a long moment. "My rationale is the fact that we're sitting here right now, that our lives changed in every way imaginable after you stumbled out of that wasteland covered in crude. Look, I don't know if that rock thing is a turd left by God himself or a piece of the asteroid that wiped out the dinosaurs. But I do know nothing's been the same since you grabbed hold of it. You want to tell me I'm crazy, go ahead. But if I'm not, maybe, just maybe, we're on to something that'll make our oil strike in the Yucatán look like a drop in the bucket. Literally."

Denton and Younger were still staring at each other, when Denton's cell phone rang.

"I'm going into labor," Danielle told him.

A moment later, Ben's cell phone rang too.

"I'm on my way to the hospital," Missy said, an edge in her voice as if something was wrong. "Hurry, Ben, please."

# TWENTY-NINE

**Nigeria, 1991**

The last fifteen miles to the site from Father Josef Martenko's Catholic mission had to be covered on foot with native guides arranged by the Nigerian government, who cleared the way through the jungle with machetes while Cambridge and his men remained forever wary of a potential ambush.

"What is it you're not telling me, Commander?" Jimenez had asked him at one point.

"It's Cambridge, just Cambridge. And if I haven't told you, it's because you don't need to know."

"I'm not sure if I can accept that."

Cambridge nodded, undeterred by Jimenez's response. "What's your specialty exactly?"

"Planetary science and astrobiology."

"Would you expect me to understand your specialties without proper training?"

"Of course not."

"Then don't ask me to explain mine."

There was something about the man that made Jimenez distinctly uncomfortable in his presence. At first, Jimenez passed it off to the man's military mindset that he could not even begin to comprehend. The problem, though, was it seemed more than that, although Jimenez couldn't explain exactly why.

Cambridge's features were dark, his face forever cloaked in shadows further accentuated by high, ridged cheekbones and a thick forehead beneath a scalp showing only a thin layer of black stubble. Those features added to the illusion that his skin was actually two-toned, the lighter and darker shades more liquid than solid, forever shifting in their battle for supremacy. His hooded eyes were unnervingly intense, seeming to see ahead into the next moment, rather than ponder the last. Nonetheless, Jimenez was grateful for the presence of Cambridge and his team, especially after Father Martenko's warning about Maitatsine rebels being concentrated in the area.

The good news was that seismological and air-quality studies of the area conducted by robotic aircraft indicated the air quality in the affected area showed no signs of contamination. But a vast, fog-rich cloud still enveloped a fifteen-square-mile area around the point of impact, growing thicker the closer Jimenez and his party drew to the actual point of impact.

A final full day's walk had brought his party into that cloud, the lack of sunlight stealing the warmth from the air. Jimenez had already reported to Secretary Neville that the effects of defoliation grew more and more pronounced the deeper into the jungle they ventured. Ultimately the cloud became thick as soup, the fresh smells of the jungle replaced by . . .

Jimenez had found himself at a loss for words here until the answer occurred to him: nothing, the jungle smelled of nothing. Not bad, not good, not anything at all.


They stopped to rest an hour later, Jimenez guzzling water from a canteen, when he spotted Cambridge gliding toward him, seeming to focus on the tree against which he was leaning.

"What," Jimenez started.

Cambridge snapped a hand over his head, clamping onto a snake Jimenez realized must've been about to lunge at him. He watched as the snake's fangs sunk into Cambridge's wrist instead, just before Cambridge pressed it down on the ground and stamped it to death.

"Bloody hell," he said, scratching at the indentation dribbling blood. "No worries, Professor. Just a baby boa. Non-venomous."

"Well," Jimenez said, eyeing Cambridge's swollen patch of skin, "that's a relief."


A few miles further into their trek, Jimenez detected the thick scents of blood and death on the air just short of a rolling, brush-covered meadow. Cambridge signaled the rest of the group to hold in place, while he moved ahead to investigate, gesturing for Jimenez to join him moments later.

Jimenez approached, pinching his nose against the worsening stench that emanated from a tangle of torn flesh, fur, and limbs swimming with the biggest flies he'd ever seen.

"A lion pride," Cambridge noted. "Seen plenty of them before, just not in this condition."

Jimenez advanced slightly ahead of him, swatting away the flies that buzzed toward him, realizing Cambridge and his entire SAS team were now holding their weapons at the ready.

"They tore themselves apart," Cambridge continued, scratching at his snakebite that looked even more swollen. "Took the cubs out first. You want to explain to me how something like that happens?"

Jimenez gazed into the distance, in the general direction of the blast zone's epicenter. "We might be about to find out."


Miles later, the team's local guides froze at what looked like the edge of a clearing. Jimenez drew even with them to find it wasn't a clearing at all, but an utter barren wasteland. A swath of jungle bled of trees and foliage of all kinds. Whatever bodies of water might have existed for the fifteen-mile stretch indicated by satellite reconnaissance were gone too, nothing but shallow depressions left in the ground where streams had once run between the thick canopy of the Nigerian forestlands. Now there was no canopy, and nothing beneath where it had once resided but parched, dead ground that looked like a desert.

Jimenez had never stopped thinking about the plague of dead animals washing up on shorelines along numerous rivers nearby or the tribes long indigenous to the region that had seemingly vanished. Then his team had come upon the pride of lions that had torn each other apart, further fueling the sense of dread and foreboding he hadn't been able to shake.

He and his team of handpicked scientists had taken regular samples along the way, stored now for safekeeping after he'd performed rudimentary field tests that revealed no anomalies in the condition of the foliage. So too he examined various members of his team on a regular basis, checking for any changes in appearance or vital signs. Jimenez feared that, perhaps, his own theories best demonstrated by the baby powder bursting out of the breached faux meteorite were being put to the test here. That the strike had unleashed some microbe utterly unknown in this world, with no cure or treatment that might well have been the cause of both the deaths and disappearances. But so far none of the members were showing any symptoms at all, other than uniformly elevated pulse rates that continued to climb the closer they drew to the impact zone.

Jimenez entered all his findings in a worn, leather notebook in precise handwriting, using the gold pen that was all he had left of his father. This as he wondered if there was enough ink left to compile the vast amount of data he was collecting.

He was no expert on mapping, but he'd been able to collate the satellite reconnaissance with maps both professional in design and drawn by hand by the chief guide Father Martenko had provided him named Foluke. That gave Jimenez a concrete destination where the actual crater should have been located.

He took his place closer to the front with the Nigerian guides and small Nigerian military escort to supplement the SAS commandos. The procession was led by Foluke, who spoke fluent English and was always smiling. But he wasn't smiling, as he led the way stiffly onward this last stretch of the way. Jimenez felt his work boots crunching over what felt like glass or seashells, but he knew to actually be the petrified remnants of the trees, soil, and flora. That suggested a surge of heat of immeasurable proportions, more in keeping with the effects of a nuclear blast than a meteor strike.

Strangely, the air began to clear as they drew closer to the epicenter where Jimenez expected to find the meteor's impact point. The thick haze, formed by the ash residue produced by that strike, was dissipating, allowing Jimenez his first glimpse of the sky for miles. Then another three miles in across the flat, parched earth, a gradual darkening of the ground gave way to a virtual black hole carved in perfectly symmetrical fashion.

Jimenez detected a light mist rising out of the hole, like vapor out of a pot of steaming water, drifting in a thin, constant wave toward the sun that had begun to peek out. For some reason, its presence comforted him, the same way dawn comforts a child frightened by the night.

He reached the edge of the actual impact point, the land turning black as tar and looking even darker somehow closer to the epicenter of the blast. The scope and depth of the depression it had left suggested the meteor itself was in the area of twenty-five yards in diameter, weighing nearly 25,000 metric tons. Normally, the velocity of such an object, along with the shallow angle of its atmospheric entry, would lead it to explode in an airburst and never actually strike the ground. This one, though, by all accounts, had remained whole until impact. which meant the bulk of its fractured fragments would still be intact, promising a virtual treasure trove of astronomical riches.

The guide Foluke and the Nigerian troops remained behind when Jimenez scrabbled down into the gaping chasm in the ground, accompanied by both the expert geological team assembled by the British government and the SAS troops. The ground felt soft and spongy, his boots pushing through thick black ash with the grainy texture of sand. The epicenter came up faster than he'd thought it would, the exact point where the meteor had made contact with the Earth. In spite of everything, Jimenez suddenly found himself excited, truly on the verge of what could be the find of a lifetime, until . . .

*Until* . . .

"What is it, Professor?" Jimenez heard one of the other scientists ask him. "What do you see?"

"It's not what I see," Jimenez told him, after sweeping his gaze about once more in case he had missed something. "It's what I *don't* see. . . ."

# THIRTY

## New York City, 1991

Dale Denton and Ben Younger had camped out in the hospital waiting room, neither with any intention of leaving, although it was clear Denton was getting antsy as he worked a pay phone nonstop.

Both their wives had suffered "complications" with their deliveries. That's all the doctors and nurses had said up until this point. Complications. Whatever that meant.

The explanation finally came a day before Melissa's and Danielle's expected delivery date of January 28.

"I've never seen one ectopic pregnancy go undiagnosed and undetected through the entire term, never mind two," the hospital's head of obstetrics explained, sounding genuinely baffled.

"Spare us the bullshit and just give us the haps, Doc," Denton said, in what sounded like an order.

"In normal situations, the life of the mother wouldn't be at risk."

"I take that to mean this isn't a normal situation," Ben interjected.

"In fact," the doctor began, clearly unsettled as well as surprised, "it's unprecedented. An ectopic pregnancy occurs when the embryo attaches outside the uterus. The severe abdominal pain that results, accompanied by vaginal bleeding, is usually more than enough to alert us to an anomaly, even before it's detected by ultrasound. In this case, both these cases, the normal growth pattern of the fetuses pushed them inside the uterus with any outgrowth sealed by scar tissue. Had we known about this earlier, we would've been able to try to deliver the babies prematurely through emergency Caesarean sections. Now we're faced with extremely complex and dangerous deliveries, no matter what scenario we choose to pursue."

"So neither woman had a single symptom," Denton said, trying to make sense of it all. "That's what you're saying."

"In ten percent of cases, Mr. Denton, there are no symptoms. But I can't explain how all of our regular checkpoints failed to detect what should've been obvious."

"Maybe because you're an incompetent idiot."

Denton's remark got no rise from the doctor. He'd introduced himself, but Ben couldn't remember his name, and saw now that he wasn't wearing a name tag.

"There'll be time for recriminations later," the doctor said. "For now, we're left to face some long, challenging hours that may well leave us with some very difficult decisions to make."

"You mean, whether to save the mother or the child," Ben assumed.

"I mean," the doctor told both he and Denton, "in both these cases, we may not be able to save either of them."

# THIRTY-ONE

## Nigeria, 1991

I don't think I understand," Secretary Neville said, after Pascal Jimenez had completed his initial report of the strike itself.

"Neither do I," Jimenez told him over the satellite phone. "This is entirely unprecedented in the annals of planetary science and meteor strikes."

"Surely, there must be *something*."

"No, Mr. Secretary, I'm afraid there isn't. I've spent the last day studying the crater and surrounding area. And I can definitely say I can find no trace whatsoever of any meteor."

"What about fragments, *anything?*"

"You've already asked me that and the answer's the same: no fragments. And, even if the structural integrity of the meteor was compromised upon entering our atmosphere at such a high rate of speed, there still should be plenty of evidence, at the very least, in the subterranean layers beneath the crater. But there's nothing."

Dead air filled the line, silence for so long that Jimenez thought the satellite connection might've been lost just before Neville's voice returned.

"You're saying that one of the most catastrophic strikes in recent history was caused by a meteor that, according to your report, no longer exists in any form."

"I'm saying that's not even remotely conceivable. And there's something else."

"I'm still listening, Professor."

"Remember you told me how none of the planetary observatories were aware of this meteor entering the Earth's atmosphere? That should've keyed us in to the fact we were dealing with something unprecedented and utterly inexplicable here. Meteors are normally aflame when they explode either in an airburst or upon impact, resulting in heat scoring and residue of the signature. There's nothing like that here. No evidence of scoring at all from any heat, other than from the energy released at the moment the strike occurred."

Jimenez heard Neville utter a deep sigh on the other end of the satellite line. "So you're no closer to a conclusion about the animal deaths and the disappearance of the tribes residing in the surrounding area."

"I had expected the answers to lie in samples of the meteor itself taken from the scene," Jimenez told him. "I'll have to look elsewhere for those answers now."

"Bloody Africa," Neville said, his distaste clear. "The mystery continent for as long as I've been in government."

"One more thing," Jimenez said, unsurely.

"What's that?"

Jimenez thought of coming upon the lion pride that had ravaged itself, couldn't put into words his fear that something the meteor strike had unleashed had been the cause.

"I misspoke," he continued, as a result. "It's nothing. Just my nerves acting up."

"Understandable, given the circumstances. I'll look forward to your next report, but contact me anytime with any further updates. And, Professor?"

"Yes?"

"You need to find whatever caused this nasty mess."

The line clicked off, Jimenez left with the satellite phone dead in his hand while forming his next thought.

*What am I missing here?*

That a meteor had struck the Earth and created the crater he was currently gazing down into was incontrovertible. So what had happened to it? Over twenty thousand metric tons of rock couldn't have all burned up. There should at the very least have been fragments, as large as boulders and as small as pebbles, contained within the crater with the largest concentration centered around the epicenter itself.

But there wasn't, not in the crater and not anywhere in the blast zone's radius. It was as if . . .

As if *what?*

Before Jimenez could consider the matter further, Foluke rushed up to him, out of breath.

"What's wrong?" Jimenez asked him.

Foluke caught enough of his breath to finally speak.

"*Wahala, Oga.*"

"*Wahala?*"

"Trouble," Foluke said, switching to English. "The rebels are coming."

As a young boy, Jimenez had grown up in Caracas, Venezuela, at a time when gangs ruled the street. Going to the market literally meant taking your life in your own hands. A simple trip to bring food back to his mother and younger siblings consisted of weaving his way through alleys and over rooftops while listening to the clack of both automatic and sniper fire as the gangs battled both each other and the corrupt police force that rotated allegiance depending on who was paying them. He thought he'd never know fear like that again.

For his part, Cambridge didn't seem overly concerned about the prospects of that, even after Foluke broke the news that the Nigerian complement of their troops had fled.

"That's why we're here," he explained to Jimenez, scratching again at the area where the snake had bit him.

"The British government knew about Maitatsine, didn't they? They knew Islamic fanatics were running rampant in these parts, all about the risk we were facing when they ordered up this expedition."

"Here's what I know, Professor," Cambridge said, without really responding. "We've both got jobs to do, and mine is to keep you and your team safe. And if that means killing some bad guys, I'm ready and willing 'cause that's what I get paid for. That's what we do." His dark eyes turned into black pools of ink that seemed to swallow all of the white. "But I'll let you in on a little secret: I'd do this one for free, once I find you safe passage out of here."

"Your hand," Jimenez said.

"What about it?"

Jimenez glimpsed the swelling around the area of the man's snakebite, riddled now with individual bumps that looked like boils ready to burst. "Let me have a closer look at it. The wound could be infected."

Cambridge tucked the hand behind his back. "I feel fine, Professor, and we got more important fish to fry right now."

Far more than he'd been expecting, as it turned out, when Foluke and Cambridge's own SAS scouts reported that pockets of the advancing Maitatsine Islamic radicals had managed to secure all routes leading back to civilization.

"And there's more," Cambridge reported. "Word is they're led by a man named Musa Makaniki, a psychopath who hates anything that even smells Western," Cambridge explained. "Apparently, he's been spotted in the area himself, leading the fighters who are headed our way."

Cambridge's walkie-talkie crackled and he snatched it from his belt, jerking it to his ear as he slipped away. His expression never changed during the course of whatever he was hearing; not dour or grim, so much as resigned, expectant, maybe even . . . pleased?

"We need to get you and your people hunkered down, Professor," he told Jimenez. "Looks like the bloody sons of bitches are coming."

# THIRTY-TWO

### New York City, 1991

W e may not be able to save the baby," the doctor told Ben Younger outside the delivery room. "We may not be able to save either. I already told you that."

"She can't die," Ben pleaded, feeling his knees quaking so much he thought the floor was shifting.

"The baby's a boy."

"I'm talking about my wife."

"If you had to make a choice . . ."

"There's no choice to make."

"I understand," the doctor said, even though it was clear he didn't.

"Save them both, Doctor. That's my decision. My wife's too."

"And if I can't?"

"Then save a scalpel for me."

"The kid," Dale Denton said. "If that's what it comes down to, save the kid."

"Mr. Denton, normal procedure dictates that we—"

"I don't give a shit about normal procedure. I care about my kid. If you can save my wife too, great. If not, it's balls to the wall to get the kid out alive, and let the rest of the chips fall where they may."

"It's a girl, Mr. Denton," the doctor told him.

### Nigeria, 1991

Maitatsine came from three directions at once, a two-hundred-man force, by all accounts, destined to converge inside the blast zone where they'd be able to flush their targets into the open. They knew the territory, certainly an advantage that Jimenez could only hope was more than balanced by the prowess and proficiency of SAS troops.

The bulk of the fighters wore shabby, Western-style clothing, a few in army uniforms either owned or taken off the soldiers who'd already fallen in their path. All carried guns; Russian Kalashnikovs, by the look of things, and spanking new compared to the ancient ordnance known from the days of Marwa.

Jimenez was with Cambridge when the report came down that their advance had come much faster than expected, leaving no time for him to hunker down with his team members, or retreat to the hills west of their current position. But there was still time, Cambridge assured, for his men to prepare for what was coming.

"You're outnumbered at least ten to one," Jimenez reminded, "maybe more."

"And those ten to one will be coming single file along congested jungle trails. Easy pickings for boys who know how to pick."

"But—"

"Bollocks, Professor," Cambridge told him. "Keep cover, keep still, and enjoy the show. This is our blasted expedition now."


### New York City, 1991

Ben Younger stood by his wife's bedside, feeling her squeeze his hand so hard he thought she was going to crush the bones.

"The baby, Ben," she gasped, "the baby!"

"He's going to be fine."

"Save him, *pleasssssse*!"

Ben felt the bones in his hand crackle, his knees quaking from the pain that left him biting his lip.

"Whatever it takes! Promise me! *Promise*—"

Missy's voice choked off there, like a battery had shut off in her head. All at once the monitoring machines wired to her began to flash and beep.

"We're losing her!" a nurse cried out.

"We're losing the baby too!" from the obstetrician, his expression anguished as he continued working his hands about desperately in Melissa's insides. His pleading eyes locked onto Ben Younger. "Choose! You have to choose!"

•  •  •

Dale Denton was hardly prepared to bear witness to an emergency Cae-
sarian section, but he wasn't about to show weakness. He did his best to
stand back from it all, as the obstetric team worked feverishly to deliver
his daughter. But the queasiness turned him light-headed and left the
floor wobbly beneath his feet. He leaned back against a wall and shut
his eyes to the sights, wished he could've shut his nose to the smells as
well.

He knew what Danielle would say, would want: "Fuck the kid. I'll just
have another."

Denton was glad that decision now fell upon him. Dani had been pregnant twice before, both squandered to booze, drugs, meds, or a combination of all three. This time, Denton had obsessively committed himself
to changing the paradigm by turning his wife into a veritable prisoner.
She went nowhere without escort. Denton himself checked the medicine
and kitchen cabinets, along with all her usual hiding places on a daily
basis—anything to make sure Dani stayed clean this time.

*Of course, she would've chosen herself; she hadn't given a shit about the
first two babies, so why change with this one?*

The doctor believed it was both of them or neither at this point, rob-
bing Denton of his ideal scenario:

A living daughter.

And a dead, pain-in-the-ass wife.

### Nigeria, 1991

Jimenez watched as glimpses of motion and spots of the sun's reflection
off gunmetal flashed in the narrowing distance, the radicals almost upon
them. His team of expert scientists, whom he'd barely gotten a chance
to know, were as secure as could be in a thick nest of foliage well back
from the crater with two of the SAS troops with them for protection.
For his part, Jimenez remained with Cambridge for as long as possible,
wanting to feel he had a part in this, even if that meant wielding a weapon
himself.

"Showtime," Cambridge said, just after teaching Jimenez how to shoot
the pistol he'd provided.

The rest unfolded in a haze of blast and fire. First came the Claymores and other mines tucked under the dried-out muck of the jungle trails. Bodies of Maitatsine soldiers, both whole and ravaged, were launched far and near like something out of a slapstick movie. Severed arms, legs, torsos, and heads rocketed out of the smoke plumes.

Jimenez watched, the sounds seeming to come after a lag. Then his hearing sharpened and the lag reversed, with him seeing the product of blasts his ears had already recorded, the whole time with his own Beretta held at the ready.

He realized the initial series of explosions had been replaced by the steady clack of assault rifle fire raining in on the rebels from secure positions that included tree limbs commanded by a pair of snipers. The fall of bodies was like something out of a crude children's video game, the kind played now with wires strung from a television. The precision of Cambridge's SAS troops was as chilling as it was terrifying, the Maitatsine radicals standing no chance against them. Up until today, they'd rampaged through the country, encountering minimal resistance posed by government troops more likely to run than fight. Schoolyard bullies used to trampling over those too weak or afraid to fight back, enamored now by their own sense of power and will that had yet to truly be before now.

It didn't feel like a dream or nightmare; it didn't feel like anything at all, at least anything Jimenez had ever experienced before. Gunfire continued to hammer his ears, interspersed with anguished screams of pain uttered by Maitatsine radicals until more SAS fire silenced them.

Jimenez followed it all as best he could, utterly transfixed, feeling as if his consciousness had detached from his own body. Around him, flames continued to bite at the air as smoke from both fire and blast residue wafted through the jungle, forming cloud pockets that looked like fog nearly as thick as the soupy ash mist that had greeted their arrival here before the sun had broken through.

Jimenez heard brush crunching underfoot nearby and ducked out from his meager position of cover. He froze briefly before opting to move back downhill, closer to the actual crater and the greatest concentration of SAS troops. He resisted the urge to use the Beretta Cambridge had provided, not trusting his aim and afraid the shots would succeed only in alerting the rebels to his position.

The foliage thinned as he neared the soot-covered ground of the blast zone, entering the open charred space in which the crater was centered, just as the SAS commandos, a few of them wounded, emerged from the jungle. Having killed or chased off the rebels.

Jimenez was staring right at them, when a blistering torrent of bullets rained down from everywhere at once.

# THIRTY-THREE

## New York City, 1991

Ben Younger prayed, which was strange because he couldn't remember the last time he'd done so. He also couldn't remember the last time he'd felt so utterly helpless, including falling down a cave in the Yucatán the year before. Ben felt like he was back in that cave right now, lying at the bottom and gazing up at what remained of his life.

He was leaning against the wall, a closet door he realized now. Before him the hospital room had gone silent, his anxious mind suspended between levels of consciousness, unsure whether to fade to black or not. He could see the shapes in blue hospital garb working feverishly, frantically. Lights on all the monitors hooked up to both baby and mother flashing soundlessly and providing his only hope.

Then the machines went dark.

They had gone dark a few rooms down the hall too. Dale Denton came right up to the damn doctor who was skinny as a rail with big eyes that looked like big marbles sticking out of his head.

"You save my damn daughter, you hear me? You fucking save her!"

"We're doing our best," the doctor managed, between whatever desperate measures he was performing on a fetus exposed amid the blood, slop, and rearranged organs.

A trio of nurses, meanwhile, were working on Danielle. Denton couldn't help but blame all the drinks, all the butts, all the drugs. Goddamn pharmacy for a medicine cabinet. Going cold turkey for nine months, when it probably would've taken nine years to get her system really cleaned out.

*You killed the first two. And now you've killed this one too.*

Denton thought he'd only spoken the words in his head, but the looks cast him by a couple of nurses working feverishly to save his wife suggested otherwise.

*Go fuck yourselves.*

Maybe he'd said that out loud too.


### Nigeria, 1991

Jimenez watched, still breathless, as Cambridge stepped out from the tree line into the sprawl of earth scorched by the meteor strike. Grinning, his assault rifle barrel still smoking, eyes wide and gleaming in what could have been ecstasy.

He'd gunned his own men down in a torrent of fire!

Jimenez ducked back into the cover of the dense brush, as the surviving Maitatsine radicals trailed Cambridge out of the jungle, herding the members of Jimenez's team before them. They prodded the eight shapes forward until the scientists reached the edge of the crater, at which point the fighters kicked or swiped their legs out, forcing them to kneel with their backs to Jimenez.

*This couldn't be happening. . . .*

And it didn't seem real when Cambridge casually strolled straight down the line, shooting each of the scientists in the head. A few tumbled down into the crater, while others collapsed straddling the rim.

Jimenez realized his mouth had dropped open, each breath making his chest and lungs ache. The pistol had remained frozen in his trembling grasp; he couldn't even raise it, never mind try firing. He wanted to move, but couldn't, a wave of fear seizing him so firmly that it trapped the breath in his throat. He had to remind himself to breathe, and even then could only manage short desperate heaves that left him light-headed, on the verge of hyperventilating and passing out.

But that would've been too easy, surrendering to unconsciousness, while the bodies of brilliant men and women lay rotting in the sun. Jimenez felt his eyes welling with tears and his knees starting to wobble, when something cold pressed up against the back of his head, and he felt the Beretta snatched from his grasp.

• • •

The Maitatsine rebel shoved him forward into the clearing, straight up to where Cambridge stood, stumbling as he tried to avoid the bodies of the fallen SAS troops their leader had just shot.

"I was wondering where you'd disappeared to, Professor," Cambridge grinned.

"What is this?" Jimenez managed. "What have you done? In the name of God, are you mad?"

Cambridge kept grinning, as he snapped a fresh magazine into his pistol. Then he used his free hand to shove Jimenez on toward the crater.

"God," he repeated. "Are you a religious man?"

Jimenez gazed at the frames of his team members, twisted and frozen in death. "Does it matter?"

"Not a bit."

And then Cambridge's eyes grew so cold they seemed to recede deeper into his skull, the dark portions swallowing the whites. He yanked the necklace from Jimenez's neck and snapped off the cross, regarding it indifferently before tossing it aside into the bushes.

"Because your God is not here." Cambridge racked a round into the chamber and aimed his Beretta at Jimenez. "Now, get on your knees so we can be done with this."

From his knees, Jimenez looked up at the Beretta's bore in line with his forehead, wanted to close his eyes but couldn't. " 'Shall I leave their innocent blood unavenged? No, I will not,' " he said, in what sounded like someone else's voice.

Cambridge's grin grew wider. Jimenez noticed the tiny bumps rising out of the snake bite on his other hand were oozing puss and blood amid the now hideous swelling. Cambridge rubbed it against his pants, leaving a thick stain, as he tried to relieve the itch.

"So you *are* a religious man, Professor, relying on God to do something you can't. Don't you remember? Your God isn't here. If he is here, beg him to give me a sign and I'll spare your life. But he won't, because he isn't."

With that, Cambridge viciously jerked Jimenez's head around to look at the bodies sprawled about the ash-covered clearing, the coppery stench of their blood starting to claim the air now.

"I'm the only god here now, Professor." Cambridge leaned over and plucked the gold pen from Jimenez's lapel pocket. "How'd you like me to write your epitaph?"

Jimenez turned and gazed up at an expression as flat as it was cold, splattered with the blood of the men he'd just killed that had coated portions of his coarse, stubble-laden scalp as well. If the devil had a face, this was it, he thought, as Cambridge pocketed the pen that had belonged to Jimenez's father.

Cambridge holstered his pistol and yanked a shiny, razor-sharp knife from his belt in its place. He stepped around Jimenez and pressed the icy-cold blade of his knife against his throat, speaking softly into his ear from behind.

"I think we'll take your head, Professor. You won't be needing it anymore anyway."

Jimenez felt the chill of the blade against his throat, prayed there would be no pain, and closed his eyes.

### New York City, 1991

Ben Younger thought the flashing lights were only in his mind. Then he realized the medical team desperately working to save both his wife and newborn son had seen them too. But the beeps were slowing, the blips on the screen rising between longer intervals.

They were dying, both his wife and unborn child, and there was nothing he could do. Then he saw something out the window, the sky darkening from twilight to pitch, all trace of light stolen from it.

*An eclipse, it must be an eclipse. . . .*

He gave no further thought to the scientific rarity, until a coldness seemed to join the darkness spreading beyond, a chill that rose from the depths of his own being he expected would frost the windows.

Suddenly, the monitoring machine by Melissa's bedside lit up like Christmas trees, faded to black, then blipped to life again. The lines and LED readouts weak, but brightening.

*Beep, beep, beep, beep . . .*

Two sets, signaling life while darkness continued to thicken beyond the window.

*BEEP, BEEP, BEEP, BEEP . . .*

Louder now, followed by something even louder:

A baby crying.

Ben watched the doctor swing toward him, having just clipped the umbilical cord from his flailing, thrashing, and muck-covered son.

"You're a very lucky man . . ."

". . . Mr. Denton," the doctor, drenched in blood and sweat, said in the room a few doors down, "to have a healthy daughter. But your wife, I'm afraid she . . ."

The doctor's dour expression, accompanied by a slow shake of his head, completed the thought for him.

"I'm sorry," he finished.

"For what?" Denton asked him, as thin light began to cut through the blackness beyond the window. "You did your job, best you could, and delivered my daughter. All in all, a fair trade, I'd say."

### Nigeria, 1991

*Am I dead?*

Jimenez was afraid to open his eyes, for fear of finding the knife still poised against his throat, Cambridge yet to finish the job. And when he finally pried them open, there was only darkness, making him thankful that death had come without pain.

*Then how am I opening my eyes?*

He realized he was still alive, realized darkness had dropped like a curtain from the sky and sucked up the light around him. Swept his eyes about the area of the crater, all by himself in the clearing now.

*Your God isn't here.*

But He must have been, because Jimenez realized he was witnessing a total eclipse, a true once-in-a-century phenomenon being so isolated down here had kept from his attention. This was different from any darkness he'd experienced before, as if the world had been sucked utterly dry of all light and this was what was left. And it wasn't just the light; the heat had been bled from the day as well, a strange chill prevalent where the air had been steamy just a few moments before.

The Maitatsine radicals were gone.

Cambridge was gone.

*"If He is here, beg him to give me a sign and I'll spare your life."*

And Cambridge had.

## New York City, 1991

Ben and Missy named their son after Ben's grandfather:

Maximillian, Max for short.

Dale named his daughter after a queen of England his now late wife Danielle had read a book about in the last, difficult stage of her pregnancy:

Victoria, Vicky for short.

Ben shared the glorious occasion at the bedside of the only woman he'd ever loved. Looking down at Missy cradling their son. Mere minutes old, Max Younger had been born happy and healthy, wrapped in a blanket now and smelling of heaven itself. Ben finally took his son in his arms, reveling in his warmth and breath while unfalteringly amazed at how miniaturized everything about him was.

*I've never held a baby before.*

The realization almost drove Ben to return Max to his mother, but he held fast instead, bouncing slightly and seeing if he could get the baby to grab his finger in its tiny hands. That's when he saw a blotch on Max's palm that at first glance looked like no more than a bruise, but on second took on the impression of a shape Ben had come to know all too well: a scratchy assemblage of crossed lines that looked randomly sketched.

Identical in miniature to the mark embedded in his own palm, left by the rock he'd grasped in a Yucatán cave nine months before, emanating that strange dark light. Ben felt his stomach tighten, as if that strange coincidence had already defined the bond between father and son.

Ben heard Max gurgle, watched the infant cough some mucus from his mouth, emotions rampaging through him like nothing he'd ever experienced before. The baby looked up and seemed to smile at him, and Ben couldn't help but smile back, kissing his newborn son lightly on the forehead.

"I love you, Max."

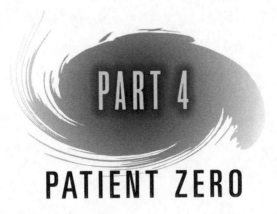

# PART 4

# PATIENT ZERO

## The Present

Who holds the devil, let him hold him well,
He hardly will be caught a second time.

—Johann Wolfgang von Goethe, *Faust*

# THIRTY-FOUR

**New York City**

P lease tell me I'm not dead," the man behind the desk said to Max.

Max grinned and closed the office door behind him. "Not unless I am."

The man rolled his wheelchair out. "Then give me a hug, hoss."

Weeb Bochner's voice still carried a trace of his backcountry Georgia roots. It had taken him three tries to get through SEAL BUD/S training, all of thirty-three years old when he and Max had been assigned to the same SEAL Team 6 unit.

They met halfway across the office, Weeb on his wheels and Max on his feet. Max bent over, half crouching, to give Bochner a hug, witnessed by the maybe hundred pictures that plastered his walls. All of him standing on two legs in various uniforms shown with various dignitaries on any number of deployments, except for the one of him receiving the Congressional Medal of Honor. Max wasn't included in any of them; nor was any other SEAL who was still active. There were a dozen elegantly framed commendations as well, evidence of Weeb's distinguished service.

"I've got a problem, brother."

"Of course you do. Otherwise you wouldn't be here." Bochner looked Max over from his wheelchair. "Still doing your time?"

"What do you think?"

"Right, stupid question. But we normally don't deploy in Manhattan."

"There were some issues on my last mission."

Bochner smirked. "Par for the course."

He'd been just over six feet before landing in his wheelchair, but Max could still see the powerful muscles rippling across his chest, shoulders, and arms. Compensation, Max knew, having seen it often enough. Obsessively working what you could control to distract from what you couldn't.

They'd been on a raid in Afghanistan's squirrelly Kandahar Province that had turned out to be a Taliban trap. Half the team inside the building, the rest holding at the perimeter, when the explosions shattered the stillness of the night, swiftly followed by strafing fire from inside what seemed like every other building in view. A chunk of steel ended up lodged in the lower part of Weeb's spine when he fell through a crumbling floor. Max had gone down after him and carried him out of the building. Over his shoulder, with one arm holding Weeb in place while the other returned fire. Two other team members died in the raid, Weeb certain to have joined them if not for Max's efforts.

*"The fuck you think you're doing?" Bochner had managed to rasp, as Max scooped him up amid the gunfire ratcheting beyond.*

*"What's it look like?"*

*"You got better things to do today than die, hoss."*

*"So do you."*

Weeb had rejoined the world when the need for his particular brand of expertise exploded in the private security field. For a price, companies like PRO-TECH, short for Protective Technologies, could do pretty much anything a regular army could, their clients culled from Fortune 500–type companies that required personal protection for their executives while traveling abroad. Weeb, last Max had heard, was responsible for coordinating the most at-risk assignments in the most dangerous arenas where gunplay often proved necessary. As such, he and the company as a whole had built a wealth of contacts across all levels of law enforcement that could be called upon at anytime to aid their efforts.

"Issues," Bochner said, echoing Max's previous statement. "I'm guessing lives got saved in the process, Commander. Though back in Kandahar, I said not to bother with mine."

"I must not have heard you."

"This coming from a man who can hear mosquitoes buzzing a half mile away," Bochner quipped.

"What?" Max mocked, cupping a hand behind his ear.

"So what can I do for you, Pope?"

Max sketched the broad strokes for him, including the fact his real name was Younger, Max Borgia being an alias built to hold up to all but the most extreme scrutiny. But he left out the peripheral details like visions and stinging pain in his palm from the birthmark that was a spitting image of the mark burned into his father's.

"Creedmoor," Bochner said, offering no further comment, as he slid a pad closer to himself on the desk to make some notes. "And that's where the attack happened."

"Yesterday. I've been pretty much tied up with the police ever since."

Bochner regarded him closer. "How'd that go?"

"Well, I did kill two men."

"Who were armed and dangerous and trying to kill you, as they say."

"The police couldn't have been more respectful," Max said, not bothering to add how relieved he was that the identity he'd been living under had held after ten years. "Stopped just short of asking me for my autograph, especially when my classified file came through."

"You mean, Max *Borgia's* classified file." Bochner leaned forward. "Those two gunmen, you didn't recognize them?"

"Not a clue. But they moved like pros, and they didn't even blink when they zeroed me in the corner."

Bochner nodded, sorting through what Max was telling him. "Sounds like the NYPD is on top of things here. What would you like me to do exactly?"

"Start with the identities of the two gunmen. They weren't acting on their own. Somebody sent them to Creedmoor to kill me, as crazy as that sounds."

Bochner nodded slowly. "That what you told the police?"

"No. I'm telling you. I'd also like you to arrange security for my mother at the facility, make sure she's not targeted in my place."

"I've got a couple of ex-marines on the payroll I can put on the job. Your mother'll be safe, you can count on that." Bochner leaned back, rocking his wheelchair slightly. "But none of this makes any sense. Whoever's after you didn't have to set up such an elaborate hit in New York. They could've nailed you in transit, after the Navy had you stand in the corner."

Max swallowed hard, having trouble forming his next words, even though he'd rehearsed them. "This isn't about the Pope, Weeb, it's not about Max Borgia. It's about somebody else entirely, named Max Younger."

"Keep talking," Bochner urged.

"Let's just say I've got some skeletons in my closet. Family shit. You need to know my mother's name is Melissa Younger. Her husband, my father, was Ben."

"Was," Bochner repeated.

"He died ten years ago. Check him out, and you'll see why I changed my name. What happened at Creedmoor, maybe it's connected to him."

"And?"

"And what?"

"Whatever it is you're not telling me."

"I've told you everything you need to know to help me," Max said, leaving it there. "If that's a problem . . ."

"It's not, hoss." Bochner finished jotting down some notes and wheeled himself out from behind his desk. "You've come to the right place. I've been waiting a long time for this day, the opportunity to do something for the man who made it possible for my life to have a second act. I'm going to keep this off the books, call in some favors if I have to."

"I appreciate that, Weeb. Thank you."

"Don't thank me until I've got something for you other than lip service. How long before you're due back?"

Max rose from his chair. "They haven't told me yet, so I'll be in the city for a while, at least until this gets sorted out."

Bochner took Max's extended hand, squeezed it tight, and held it. "Watch your back in the meantime, Pope."

# THIRTY-FIVE

**Cairo, Egypt**

hey're stalling," Vicky said to Neal Van Royce. "We've wasted an entire day sitting around."

"Not wasted. The Centers for Disease Control is mobilizing, the same minds that licked Ebola ready to take on whatever we're facing here."

"Which is nothing like Ebola. We've lost a day when we can't even afford to lose a minute. We've issued our initial reports to Washington, and we need Washington to secure the cooperation of every government in the Middle East. They need to be ready to ground all air traffic in and out of the region to keep this from spreading further." Vicky watched Van Royce scanning his e-mails yet again. "How bad?"

"Reports of a dozen more outbreaks still confined to the Middle East, mostly localized."

"Mostly?"

"There's anecdotal evidence of possible victims in both Beirut and Amman."

"Anything outside the Middle East?"

"Not yet, no." Van Royce hesitated, looked down and then up again. "I need to ask you again, Vicky."

"Ask me what?"

"Back in that village, how you knew to warn us. How you knew what was coming."

"I had a feeling."

"It seemed to be a lot more than that at the time. So I'll ask you again: What tipped you off, how did you know?"

Vicky could've told him her dead fiancé had sent her a text message telling her to GET OUT of the village, but the evidence was gone from her phone, leaving her not quite believing it herself. She knew she hadn't imagined what had transpired back in the Sinai, just as she knew there was no rational way to explain it. And, as when diagnosing a disease, her training dictated that she consider all options before settling on the most logical and also the most ludicrous one:

That Vicky's dead fiancé really had saved her life.

She'd found herself checking the phone constantly, reluctant to ever let it leave her grasp at times, on the impossible and utterly irrational chance another message from Thomas might come through. And every time the soft chime signaling an incoming e-mail or text sounded, her heart jumped.

Where was the rationality in that?

A lieutenant in the Egyptian army emerged from the office they'd been sitting outside of for hours, sparing Vicky from having to answer Van Royce's question.

"The general will see you now."


"I apologize for making you wait," said General Azmir Malik, chief of staff for Egyptian president Abdel Fattah al-Sisi. "Please, sit down."

Vicky and Van Royce took matching fabric-covered chairs set before his desk, Malik waiting until they were seated to follow. His office over-looked Tahrir Square from the gleaming governmental ministries built atop the demolished refuse of former president Hosni Mubarak's National Democratic Headquarters. The general had served al-Sisi in various roles since he began his historic rise through Egyptian military rankings to his current position as president.

He was a short man with unnaturally broad shoulders that made his uniform look as if it were full of stuffing. His eyes were dark, somewhere between black and brown, his furtive gaze reluctant to meet either of theirs directly in what Vicky took to be well practiced to avoid roiling allies or provoking enemies.

"I apologize for the delay," he resumed, "but it was unavoidable, given the unprecedented nature of the events we find ourselves facing."

"We understand the gravity of the situation," Van Royce said, jumping in before Vicky had a chance to. "We barely escaped Al Arish with our lives. You should've taken steps to alert us, done whatever was necessary. My bloody God, man, we're on the same side here!"

"You're right, of course, and we did try to reach you via the cell and satellite phone numbers the WHO provided. But none of those communications went through and the WHO was similarly unable to reach you. I imagine you encountered much the same thing."

"We did," Van Royce confirmed.

Malik shrugged. "Our investigation into the breakdown in communication remains ongoing. In the meantime, you have my deepest regrets to go with a formal letter of apology from our president to your superiors at the World Health Organization."

"What about your assistance in determining what we're facing here?" Vicky chimed in. "Can we have that too?"

Malik's chest puffed forward as she said that, as if the gesture was supposed to mean more to them than it did. "Of course," he said, clearly not used to being deferential to a woman.

"Then let's start with why you bombed the village."

"We must speak theoretically," Malik said, aiming his words at Van Royce.

"Of course."

"Then, theoretically, our government could have received cryptic, garbled communications from the village suggesting some kind of hostile action, even an attack. Theoretically, we could have dispatched the appropriate military personnel to investigate. Theoretically, we could have lost contact with that team after a series of desperate exchanges, suggesting something even more serious than an attack."

"We're talking about suspected outbreak here, a potential epidemic," Van Royce suggested.

"And what did you find when you investigated this potential epidemic?" Malik asked, addressing them both this time.

Vicky leaned forward. "Nothing. The patients and staff were all missing, like we told you. And there was no evidence of anyone about in the village either," she added, not bothering to mention the shapes both she and Van Royce thought they'd glimpsed scurrying about the town proper.

"And if the cause of all that was, theoretically, this potential epidemic," Malik said, seeming to weigh his next words carefully, his voice growing more measured and flat, "and if the final cryptic reports from the military personnel dispatched to the scene indicated they were under some kind of attack. Gunfire could be heard, screams too. Then nothing, no further contact." Malik's lips trembled for a moment before he took a deep breath to regain his composure. "In such a scenario, eradication would be the primary strategy to consider. In a theoretical sense, of course." Malik laid his arms on his desktop and tapped his fingers together. "For something less theoretical, you need to go to southern Lebanon, fifty miles from the Israeli border."

"And what will we find there, General?" Vicky asked him.

"A secret installation once involved with bio-weapons development. All contact has been lost with the facility, again following a series of panicked, cryptic messages. We've already arranged safe passage there for you with the Israeli and Lebanese governments. I'll have a plane take you to southern Lebanon where you'll be met by a Lebanese army escort. Lebanese troops are in the process of securing the perimeter, but won't approach the facility until you arrive," Malik told them both.

"Secured against what?" Vicky wondered.

Malik was suddenly reluctant to meet her gaze. "It's better if you see for yourself."

# THIRTY-SIX

## Over the Atlantic

W hat am I supposed to call you?" Father Jimenez said, early into the flight aboard a U.S. military jet to the Middle East with the stranger who'd dropped out of the sky, literally, back in Brazil.

"Red."

"That's your name?"

"No," the man told Jimenez, "but it's my favorite color."

The men who'd accompanied him to Brazil, well armed and virtually indistinguishable from one another, sat silently in the back of the plane not seeming to move through the entire duration of the flight. For his part, Jimenez quickly tired of trying to engage "Red" in conversation, lapsed into sleep several times over the course of the flight instead, only to be jarred awake by nightmares he couldn't remember.

"What does this all really have to do with me?" he finally asked, after the jet had hit its cruising altitude, already streaking across the Atlantic.

"Goes back to your experience in Nigeria, almost thirty years ago now. That ring any bells?"

"Too many," Jimenez managed, through the clog that had formed in his throat. "Can you be more specific?"

"No, I can't. Remember I told you the world was going to hell? What would you say if I said that you were a part of it?"

"I'd say you were crazy. Who do you work for, and what is it you do for them exactly?"

Red's gaze narrowed. "Well, you might say we're in the same line of work, actually."

"Religion or science?"

"Miracles or, more accurately, inexplicable phenomena. The difference being I do it on behalf of the United States, a branch of the government

that nobody's ever heard of. This isn't the first time I've chased something like this, but it just might be the most dire."

"Something like *what*?" Jimenez asked him.

"My job started out chasing weapons, or anything that could be wea-
ponized. If there was a mass death, humans or animals, I'd be on the scene
to see if the cause could be exploited. When NASA sent probes into outer
space, I was there when they came back to see if any intergalactic men-
aces we could utilize had hitched a ride. If some armchair scientist pat-
ented something that could work to our advantage, I'd be knocking on
his door the next day."

"Just knocking on his door?"

"Figure of speech. You get the idea."

"I'm trying very hard not to."

"We're both chasing miracles, Father; we just define them differently.
For me, it's inexplicable phenomena and nothing more. But what's uniquely
terrifying is how much of it as of late seems to be occurring across the
globe. A veritable epidemic of the bizarre. And I happen to believe all the
random, disparate pieces are connected. That's where you come in."

Jimenez leaned back, feeling a bit chilled. "Science, superstition. Not
one or the other—both."

Red didn't nod, didn't react, remaining noncommittal. "Let's just say
that the net I cast is substantially wider than the Vatican's and I've got a
whole floor of staffers checking what's been reeled in. I've got an unlimited budget and all the resources I need. And, even with all those resources,
we can't keep up with all the data coming in right now. You know what
that means?"

Jimenez felt turbulence shake the jet, bothering him far more than it
normally would, as if in response to their conversation. "I haven't a clue."

"Patterns, connections. A surge in the kind of phenomena both of us
are chasing, to the point where I find myself questioning what it may be
leading us toward, how everything fits together."

"I've managed to explain on a scientific basis every so-called inexplicable event I've investigated."

"I'm aware of that, Father. But that doesn't include Nigeria, does it?"

Jimenez stiffened. "I wasn't working for the church yet."

"No, but your signing on was directly related to what happened down
there, wasn't it?"

"You seem to know an awful lot about me."

"It's my job to know, Father."

Jimenez realized his mouth was very dry but stopped short of asking for something to drink or getting it from the galley himself.

"And your involvement with what happened in Nigeria is why you're on this plane, Father. But I've also gone back and read your books, particularly the passages on the origins of the Universe and the existence of dark energy. Thought I may have found a kindred spirit, someone who could appreciate the concerns that have come to dominate my experience, especially after you experienced your own miracle in 1991 that brought you into the priesthood."

"An eclipse isn't a miracle, it's a naturally occurring scientific phenomenon."

"And if it had happened no more than a few seconds later, your head would've been rolling around on the ground."

"You want to call that a miracle, go ahead," Jimenez told him, his mouth so dry that his voice cracked a bit.

Red raised his shade and spoke with his gaze focused outward, into the emptiness of the sky. "Something I didn't tell you about my job description, Father: it comes with a whole lot of study and analysis. Call it an accumulation of necessary knowledge. Old texts, ancient writings, many dealing with what passed for science in their respective times. Books where the scribes were trying to make sense of what their world at the time told them couldn't be. Like infestations and plagues and famines and droughts. Fish raining from the sky which everyone thought was a joke until it actually happened in Australia in 2010, then again in Alaska in 2015. The fact of the matter, Father, is there's *always* a scientific explanation, if we try hard enough to find one. I've seen one for each of the Ten Plagues of the Pharaohs. Hell, I've even seen one for Moses parting the Red Sea that discounted the whole thing as a tidal anomaly in convincing fashion, but quite a coincidence, wouldn't you say? My point being that the line between myth or legend, and what we know as reality, is absurdly thin. I've been at this job a long time, and if I've learned nothing else, it's that."

Jimenez looked past Red out the window, as the jet settled into a softer pocket of air. "What does all this have to do with Nigeria?"

"You mean, beside the fact that it wasn't an ordinary meteor strike at all, any more than Brazil was?"

Jimenez tried hard not to look surprised that Red somehow knew that. "How much do you know about meteor or asteroid strikes?"

"What I need to, Father."

"Then here's some more. A meteor capable of doing the damage on the scale done at the Nigerian site would be of sufficient size to give off a decidedly audible bang that could be heard for hundreds of miles, like a sonic boom."

"Your report mentioned nothing about that."

"Because there wasn't one, nor were there any infrasound components either."

"Infrasound?" Red asked, the level of his technical expertise clearly not including that.

"Extreme low frequency sounds inaudible to the human ear that travel in what's generally known as a wavefront. Take the relatively recent Chelyabinsk meteor strike in Russia as an example. The infrasound given off not only radiated across Chelyabinsk and much of Russia, but around the world several times. I use that as an example because in terms of mass and force, it should've been close to what we encountered in the Nigerian strike twenty-seven years ago. And yet no infrasound whatsoever was detected. Then there was the site itself."

"What about it, Father?" Red prodded, again as if seeming to know where Jimenez's thoughts were headed.

"It's inconceivable for a strike of that magnitude, coupled with atmospheric entry, not to rupture the structural integrity of the meteor, and reduce it to smaller chunks of rubble. So in addition to our examination of what we determined to be Ground Zero at the scene of the strike, my team reconnoitered a large stretch of area in search of pellet-sized holes in the ground, samples left by the shotgun-like spray the meteor's rubble fragments gave off. Again, nothing."

"Impossible or unprecedented?"

Jimenez weighed the distinction. "I'd say both, at least based on the limitations of science both then and now. Unprecedented because even the most shallow angle of descent couldn't account for such an anomaly. Impossible because every other bit of visual and anecdotal data we collected told us it had absolutely had to be there. So take your pick. But, based on the degree of damage we encountered, we should've been looking at a meteor at minimum twenty meters in diameter. And yet we found absolutely nothing."

"Just like Brazil, eh, Father?"

"Brazil was no meteor strike."

"According to you, neither was Nigeria. And what both these incidents have in common is that neither can be explained away by applying scientific principles, at least those within the limits of current knowledge." Red settled back into his seat, the soft fabric seeming to absorb him. "That's where I come in. That's what I do. And I can tell you, without violating any security clearances, that I've been doing it a hell of a lot over the past few months. And this pattern, if it can truly be called that, could potentially date back to well before Nigeria."

Something scratched at Jimenez's spine, just as a fresh wave of turbulence shook the jet. "So what do you need me for? What does all this have to do with the latest crisis in the Middle East that I have nothing to do with?"

Red stopped just short of a smirk this time. "Actually, Father, we think you do, more than you can possibly imagine."

# THIRTY-SEVEN

### New York City

"Close the door, Pope," Weeb Bochner told Max, twenty-four hours to the minute after their first meeting had concluded.

Max sealed it behind him and held his ground halfway to Bochner's desk.

"I'm gonna give you some advice, hoss," Bochner continued. "Turn around, walk back out that door, and forget you ever came to me. Because you're about to hear things you can't *un*-hear, and maybe it's better if you don't hear them at all. That's the thing about truth: it really *does* hurt. The older it is, the more it hurts."

"I've never had a problem with pain," Max told him.


Max had spent much of the past day walking the city, refreshing himself with a world he'd abandoned, for good he thought, a decade before when he'd become a different person. New York was remarkably unchanged, frozen in time. The smells, the sounds, the sights. Different storefronts, of course. More chain stores, comfortable in familiarity and, he supposed, capable of affording the incredible rents. He strolled past these where they mixed with massive skyscrapers rising like steel and glass monoliths, as if birthed by the razed establishments, the names of which Max couldn't recall.

He walked not so much in search of a memory, as a feeling. Something that would take him back to growing up in Manhattan through a succession of schools both private and public. His father absent through much of it, always away at work, as he and his partner Dale Denton expanded their energy empire to a corporate headquarters in Houston. It was Max and his mother, she seeming to sense in him what his father always denied. She'd tried to understand what was happening, just as he had, neither of them succeeding very well at all, while her sanity fled her in leaps and then bounds.

Max had told Weeb Bochner nothing of this, only of his real identity accompanied by a highly sanitized version of his background and the circumstances that led him to shed his father's name and reinvent himself as an entirely new person.

Something else he hadn't shared with Weeb Bochner.

Bochner wheeled his chair out from behind his desk and positioned it alongside the armchair in which Max was seated.

"You need to know this information is privileged," Bochner continued, his voice deep and somber, "not just by blood, but also by law, like attorney-client. Everything we're about to discuss stays between us, no paper or electronic trail whatsoever, and as far as the world knows you were never in this building. That includes the security tapes. I want you to understand that."

"Understood."

"First off, I got IDs on the shooters from Creedmoor. High-end mercs, each with a dishonorable discharge to his credit. Unfortunately, these are the kind of guys who don't leave trails back to their employers. Given time, I might be able to come up with something, but time's something I know you're short on right now, so let's just table that for now."

"You did say 'first off,'" Max said.

"I did at that," Bochner nodded, his expression looking like a video frozen in the midst of buffering. "Because you suspected the attack on you at Creedmoor involved something from the past, I had to go back into the Younger family history, jumping off from what you provided me to look into your father. I was able to get some medical records, dating back a long time, along with the autopsy report following his death," Bochner said, after another pause. "You would've been . . ."

"Seventeen, almost eighteen," Max completed.

"A kid. Explains why you didn't notice the signs."

"Signs?"

"Your father, Pope."

"He jumped out a window on the sixtieth floor of an office tower," Max said, not bothering to disguise the bitterness in his voice. "I always figured it was because of the scandal that followed, the investigation that turned up the fact that he'd embezzled tens of millions of dollars from his company."

"There's more. He was sick, dying."

Max felt his stomach drop, the same way he did when a big transport plane dropped straight out of the sky over an airfield to avoid taking enemy fire.

"I didn't know," he heard himself say.

"According to the autopsy report, it was some kind of blood cancer nobody could identify, or had ever seen before. He went all over the country, seeking out second opinions on both the diagnosis and potential courses of treatment, regardless of cost. From all I can gather, he spent a fortune on tests and specialists, keeping the transactions entirely off the books to prevent his insurance company, and business associates, from learning anything about what was happening to him, and that clearly included his family. It might also help explain the embezzlement. His last stop was a genetic testing lab right here in New York City, place called CyberGen. All those years ago, CyberGen was on the cutting edge of targeted treatment based on a specific patient's individual DNA."

"He was pulling out all the stops," Max managed, through the thick clog building in his throat. "My father was never one to give up."

"And yet he killed himself. How do you reconcile that?"

"I can't. I never could. It never made any sense to me, any more than the embezzlement charges did, but I was too busy running away from my past."

"I'm sorry, Pope."

"For what?"

"Dredging up that past."

"I asked you to do it."

"This isn't what I expected to find; I'm not sure what I expected to find." Bochner looked down, as if to check the condition of the legs that had died half a world away. "And that's not all."

Max just looked at him. "I'm still listening, Weeb."

"You know how I found CyberGen, hoss? I followed the money. Your father did a pretty damn good job of hiding his tracks—the truth, in other words. And his efforts would've held up to scrutiny a decade ago, but not today and not to a man with resources like mine. Payments were made through a shell company in the Bahamas and rerouted via wire transfers from offshore accounts in the Caymans where my company maintains close contacts. Your dad was one determined son of a bitch."

Max almost smiled. "Indeed, he was."

"The last transfers went to CyberGen. After that, nothing. CyberGen was Ben Younger's last stop and, I'm guessing, his last hope."

"Which didn't pan out, obviously."

Bochner wheeled himself slightly closer to Max. "I'm guessing you're not one to believe in coincidences."

"Like what, Weeb?"

"Like about a month after Ben Younger jumped out of that window, CyberGen blew up. Gas leak was blamed and left pretty much nothing behind. I got hold of the police and fire reports from the time. The explosion was caused by gas all right, but no evidence of the leak in question was ever found. So, if you ask me, somebody went through great lengths to destroy all of CyberGen's records and killed twenty people in the process, including the geneticist your father was seeing, a doctor named Kirsch."

"Dead end then."

"Maybe."

"Maybe?"

"After Kirsch died, his daughter inherited his brownstone," Bochner explained. "If he left anything behind about your father, that's where you'll find it."

# THIRTY-EIGHT

### Southern Lebanon

The plane General Malik had arranged for Vicky and Neal Van Royce landed at a tiny airport in Nabatieh, Lebanon, with a single runway barely long enough to accommodate it. Vicky had expected a minor Lebanese military escort to accompany them the rest of the way. But what looked to be an entire platoon was waiting for them on the tarmac. A whole convoy of trucks, Humvees with heavy machine guns poking out from their turrets, and a bevy of troops in full battle gear, to take them to a location in the barren reaches of Lebanon's Nabatieh Governorate.

The commander was a tall man with a brusque, impatient demeanor who introduced himself as Major Mohammed el Musa. His face was dominated by a combination of scars that crisscrossed his cheeks and a neatly trimmed beard dotted with empty patches where more scar tissue pervaded. He had eyes that looked like pools of black ink spilled from a pen left sitting for too long, and the expression of a man already somewhere else in his mind.

In addition to the Lebanese troops, Vicky spotted a man wearing an Israeli Defense Forces uniform standing off by himself and holding his stare on her. She nodded his way, but the man didn't acknowledge her beyond his steely gaze.

"A bit more than we were expecting," Vicky said, as she surveyed the scene, falling into step alongside Musa and Van Royce en route to the armored Humvee.

"Precautions," the major said gruffly.

"And do those precautions include a member of the IDF?" she asked, looking toward the man she was certain was Israeli army.

"His name is Raviv. He says he's a captain, but I suspect his rank is actually much higher. Our nations are working cooperatively on this,

Doctor, given that we may share an unprecedented threat. It's better if we leave things at that."

"Rather unprecedented, though."

"There's good reason for the exception, as the two of you will soon see for yourselves."

"Major?" Van Royce posed, slowing and then swiftly resuming his pace when Musa kept right on going.

Musa responded without regarding either one of them. "The facility in question doesn't exist. It was originally a bio-weapons facility moth-balled when the Israelis learned of its existence and threatened to bomb it and the surrounding countryside. It remained dormant for a long stretch, until a private pharmaceutical concern decided it was the perfect place to house their research and development division."

"What triggered the alert?"

"A worker who fled the facility is now hospitalized in a Bedouin vil-lage between our current position and the facility itself further to the south. He's a Turkish native who's been identified as a Muslim Western intelligence operative out of Germany who'd managed to infiltrate a team of scientists believed to be connected to the terrorist group the New Islamic Front. The facility in southern Lebanon was a virtual dead zone when it came to issuing reports, but something must've spooked him enough to make a run for it."

They reached the Humvee but stopped short of climbing into it.

"The village elders called us. This would have been eighteen hours ago now. The village itself has now been quarantined, more of my men having established a perimeter. Nobody in, nobody out."

Vicky felt the familiar tug of unease inside her. "Is that a normal re-sponse?"

"For this particular set of circumstances, it was."

"And why is that exactly?" from Van Royce.

"I'm not authorized—"

"—to say," Vicky completed. "What *are* you authorized to say?"

"I'm authorized to take you to the village and the facility located fur-ther to the south that we've also secured a one-mile radius around. The order is up to you."

"Then let's start with the village," Vicky told him.

• • •

Abu Siddar was like any number of quaint, desert-based villages she'd visited over the years, dominated by a ramshackle sprawl of shacks, shanties, and modest houses. But a smattering of small satellite dishes dotted the rooftops, and power lines weaved a twisting path from poles fed by what must've been underground power lines.

Over the course of the drive, Major Musa had explained this particular village supplied a number of workers to Lebanon's high-tech industry sprouting in the directorate's capital of Nabatieh, specifically Sadel Tech, a company owned and operated by an offshoot of this particular Bedouin tribe based in Israel. The company's location required residents to take a pair of buses on a circuitous ninety-minute drive both ways every day. The irony being that Abu Siddar lacked sufficient electricity at night to power either the small satellite dishes or the laptops on which residents brought home their work. A pair of propane-fueled generators alleviated the resulting strain somewhat, while the village remained otherwise suspended between the past and the present, even as it fought to claw its way toward the future.

Their convoy was passed through a hastily erected checkpoint manned by more Lebanese soldiers and motored on toward Abu Siddar where, much to Vicky's surprise, they were met by a woman.

"Rabaa al-Hawashleh," she greeted, extending a hand toward Vicky first, as if seeing them as kindred spirits.

Vicky recalled Bedouin society as being both tribal and patriarchal, but al-Hawashleh had apparently inherited her position of sheikh from her late father.

"Dr. Victoria Tanoury."

"You're from the WHO? An American with a Lebanese name?"

"We are, and I am, yes."

"Then you've come to the right place. Follow me."

They walked under the protective umbrella of Musa and a hefty complement of his troops, steering toward a freestanding structure set off by itself and marked with the familiar symbol of the Red Cross over the door. The Israeli officer who called himself Raviv remained behind, still having not uttered a single word to either Vicky or Van Royce.

A pair of Lebanese soldiers, assault rifles shouldered over full hazmat gear, stood guard on either side of the clinic entrance.

"We were told someone who fled a former bio-weapons facility found his way here," Vicky said, her voice crackling slightly.

"El al-Lacosh, as we call it," al-Hawashleh told her. "We were able to ascertain that from the security badge he was still wearing from the private concern he was supposedly working for."

"Supposedly?"

"Our government has since contacted this research and development's concern home office. Apparently, they know nothing of its existence and claim the government was the victim of some sort of ruse. And the subject in question didn't find his way here," al-Hawashleh corrected. "We found him in the desert a few miles away."

"Back in America, I was practically raised by a Lebanese woman," Vicky told her, "so I speak Arabic quite well. But the phrase *El al-Lacosh*, that's one I'm unfamiliar with."

"That because it's an old, colloquial term, Doctor," al-Hawashleh told her. "Roughly translated, it means 'the house of evil.'"

During daylight hours, the village maintained sufficient electricity to fully power the clinic currently being guarded by the Lebanese soldiers wearing biohazard suits. Inside, Vicky and Van Royce pulled similar garb up over their clothes and tested their respirators.

"Right this way," al-Hawashleh said stiffly, having pulled biohazard gear over her clothes as well.

"You're a doctor?"

"You sound surprised. What I trust won't surprise you is what you're about to see, given your familiarity with the infection's symptoms."

Her words aimed toward Vicky, as she ushered them down a hall sheathed in clear plastic toward a single examination room.

"As I mentioned, we know he came from the pharmaceutical facility to the south because he was still wearing his ID badge. He was already showing symptoms then, and the infection has progressed steadily since, his symptoms worsening in a pattern and extreme that's like nothing I've ever seen or studied before," al-Hawashleh said, passing the badge in question from her glove to Vicky's.

"Gunther Brune," Vicky recited, reading off the laminated tag that featured a young face with thick hair and a neatly trimmed beard. "Have you been able to speak to him?"

Al-Hawashleh pulled back another sheet of dangling plastic draped over the door. "It's better that you see for yourself," she said, and pushed the door open.


*beep . . . beep . . . beep . . .*

Vicky heard the steady whir and wheeze of the various machines to which Gunther Brune was hooked up, as she approached the bed. The patient was covered up to his neck by a pair of sheets sandwiching a thin blanket, leaving only his head exposed.

She heard her own breath picking up inside her helmet. Brune's thick hair and beard were gone; so were his eyebrows. The shading of his skin was eerily akin to the patient she'd examined in the Jordanian village three days before; a dull, grayish ash color. Whereas the gray tones of that patient's skin had been mixed with pale patches of flesh, though, Brune's entire face looked coated in ash segmented into jagged, irregular patches separated by what looked liked stitching dug into the skin. His eyes were mere slits, unseeing by all accounts through pools of what looked like spilled black paint, showing nothing of the whites or what passed for pupils whatsoever.

Vicky checked the readouts on the monitoring machines, figuring such advanced equipment must've been provided by one of the many humanitarian aid charities familiar to the region. She blinked rapidly and swabbed a sleeve across her facemask to make sure she was seeing the readouts right, because they were . . . blank. Reading all zeroes, as if Gunther Brune was already dead.

"His flesh has become too rigid and coarse for the leads to penetrate," al-Hawashleh explained.

Vicky had a strong sense of what awaited her examination before she touched the fingertips of her right hazmat glove to the ash-toned flesh. It was hard and rigid to the touch, no give or depression at all when she pressed. More like touching bone than skin.

Or stone. That's what Vicky thought in that moment. Stone. As if that's what the German's skin was turning into.

"Medusa," she heard Van Royce say through the microphone built into her helmet.

She looked his way.

"The Gorgon," Van Royce continued, "monster from Greek mythology punished for neglecting her vows of celibacy when she married Poseidon. Her punishment was a head of snakes and eyes that turned anyone who looked at her to stone. Medusa," he repeated, moving up closer to Brune on the other side of the bed. "If I didn't know better . . ."

"We don't know anything," Vicky said and looked back toward al-Hawashleh. "I want to take flesh and blood samples from beneath this hardened shell."

Al-Hawashleh reached back to a wheeled tray and trapped a thick, knobby syringe between her gloved fingers. "Ten-gauge, thickest we have on hand."

Before taking it from her, she started to gently ease back the bedcovers. In that moment, she thought the liquid slits Gunther Brune had left for eyes shifted a bit, giving her the sense he was following her motions.

A trick of the light, that's what it had to be, Vicky thought, but the condition of his mouth was anything but that. His lips were gone, or had receded in place of a gaping mouth squeezed so full of teeth, no exposed gums were visible either. The teeth were of varying sizes, the largest seeming to pulse, leading Vicky to recall the fresh set of teeth that was emerging in the Jordanian patient's mouth.

Vicky forced herself to stop regarding them and folded the covers back further to expose Brune's arms and torso. Found them utterly bare, the flesh having hardened to the same shell-like consistency of his face. The pattern his hardened, ash-colored flesh had divided itself into reminded Vicky of a jigsaw puzzle with evident seams left between the fit-together pieces. His chest rose and fell slightly in rhythm with his splotchy, irregular breathing that came in fits and starts as if retarded by the excess weight of the chest cavity.

She approximated the position of the vein where the bend between his forearm and elbow should have been, and took the ten-gauge syringe in her grasp. Easing the needle inward with pressure on the plunger.

Brune's eyes shifted again, narrowing into even tighter slits, seeming to scold her; she was certain of it this time.

Vicky gave the plunger a bit more pressure and the ten-gauge needle snapped, broke off, and rattled against the floor surface.

"We brought in a portable MRI scanner," al-Hawashleh reported, "but it couldn't penetrate the increased hardening condition of his flesh."

Vicky was familiar with several diseases, most notably the autoimmune condition scleroderma, known to cause hardening of the skin as well as internal organs. But even at its most advanced stages, neither that, nor any other known infection, microbe, virus, bacteria, or autoimmune response, had ever been known to produce symptoms this extreme.

"When was he found?" she asked al-Hawashleh.

"Just over ninety-six hours ago now."

Vicky did the rough calculations in her head, contrasting the timing against the first reported case to the WHO that had sent her and Neil Van Royce to Jordan. This victim's infection was advanced a full day beyond the first victims struck down in that village.

She thought back to the Egyptian village in the Sinai her team had barely escaped when it was shelled. Vicky was certain General Malik hadn't told her and Van Royce everything, just as she was certain she was facing something here that was utterly unprecedented in the annals of medicine.

Vicky looked down at Gunther Brune.

Gunther Brune looked back through his inky slits.

And that's when she heard Van Royce scream.


Brune had latched a stone-like hand onto Van Royce's wrist, somehow managing to flex his fingers, fastening them in place like a pit bull's bite. Vicky watched Van Royce's hand trembling madly and going beet red, his fingers spasming in an odd, melodic fashion like a madman playing the piano.

"*Vicky!*" he cried out, his voice more a high-pitched wail.

Dr. al-Hawashleh had already started trying to pry the fingers off, Vicky realizing immediately she wasn't having any luck and wouldn't.

*Crack!*

Van Royce's orange-sheathed wrist bone snapped audibly, loud as a gunshot, and he gasped, only air flooding out his mouth when he tried to scream. His knees went out, as if the floor had been ripped from under him, prevented from collapsing only by the ash-colored hand that seemed to be tightening its grasp upon him even more.

Vicky rushed over to the other side of the bed and lent her efforts to al-Hawashleh's in trying to pry Gunther Brune's hand off Van Royce. Her gloves made the task difficult, but it was the rigidity and power of the fingers that made it impossible. Like trying to bend back steel.

*Crack!*

The sound softer this time, a smaller bone snapping like a twig or chicken bone, one of the soldiers lending his efforts to free Van Royce as well, to no avail.

Vicky burst out of the examination room into the hallway, recalling the fire axe and commercial extinguisher hanging from a hallway wall. She ignored the extinguisher.

Grabbed the axe, so heavy she more dragged than carried it back into the room.

Van Royce's face had gone white as a sheet, the agony of having his wrist literally crushed pushing him into the shock.

"Stand back!" Vicky ordered al-Hawashleh and the Lebanese soldier, finding the strength to hoist the fire axe overhead with both hands.

Aiming it was something else again, but she knew she had no choice. Brought the axe ringing downward as close to Gunther Brune's wrist as she could.

The blade ended up striking further up his forearm with an ear-numbing clang, steel to stone. And, worse, his grayish, ridged hand tightened even more, whatever was left of Van Royce's bones crackling audibly.

Vicky watched his eyes roll back in his head from the pain, the poor man unable to speak, barely able to breathe. She brought the axe back overhead a second time, felt it freeze in the air when a *pop* sounded.

And Neal Van Royce's hand from the wrist down broke off, left in the grasp of the stone-like fingers which continued to tighten around the severed limb. Van Royce dropped all the way to the floor, blood shooting from his stump in a soft geyser, clearing the path for Vicky's next strike.

She tilted the axe lower, so the blade was even with her shoulder blades to build more momentum. Felt more speed building as she let it slash downward.

Vicky thought she'd missed when the blade sank into the mattress, coughing stuffing into the air. But she followed its path to see a gap between Gunther Brune and his severed hand, the now disembodied stone-like fingers still digging hard into Van Royce's similarly disembodied wrist.

Blood, thick and black as ink, oozed out from Gunther Brune's severed hand, pooling on the floor in thick globs.

Vicky took the axe blade up and started hammering the back of Brune's severed stone hand. Each blow sent shockwaves of tingling pain up her own arm into her shoulder, like trying to hammer a nail through steel, until the stone-like fingers finally locked open.

Then Gunther Brune lurched from the bed, his entire body minus the missing hand moving in what looked like stop-motion animation, one frame at a time.

The closer of the two Lebanese soldiers moved to restrain him, the other frozen in place. The closer soldier succeeded briefly in pushing Brune back down, but then his remaining stone-like hand closed over the man's face. Vicky heard the sounds of bone and cartilage cracking, a muffled raspy whoosh of air pouring out of the soldier's mouth in what had started as a scream. Suddenly he was airborne, striking the wall with enough force to crack the plaster. Sliding downward with his face mashed to pulp, features utterly unrecognizable. Cheekbones exposed through his flesh, eye sockets turned into black holes shoved backward in his skull, nose and mouth morphed into one mangled assemblage.

"Shoot him! Shoot him!" Vicky cried out to the still-frozen soldier, al-Hawashleh dragging the helpless Van Royce across the floor, as the now standing Gunther Brune started toward them. *"Shoot him!"*

Before the soldier could move, Brune charged him in a motion so swift, it was lost to a blur. Vicky watched the teeth, all of them, emerge as if no longer part of his mouth, again recalling the fresh set she'd detected the patient in Jordan was growing. Digging those teeth deep into the soldier's throat, shredding it the way a wild animal would and splattering blood through the air against the walls and floor.

Vicky saw the soldier's feet twitching, realized Brune had hoisted him off his feet, continuing to rip and shred until his head came free and landed with a sickening plop. She choked down the shock and recovered enough of her bearings to bring her axe up again, then slash it down hard, lurching forward in the same motion.

*Clunk!*

She'd buried the axe blade to the hilt in Brune's chest. But he still kept moving, cutting off al-Hawashleh's path to the door with Van Royce in tow.

Out of the corner of her eye, Vicky saw the hospital room door burst open, banging against the wall under the force of a combat boot. Major Musa, biohazard suit pulled over his uniform but wearing no helmet, sprayed Gunther Brune with automatic fire, the bullets punching him backward. Flecks and shards of what looked like granite spewed into the air, formless divots dug out of Brune's torso instead of bloody holes.

"The head!" Vicky cried out. "Shoot him in the head!"

Musa turned his fire on Brune's face, his features vanishing in a burst of gray, jagged fragments Vicky knew were as much hardened flesh as bone.

*Click.*

Musa was trying to snatch a fresh magazine from the confines of his biohazard suit when Gunther Brune finally swayed like a felled tree, bounced off the bed and struck the floor with the force of a toppled statue. Shedding more granite-like flecks on impact that hit the air like a dust shower, Vicky unable to take her eyes from him.

Gunther Brune had fled that former bio-weapons facility just a few miles to the south, and that's where she needed to go now.

# THIRTY-NINE

**Houston, Texas**

ou need to put your goggles on," Orson Beekman said to Dale Denton, extending a pair toward him.

Denton looked at the glass wall before which they were standing. "That's twelve inches thick."

"Eighteen. It was replaced this morning after the twelve-inch glass cracked last night during our first series of experiments on the rock."

Denton peered through the glass at the rock currently resting in a slot scooped out of a thick granite table that extended all the way to and, actually, through the floor.

"Didn't you read my report?" Beekman asked him.

"I saw the e-mail while I was traveling home. Thought it could wait until this morning. Why don't you give me the broad strokes?"

They were standing five stories beneath Western Energy Technologies' corporate headquarters along the West Houston Energy Corridor. Denton had purchased the twenty-story building for a song from a renewable energy company whose best intentions had led to bankruptcy. Then he'd used just about all the money he'd saved on the deal to construct a research and development lab worthy of NASA five stories down amid layers of steel and concrete to immunize the efforts undertaken there against corporate espionage and exposure if anything went wrong. Denton had built the facility a decade back to develop the most secretive, and potentially lucrative, of WET's experiments on new means to potentially power the future. Chief among these, of course, was the rock that had been his personal obsession ever since the day they'd struck oil in the Yucatán. All things considered, it had been the best and happiest day of his life, and recovering the strange object that had left its mark on Ben Younger's hand had rekindled that feeling.

Denton stood with Beekman today feeling the flutter he'd last experienced when oil had inexplicably burst from the leased grounds around him in Mexico, dousing him and his workers in a black sheen that had become the foundation for everything he'd built since. Including this twenty-thousand-square-foot facility that was one of the most advanced of its kind within the private sector anywhere in the world.

"We powered up the machines to run our initial series of diagnostics on the object yesterday, while you were in transit," Beekman explained, getting Denton up to speed.

"And?"

"And the glass cracked."

Denton tightened the goggles over his eyes. "Wait a minute, all you did was flip a few switches?"

"More or less. And it wasn't just the glass. There were four technicians down here with me. All but one of us made the mistake of carrying our smart phones."

"Mistake?"

"They all stopped working. No damage, visible or otherwise. They turned off and wouldn't turn back on. When I finally got mine powered up this morning, everything was gone, including the operating system. Just a metal shell that lights up."

"Suggesting?"

"What I've suspected all along, ever since 1990," Beekman said, trembling from the mere thought the memories evoked. "What today's experiment will hopefully demonstrate."

Denton looked toward the object recently recovered from the Yucatán. "If the glass holds up this time, you mean."

"It's been replaced by a far thicker polymer. And both the housing in which the object's been placed, and the chamber itself, are sealed from the inside, completely airtight. As an added precaution, we can shut the experiment down immediately in the event our monitors record an energy spike."

"Is that supposed to make me feel safe?"

Beekman turned his gaze back to the fist-sized rock to avoid answering the question. "Upon initial inspection, and from Ben Younger's description, I thought we were dealing with some kind of igneous volcanic fragment. That's what the appearance, scaling, weight, and general physical characteristics suggest. The problem is the density levels are all wrong."

"Wrong?"

"To the point where none of our X-ray, magnetometer, or magnetic resonance devices can approximate a three-dimensional rendering."

"In other words," Denton elaborated for himself, "we've got no idea what's going on inside it."

"Or what elements it's composed of. Since I don't dare risk removing any surface samples, I was relying on structural and quantum analysis to tell us what we need to know. Now I realize that even if such an analysis was successful, we'd still be left scratching our heads."

"It's not of this world—that's what you're suggesting, isn't it, Professor? It's the product of a meteorite, not a volcanic eruption."

Beekman shook his head, a reflection of it caught in the thick glass that looked into the chamber holding the rock. "No."

"No?"

"The odds of a meteorite fragment being perfectly spherical is a statistical impossibility."

"Any more than what we experienced in the Yucatán? All I'm saying is we've been chasing the impossible for over twenty-five years. We should've been prepared."

"I don't think preparing for what's in that chamber was ever possible. We should have known that from the moment Ben Younger uncovered it. From the moment wells without a power source uncovered one of the largest oil strikes in history. From the moment Ben Younger regained consciousness over a mile from where he had been with no recollection of how he got there or managed to climb out of the cave. From the moment the animals anywhere close to the site went crazy for no apparent reason."

"Riddles, Professor."

"No—facts. Allow me to demonstrate."

With that, Denton watched Beekman nod to his technicians who went to work behind their various displays and computer controls. Almost immediately, he felt a hum in his ears, like a buzzing he couldn't shake with all the annoyance of a mosquito he couldn't squash. A sound at the outer limits of his hearing's range.

"We're hitting the rock with electricity in the amount of point zero zero zero zero five kilowatts, the equivalent of what it takes to make your cell phone screen light up," Beekman explained.

"Not much, in other words."

"Virtually immeasurable, in fact. Virtually—"

Something more like a whine, or a harmonic growl, froze Beekman's words there. In the next instant, the plastic polymer showed a small fissure line that quickly branched outward like a spiderweb being stitched by an Etch A Sketch toy. The cracks spread, converging and crossing to the point where they riddled the entire clear wall.

"The rock's doing that," Denton said, transfixed by the process.

"It's sending back out what it received."

"It only received enough energy to light a phone screen."

"And that's what it radiated back, when factoring in its own quotients and relative ratios, multiplied on the level of ten to the fifth power."

"In English please, Professor."

"The rock, as you call it, doesn't generate any power on its own—it's not a source of energy in and of itself, in other words. Instead it acts as a magnifier, an amplifier, scientifically speaking. It seems to absorb energy and radiate it back out, amplifying it on a virtually immeasurable, quantum level."

"Ten to the fifth power, you said," Denton recalled.

Beekman nodded. "So assume one megawatt of electricity can power as many as one thousand homes. Fifty megawatts is what it takes to generate energy for a city of a hundred thousand, while it would take in the area of seven hundred fifty megawatts to supply power to a city of one million." Beekman stopped, either to compose himself or form his next thoughts. "In order to power that city of one million, our object would need a kilowatt base equivalent to the energy expended by a sixty-watt bulb."

Denton actually pinched himself in the forearm to make sure he was awake. "You're saying we can power a city of one million with the energy produced by *a lightbulb?*"

"A bit more, if you want to do it for an entire day, say *two* lightbulbs."

"Because of that thing in there, what by all indications is what Ben Younger found down deep below the surface of the Earth," Denton said, bobbing his head toward the spiderwebbed wall. "Because of its ability to magnify the output of an existing energy source exponentially."

Beekman kept looking at him but didn't nod this time. "Harness that ability, find a way to channel the energy it produces through amplification, and all other energy sources would be rendered obsolete."

"Does it put out any radiation, or anything else that's potentially dangerous?"

Beekman shook his head. "Not that our instruments can detect. But that's hardly surprising."

"Why?"

Beekman ran a hand through his thinning wedges of hair atop his round head and looked through the cracked glass as if to wonder if the rock was still there. "Because it's not of this world. It doesn't play by our rules of physics. We don't know where it's from or what it's made of. And we have no idea yet of the range or the extent of its capabilities."

"When Ben touched the thing, it left that mark on his hand. Then his son was born with a matching mark on his palm, identical in all respects. You want to tell me how that's possible?"

"DNA," the older man said, his thoughts seeming elsewhere. "Touching it must've altered something in Ben Younger's genetic structure, something he passed on in the form of the mark. But for some reason . . ."

"For some reason *what*?" Denton prodded, when Beekman's voice tailed off.

Beekman's face had paled. "I saw firsthand what touching that rock can do," he reminded. "So why didn't it affect Ben Younger the same way?"

"Don't know, don't care."

"You should; we all should, because it doesn't make any sense. What happened down in Mexico, what I saw, can't be explained in any rational or scientific sense."

"And that leaves . . ."

"Something inexplicable, even paranormal. You didn't see what I did in the Yucatán three days ago."

"I'm not convinced you saw what you think you did," Denton said, his gaze narrowing on Beekman, flashing sudden concern. "Your ears, Professor, they're bleeding."

Beekman touched a finger to one ear and then the other, coming away with twin dabs of blood. He realized he was feeling light-headed, looked at Denton to tell him.

"Your nose," he said instead.

Denton touched his nose, pressed the blood dabbled there between his thumb and middle finger. He and Beekman turned toward the technicians gathered in the control and monitoring room to find them similarly afflicted. They noticed a woman in a white lab coat with red rivulets leaking from the corners of her eyes, as if she were crying blood.

"I think," Beekman started, before his thoughts betrayed him. "I think . . ."

As his voice drifted off, Denton heard a sound like popcorn crackling inside a microwave, at the same time the crack lines in the polymer seemed to consume the wall. Then it erupted in a storm of marble-sized shards that sprayed the room like shrapnel.

Denton took Beekman with him to the floor. "I see what you mean by immeasurable power, Professor," Denton said when the shower of shards passed, sliding off him.

"No, you don't," Beekman said, still trembling. "You have no idea. None of us does."

# FORTY

## New York City

T hank you for seeing me, Ms. Whitlow," Max said to the daughter of the late geneticist, Dr. Franklin Kirsch.

"Call me Laurie, please, Mr. Borgia. Outside, you said this was about my father?"

Max nodded. "My father was a patient of his. And call me Max, please."

"I see," Laurie Whitlow said, even though it was clear she didn't.

She closed the door behind them and ushered Max from the foyer into a den looking down over the street, dominated by a big widescreen television built into an elegantly paneled wall that otherwise looked untouched. Max had the feeling the brownstone was pretty much as Kirsch must've left it, the design and layout clearly dated.

Max had been waiting on the stoop of the West Side brownstone when Laurie Whitlow got home from teaching at PS 11, William T. Harris Elementary School, in Chelsea. According to Weeb Bochner, Whitlow had spent her entire teaching career at that school, nearly twenty years now and ten since her father's death. Max could only imagine what the three-story brownstone might be worth today and figured the taxes alone might well have eaten up a teacher's normal salary. Given what Bochner had learned about Kirsch's considerable investments, and the hefty insurance settlement his daughter and sole heir had received following the explosion that had leveled CyberGen, though, meant money should never be a problem for her.

Max noted a number of framed photos picturing Kirsch with a woman who must've been Laurie Whitlow's mother. The resemblance was uncanny, both women with a mousy look and cursed with stout frames that made them look overweight, even though they weren't. Both women's straight hair hung limply to their shoulders, as if Laurie were purposely imitating her mother's style.

"Please," she said, offering him a chair, "sit down."

Max pointed to one of the pictures as he did so. "Your parents?"

Whitlow nodded. "That one was taken just before the divorce. My mother died a year before the explosion took my father. Cancer."

"That's what my father was seeing yours about, Laurie," Max said, as she took a seat on the matching leather couch adjoining his chair, laying a shoulder bag alongside her. "A rare type in the blood family of the disease."

"Is he . . ."

"He died. About the same time as your father."

"Oh," Laurie Whitlow managed.

"No records kept by CyberGen survived the explosion. I thought maybe your father kept his most important files elsewhere, that you may have by chance retrieved, hopefully the ones concerning my father. Something. Anything," he added, sounding just desperate enough. "Because if I happened to inherit that particular gene from my father," Max continued, letting his thought dangle.

"You could've just called. Saved yourself the bother of a visit."

"No bother. And I wouldn't have known what to say on the phone."

"Unfortunately, the result's the same: Any records my father may have kept were moved out years ago, all his papers. He was a hoarder when it came to such things. They were overrunning the whole house."

"Did you put them in storage?"

"No, I had them all destroyed. Didn't see the point of paying the hefty storage fees for all those boxes. The NYPD had already had their go at them, the FBI too. All part of their routine investigations, they said. I was too numb to care."

"I understand. But CyberGen must have had some means to back up their records."

"Believe it or not, all the company's assets, including any records they may have stored or backed up elsewhere, are still tied up in litigation."

"After all these years? You're kidding."

"I'm sorry to be the bearer of more bad news, Max." Whitlow dragged her phone from a pocket in her bag and jogged it to life. "Can you give me your number, just in case I come up with something?"

"Of course."

Max recited a dummy number, while sweeping his eyes about the room. The shelves were dominated by a collection of figurines, all animals that were comparable in size and all formed of beautiful porcelain.

"My father gave one to me on my birthday, each and every one," Whit-low said, noting his interest. One of our most cherished traditions."

"When's your birthday?"

"June fourth."

"Beautiful," Max said, reaching for one of the elegantly fashioned fig-ures, a horse. He turned it upside down, so he could better regard the tiny sticker he'd spotted. "My father and I used to climb mountains to-gether. Our goal was to scale the highest peak on each continent, but he died before we could finish."

Whitlow's eyes teared up, as Max replaced the horse on the table. "When I was a little girl, my father and I used to go to the Bronx Zoo all the time. Some of my happiest memories."

"I'm sorry."

"Likewise."

Max rose stiffly. "Thank you for your time."

"I wish I could've been more helpful. I'll call if I think of anything."

"Please."

Max waited until he was well down the block, out of sight from the brownstone, before stopping to call Weeb Bochner.

"How'd it go, hoss?"

"Write this down," Max said, spelling out the name of a store listed on the sticker on the underside of the horse figurine he'd inspected. "I think it's a high-end collectibles store. Find out if they've been shipping ani-mal figurines around June fourth for the past ten years to Laurie Whit-low at the address of her father's brownstone."

"And why am I doing this?"

"Because she told me her father used to give her one on her birthday every year. But my count puts her collection at forty-two, her age today. So who's been sending them to her these past ten years?"

Max was sitting in a coffee shop an hour later, when Bochner called him back.

"You'd make a good detective, Commander."

"What'd you find?"

"Return address for the ten figurines shipped over the past ten years was a post office box in Canada. British Columbia, specifically, middle of nowhere. Closest city is Vancouver."

"It's a start."

"It's more than that, hoss. Got a pen handy?"


Laurie Whitlow stepped out of the shower stall and wrapped a towel about herself, still unnerved by the man who'd come poking around about her father. She couldn't tell how much of his story was genuine, further unsettling her and wondering what the true purpose behind his sudden interest in her father had been.

She stepped into her bedroom and recorded a pair of blurs at the edge of her consciousness, before a pair of big men wearing ski masks grabbed her forcibly by either arm. Her towel fell to the floor and Whitlow found herself staring at a third man, just as big, standing in front of her and grinning through his mask.

# FORTY-ONE

## Western Iraq

W e have a problem," the scrambled voice on the other end of the satellite phone told Mohammed al-Qadir.

"I do not have time for your problems."

"This isn't my problem, it's our problem. Yours, in point of fact."

"God does not deal in facts, God deals in faith."

"You really don't know what's been happening, do you?"

Al-Qadir was pacing in the mosque located in his headquarters hidden beneath the Iraqi desert. He prayed five times a day no matter the circumstances, especially now when he needed Allah more than ever. One of his top commanders had taken sick upon returning from a mission in the field. He was getting worse by the hour, and al-Qadir was starting to believe that God was all that could have him.

"I know the final battle for the soul of the world approaches. I know all has gone exactly as God willed."

"You may want to rethink such assurances." Even scrambled, the sharpness of the voice's criticism was evident. "A plague has begun to spread through the Middle East and we've lost contact with the facility in southern Lebanon."

"As God wills, then," al-Qadir said, not bothering to mention that his sick commander had fallen ill after paying a visit to that same facility, a facility that had been producing the means by which his forces would seize power the world over.

"God has nothing to do with this. There is evidence that a pathogen escaped the lab, but it doesn't at all fit the parameters of what we've spent so long developing."

"We don't control fate, ours or any. You'd be wise to remember that."

"Just as you'd be wise to realize that something has gone terribly wrong here. We had a systematic, painstaking plan of how the pathogen was to be released. But this one barely resembles what we set out to create and it's gotten loose all on its own."

"These deaths being an unexpected reward for my service to the one true God."

"That's just it," the scrambled voice said softer. "The victims aren't dying. I've been made privy to the World Health Organization reports. The victims near death's door, but don't pass through it, undergoing some kind of transformation instead."

"Into what?" al-Qadir asked, unable to hide the surprise in his voice, thinking of his own commander with hardened, smoke-colored flesh now lying atop a mattress on the floor in another chamber, bleeding from his eyes, ears, and nose.

"Unknown, at this point. The reporting on the specifics is vague and noncommittal."

Al-Qadir stopped pacing. "You really don't understand, do you?"

"I believe that was my point to you."

"No. You feel there is a plan that was to proceed by our making. But it was never ours, it was always God's to do with as He wished. Such is the problem with men like you. You seek to control that which you cannot and never could. You seek to master fate itself, instead of serving it as I do. Whatever is happening is happening through His divine providence and we must embrace that. We are being given a final test before the End of Days are upon us."

"You haven't heard a word I've said," the scrambled voice snapped. "Whatever escaped that lab is already spreading beyond control, and there's no reason to expect we are going to be spared."

"As God wills, then."

"That isn't an answer."

"No," al-Qadir said staunchly, "it's a plan."

# FORTY-TWO

### The Mediterranean Sea

What are you holding back from me?" Father Jimenez asked the mysterious, flat-featured man he'd come to know as Red, as the military jet began its descent over the Mediterranean.

"Ever play show-and-tell as a kid, Father?"

"Of course."

"We've had our fill of telling already," Red said, looking like a two-dimensional figure come to life in the shading cast by the tinted windows. "Time to get on with the showing. What's the opening line of the Bible, Father?"

"'In the beginning, God created the heavens and the earth.'"

"And that's where we're going, Father, in a manner of speaking." Red hesitated, as if weighing how much to say. "This is right up your alley."

"And why's that?"

"Because your job is to investigate inexplicable phenomena. Believe me when I tell you, that's what we're facing in the Middle East right now."

Jimenez bristled. "I've spent the last ten years of my life watching people's retched lives collapse under the weight of supposed miracles that were nothing more than those same people wanting their faith to be rewarded. Because if that happened, then there was hope for them, for all of us. But there isn't. You know what a true miracle would've been? Not an eclipse in Nigeria, but the members of my team coming back to life, or time rewound so the massacre never happened in the first place. But the world doesn't work that way."

Red looked almost frustrated. "Then tell me how it does work, Father? Start with what we both witnessed in Brazil."

Jimenez nodded, glad for the opportunity to return to the scientific dogma with which he was infinitely more comfortable. "An ordinary meteor strike couldn't cause that kind of mass destruction. It would take an asteroid of a mass and speed capable of generating an explosion measured in kilotons upon impact and, as I've already explained, that doesn't conform in any way to what I found at the blast site."

"Go back to the beginning, Father," Red said, instead of arguing his point.

"As in God creating the heavens and earth."

"Another word for what?"

"The birth of the Universe."

"As in the Big Bang, the single largest release of energy for the last fourteen billion years or so. Molecules formed of light and dark matter colliding with each other to create a force that can't be measured or comprehended."

"What does the Big Bang have to do with all this?"

"Go back to all those light and dark particles colliding. Only they didn't all hang around, did they?"

"Yes, they did. But we can only quantify half of them, the light ones. The dark matter is still there, all around us. We just can't see or measure it. Maybe isolate it for a thousandth of a second inside a particle accelerator, but that's about it."

Red was nodding now. "I think you're starting to get the point."

Jimenez felt the jet's landing gear engage. "I am?"

Red had turned his gaze out the window, toward the sea below. "Nigeria and Brazil. Both sites struck by phenomena that weren't meteors at all according to all the rudimentary principles of geophysics and astrophysics. Right?"

Jimenez shrugged. "I suppose."

"Don't suppose. You're a scientist. Consider the data. But you're also a priest. So consider the underlying context of that data. Think like a priest."

"Light and dark matter. Good and evil," Jimenez said, as if drawing a likeness between them.

"Now, think like a scientist."

"What happened to all the dark matter, the residue?"

"Say it splintered off," Red picked up. "Blown into the celestial ether billions of years ago. Spending those billions of years roaming the darkest reaches of the Universe, following the lines, curves, and folds in space. What would happen? Tell me."

"Speaking as a scientist or a priest?"

"Both."

"It could, *would*, inevitably come back. Billions of years to circle back."

"Exactly," Red nodded, almost buoyant for that brief moment at the conclusion he'd wanted Jimenez to reach, the connection he wanted the priest to make. "Nigeria, Brazil, the Yucatán in Mexico sixty-five million years ago."

"You're talking about the meteor strike that brought on the Ice Age," Jimenez said, suddenly feeling chilled again.

"And something else, Father: What if evil, the ultimate evil as detailed in the Bible, exists to destroy all life, as we know it? I'm not a religious man, but I go where the road leads me and, in this case, the signposts couldn't be any clearer."

"Care to point them out to me?"

"That's exactly what I intend to do, Father."

# FORTY-THREE

### Southern Lebanon

The former Lebanese military bio-weapons complex, what the doctor in the Lebanese village had called *El al-Lacosh*, or House of Evil, was a sprawling single-level, sand-colored building that looked as if it had sprouted from the desert floor. That single floor had almost surely been constructed over any number of comparably sized levels beneath the earth. The heavy security fence that enclosed its perimeter was similarly sand-colored and the one thing that gave away the facility's presence.

The convoy rumbled through an open gate blown weakly back and forth by the wind. The entrance to the building was ajar too, a big dark gaping mouth open to the night beyond. No signs of life whatsoever, or death for that matter. Just nothing.

The wind increased, kicking up miniature funnel clouds as the four Humvees drew to a halt abreast of one another.

"Let's have a look inside," Major Musa said to Vicky.

She was on her own now. A helicopter had been dispatched to the Bedouin village of Abu Siddar to rush Neal Van Royce to a hospital in Beirut, memory of the sight of his hand being snapped off and blood shooting out from the stump making Vicky feel queasy.

His attacker, the German intelligence operative Gunther Brune, had no longer appeared to be human. Barely alive, according to his vitals, and yet capable of incredible physical feats of strength and speed. Vicky had been searching her mind and experience for a plausible scientific explanation for what she'd witnessed, but had so far drawn a complete blank. She could only hope the answers she was looking for rested in this former bio-weapons facility, reconfigured under the guise of a pharmaceutical concern by the terrorist group Gunther Brune had managed to infiltrate.

*El al-Lacosh . . .*

The House of Evil.

Before entering the facility, Vicky redonned her biohazard gear, accompanied this time by Major Musa and four of his men because they'd only brought six of the suits with them. The remaining soldiers would stand guard inside the fence line and contact them immediately if any additional parties arrived on the scene.

With Vicky trailing him, Musa moved toward the Israeli officer named Raviv. "I've already ordered my men to shoot anything that comes out that's not us," Musa said, the Humvees already positioning themselves so their turret-mounted heavy machine guns were poised directly before the doors. "If we don't come out, and you can't reach us, you know what to do," speaking to him for the first time since Vicky's arrival in Lebanon.

The man nodded, his voice gravelly and hoarse when he responded. "We have two F-16s already in the air, circling overhead."

Just like the Egyptians must have two days before, Vicky thought, certain now that government knew far more than they were saying about Medusa. She had no concept of what they were about to encounter once inside, but couldn't stop picturing an army of the infected, unleashed on the world in the event the pathogen couldn't be contained.

"I want a gun," Vicky said to Musa.

Musa took a pistol from one of his men and handed it to her. "Just don't shoot me. And remember to aim for the head," he added, recalling her own words back at the clinic.


The facility's fate became quickly and abundantly clear from the moment she, Musa, and the Lebanese soldiers stepped through the black hole of the entrance.

The facility had been ravaged, looked to have been the target of a savage and concentrated attack, the level of damage and destruction growing worse the deeper they waded. Blood was splattered everywhere, dried and chalky. Equipment was toppled, doors blown or torn from their hinges. The shattered refuse of computers and other diagnostic equipment was strewn everywhere, little of it recognizable. Emergency lights were sputtering or flashing in strobe-like fashion, making it difficult to focus. And a dull whine, evidence of an emergency alarm that had burned itself out, toyed with the edge of Vicky's consciousness, unsettling her even further.

But what stood out most were footprints, footprints frozen in the blood. Crisscrossing each other, all seeming to head in the same direction:

The facility's main doors, through which Vicky had just entered.

The intensity and level of destruction worsened the deeper they drew into the facility and approached a stairwell that descended to the first sub-level.

Vicky could see Musa swallow hard through the orange fabric covering his throat. "None of this makes any sense."

"Not yet, anyway," she told him.

Continuing on, they encountered a series of hastily erected barricades, now breeched, formed of office furniture placed at strategic points to block access to the stairwells leading to the first sub-level. The elevators had been disabled, wiring exposed from within their operating panels.

Some portion of the facility's staff had seemingly made a concerted effort to contain the crisis here and not let any of the infected escape El al-Lacosh, as Vicky had come to think of it. But Gunther Brune's presence in Abu Siddar clearly indicated that effort had failed, along with the fact none of those who'd made their stand here were anywhere to be seen.

One of Musa's men continued to lead the way deeper into the facility. Vicky walked immediately behind him, Musa on her right with another soldier, the remaining two having gone off to sweep additional areas of the facility in search of survivors. She wished they'd brought more bio-hazard suits to accommodate more soldiers, but squandering the time it would take to get them to the site was unthinkable under the circumstances.

"Security tapes," Vicky told Musa, gesturing toward a wall-mounted camera.

"I'm familiar with the system," he said, after inspecting it closer. "Digitally based, content stored on a hard drive."

"We need to bring the computers that are still whole with us. They'll be able to tell us whatever was created here. And what got loose," Vicky added after an uneasy pause.

They forced their way through the next, bulkhead-type door to find it had been blocked by a desk and assortment of chairs. The inside of what looked like a more administrative area was lined with spilled-over desks, save for one where a single figure lay facedown atop a blotter soaked in blood and gore.

Vicky eased him upright and saw what was clearly a gore-splattered entry wound on the side of his head.

"He shot himself," Musa said, noting the presence of a fallen pistol at the man's feet.

Vicky barely heard him, too busy examining a series of bite marks on the man's side and upper legs. "He was infected, knew what he would soon become."

"What, like Gunther Brune? You're saying there are more of them here?"

The other two soldiers returned from their sweeps with a collection of assault rifles they handed over to Musa.

"They've all been fired," he reported, after inspecting the first few. "All of them empty."

Damage from more gunfire was evident in the walls and toppled equipment as well, but that didn't tell Vicky who, or what, they'd been shooting at.

"Where are the bodies? Where's the blood, the carnage? If they went up against a horde of what we saw back in that clinic, it should be everywhere."

Musa could only shrug.

"And what happened to them once the barricades were breached? If they'd survived, they would've reached civilization by now. If they didn't, as all indications would suggest, whatever's left of them should be in front of us now."

Musa didn't bother to shrug this time. "This is where it started, isn't it? This is Ground Zero."

And that's when they heard the crash.

# FORTY-FOUR

## Southern Lebanon

The Lebanese soldiers who'd accompanied Vicky and Major Musa inside the facility tensed, the faceplates of their helmets gone misty with condensation. They aimed their assault rifles back across the floor riddled with toppled equipment, toward the door beyond which lay the barricades erected by workers who seemed to have vanished along with everyone else.

"We should get out," Vicky said, readying her own pistol in her gloved hand.

"My thoughts exactly," Musa agreed, already backpedaling.

They were almost to the heavy, swinging doors, when both crashed open and a surge of motion engulfed them in the same moment the single door leading to where the survivors had made their last stand burst ajar behind an identical wave. Vicky processed the scene in slow motion, catching glimpses of the pathogen's victims in the next phase of the disease, what Gunther Brune was becoming before he was gunned down.

Her first thought was that their skin had turned inside out, an illusion cast by the fact that the hardened, pulsing ridges layered atop the surface looked like veins and arteries running externally instead of internally. Their eyes were like black marbles wedged into their hairless skulls. The faces of the creatures were dominated by the same crisscrossing, overgrown rows of teeth as Gunther Brune had displayed, looking more like snouts as a result. Their arms and legs appeared vaguely simian, but hairless to reveal those sinewy growths Vicky had already taken for veins and arteries layered outside the skin instead of within it. Encased likely in some form of hardened shell comparable to what she'd witnessed in the patients she'd examined.

No longer human at all, their recombinant DNA reengineered by the infection, turning them into . . .

Into *what* exactly?

Musa's soldiers turned their fire on the creatures, two in each direction to protectively enclose Vicky and the major. But the creatures were on them before the bullets could even slow them down, engulfing the soldiers in twin waves, a blur of time and motion. Amid the horrible screams and red mist wafting into the air, Musa and Vicky bolted for the now cleared path to the door and potential escape. This as the screams of the soldiers being ravaged turned wet and wheezy, and Vicky felt their blood splashing against her.

"*What are they?*" Musa managed, as they dashed up the stairs, back toward the facility's aboveground floor.

They shoved their way through a heavy bulkhead-type door. Musa sealed it closed after them, but found no locking mechanism to slide into place. They'd started to rush toward the same doors they'd entered through, when the bulkhead door crashed open, the flood of creatures from the sub-level surging toward them.

Musa swung and drained the magazine of his assault rifle, aiming for the head and downing a dozen of the creatures that were immediately trampled by the remainder of the advancing horde. Vicky heard it clack empty, Musa exchanging it for a pistol in the same moment she readied her own. The two of them firing shot after shot, more hits than misses, the hits obliterating the features of the creatures, spraying blood and bone matter into the air and walls.

Vicky felt the 9mm pistol kick upward in her hand, sending her bullets wildly off target, when she picked up her pace backward. She realized Musa was tugging her on by the wrist, but she kept firing until her pistol's slide locked open and the main doors were upon them.

They surged into the night toward a pair of Humvees that had positioned themselves so their heavy machine guns were facing the door. The twin guns opened fire as soon as she and Musa were clear, dual streams of bullets pouring into the creatures, as they seemed to congeal in the doorway.

"The heads!" Musa cried out. "Shoot for the heads!"

Vicky was already at their vehicle by then, Musa leaping inside and slamming the door just behind her. Her thinking halted abruptly when she realized her Humvee was reversing, twisting and turning, the constant din of the .50-caliber machine gun's fire deafening her to the screech of tires, crack of the big bullets' multiple impacts, and the blare of the constant stream of fire itself. She had the same sense she recalled as a little girl when the merry-go-round started spinning so fast, she could barely spot the sea of faces waiting beyond.

The things that had managed to escape the initial barrage were surging toward them.

*Thud!*

Vicky felt rather than heard the thump of her Humvee striking one of the men-turned-monsters by the deadly pathogen that had been conceived within the walls of the facility they'd just fled. She knew Musa was barking out orders, screaming into the vehicle's radio to report what was happening or summon reinforcements or airstrike, *anything*, in words she still couldn't hear. Or, if she heard them, they didn't register, lost in the haze bred by panic that had consumed the night.

There was a large blast she *did* register, followed by a flame burst that split the black air. One of the Humvees had crashed into a concrete pillar supporting the fence. Vicky thought she detected screams at the edge of her consciousness, caught strobe glimpses of motion descending upon the wreckage. This while her Humvee was tearing on, whipsawing and fishtailing, the fire from its turret-mounted heavy machine gun deafening.

Musa swung toward the Israeli soldier Raviv to find him already on his satellite phone, calling in the air strike on the facility from the F-16s that were circling overhead now. They'd use bunker busters to make sure nothing was left, whatever creatures might still be gestating inside the hardened shells obliterated before they could complete their transformation into whatever these things were.

Their Humvee and a second one that had managed to survive surged out into the surrounding desert mere moments ahead of the initial blast that impacted with a fury that coughed a huge dust cloud into the air ahead of the fireball. A second blast rattled the Humvee again, before a third actually lifted it off the road, the driver barely able to retain control when it smacked down again.

"We just came from hell, didn't we?" Musa managed, settling back in his seat, with the glow of the fires wrought by the blast dissipating the farther away they drew.

"Close enough," Vicky told him.

# FORTY-FIVE

## British Columbia, Canada

Max flew into Boundary Bay Airport just over the United States border, ten miles from Vancouver. The address associated with the post office box that formed the return address for the animal figurines Laurie Whitlow continued to receive after the reported death of her father was located in the town of Maple Ridge. Max had already reserved a rental car preloaded with directions to cover the roughly one-hour drive.

When he landed, there was a message waiting for him on his phone from Admiral Darby, summoning him back to station. Not just him, either, Max recalled now: All personnel were being recalled to duty or redeployed to the region, something big and bad obviously going down.

But Max had to pay a visit to Dr. Franklin Kirsch first. Four, five hours maybe, was all he needed. Then he could hop whatever series of flights to return to the Middle East, from Vancouver International Airport, instead of Boundary Bay.

It was misty and damp, with rain in the forecast, a fact that hardly diminished the beauty of the countryside Max passed on the drive. He kept his cell phone handy in one of the console cup holders, in case Bochner uncovered anything else awry in the circumstances surrounding Dr. Franklin Kirsch's passing. Because his instincts had convinced Max that Kirsch had somehow survived the explosion at CyberGen and had been hiding out here ever since. Land records indicated no deeds or transfers in his name, but that was hardly surprising, given that Kirsch would've taken all necessary measures to disappear forever. Add that to the timing of the explosion coming so close to Ben Younger's visit to Kirsch, and a connection seemed at the very least plausible.

Max reached the fence line of the farm in question, just as the sun broke through the dusk sky. He figured it to be around four hundred acres, average for this area. There was no gate at the entrance, located along-

side a mailbox, and he drove onto the property toward a farmhouse, passing acres of apple orchards on the way.

Max slowed near a large fenced pen where a quartet of horses were
grazing not far from him. They looked like draft horses, working animals.
Suddenly, the four horses reared their heads back, sniffing at the air. Their
eyes seem to lock on him, freezing for a long moment before they began
baying and snorting. Kicking their front legs into the air before galloping
toward the other side of the pen, as far from him as possible.

*Was it something I said?* Max quipped to himself, sliding up the window
again. *Guess I'm not your type.*

Drawing deeper onto the property, Max saw that the postcard perfection of the initial acres he passed were shadowed by empty, barren lands
beyond riddled with overgrowth. Closer to the farmhouse, he spotted a
horse barn before which lay a hog pen, the animals turning his way as he
eased his car to a halt.

Max climbed out, eyes on the front door, when he heard the unmis-
takable clack of a shell being ratcheted into the chamber of a shotgun.

"That's as far as you go, mister," a voice warned ahead of a young man
in denim overalls emerging from the darkness of the barn. "Keep your
hands were I can see them."

Max raised them into the air. "I'm not armed."

"You better not be," the young man said, his thick hair looking like a
tangled bird's nest atop his head, acne riddling his face. "You lost or something?"

"I'm here to see Franklin Kirsch."

"Then I guess you are lost, since I don't know anybody by that name."

"But he'll know mine. It's Younger, Max Younger. My father Ben was
a patient of his."

"I don't know anything about that and I don't know nobody named
Kirsch," he said, extending the shotgun further forward. "That means
you're trespassing and I'll shoot you, if you don't get yourself gone."

Max had started to backpedal, to mollify the young man, when he felt
a presence to his right, like a ripple in the air, the same way he sensed an
enemy in combat.

"It's all right, Teek," a voice called out from the area of the house. "You
can lower the gun."

Max turned slowly to find an old man approaching. Slightly stooped
over, wearing corduroys, his white hair now a gangly mess atop his head,

but still recognizable from the pictures Laurie Whitlow kept displayed in the den of the brownstone she'd inherited from him.

"Dr. Kirsch," Max greeted.

Kirsch stopped a dozen feet away. The light was bleeding fast from the sky, the clearing set between the farmhouse and the barn holding the last measure of it.

"Is it true what you just said, that you're Ben Younger's son?"

"I see you remember my father."

"And I remember he had a son named Max. I remember that all too well," Kirsch added, his voice cracking. "What I need you to do," he resumed, after clearing his throat, "is climb back in your car and drive off. Whatever you came here for, you won't find it."

"I'm Max Younger and I came here for information about my father, Dr. Kirsch."

Teek started to raise the shotgun's barrel again, and Kirsch made no move to stop him.

"I have nothing to say to you, young man."

Kirsch turned and started to walk off, into a patch of ground already darkened by shadows.

"Someone tried to kill me," Max called after him.

Kirsch stopped.

"And I think it's connected somehow to the destruction of CyberGen," Max continued.

Kirsch turned back around.

"How did you manage to survive, Doctor? Why did you fake your own death?"

"Because if I didn't, I knew they'd finish the job. Because I had stepped out of the office for a meeting and when I came back the block had been cordoned off and the building was reduced to rubble. Do you know what blood smells like?"

Max nodded, not bothering to elaborate.

"Because I think I smelled it on the air." Kirsch took a few steps forward, back into what little remained of the light. "You believe the oddities of your father's . . . condition was somehow to blame for what happened? Well, so do I."

•  •  •

Kirsch led Max inside the farmhouse and locked the door behind them, after dismissing Teek.

"Were you followed?"

"No," Max said, calmly.

"Are you sure?"

"I'd know if I was. Believe me."

Kirsch moved further away from him. "How, how did you find me? It couldn't have been my daughter. She's never told anyone, never, and she sure as hell wouldn't have told you. Unless . . ."

"Doctor—"

"You didn't hurt her, did you?" Kirsch demanded, his features flaring. "Tell me you didn't hurt her!"

"I didn't hurt her. I played a hunch and it led me here."

"A hunch? It would have taken far more than a hunch to lead you here. Then again, your father . . ."

"What about my father?"

"As I recall, he mentioned something about your hunches."

Max explained to Kirsch how he'd made the connection with the figurines.

Kirsch nodded, appearing impressed. "Are you police?"

"Military. With plenty of retired friends who know which stones to turn over and how to find them."

"Just tell me my daughter's okay."

"She was when I left her."

"Because we had a call scheduled. She didn't pick up."

The anomaly tugged at Max, but he let it go. "I can have someone check on her, if you'd like," he offered, wondering if he should have asked Weeb Bochner to put a man on the brownstone too.

"Yes, can you do that? Please."

Max reached into his pocket, Kirsch tensing until his hand emerged with only a phone. "I'll text my friend, Doctor. The process will take some time, give us the opportunity to talk."

"If anything's happened to her, if something you did . . ."

"I'm sure she's fine," Max said, even though he wasn't.

"I haven't seen her in ten years, not even once. Too risky."

"Ten years is a long time, Dr. Kirsch."

"I'm not a doctor anymore and my name is Farrell now. For all intents and purposes, Franklin Kirsch really did die in that explosion at Cyber-Gen."

"You know who was behind it."

"I have my suspicions."

"I'd like to hear them."

"We're a long way from that. You need to prove you really are Ben Younger's son first. If that's who you really are, you'll know how."

Max held up his palm, featuring the mark identical to his father's. "This good enough?"

The color seemed to drain from Kirsch's face. He nodded, the motion slow and drawn out.

Max fought to maintain his calm. The farmhouse's interior had a stale, musty odor to it. He noticed a vein pulsating along Kirsch's temple, evidence of his blood pressure running in the red.

"My father came to you because he was sick, dying."

"Thanks to what happened in Mexico in 1990." Kirsch looked at Max closer, perhaps trying to gauge his age. "Not long before you were born, I imagine. He told me your conception was supposed to be impossible, that your mother had been judged infertile by the best experts in the city. He came to me once his symptoms became pervasive. Other experts had diagnosed it as a rare blood cancer. Well, it was rare all right, but it wasn't cancer. At least not any cancer any expert, including me, had ever seen before."

"You're right about my mother being unable to conceive, Doctor. Then my father and his partner struck oil in Mexico, and when he came back the whole world changed. Like he dragged something back. Or maybe it followed him."

Kirsch's expression flattened, the edges in his plump round head softening, his eyes losing a measure of their suspicion. "Keep talking."

"He told you this."

"Keep talking," Kirsch repeated.

Max flashed his right palm before the man instead, making sure he angled it so enough of the light would reveal the birthmark that looked more like a tattoo. "He came back from Mexico with an identical mark on the same palm. Then, around nine months later, I was born with this."

Kirsch was still staring at Max's palm, transfixed by it, looking almost hypnotized.

Max lowered his hand. "Something in his DNA," he resumed. "Something in my father's DNA must've passed the mark to me. But that means what happened in Mexico altered his DNA. That's why he got sick. That's why he came to CyberGen."

"No," Kirsch said, looking away now toward the uncovered window. "He knew it was too late for him. He came because of *you*, because he was afraid the mark wasn't the only thing you'd inherited from him. He wanted me to check your DNA, compare it to his, see if you were headed down the same path. He had taken a sample of your hair for me to analyze. But I remember distinctly he didn't want anyone to know about his sickness, especially you—he was adamant about that. He wanted to protect you. That was always foremost on his mind."

"What else, Doctor?" Max asked, feeling his heart hammering against his rib cage. "What else?"

Kirsch turned his gaze toward the staircase. "Let's go upstairs. To my office."

Kirsch's *office*, as he called it, was nothing like Max expected, although he really hadn't known what to expect. An assortment of mobiles normally churning over an infant's crib hung from the ceiling, battling for space and shifted about by an unseen breeze.

The office was otherwise unremarkable. The wheeled, leather desk chair matched a Chesterfield sofa tucked comfortably against a wall beneath an old window with a built-in seat before it. Max counted three computers, a pair of printers, and a scanner amid the cluttered confines— all gathering dust. There were beautiful built-in bookshelves but Kirsch's library was in neat piles set before them instead. Spines turned out in alphabetical order so he'd have no trouble pulling whatever title he needed from the stacks set on the floor.

"Mexico," Kirsch said, after steeling himself with a deep breath. "You mentioned Mexico. What did your father tell you about it?"

"Not much. Almost nothing. Just the fact that's where he made his first fortune, the basis for the company he and his partner founded."

"Nothing about a cave? A stone he found down inside it?"

"Stone?"

"The mark on your father's hand, the mark he passed on to you. He grabbed hold of the stone and that's how he got it. He came to Cyber-Gen because he blamed the stone for what was happening to him, what the doctors he'd been to mistakenly labeled cancer. Because it wasn't an ordinary cancer. It wasn't like any cancer they'd ever seen before at Sloan Kettering, didn't respond or react according to any existing parameters and specifications for that time or this one. Utterly unprecedented and, unfortunately, untreatable. And that, young man, was just the beginning."

# FORTY-SIX

## British Columbia, Canada

To tell you the truth," Kirsch continued, "I'm surprised you're still alive."

"Because of my DNA. Mine was altered too, wasn't it? Just like my father."

"Altered, but not like your father, not at all. Your father's DNA was altered by an external stimulus. Yours was what you were born with. You inherited it from him, like hair or eye color. Brains, body shape—it's all connected."

"What was wrong with my father's DNA?"

"After his encounter with that stone, simply stated, it was killing him. Slowly and methodically, but killing him all the same. What do you remember of your father from those days?"

"He was hot all the time, like he had a fever."

"Because his body wasn't compatible with his evolving DNA. It was trying to change him, but his body wouldn't go along. Activated antibodies to fight it, but those antibodies had no better luck finding a disease to kill than his oncologists did because there was no disease. Your father wasn't sick per se. His affliction was symptomatic of going through a radical physiological metamorphosis. You never noticed the pain he was in?"

"No," Max said, through the clog that had formed in his throat.

"I imagine it must've been excruciating at times. I offered him prescriptions, but he refused to take them. Didn't want to live his final days in a fog, he said."

"This cave, this rock," Max concluded. "That's how he was exposed, wasn't it?"

Kirsch nodded. "It all goes back to the moment he touched it; he was certain of that. He believed the rock was somehow behind your birth.

How else could you be born with the same mark? Show it to me again, please!"

Max held up his palm.

"Identical in every respect," Kirsch nodded.

"How can that be?"

"I don't know. That's why I've squirreled myself here, why I pretended to be dead, because I don't know. I have no phone, no Internet, no television. No signals coming into the house, no wires, and with good reason. Because I believe, I'm convinced, that CyberGen was destroyed so all trace of the records associated with your father would be lost forever. He insisted they not be backed up, forbade me from entering anything onto the computer. You see what I'm getting at?"

"No."

"Then let's back up a bit. It's a well-known fact that environmental factors such as food, drugs, or exposure to toxins can cause epigenetic changes by altering the way molecules bind to DNA or changing the structure of proteins that DNA wraps to. These structural alterations can result in changes in gene activity, and these changes can be passed on from parent cell to daughter cell within the body, and from parent to child."

"So I inherited my father's altered DNA," Max concluded. "That's what you're saying."

"But that in itself doesn't explain the identical mark on your palm. That suggests something else entirely, outside the bounds of rational, scientific thought, something that cannot be explained."

"Like what?"

"Energy. Quantum fields capable of changing the organic nature of those exposed to them. Your father was dying because he was becoming something else, something different. You were born as whatever that is. Your DNA doesn't match up to any existing models, thanks supposedly to your father touching the stone in that cave. If I'd had more time, if your father's life hadn't ended so tragically, maybe, just maybe, I would've been able to help him—and you."

Max considered Kirsch's words in a different light, one cast against the backdrop of his own experiences growing up that carried over in the military. The feats of strength, speed, and endurance he was capable of when agitated. The visions he got of things he always seemed capable of changing, like he could alter the future and, with it, fate itself. How those abilities had continued to expand through his tenure as a SEAL. How each time they surfaced represented an escalation of sorts, a progression he'd always accepted but never understood.

But the mark on his hand had never bled until recently. That suggested something else was happening.

"That stone my father touched in the cave," Max heard himself saying, feeling detached from his own mind, "the one that left its mark on his palm and set me down this road—what was it, Doctor?"

Kirsch frowned, then shrugged, suddenly reluctant to meet Max's gaze. "I don't know."

"I think you do, suspect something anyway. You wouldn't be living like this if you didn't have your suspicions."

Kirsch nodded, speaking so softly Max could barely hear him. "Do you believe in evil?"

Max thought back to Yemen, and dozens of other places that might as well have been the same. "More than you can possibly realize."

"I'm not talking about evil as in the deeds that men do, I'm talking about evil as an entity in itself, a force of nature. A dark energy we can't see, measure, or quantify, similar to that which was involved in the creation of the universe."

"You mean in a religious sense, like the devil?"

"That's for you to decide. I'm talking purely in scientific terms here, not religious ones," the old man said, as much excited as anxious now. "That's the problem with a world that constantly creates false, diametrically opposed categories of thought when such things are and always have been intrinsically connected. Like science and religion in this case, as impossible as that seems."

"A scientist who believes in the impossible?"

"We call impossible what we can't explain or comprehend, 'impossible' only within the limits of our understanding. And your father's experience challenged those limits. I don't know what that stone was your father touched or where it came from," Kirsch resumed. "But maybe it was waiting down in that cave where it had been for millions and millions of years, waiting for *someone* to take it in hand. And maybe it was written in the cosmos that your father would pass whatever touching that stone did to him on to you. I know that doesn't sound very scientific; in fact, it sounds crazy, because it is. According to the Old Testament, there are no coincidences in the Universe. Everything happens for a reason. And the fact that I'm not religious doesn't change the fact that all of this is crazy and inexplicable, but that doesn't make it any less real. And what your father experienced was just the beginning, I suspect, of something far greater and more ominous. He was an unwitting accessory to a chain of events that, once triggered, cannot be stopped."

"What chain of events?"

Kirsch looked away. "I've said enough."

"No, you haven't. Not even close, Doctor."

"Don't call me that. I'm a farmer now, way out here where the world might leave me alone."

"Then who are you hiding from up here?"

Kirsch looked away, as if suddenly reluctant to meet Max's stare. "About a month after your father's death, a man came to see me at CyberGen. Offered me a fortune to give him the files I had on your father and his inexplicable condition. I asked the man who he was working for, and all he said was it was someone I didn't want to risk disappointing."

"Did you give him what he wanted?"

"Of course not. But I knew he'd be back. Whoever he was working for didn't sound like the kind of man who took no for an answer." Kirsch suddenly looked terrified, the memories returning in force. "I was afraid to go to work the following day."

"The day CyberGen was destroyed . . ."

Kirsch nodded, even though Max hadn't posed it as a question. "All my co-workers killed, for no reason," he said, tears welling in his eyes. "Not being there is all that saved my life. But the blast was so massive that not all the bodies could be positively identified."

"So you decided to disappear," Max concluded. "You came up here, so they couldn't threaten you again."

Kirsch swiped a sleeve across both his eyes and sniffled. "As a scientist, I believe in cause and effect, not coincidence. And the timing of the blast, so close to that man showing up at my office, couldn't be ignored. It wasn't hard to figure what they'd do, if they learned I was still alive. My daughter's the only one who knows. But she was raised by her mother and has a different last name, so she must've escaped their radar screen. I had decided to quit the day CyberGen was destroyed, was planning to tender my resignation. That's why I wasn't there, what my off-site meeting was all about. The explosion likely saved my life, allowed me to fake my own death and disappear. Live out the rest of my life up here, safe from the truth."

"And what truth is that, Doctor?"

Before Kirsch could respond, Max spotted an all-too-familiar red dot on his forehead, an instant before his skull erupted in a spray of blood and bone.

# FORTY-SEVEN

## British Columbia, Canada

Max hit the floor, not far from Kirsch's fallen body, feeling a whip of cold air sifting through the window just shattered by a sniper's bullet. He had no idea of how many more were out there, what weaponry they were carrying.

Since he wasn't carrying any himself, that didn't seem to matter, but it could also be remedied.

Once he slipped outside to confront the attackers.

Max had never seen a night as black as this, the sky moonless and a ground mist combining with the dank, fetid air to create rolling blankets of utter pitch. He knew the attackers would have come with night-vision goggles, so he unscrewed the dim porch bulb for good measure. But a few lights still burned inside Kirsch's farmhouse, enough anyway for the goggles to make use of.

*Should have turned those off too.*

No sense in considering his omission further. A tall shape was slinking Max's way, motions awkward, rifle barrel struggling to shimmer in the thin patches of light sprayed from the farmhouse. Max slid behind the shape, mirroring its steps, until he jerked a hand over the figure's mouth.

"Down," he whispered in Teek's ear. "And give me the shotgun."

The young man did as he was told, ducking down behind the cover of a thick fence post in the hog pen. The motion disturbed the napping animals, kicking them into motion, their snorting breaking the silence of the night.

*Good*, Max thought, which gave him another idea.

He crouched down, until he was even with Teek. "I want you to get to the barn. Hide in there until I come get you. But first I want you to do something for me."

Max realized the birthmark on his palm was throbbing again and could feel the moist soak of blood oozing from it. Its coppery scent permeated the air, setting him on fire inside, as if it were molten steel rushing through him instead of adrenaline. He knew these attackers were pros by what he didn't see, rather than what he did, just like the mercenaries who'd come after him at Creedmoor. Two black-garbed figures wearing neoprene commando masks followed the line of the drive forward toward the house, clinging to the darkness. Max knew they were decoys, meant to draw him out, expose his position for the other gunmen who would've already taken up positions closer to the barn and farmhouse. Max wondered how much they'd been prepped, if they'd been made aware of the prowess of their opponent.

He did a rough count in his head, picturing the enemy force out there in the darkness, invisible for now. He was sure of the sniper who'd fired through Kirsch's office window at the rear of the house, and the two decoys approaching now. Beyond that, he expected another five or six, although it could be more. Coming in numbers any more superior to that would've likely allowed for a full frontal assault.

Max counted down the seconds in his head, picturing Teek in the barn, just as he heard the first of the horses neighing. The sound stirred the hogs even further, sending them careening about their pen as if aware something was awry. A half dozen horses burst from the barn in the next moment, Max using the flash of their motion and disruption caused by the pounding of their hoofs to spring.

He stepped out and fired four shots in rapid succession, going against the grain of practiced dogma by taking out the decoys with a pair of twelve-gauge blasts each. The return fire poured his way was incessant and immediate, Max already in motion away from its anticipated path toward the spot he'd just occupied.

The blur and sound of the horses threw the enemy off just enough to buy him the time and space he needed to reach the gate of the hog pen. Throwing it open and herding those animals into the night as well. Crimped low and shuffling between them for cover, until another masked figure disturbed by their release popped up from behind an old-fashioned gazebo well.

Max wielded the shotgun like a baseball bat and slammed the gunman across the face with the butt, blood spraying from his palm with each strike. He felt facial bones shatter under the blow, the man's feet swept violently out from under him. Still alive and spitting blood when Max drew the now cracked butt upward and slammed it down across his nose and cheekbones.

The man made a sound like a vacuum cleaner winding down. Max hit him again.

And again.

And again.

The man's sputtery wheezing ceased, his mashed face reduced to pulp that left only bone splinters amid the gristle and gore.

Lightning flashed before Max's eyes, illuminating the night for an instant that lingered from one breath into the next. Except there was no storm, no thunder, the lightning his and his alone. Finding the enemy for him like a spotlight.

He crushed the heel of his boot into what was left of the dead man's face, ground it around a bit. The sight in the sudden day-glow brightness recharged, refreshed him. He could smell and taste blood, felt its warm soak dotting his face.

*What was happening?*

His mind flashed back to Yemen, when the same inexplicable feeling had seized him. Everything again seemed to be happening a fraction of an instant ahead of itself, not a vision so much as a glimpse of the next moment as it unfolded. Not a measurable bit of time, so much as a gap between seconds that Max claimed as his own.

The light shined around him, turning when he turned, illuminating all for him to see while the true blackness of the night cloaked him from the enemy. Killing the rest of them wasn't enough, any more than killing this one had been.

The dead man's assault rifle had fallen just beyond his feet that had finally stopped twitching. Max could have picked it up, but chose not to, another strategy starting to form as jumbled pictures in his head tumbled together.

He knew Laurie Whitlow was dead. Saw her lying in a bathtub with

her wrists cut, someone who'd paid her a visit in the wake of Max's trying to make it look like suicide. The same someone must've been behind
these gunmen. Max did the math, the timing indicating no wasted time
behind getting a fix on Kirsch's location and a professional team being
dispatched.

No wasted time at all, Max thought. Someone with resources, then,
unlimited resources, the same someone whose thug had visited Kirsch at
CyberGen in search of answers about Max's father.

With no time to ponder that further now, Max lurched into motion,
melting into the darkest reaches of the night. He felt the same way he
did when a big wave took control of him while bodysurfing with his
father as a boy. It swept you up and you went with it, because you had
no choice, the power of even a small wave incredible, no man a match
for it.

Right now, Max felt swept up by a different kind of power, but one
that felt equally relentless. An unstoppable wave of violence that brought
with it not just a craving for blood, but also a love of it. A feast of killing,
like he could gorge himself and never get enough of it.

The wave again . . . Only he wasn't getting swept away by it, he had
become the wave, sweeping away all else in his path until there was nothing left to rise before him.

The night took on such a surreal quality that he actually questioned
whether this was happening at all. Detached from himself, as if a spectator to his own life, a movie reel unspooling before him, and he couldn't
take his eyes away, captivated and riveted by the sight. Feeling nothing
as he watched.

And moved.

He was moving so fast and purposefully that it felt like gliding, virtually surfing the ground on a path that brought him to the next closest
gunman. The man swung at the last moment. Max thought he saw the
assault rifle barrel flare, before he clamped a palm over the gunman's face
and drove him backward toward an old birch tree. The man's skull rattled
on impact, his brain banging about his skull. Only the tree must've been
rotten as well as old, because the force of Max's thrust pushed the man's
head through the bark and buried it deep in the tree's base. It literally
disappeared, leaving only the man's neck visible, craned backward over
his twitching feet.

Max ducked, and a bullet smacked the tree man's torso instead of his. He twisted and a second bullet, seeming to move so slow that Max thought he could follow its flight through the air, buried itself in the birch bark. In the darkness he could estimate the positions of the gunmen from the fire angle that had probably changed already. In that surreal wave that had swept him up, though, Max felt himself dipping his hands to his belt and coming away with a pair of sharp-bladed military knives he must've plucked from the men he'd downed, even though he had no memory of doing so.

He hurled them outward, snapping his wrists in perfect motion, going with the flow of the night wave just as he had the ocean variety so many times. A pair of gasps followed, splitting the night.

Then he was on another of the gunmen, again with no gap in time recorded in memory, as if he had teleported here. The man's legs folded up and he crumpled to the ground like a rag doll, spewing blood even darker than the night in all directions. Splashing Max with its coppery scent and wet, oozing warmth. He looked down and realized he was holding the man's head in his grasp, with no memory again of how it had gotten there.

Max licked the blood from his lips, then swiped another spray from his eyes and forehead and licked it from his fingers. He wasn't sure how many more gunmen there were, only that they'd all been reduced to steaming mounds atop the ground, his actions lost to the night wave. The lightning was gone, replaced by a strobe light that caught only bits and pieces of the night, leaving the bulk of it as blanks to be filled in.

Max felt the warmth of more blood soaking him, his palm feeling as if somebody was sticking a knife into it now. He remembered thinking this had to be a dream, because all he felt was glee, buoyant in the night wave he found himself welcoming now, surrendering to.

*My clothes . . .*

He couldn't leave the farm like this, had to change clothes at the very least and started back toward the farmhouse to see what he could find. Halfway there, he spotted a body askew on the ground, hand extended as if to reach for the home's front steps. Max knelt and recognized Kirsch's farmhand Teek from a face left whole by the barrage of bullets that had obliterated the rest of him.

*I told you to stay in the barn.*

And now the young man was dead, because he hadn't followed Max's

instructions. Teek lying dead out here, Kirsch upstairs. Two more innocent victims, to go with Laurie Whitlow.

He rose back to his feet and swept his eyes one more time about the
blackness around him, checking for any lingering movement and drinking in the stench of blood that hung heavy in the air.

# FORTY-EIGHT

## Galveston, Texas

'm sorry, sir," the big man said to Dale Denton, standing rigid over the drainage ditch dug to protect the nearby, mothballed natural gas pipeline.

Denton swung back toward him, his face looking red and shiny in the spill of the floodlights installed to ward against vandalism. The chopper sat nearby on a flat patch of ground, turned makeshift landing pad, its dull black finish barely reached by the glistening bulbs.

"That all you have to say, Spalding? First, the mess at the nutso palace and now this, and you can't do better than that? How many shit storms can you unleash in a single week?"

"I'm confident the damage can be minimized," Spalding said stiffly. "The operators weren't carrying ID and, even if the Canadian authorities manage to identify them, there's no link back to us. I made sure of that."

Denton nodded, gnashing his teeth. "These would be the same men you assured me were reliable. Up to the task, you said. Big, bang, boom was the way you described it. Big, bang, bullshit is what I ended up getting. One man, how hard could it be to take out one man for these special operators of yours?"

Spalding started to swallow, then stopped. "Maybe Younger wasn't alone. The reports I'm getting from the scene in Vancouver . . ."

"What?"

"One man couldn't possibly have done it. At least, no one man I've ever come across."

"You're the one who told me Max Younger, or whatever he's calling himself, is a Navy SEAL now."

"What happened on that farm wasn't the work of any SEAL I've ever known."

Spalding sighed audibly, standing at attention out of habit. He stood as close to seven feet as six, even without combat boots, though his 5.11 Tactical gear made him look even bigger. He was strangely, and utterly, hairless, not from birth, Denton had read in his dossier, but from the heat wave loosed from a terrorist bomb. He had no eyebrows or hair, and his arms bared beneath a tight short-sleeve T-shirt looked slathered in oil. The heat had been so intense that it had burned off Spalding's tattoos as well, something Denton hadn't thought possible, leaving a patchwork of embroidered scars behind. Denton liked the fact he'd been dishonorably discharged for acts of brutality against civilians; specifically, torture to make members of an Afghan village give up Taliban fighters hiding in their midst. It showed he was a man with an edge, willing to go to extremes when called for.

Denton had never stopped looking for Max Younger after he'd disappeared a decade before, knowing even if those efforts failed, someday he'd return to New York with his mother committed to Creedmoor Psychiatric Center. While it had taken far longer than he'd expected, the patience he'd displayed by keeping certain security and reception desk personnel there on the payroll had finally paid off. At long last, Max Younger had shown up, even more fortuitously after-hours since it meant he had to return the following day, giving Spalding time to get a team together.

"It was the woman's birthday, you know," Denton told him, stepping out of the spill of the floodlights into the shadows.

"No, sir, I didn't."

"I did. Celebrated too goddamn many of them, while my partner was still alive."

After the attempt on Younger's life failed at Creedmoor, Spalding got his chance for redemption when a handsomely paid contact in the NYPD's Intelligence Division got a hit on Max Younger's photo through facial recognition software keyed to the city's security cameras. A series of those shots captured Younger standing outside a fancy brownstone on the West Side. Once the address was confirmed, Spalding dispatched a team to, of all people as it turned out, the daughter of Dr. Franklin Kirsch, learning the missing doctor's location where Younger must've been headed.

Talk about killing two birds with one stone, Denton had mused at the time, blessing the same fortune he was now cursing.

He pointed Spalding's attention toward the natural gas pipeline. "Protests by so-called environmentalists led to its shutdown. Cost me millions. Know why I'm telling you this, why I wanted to meet here?"

"No, sir."

"Because the only thing I hate more than setbacks are failures. I hired you, because I like a man willing to play by his own rules, if that's what it takes to get shit done. Problem is, Spalding, you haven't been able to get this particular shit done, have you?"

"I will, sir."

"That a promise?"

"A guarantee."

"Money back and all that? Save that shit for somebody who cares. You think I haven't had other men like you on the payroll from time to time? You think maybe this pipeline holds a whole bunch of bodies under all that corrugated steel?" Denton grinned, as much to disguise the accuracy of his statement, as make light of it. "Use your imagination, Spalding, use your resources. Just get me another body to bury."

# FORTY-NINE

### Western Iraq

Mohammed al-Qadir stood in the spreading shadows cast by the sun setting over the desert landscape beyond. From this vantage point, at dawn, the sun looked blood red, as if it wasn't rising so much as about to crash into the Earth and paint the planet with the blood it was leaking.

He was convinced his entire life's work had been building toward the moment that was coming now, and a lot faster than he'd ever imagined.

It was worse than the voice on the other end of the satellite phone had intimated, in part because the situation in the Middle East was dissolving further by the minute. If initial reports were to be believed, contact had already been lost in parts of the region. So too reports of outbreaks, attacks, and spreading swaths of dead zones had come in from Jordan, Lebanon, and Egypt just for starters.

The pathogen his holy reverence had delivered unto him years before had mutated into something it was not supposed to be. He had borne witness to this in the form of the trusted New Islamic Front commander who'd returned from the facility from which the disease had escaped carrying it inside him. And now al-Qadir understood the crucial role he was playing in the grand plan for delivering the End of Days, rubbing the arm covered from wrist to shoulder by a flesh-colored sleeve normally concealed beneath his robes. At long last, he grasped the true place set for him years before, a great puzzle finally falling together.

By guiding his transformation, al-Qadir believed Allah had taught him that the ends were all that mattered, the means generally irrelevant. Being spared death filled him with a sense of purpose that was first realized in the hatred he felt for Westerners. But that child from the refugee camp was a stranger to him now, a relic from a different world and different life. He knew nothing then of how his initial exposure to violence and hate would ultimately turn him toward God. All fated, every bit of it, to make him into the man he was today.

Allah did indeed work in mysterious ways.

Al-Qadir thought he understood his role in this. Now he realized the total view of Allah's grand design was obscured even to him. Something else had been created in southern Lebanon and now it had been unleashed on civilization to punish man for his sins and failure to accept God's true word.

Al-Qadir watched the rising sun continue to brighten, creating a blinding shimmer over the endless desert around him. His work was not done yet. He could feel a flutter inside his head he took for God whispering in his ear, speaking of enemies who still posed a threat and needed to be vanquished.

The dry, stifling air prickled with static, supercharged with sparks he could feel snapping against his skin. Al-Qadir felt Allah's touch in each and every one of them. He didn't want to return to the cold dark of the cave, wanted to stay out here until the blistering sun melted his skin, so long as he could feel God so close and so strong.

*Something was coming.*

And al-Qadir would rise to meet it, standing, undaunted, by Allah's side in the final battle that was to come.

# FIFTY

## George H. W. Bush

Red's government-issued Gulfstream was equipped with a tailhook that allowed it to snare one of the arresting wires on the deck of the *George H. W. Bush*. Being jolted to such a sudden stop was like nothing Jimenez had ever experienced before, and he realized in that moment the reason why each seat was outfitted with an entire restraint apparatus, instead of just a seat belt. His feet hit the deck in wobbly fashion, to find an officer waiting nearby to escort them to a ready room that had been transformed into a command center with both electronic and paper maps filling the walls amid current troop deployments and units in transit.

Units making up tens of thousands of troops, the progress of their mobilization charted the way the news stations follow that of Santa's sleigh on Christmas Eve.

"Father Pascal Jimenez," Red said, after escorting him up to a man wearing admiral's bars on his uniform's shoulders, and more ribbons than Jimenez could count under his lapel, "may I present Admiral Keene Darby."

Darby nodded, an unlit cigar in his mouth, and didn't bother to shake hands. "He know why he's here?"

"Not yet. I thought it best for him to hear it in the proper context."

They moved through a door into an adjacent larger room, a conference table squeezed in before a single wall-mounted widescreen television.

"I told you we're facing an unprecedented threat to the future of civilization," Red said.

"Not in those words."

"Then let me be more specific, Father," Admiral Darby offered, working a remote control to bring up a map of the Middle East on the widescreen television. "Take a look."

The map was dominated by a mass of colors scattered in patches and swatches across the region: a mix of blue, red, and yellow across a white background; actually just a smattering of blue amid much larger swatches of yellow and a pale red color having usurped the bulk of the white.

"Ninety-six hours ago, the World Health Organization received a report of an outbreak of an unidentified, potential pathogen in Jordan," Red started, sounding almost casual. "Within twenty-four hours, their efforts had uncovered all the blue you see on the map, denoting areas where an outbreak in its initial stages was detected. The yellow patches indicate the spread of this potential pathogen over the past seventy-two hours, and the red denotes our estimates on the reach of the spread within the next seventy-two hours."

Jimenez blinked several times to reset his vision, hoping that might change the sight before him. "The entire Middle East, virtually."

"Air, and all other forms of travel in and out of all affected countries, has been shut down," Red resumed. "Any plane, train, or ship that violates that order will be shot down or destroyed. Financial markets are collapsing, and countries all over the world are panicking over oil normally shipped from the Middle East never reaching them. Add to that the fact that there's a feeding frenzy going on with the press we won't be able to fend off much longer either. And when and if this story pops, we're looking at a full-scale panic certain to plunge this region, and maybe the entire world, into utter chaos and anarchy."

"That's not all, Father," Darby interjected, looking toward Red. "Show him the next slide."

Red clicked on the remote, a map of the world replacing the one of the Middle East. "Thus far, no cases of the pathogen have been reported outside the Middle East. But our computer simulations universally show that won't remain the case for long. Here's the world a week from now."

Jimenez saw pockets of red displayed all over the map, larger closer to the Middle East and growing progressively smaller the farther away.

"And two weeks," Red resumed, giving Jimenez time to process what he was seeing.

In this case that was red occupying far, far more of the screen, including a clear spread to the United States.

"Now three weeks."

The red was everywhere now, in congealed pockets that looked like somebody's spilled blood had dried all across the map.

"We're looking at this as a potential Extinction Event," Darby resumed. "Ebola to the zillionth power."

Jimenez was having trouble processing all of what the admiral and the man named Red had just laid out for him. "So why am I here?"

"Because you can help us."

"Me? How is that even possible?"

"Let's start with this," said Red, jogging the screen to one of the few pictures ever taken of Mohammed al-Qadir. "Do you recognize him, Father?"

Jimenez nodded. "The leader of the New Islamic Front, who's pledged to destroy all of Western civilization."

"Thanks to an apparently inexhaustible supply of funding, originating in non-Muslim countries, that we've been powerless to trace. So maybe the NIF has some kind of financial angel on their shoulder, your guess is as good as mine."

Jimenez's gaze returned to Mohammed al-Qadir, meeting his eyes close up on the sixty-inch screen.

*Those eyes, piercing in their intensity, their emerald shade making them appear almost translucent.*

Jimenez felt sick to his stomach, because he'd seen those eyes before, a long time ago, up close and personal.

And then he doubled over, retching.

# FIFTY-ONE

## West Houston, Texas

A lightbulb?" Dale Denton asked.

Orson Beekman nodded. "You'll see why in a moment."

Denton didn't bother to nod. His chopper had landed on the roof of WET's West Houston offices just minutes before, having ferried him back from his meeting with Spalding in Galveston. And now Beekman's chattering drew Denton's attention back to the control room, a fresh polymer having been installed to replace the glass that had shattered in the midst of their last experiment. Just in case that turned out to provide inadequate protection, they were viewing this latest demonstration from the safety of Denton's office via video projection upon his computer monitor.

The lightbulb in question shared the same table as the mysterious rock Ben Younger had first come upon, secured inside the chamber between that clear wall ten times as thick as the one that had virtually dissolved before their eyes. It was screwed into a simple socket, but not switched on yet.

Beekman looked back toward Denton. "On a scale of one to ten, Manhattan being a ten, when it comes to the energy required to power an entire city, Houston would be a five, roughly a billion times what it takes to keep that lightbulb burning."

"I've had a difficult day, Professor. Can you get to the point?"

This time, Beekman physically pointed at a bar grid occupying the far-right side of the monitor. "We're going to measure the degree to which the rock can amplify minor ratios of energy. The lightbulb wouldn't even register on the grid. A city block would move the needle ever so slightly, a small town only a bit more."

"What if the needle reaches the top?" Denton wondered. "What kind of energy output would we be looking at then?"

"Enough to power the entire city of Houston."

"Through a lightbulb?"

Beekman nodded. "Thanks to amplification."

Denton turned his gaze on the replacement glass polymer, visible on the wall-mounted television. "Then what are we waiting for?"

### British Columbia, Canada

Max snapped alert with a start, totally disoriented, gazing about to find he was seated in an airport terminal waiting area. His cell phone was ringing and he jerked it to his ear, recognizing Weeb Bochner's number.

"Weeb?" Max managed in a scratchy voice.

"He speaks! At long last, he speaks. What the fuck, Pope, what the *fuck happened*?"

Indeed, what *had* happened? A thick fog, more like a blanket, covered everything else that had transpired up until this moment. There were snippets of memory, including sorting through some clothes hanging in a spare bedroom of Kirsch's farmhouse. Max realized he was wearing a selection of those clothes now, jeans and shirt that fit well enough because they must've belonged to Teek, who was about the same size as him. They scratched at his skin a bit and smelled like chlorine bleach, still far better than the blood-soaked garb he must have discarded at some point.

"At least you're not dead," Bochner was saying.

Max realized his mouth was dry and pasty. "But Laurie Whitlow is, isn't she?"

"Her body was found this morning, by the man I sent over there to check on her, like you asked. She'd slit her wrists in the bathtub."

"She didn't kill herself, Weeb, she was murdered."

"How can you know that?"

"I can't explain. I just do."

Max tried to swallow again, realized he was sweating so much it was beginning to soak through his clothes. He scanned the waiting area, especially those sitting close to him, to make sure no one was watching or listening.

"What time is it?"

"Nine a.m. here. Six a.m. where you are. Shit's hitting the fan, Pope."

"I've been recalled to duty, Weeb."

Max remembered the voice mail from Admiral Darby he'd listened to upon landing at Boundary Bay Airport hours ago. From Kirsch's farm, though, he'd driven his rental car to Vancouver International Airport instead, where he booked the quickest route he could back to the Middle East, his military ID thankfully earning him a complimentary first-class upgrade on the flight he was now waiting to board.

"Listen, hoss," Weeb Bochner was saying, "even our friendship, all the shit you did for me, only carries so far. I can't help you with what went down up there any more than I already have."

Max felt stiff everywhere, wished he could do some light stretching to loosen up. "What went down, Weeb? What do you know?"

"I know eight unidentified males were found dead on Dr. Kirsch's property, along with Dr. Kirsch himself. Had the makings of an all-out firefight, except it wasn't bullets that killed a whole bunch of them."

Max felt his insides sink, more memories flooding back. As Bochner resumed, he groped through his pocket for the old mood ring that had long served as his lucky charm, the one and only thing he'd kept from his former life, oblong plastic jewel superglued in place, and squeezed it onto his finger.

"Royal Canadian Mounted Police are heading up the investigation, but they don't have shit and no clue you were there." Bochner paused, the edge leaving his voice when he resumed. "What do you remember exactly?"

"Bits and pieces, that's all."

"Then answer me this: Does you being recalled to duty have anything to do with scuttlebutt suggesting the Mideast is about to come completely unhinged to the point where I wouldn't be surprised to get a call back myself? Rumors are rampant, and there's amateur footage out there on social media that's running on a nonstop loop on the news channels that look like the world really is going to hell this time. Looks like the goddamn zombie apocalypse wasn't as far from the truth as everybody thought."

"Admiral Darby ordered me to get my ass back on station. He didn't say what for."

"Don't bother giving him my best because, you and me, we never saw each other. As far as I'm concerned, after what happened in Vancouver, you don't exist. As much as I want to believe you, there's too much that doesn't add up, and I can't risk it leading back to me."

"My mother, Weeb," Max managed.

"I won't let you down there, Pope, on the condition you lose my name and my number. Old times' sake only carries so far."

"I understand. Thanks for everything. Weeb?"

Too late. He was already gone.

### West Houston, Texas

"You're telling me that, thanks to our rock, a single lightbulb might be able to power all of downtown Houston?" Denton posed, after Beekman's remarks had a chance to sink in.

"That's a rather rudimentary way of putting it, and that's the purpose of this test: to find out if the preliminary algorithms were correct. We're going to turn things up slowly this time. Do our best to avoid any repeats of what happened the first time. The amount of energy is so potentially vast, we'll need to come up with an entirely new storage mechanism. The difference between the size of a gas tank and an entire tanker, maybe an entire fleet of them—and I mean that quite literally."

"Start the test, Professor," Denton ordered. "Let's see what we can see."

Beekman hit a button on his keyboard and the lightbulb switched on. Almost instantly, the vertical bar grid begin to fill in from the bottom up. Rising in deliberate fashion toward the one-tenth mark.

Denton studied the screen closer. "What's happening to the energy we're generating?"

"Flushed out into the ether beyond where, I suspect, it will become static electricity or something similar. That way, it spreads out and we avoid pockets of concentration."

"And what could those pockets do?"

"Act in the same manner as some sort of an electrical storm, even a very minor electro-magnetic pulse, I suspect."

"You *suspect*?"

"We've squarely entered uncharted territory here," Beekman explained. "Everything is supposition."

The bar grid had reached the line one-fifth from the bottom, still moving in deliberate fashion. Denton thought he must have seen it wrong, because his next glance an instant later showed the grid to be a third full. But one look at Beekman told him, no, he'd seen it right.

"Professor?" Denton said.

He looked back toward the laptop screen to find the arrow marker had reached the halfway point, picking up visible speed, until it filled in all the way to the top. The colored portion continued to pulse, as if surging beyond the machine's capacity to measure the energy being generated, and Denton half expected the top of the bar grid to rupture under the pressure.

Something, misplaced motion or something else that didn't seem to fit, drew Denton's gaze to the left-hand portion of the screen, where lab technicians five stories underground were beginning to scurry about, something clearly amiss.

"Oh my," Beekman managed. "Oh . . . no."

## Canada

Max had boarded the plane without incident. He made sure to exchange just enough pleasant smiles with his fellow passengers in the first-class cabin, before taking his seat, the one next to him empty.

He vaguely heard a recorded voice reviewing the aircraft and the proper steps to take in the event of an emergency, before his eyelids grew heavy and he felt himself nodding off. Max didn't actually think he was asleep, because he could feel his own breathing, could still think. Then he felt himself twitching, powerless to rouse himself from whatever dream was opening like a curtain before him.

*Somebody, wake me up!*

He thought those words, but never spoke them. Couldn't speak in his restive state, couldn't make any sound other than the low whine, like an elongated guttural grunt, he could hear in his own ears.

The curtain continued to open, the nightmare into which he felt he'd fallen about to begin like some kind of twisted movie.

## West Houston, Texas

"Professor!" Denton said, twisting Beekman around in his chair toward a wall-mounted widescreen television, tuned to CNN. "A sub-sea earthquake detected in the Gulf Stream off the coast of Houston?" he continued, reading the bulletin scrolling across the bottom of the screen. "Is that even possible?"

Just then, the Emergency Broadcast System cut into that, and all local broadcasts, signaled by a high-pitched, repetitive squeal.

"It's us," Beekman barely managed, his voice cracking. "We did this."

"That's fucking insane."

The room erupted in high-pitched screams and wails, both men swinging back toward the computer monitor picturing the control room five stories beneath ground level.

"Oh my God," Beekman muttered.

### Over Canada

In his nightmare, Max could feel himself still twitching, muttering incoherently as he soared through history, a kaleidoscope of events rippling before him like a staccato montage.

The spear that had just pierced the side of Christ being crucified dripping blood onto a flattened dirt road . . .

A muck- and blood-riddled field of corpses and severed limbs with sword-wielding Crusaders gazing over their plunder . . .

Women being hanged as witches as pious puritans looked on, enraptured by the sight . . .

Soldiers still in their teens in blue uniforms crashing up against boys in gray uniforms, as musket balls and cannon fire showered blood into the air . . .

A slow-moving parade of emaciated souls in tattered concentration camp rags being led to a flat slab of a building beneath a sign that read AUSCHWITZ . . .

Flesh and bone being vaporized in the mushroom cloud spreading via a shock wave through Hiroshima . . .

Masked men lopping off the heads of men, women, and children in an Iraqi Christian village . . .

He bore witness to it all happening in the same moment of time, history rewound for his private view.

### West Houston, Texas

Beekman and Denton heard a rippling series of crackling sounds, like branches breaking, accompanied by horrible, high-pitched screaming that quickly turned to hoarse rasps desperately heaving for breath. The technicians dropped in what looked like a single unbroken wave; no, not dropped so much as crumpled, folding up accordion style, even as more crackling sounds resonated through the widescreen's speakers.

## Over Canada

The ugliest moments in human history continued to unfold, with Max bearing witness. He was a spectator in a vast void that could have stretched to infinity or occupied only the area of the jet's cabin. It seemed not to matter, the scope of the world no longer relevant.

Because he felt the world in his grasp.

The surge of power he felt seemed to superheat his blood, lending him a sense of pleasure he could feel all the way to his very core. It filled him with a calm reassurance that consumed all the doubt, all the uncertainty. If he could find a way to surrender to this power, join with it, the vagueness and mysteries of his past would melt away.

As he would melt away.

Into something unimaginable.

## West Houston, Texas

The screams of the technicians grew so loud Beekman was left covering his ears as he watched them drop, watched them clutching for various limbs, confronted by the impossible reality that exposure to the energy released by the rock was actually shattering their bones. Their spines seemed to go last, stilling their desperate flailing even as they continued to cry out in unspeakable agony, their gnarled bodies twitching and racked by spasms. He thought he saw, actually *saw*, splintered vertebrae break through the skin ahead of blood splatter showering the air, before he turned away, unable to watch any longer.

"Cut the power, Professor!" Denton ordered. "Cut the fucking power!"

Beekman had just hit the key that switched off the lightbulb, when the television fizzled, sparked, and exploded with a *poof!* right before their eyes.

"Shut it down!" Denton ordered again.

"I tried, I tried!" Beekman wailed back at him.

## Over Canada

Wherever Max was now, his feet were back on the ground, the nebulous nature of vast, opaque nothingness replaced by a darkened room that felt stuffy and stale, the air rank with a stench of plant or tree rot. A dim cone of light shined downward, from a ceiling he couldn't make out and a fixture he couldn't see. He felt a shrill, dry wind, like one bred of a desert blowing, not so much into, as through him, leaving his mouth feeling like sand grit was coating it.

He realized the light was centered over a table enclosed by black-cloaked, hooded figures who seemed not to recognize his presence. The ones on the near side parted, squeezing into a semi-circle rimming the table, to reveal the figure of a young, incredibly sexy woman, so beautiful and perfectly formed that she seemed the product of a sculptor's chisel, lying motionless upon it. Naked everywhere, except her face, which was covered by a mask zippered up from the top down the back of her skull. A snake, shiny black and glowing in the thin light, coiled about the woman atop the altar, caressing her skin lightly, almost affectionately.

Max felt a stirring inside him, wanting to see more of the woman, wanting to see *all* of her. Consumed, obsessed, and aroused like nothing he'd ever experienced before. He tried to approach her, but he couldn't move, his feet feeling as if they were glued to the chalky floor. He looked down and realized he couldn't see them. Maybe they were gone. Maybe they'd sunk through the floor.

As Max watched, still trying to pry his feet free, the hooded, faceless figures seemed to dissolve, robes dropping in ruffled heaps to the floor. But in their place, a like number of black snakes joined the first in slithering about the beautiful young woman's naked body, their paths crisscrossing, hissing as their tongues probed the air.

Suddenly the woman sat up on the pedestal and swung toward Max, shedding the snakes from her. She stepped down lightly, bare feet touching the floor amid the snakes circling about. Then she started toward him, seemingly carried by the winds that still swirled about the room, the snakes trailing her in matching S-patterns.

She stopped, close enough to Max for him to feel her breath through the mouth slit of the mask. His insides felt like jelly, the breath catching in his throat at her absolute perfection.

And then they were kissing, deeply and passionately.

### West Houston, Texas

Dale Denton's eyes flitted between CNN, playing on a computer screen now, and Beekman desperately pounding keys behind his computer linked to the control room below ground level.

"Professor!"

"It's not working, nothing's working!"

Denton thought he could feel, actually feel, the air lighten, the shrill siren wailing beyond seeming to ebb. The LED readout measuring the power output generated by the stone was steadily falling, just as fast as it had risen.

"You've done it, Professor! You've done it!"

But his relief was short-lived, his gaze drifting back to the technicians who'd crumpled to the floor, their limbs askew and twisted at inconceivable angles. Nothing other than a few twitches and spasms for movement. All of them dead now.

### Over Canada

The touch of the masked woman's lips felt somehow familiar to Max, even before she stepped slightly back. Still at arm's distance . . .

*"Sir! Sir!"*

. . . when Max reached out to unzip her mask to reveal her face.

*"Wake up, sir! Wake up!"*

Max awoke with a jolt that snapped him forward in his seat, in full view of the other passengers in the first-class cabin. The flight attendant who'd been jostling him lurched back into the aisle.

"You were having a nightmare, a nasty one. I'm sorry, I didn't know what else to do. I brought you some water."

Max took the glass and guzzled it down, then gazed about the cabin apologetically. "I'm sorry," he said, clearing his throat while still trying to clear the fog from his mind. "Sorry for all the commotion." He forced a smile. "Guess I better have some coffee."

The flight attendant forced a smile too, while looking just as anxious and frightened as the rest of the cabin's passengers, unnerved by what she'd just witnessed. "I've got a fresh pot on."

Max settled back in his seat, started to close his eyes but stopped for fear of drifting off to sleep again.

He realized the other passengers in the first-class cabin were still staring at him.

"It's okay," he said, trying to reassure them. "Everything's okay."

Even though he knew it wasn't. Not even close.

# PART 5

# ORIGINS

I have never met any really wicked person before.
I am so afraid he will look just like everyone else.

—Oscar Wilde

# FIFTY-TWO

The news isn't good, I'm afraid," Dr. Franklin Kirsch told Ben Younger. Ben had suspected as much as soon as Kirsch had closed the office door behind him, reluctant to meet Ben's eyes until safely insulated behind his desk.

"How much do you know about DNA?"

"What I learned in high school, which means not much," Ben said, his mouth gone suddenly dry.

"Well, the science has evolved quite a bit since then, but the basic fundamentals remain the same. The double helix, a visual depiction of what makes humans both different and the same. Human DNA consists of about three billion bases, and more than ninety-nine percent of those bases are identical across the board—that's what makes us the same. The order, or sequence, of these bases determines the information available for building and maintaining an organism, similar to the way in which letters of the alphabet appear in a certain order to form words and sentences—that's what makes us different."

Here, Kirsch's expression sombered, his gaze suddenly furtive once more. When he finally met Ben's gaze across the desk again, Ben was certain he detected something else he first mistook for confusion but now realized was fear.

"An important property of DNA," Kirsch resumed, "is that it can replicate, or make copies of itself. Each strand in the double helix can serve as a pattern for duplicating the sequence of bases. This is critical when cells divide, because each new cell needs to have an exact copy of the DNA present in the old cell. That's where the anomaly in your case, and the root of your illness I believe, lies."

Ben had come to CyberGen for answers, for hope, after finally receiving a diagnosis for a baffling illness that had been plaguing him almost from the very day of his son Max's birth nearly eighteen years before. The first symptom was a strange sensation in the mark on his palm left by grasping that scaly, crater-riddled rock the size of his hand in the cave down in the Yucatán. The mark had started to tingle, followed by a chilling numbness that made him feel like he was squeezing cotton.

"You don't have a blood cancer," Kirsch resumed. "The doctors you've seen are calling your affliction that, because they don't know what else to call it. It's only related to the blood, because it's blood that carries cells, and your problem lies there. At the base genetic level. To put it plainly, the process of your cells dividing—the de facto definition of life—is slowing, has been slowing, and continues to slow. But there's something else."

Ben continued to listen.

"Your cells aren't producing replicas, they're producing hybrids, as if your body is rewriting its own genetic code from second to second. Never mind not being the same man you were yesterday or the week before; you're not the same man you were since your last heartbeat."

"So what can we do about that?" Ben heard himself ask, as if someone else were posing the question.

"Do?" Kirsch shrugged. "Truthfully, I'm not sure. My specialty is diagnoses aided by genetic analyses, not treatment. We're dealing with an empirical mystery. The simplest, most basic answer to your question is, first and foremost, we find the source of the mutation that turned your genetic system haywire and try to reverse it."

"Is that even possible?"

Kirsch shook his head. Slowly. "What you're experiencing is utterly unprecedented in the annals of genetic science. I think we need to look outside of infections, viruses, autoimmune responses, and the other standard medical fodder." Kirsch crossed his arms and tightened them across his chest, making his shoulders look very small. "I think we need to look toward the normally inexplicable."

"And what would that entail?"

Kirsch looked away. "Not my area of expertise, I'm afraid."

"No, Doctor," said Ben, leaning forward with a start, "*I'm* the one who's afraid. I'm paying you a fortune to learn what's happening to me. So who else am I supposed to go to? Whose area of expertise is this exactly?"

Kirsch nodded and let out a deep breath. "Okay, as far as the inexplicable goes, my first thought would be your . . . condition was caused by exposure to some kind of foreign-based organism."

"By foreign, I don't suppose you mean something I caught on a business trip outside the country."

"I'm talking about some sort of virus or pathogen not of this world."

"Meaning?"

"Meaning an unknown organism we can't identify or quantify, much less come up with a predictive diagnosis," Kirsch explained. "You need to understand that science is based as much on theory as fact. We can try to pass off the genetic mutation you're afflicted with as due to exposure to some especially rare and virulent pathogen, or we could simply accept it as an inexplicable genetic anomaly. But we must at least consider the possibility that your unprecedented affliction was caused by exposure to something similarly unprecedented, in the form of something not necessarily of this world."

Ben looked down at his palm. "You're referring to the rock I touched, the mark it left on my hand."

Kirsch unfolded his arms and leaned forward. "That mark wasn't burned into your skin like a brand. It wasn't inked into your skin like a tattoo. And it wasn't carved into your skin either. There's no scar tissue, it doesn't extend beyond the dermas. If you asked me what the mark most resembles, I'd tell you a child drawing on your palm with a red crayon. And yet you tell me all attempts at having it removed, including chemical peels, produced no effect whatsoever."

"So you're saying," Ben started, and stopped just as quickly. "What are you saying?"

"Because we're dealing with something utterly unprecedented, its origins must be similarly unprecedented. If you'd allow me to consult with some experts, share your—"

"I'm also paying for your confidentiality, Doctor," Ben interrupted.

The experience deep down inside that cave in the Yucatán eighteen years earlier had scared Ben. But finding out he was sick with a deadly, incurable disease had scared him even more. And now this. Kirsch had said little, virtually nothing, Ben hadn't considered himself at some point. Confirmation of his worst suspicions, though, added a grim finality to the picture. But he couldn't let the truth get out at this point, not under any circumstances.

"I'm well aware of that, Mr. Younger, and I signed your nondisclosure agreements to that effect. But I'm hoping the circumstances call for an exception, so I can contact specialists who may be able to help where I've failed."

"And turn me into a pincushion with tests and experiments? Spend my last days as a lab monkey?" Ben shook his head demonstrably. "I don't think so, Doctor. And, besides, there's something else I need to tell you," he said to Kirsch.

# FIFTY-THREE

### New York City, 2008

You disappoint me, Professor," Dale Denton said to Orson Beekman, in his sprawling office on the sixtieth floor of the tower housing the New York headquarters of Western Energy Technologies.

"I wish I had better news."

Denton rose from his desk and moved to a sun-drenched section of the floor-to-ceiling window glass that followed the office's rounded edges. The illusion created was that it was a single, unbroken pane, as if blown into place from scratch to conform to the building's odd shape, which wasn't far from the truth. The sun was so hot and strong, it baked Denton's skin, made him think he was out exploring an oil field somewhere years back when such things were important. When an especially solid yield seemed like all the money in the world, starting back in the Yucatán.

He turned from the glass, face flushed red from the burn and heat of the sun. "Eighteen years," he said, shaking his head. "Eighteen years I've been giving you everything you've asked for. Never skimped when it came to filling your shopping list. And this is what I've got to show for it? Nothing. Nada. Shit."

"You know the phrase a needle in a haystack?" Beekman said, defensively. "This is ten thousand times harder, because we can't even find the haystack, not after that earthquake destroyed the cave system where Ben Younger first found the rock. And we need to consider something else."

"What?"

"That maybe we can't find the rock because it *can't* be found, by us or anybody else, because it doesn't want to be found, or isn't supposed to be found."

"That's insane."

"Is it?"

"It's a rock, Professor."

"If it was just a rock, you wouldn't have spent all these years and all this money trying to find it."

"Figure of speech," Denton retorted. "And once we find it, I'm convinced we'll be looking at that money as the most worthwhile investment Western Energy Technologies has ever made."

"Or something we'll be regretting for the rest of our lives. Theoretically," Beekman qualified.

"Like there was *theoretically* oil in the Yucatán, the field that saved our collective asses, you mean? I've got a pretty good track record when it comes to such things. Risk equals reward, something I don't expect you to understand, because you follow science, while I follow my gut. That's what makes who we are." Denton's gaze bore into Beekman sententiously. "And who we're not. Ben Younger touched that rock you can't find, and all of a sudden oil blows into the air. He ends up more than a mile away, with no memory of how he got there. Then he goes home and his infertile wife gets pregnant, his son born with a mark identical to the one touching the rock left on his palm. I miss anything theoretical there?"

Denton waited for Beekman to answer, resumed when he didn't.

"How many times have I asked you for a rational explanation to any of those things and how many times have you provided one? Zero, Professor, because they don't exist. Remember what you said after your initial evaluation, weighing all the available data, the power it would take to force all the oil up through the ground, so much so fast?"

Beekman nodded. "Speaking hypothetically, I called the rock an immeasurable, but also inexplicable source of energy."

"And I've never forgotten that original assessment. Give me instinct over knowledge any day, Professor, and on that day you were speaking from your gut, what you believed that rock had done and could do—that's what I still believe, even if you don't. And I'm going to tell you something else. We're going to find that rock, no matter what it takes. And if you can't get the job done, I'll bring in somebody who can."

Beekman looked chilled, even through the streaming rays of sunlight striking him. "It doesn't matter who you bring in. The earthquake that struck the region a decade ago was a seven-point-three, spawning aftershocks more than powerful enough to bury that rock in a billion tons of rubble."

Denton scowled, his face glowing in the sunlight. "We're going to find that rock. You want to call that a fool's errand based on greed, go ahead; I call it ambition."

Denton was waiting for Beekman's response when he heard the voice of Ben Younger instead.

"You mind giving us a minute, Professor?"

"Leave it alone, Dale," Ben resumed, after Beekman had shuffled past him, taking his leave and closing the door.

Denton stepped away from the glass into a dark, shadowy patch between decorative pillars, the one spot in the office untouched by the gleaming light. "This isn't your call, partner. You should read the nuts and bolts of our partnership agreement again."

"I have and I've also been reading the balance sheets. And, you know what, they don't add up. Whole bunch of money's missing—tens of millions, maybe much more, siphoned off over a whole lot of years. Started when we were a private company, just you and me, but we're not going to be private much longer and how do you think our shareholders would react to learning the IRS was coming to do a forensic audit?"

In the shadowy patch of his office, Denton's face looked drained of color. "They aren't."

"They will be, if you don't give up the hunt for that rock now, Dale. I can see the headlines in the *Wall Street Journal*: 'Oil Tycoon Indicted on Fraud, Corruption, and Embezzlement Charges.'"

"It's your company too, Ben, at least it was until your marbles deserted you. Is crazy something you can catch? Because your goddamn wife's been singing loony tunes since your loser of a son was born, and now she must have you singing along. Why don't you just stand back and smell the money? Jesus fucking Christ, we're about to go public here and become richer than we ever imagined."

"It's not just me," Ben said, leaving it there as he glanced at the mark on his hand. "And you misappropriated funds to keep this search going and keep the shareholders in the dark. In the corporate world, that's called stealing. Think that might scare off an investor or two when we issue our IPO?"

"Is that a threat, partner?"

"Does it need to be?"

Denton shook his head, trying to chuckle. "You'd destroy everything we've built?"

"The rock you're looking for, if found, could destroy a shitload more than that."

"You can't know that."

"Yes, I can, and I do. I'll spare you the details for now. That will change if you don't pull up stakes and suspend the search, in which case all bets would be off."

Denton took a few steps closer to him. "You really don't look too good, Ben. You should go home, get some rest, and leave all this to me."

"I think I'll stay right here."

"Suit yourself." Denton stopped, his expression changing, as if he'd donned a different mask. "Maybe I was too generous."

"Excuse me?"

"Remember what your initial investment was in us, in all this, in the Yucatán? Zero. You came to me with a plan to get rich without a single penny to your name. I'm sure I wasn't the first. How many others turned you down, before you came to me and played the friendship card?"

"None," Ben said, with no hesitation at all, his tone remaining surprisingly measured, "because you *were* the first. First and only. But that would never have happened, if I'd known where the money came from."

"Not all of it, partner," Denton said, advancing toward him and stopping just short of a wide swath of sunlight which now seemed to form a barrier between them. "I lost all my cash in securing the permits, the initial surveys, the crews, the equipment, the digging. And when that ran out, I went to the street, because that's the only place I could get the kind of money we needed to finish the job."

"What would've happened if we hadn't found oil?"

"We would've been dead," Denton told him bluntly. "Broke, failures, done, dead—I don't really see the distinction. Who gives a fuck?"

"You should have asked me," Ben insisted, staring him in the eye. "Just like you should've asked me about this search of yours, for that rock. And just like going public with the company."

"We discussed that."

"It was more you informing me of your plans."

"Right, my plans to make us both richer than rich. And, as I recall, you didn't argue much at the time. Hey, you want out, Ben. Just say the word."

"I want out. I'm saying the word."

At that, Ben watched Denton prance behind his desk, looking more through than at him, as if he wasn't even there.

"Okay," Denton said, pretending to check his stack of accumulated mail, "bye. It was nice while it lasted."

Ben didn't move. "That's it?"

"You were expecting a gold watch, a severance package, a kiss and a hug maybe?"

"I still own half of this company. It's not as simple as walking out the door and closing it behind me."

"Yes, it is, because you own squat."

Ben drew up even with Denton's big desk. "You want to say that again?"

"You heard me. And, on the chance you didn't, check our original partnership agreement. See what you got for all your sweat equity."

"I don't have to. Everything's fifty-fifty, an even split."

Denton grinned, a poker player knowing he was holding the winning hand. "I'm talking about the fact that if you want to sell your shares, you can do so only to me. And, guess what? I'm not interested in buying them right now. Means you're stuck, partner. In addition, any distribution or profits on an annual basis, according to our partnership agreement, is to be decided by management. And since I'm the CEO and Chairman of the Board of Directors, I've decided to distribute zilch, zero, nada. But I'm a nice guy, so you can keep drawing your salary, for as long as you're alive. After you're dead and buried, it'll be like you were never in the building."

"That's bullshit."

Denton shook his head. "It was. It isn't anymore. If you want to try and sue, go right ahead. But then the facts that our books don't balance would inevitably come out and then we'd both get nothing. One of us goes down, or to jail, we both go. How's that tune ring to you?"

Ben felt something tugging at his insides. "So buy me out and let's be done with it. Just because we share the same skyscraper doesn't mean we have to share the same jail cell."

Denton stifled a laugh. "Buy you out? Why would I do that, why would I consider giving you even a penny with you knocking on death's door?" He let his point sink in, watched the color drain from Ben Younger's face before continuing. "You think I wouldn't find out? You want me to buy you out? I'll bury the goddamn check in your grave. I shouldn't have to remind you that, according to our partnership agreement, in the event one of us dies, he grants full ownership to the other partner. Unless I buy you out, which I have no intention of doing, since I'll own all your shares free and clear once you kick the bucket. Know what that means, partner? It means your crazy wife and, especially, your whack job of a son won't get squat. I'd rather eat the money and shit it out, before letting him get his hands on anything. 'Mad Max,' I hear they call him in school, according to Vicky."

Ben's phone buzzed with an incoming text message before he could respond.

"I have to go," Ben said, after reading it.

"The hell with that."

Ben had already started for the door. "We can finish this later."

"Hey, as far as I'm concerned it's finished already, and so are you. But I'll tell you this, partner. You keep your piece of shit son away from my daughter. You think I don't know where he gets his genes, that what's killing you is probably the same thing that's made him batshit crazy? You think that mark on his palm is the only thing he inherited from you? Man oh man, does nutso run in your family or what?"

Ben held up his palm for Denton to see. "You've spent millions of dollars looking for the rock that did this. Maybe you should look in the mirror."

# FIFTY-FOUR

### The Vatican, 2008

I have a new assignment for you, my friend," Cardinal Josef Martenko told Father Pascal Jimenez, as they strolled through the Vatican gardens. "One I believe is a better fit for your area of expertise."

"My work spreading the word of Christ along the Horn of Africa disappoints you?"

"No, Pascal. In fact, it's exemplary. You've proven a wonderful emissary for the church and His teachings."

"That is my area of expertise, Your Eminence."

"Pascal, please. Do you recall what transpired in the aftermath of the eclipse?"

Jimenez nodded. "How could I forget? I'd been wandering in the jungle for who knows how long when I finally made it back to the Catholic mission you were running."

"You'd been wandering for days."

"I don't remember much of it, hardly anything."

"But you recognized that a miracle had saved your life, Pascal. How God made that heathen traitor spare you. How the sky darkened, and when the light returned, he was gone."

*Your God is not here.*

Cambridge's words, spoken with smug self-assurance, had haunted Jimenez ever since. As it turned out, though, God must've been there, and that fact had left an indelible impression on Jimenez, making him see the world in an entirely different light. His dazed trek through the jungle that followed ended when he collapsed at then Father Martenko's feet, dreaming in his fugue state of the priest framed by an ocean of light extending a hand down to show him a new way. In that moment, Pascal Jimenez had glimpsed his future, and for the last fourteen years had served the church to the best of his ability, never letting his own experience with God stray too far.

Jimenez watched Martenko's flat expression grow reflective, even nostalgic, his robes billowing in the stiff breeze, casting the illusion that he was floating rather than walking. "You described it all for me, once you regained consciousness. You told me you wanted to give yourself to the church, that it was the only outlet for your newfound faith. And who could blame you after what you'd experienced? And yet you chose Africa for your posting. You think I didn't know why?"

"I know you did."

"Because you thought your path might cross with that lunatic monster again."

"Because I wanted to protect others from him. Turn them to the graces of God, so they'd know how to fight the devil. I felt I owed that much to God, after He spared my life."

Martenko nodded, as if Jimenez had made his point for him. "And that mission has served you well, prepared you for the next stage of your service to Him and His holy church. These are difficult times for the world, Pascal.

"There is so much violence taking place everywhere, on a scale unprecedented since the horrors of World War Two. With wars over religion breaking out and continuing everywhere, people's faith is being put to the test, and they are searching more than ever, even groping at times, for something to believe in. That has led to an unprecedented rise in the reporting of very odd events or, as they are prematurely labeled, purported miracles. Unexplained phenomena the most faithful of our flock wish to leave at God's door."

"So long as they come to God's door, what does it matter what brought them there?"

"Because they have come to Christ, hoping Christ will come to them. Better that faith be kept to achievable limits lest the church become a victim of their misplaced expectations. Indeed, we must manage those expectations, Pascal, control them before they create their own narrative."

"And where do I come in?"

Cardinal Martenko, a lowly priest himself when they'd first met seventeen years before, stopped and turned to face Jimenez. "The Miracle Commission I oversee is woefully understaffed. I'd like you to come on board as the chief investigator, reporting directly to me."

Jimenez stiffened, gazing back as if wishing he could rewind the path they'd taken through the garden. "I'm happy in Africa, Your Eminence."

"The church has bigger plans for you, my friend, important plans."

Jimenez felt Martenko lay both hands on his shoulders. He wasn't a strong man, nor a big one, but his hands held a strength and heaviness that had always been able to mold Jimenez in their grasp. He felt that happening now, felt himself bending to Martenko's will.

"You think it wasn't God who brought you to my door all those years ago, Pascal? You think you weren't delivered on to me for a reason? A *scientist* who had suddenly found God? We helped that man find his faith, salvage hope from a horrible experience, lend renewed purpose to his life. We took that man and made him a priest." Martenko's soft stare became pointed. "Now we need the scientist again. What better qualifications to investigate these proclaimed miracles and determine their efficacy? Who better qualified, and with more credibility, than a servant of God who is also a man of science?"

"I haven't been a man of science for many years, Your Eminence."

Martenko's gaze narrowed, and then slowly widened again. "You've taught natives the principles of irrigation, food preservation, gotten them to accept inoculation from disease. Apparently you've never stopped being a man of science."

"I was speaking figuratively."

"So was I. Your skills are exactly what the church requires, Pascal. The world is changing. We never beat the media to the site of a purported miracle any longer—sometimes we even learn of them *from* the media. I'll make sure your assignments are kept to areas where science is involved and an assessment based on your particular areas of expertise is required." Cardinal Martenko paused briefly. "Do you trust me, Pascal?"

"I owe you so much, Your Eminence, everything."

"Debt isn't the same thing as trust, my friend."

"I trust you."

"Then you must trust I'm proposing this reassignment, this *promotion*, in keeping your best interests in mind as well. Your base of knowledge makes you a valuable asset for the Vatican in these difficult times, if utilized properly. When we debunk a miracle, it's because we didn't know enough, and on the rare occasions that we acknowledge one, we're told we know too much. You represent the happy medium, possessing a rare credibility for someone in this position." Martenko stopped again and squeezed Jimenez's shoulders affectionately. "So, have I convinced you?"

"I'm afraid."

"I told you, we'll keep you away from areas where you're more likely to revisit the past."

"I'm afraid of losing my faith, Your Eminence," Jimenez elaborated. "It's all I have now, and disproving miracles is no way to maintain it."

"And what if there were some miracles you weren't expected to disprove, one especially so that requires immediate attention?"

Jimenez leaned forward, his attention captured. "If this is the path you've chosen for me . . ."

"It's not me who's chosen it for you, Pascal, it's our heavenly Father Himself."

"In any event, I shall take it."

Martenko nodded, smiling tightly. "That's good, because we have a private jet at Ciampino Airport waiting to take you to your first assignment."

# FIFTY-FIVE

## Western Iraq, 2008

The air smelled like blood for good reason, Mohammed al-Qadir thought, as he walked amid the aftermath of the ambush.

Al-Qadir heard a moaning sound and moved to the far side of a toppled troop carrier where an American soldier missing a leg had crawled into the lee of the vehicle, the stench of the man's blood adding to the soak of the smell in the air. The man looked at him, following his approach weakly with his eyes. Remaining silent when al-Qadir stood over him.

Al-Qadir could feel death coming to take the American soldier, and knelt by the dying young man, feeling the life, the very essence, ebbing out of him. Felt around through his fatigue pants pockets until he found what all Western soldiers carried: pictures of their loved ones.

He'd been waiting for the convoy at this spot along the hard-packed road that wound through the desert, stitching the desolate villages, towns, and cities together while providing a lifeline in the form of supplies and security. The IEDs, improvised explosive devices, had gone off both around the convoy and beneath the roadbed. Not all the trucks were hit, but enough were struck to send them spiraling into each other, kicking up huge plumes of dust and gravel. And when the plumes cleared, there were the horrible screams and the smell of blood that continued to thicken in the air, as al-Qadir's men emerged to gun down the survivors offering further resistance. Gleefully massacring them.

Al-Qadir watched his men then round up the survivors who'd surrendered to exploit as prisoners by beheading or burning them on camera. As one of the leaders of Al Qaeda in Iraq, he looked at this blessed moment as payback for the military surge that America had already proclaimed a smashing success. A violent response to the violence the Americans and the West in general had brought to this country.

Al-Qadir stood back up over the one-legged American soldier who was slowly bleeding to death, holding the two pictures of the man's family in either hand. Wife and kids in one, just the kids in the second. Plump cherubs with sweet faces and loving eyes.

Al-Qadir looked back down at the American who had raised a shuddering hand into the air, as if to ask for the pictures back. Instead, al-Qadir dropped them onto the roadbed pooled with gasoline spilled from the trucks' ruptured tanks. He watched the American grope for the snapshots, straining to grab hold but failing, since al-Qadir had placed them purposely mere inches out of the man's grasp.

"I know where my road leads now," he said suddenly, addressing the dying soldier without having planned to. "And I want to thank you, thank all of you, for helping to show me the way. My destination isn't a country or a place; it's a fated place in the history I am determined to change. The road leads to your wife and children, who will be struck down brutally in the passage of time, just as you were here today."

The American launched a final, desperate push to reach the pictures, almost grasping them, before al-Qadir eased them aside with the toe of his boot.

"I didn't realize all of it until recently," al-Qadir continued, "or what my fated role was to be. But your petulance, your arrogance, your invasion and surge has helped guide me the rest of the way toward fulfillment. I see now that we need not come to you, that you will continue coming to us, as the war our two sides are fighting sets the stage for the End Times.

"Smell that?" al-Qadir continued after a brief pause. "It's the stench of death and defeat and someday soon, your entire world will be rich with it."

The dying soldier kept clawing for the old, dog-eared snapshots and al-Qadir kept easing them away from his grasp, while always leaving them tantalizingly close.

"You are blessed, truly blessed, to face the man who will visit the wrath of the one true God on mankind. That makes you a pioneer of sorts, the first of the infidels to venture down a road as figurative as it is literal, in your case anyway. Your reward for that is being spared the pain of what is to come."

Al-Qadir lit a match and shielded the flame from the wind with his sinewy frame that was knobby with muscle.

"Now you must witness the pain of what it is to be, a pioneer once more."

Al-Qadir dropped the match directly atop the snapshots that had frayed even more under his boot. Watched the American flail for them one last time, before realizing that the flames consuming them were already following the line of gasoline toward him.

Mohammed al-Qadir had already walked away when the American's high-pitched, shrill screams started. They persisted for several moments, during which al-Qadir stepped back to watch the smoke rising over the remnants of the convoy. As the dying soldier's screams reached their peak, he saw the smoke twisting around itself and seeming to thicken. Forming into *something*, terrible and wonderful at the same time. Al-Qadir thought he glimpsed a gaping mouth, eyes that were actually flames, and teeth formed by the light sneaking through. Something was coming to life, finding shape and purpose in the air and the blood and the despair of dying men.

Al-Qadir reveled in the sight, awestruck in anticipation of what its final shape might be. Those flaming red eyes seeming to regard him for one blessed moment before the American's screams began to fade, and whatever was forming faded with it.

It was gone the moment they ended, just coarse black smoke before him again, that rose in diminishing clouds for the sky. But al-Qadir didn't fret, because he knew something far larger, and more ominous, was forming even now, adding strength and sustenance with each life he took. He had no idea what it would look like once complete, or when that time would come exactly.

Only that he would be there when it did.

# FIFTY-SIX

## New York City, 2008

Ben Younger left his car in a red zone, checking the text message from his son Max one more time to make sure he had the address right. A flophouse on the lower West Side with a faded, washed-out marquee advertising rooms for rent by the hour.

He opened the door to the SUV and started to climb out, only to be struck by a wave of dizziness. The world turned to black and white, all the color washed out of it, the scene beyond taking on the surreal feel of an old movie. His ability to follow motion too was affected, people moving in stops and starts, the moments lost between them even though his eyes stayed open. The worst symptoms had started three months back, just glimpses of those which lingered for increasingly longer durations, leaving him, inevitably, in the kind of cold sweat he felt starting to drench him now.

Ben squeezed his eyes closed and tried to find a happy memory, a happy thought. Opened them after thirty seconds to find the color still washed from the world. When he closed them again, he tried to think of nothing, but his thoughts turned to Max anyway, what it meant for the boy's health and future that he bore the identical mark on his palm.

This time, when he opened his eyes, the color had returned to the world, and the wave of dizziness and nausea had abated. Before it could return, Ben yanked open the door and strode straight for the elevator, paying a clerk perched within a cubicle enclosed by steel grating no heed, even when his voice shouted after him.

"Hey! *Hey!*"

Ben took the elevator to the third floor, the room number from Max's text message committed to memory now. The room in question had a shiny door latch that didn't match the others along the hall, as if the last one had been broken by a well-placed boot or ram.

Ben tried the knob, knocked when it didn't turn.

His son Max answered, almost eighteen now, still looking much more like a boy than a man. Long, floppy hair covering his ears and face all the way to his brow, and a scruffy beard more the result of laziness with a razor than an attempt to grow one. His naturally athletic, muscular frame, nothing like Ben's, or his mother Melissa's for that matter, contained in a black leather jacket and shapeless jeans worn over black lace-up boots.

"Dad."

The word stretching out his lips to make it sound like two syllables.

"She's in here," Max continued, easing the door all the way open. "On the bed."

Ben closed the door behind him and spotted Vicky Denton lying on her back, arms spread eagle. Her mouth hung open, drool sliding down one side, the gaping window unable to chase the stench of vomit Max must have cleaned up from the room.

"What's she on?"

"Ecstasy. I think."

"You think?"

"It's what she told me she was buying. But she had a stash of Vikes and Oxy too," Max elaborated, referring to Vicodin and Oxycodone. "I found out who her dealer is," the boy finished, and left it there.

It was the way he left it, together with the restrained conviction painted over features gone utterly flat, that left Ben unsettled. He'd seen that look before from his son, not often but often enough, and what followed was never pleasant.

"You didn't call a rescue," Ben said, in what had started out as a question.

"Vicky made me promise not to, before she passed out. So I called you instead."

Ben was no doctor, nor a paramedic, but his many adventures and visits to exotic or, at least, distant places left him quite the expert on all things first aid, from splinting broken bones to recognizing the symptoms of some dangerous disease. But he'd had no experience with drug overdoses. Still, he moved to the bed and checked Vicky's pulse and vitals.

"I did that already," Max told him. "Besides being zonked on drugs, she's fine. Otherwise, I would've broken my promise and called nine-one-one."

Ben checked her pupils with a grimy lamp held before her eyes and made sure her breathing was regular.

"What's wrong, Dad?"

"You need to ask me that?"

"I'm talking about with you. You're sweating like you just stepped out of a steam room."

"Try raising a seventeen-year-old."

"Eighteen before you know it And, no, I'm not going to ask you for a car again."

Ben tried to smile, unsettled as always by his son's proclivity for staying one step ahead of him, always seeming to be several seconds ahead of the rest of the world. When Max was a younger boy, they'd set a goal of climbing the tallest peak on every continent. They'd climbed Kilimanjaro when Max was all of thirteen, and he'd saved both their lives by pulling both of them to safety, seconds before a world-shaking rumble preceded an avalanche that would've otherwise entombed them. Another time Max had yelled "Stop!" at a green light, and Ben had jammed on the brakes just in time to avoid a car flying through the intersection that otherwise would've obliterated their car.

Their list of peaks to scale remained unfinished, most notably Everest, and Ben felt a lump form in his throat, needing to choke off tears every time he considered they may have climbed their last mountain together.

"My car's parked just outside," he told Max, clearing his throat to disguise it cracking. "If we can get her walking, that's her taxi home."

"To our place. Please, Dad, until she sobers up."

Ben nodded grudgingly, as much because he could never say no to Max, as to spare Vicky Dale Denton's wrath, especially today. Matter of fact, he kind of liked the idea of sticking it to the son of a bitch.

He moved aside to let Max tend to Vicky, see if he could rouse her.

"What's his name, Max?"

"Who?"

"Vicky's drug dealer."

"I don't know."

"You said you did."

"I must've meant I will. After I talk to Vicky," the boy said, turning enough his way for Ben to catch that look again.

*Mad Max* . . .

That's what Dale Denton had said the kids at school called his son. It was why Max had never played organized sports, even though he was one of the best athletes at every school he'd attended. The boy had tried, really had after his father pushed him, but things had happened.

Strange things.

Bad things.

Inexplicable things.

He'd told Dr. Kirsch that Max was born with a birthmark identical in all respects to the one touching the rock had left on him, the very touch that was killing him now. And he'd already snatched a hair sample from the brush the boy seldom used to work his tangles of waves into shape, and brought it to CyberGen, so Max's DNA could be tested. See if the boy had inherited whatever was afflicting Ben.

The mere possibility set him trembling. He'd long been convinced that touching the rock that had left its mark, had been responsible for the miracle of Max's birth. The fact that it might also be responsible for his premature death was unthinkable, a strange and bizarre twisting of circumstances that threatened to render Ben's entire life meaningless.

"Leave me alone," Vicky moaned, her words slurring together, as she slapped Max's hand away.

"I'm done leaving you alone," the boy said back to her, kissing her lightly on the forehead. "Look what happens when I leave you alone. But it won't be happening again. I'm going to see to that. Promise."

The unspoken message in Max's words left Ben chilled. He shut his mind to the thought, as Vicky began to stir.

"I think I can get her walking, Dad," Max was saying. "We can get her to the car."

And they did, Max riding in the backseat of the Mercedes SUV the whole way back to their Park Avenue penthouse. They drove straight into the garage, the parking space just a short walk from the elevator that served only the penthouse levels.

Ben had doctors he could summon discreetly, if Vicky's condition worsened, or she lost consciousness again. But she was sitting up, by the time they pulled into the garage, smacking her lips dryly and begging for a mint or stick of gum to chase the bitter taste from her mouth. Otherwise, she remained silent, clearly embarrassed and not really addressing Ben until he threw the Mercedes into park.

"Thanks, Ben."

She'd called him that since she could talk, while Max always called Dale "Mr. Denton," when he called him anything at all.

They took the private elevator to the penthouse floor. Vicky clung to Max, seemed ready to melt into him, while Ben got the ornate fire door unlocked and held it open so Max could ease her through into the penthouse. Steering straight for his room, Ben noticed, as opposed to the guest room, his boots clacking against the bamboo flooring.

Ben's wife Melissa appeared moments later, strands of rosary beads threaded through both hands. She had that "glow" about her that characterized her personal prayer sessions. Maybe the rosy glow came from the warmth over communing directly with God, a practice that started almost from the day Max was born, but had been ramped up substantially as of late. Or maybe the rosy glow was more of a heat flash, thanks to keeping the spare bedroom she'd transformed into her prayer hostel too warm.

"He's not happy," she said, her expression tight and pained. "He's angry at us, Ben."

"Who?"

"God."

"I don't really have time for this now."

She moved to block his path. "You need to find it. Because I know bad times are coming, not just for us—for everyone. We must all pray, the three of us together, to forgive the sins behind what's coming. We're the ones who spawned it. Lilith told me that, and she's been right about everything she's always told me for years."

"Lilith," Ben repeated, shaking his head, "the little girl again . . . Did you take your pills?"

"No. I can't hear Him when I take the pills. I need to keep my mind lucid, be sure I don't miss anything. It makes my head hurt, but I don't care."

"You need to take your pills, Missy. I'll get them for you."

He started to move away, but she clamped a hand onto his arm. "He's worried about Max."

"Who?"

"The Lord. I've been waiting to tell you what He said."

"I want you to take your pills before you tell me."

Melissa nodded, grudgingly. "I'll come with you."

They went into the kitchen together where Ben pulled one pill each from three separate prescription bottles, handed them to his wife along with a glass of water, and made sure she swallowed them down.

"Lilith said Max's soul is soiled, that he belongs to the Beast."

"She's got things wrong," Ben said, unable to help himself. "There's nothing wrong with Max's soul. He's as good and kind a boy as there is."

"Lilith said Max was evil. And you know she's right, Ben. You've seen the things Max can do as well as I have."

Ben bristled. I have no idea what you're talking about."

"Yes, you do. You just can't see it as clearly as I can, because you haven't turned your ears to His word. Once you do, it'll all be crystal clear. We need to help Max embrace the Lord, Ben. It's his only hope."

Ben could see her eyes growing sluggish and distant, as the medication began to take hold. Just a few more minutes, he told himself.

"He brought that girl home," Melissa was saying now. "The devil's spawn."

"He just wants to help her."

"Oh, I know what he wants. She corrupts him, turns him from the good."

"They're just friends, Missy. They've known each other all their lives."

"We need to get him away from her, Ben. Lilith told me that too. She, she's bad for Max. She . . ." Melissa looked dazed, her eyes glazed over. "Where was I? I can't, I can't remember."

"I need to check on them."

"Check on *who*? I think I need to lie down. Can I lie down?"

"I think that's a good idea," Ben said, and led her into the bedroom.

"You need to watch him closely," Melissa said, as he sat down with her on the edge of the bed. "And when you watch him, you need to see what Lilith warned me about. It's there, but you have to let yourself see it."

Ben eased her back, sliding a pair of pillows in place and positioning them just the way she liked.

"Promise me you'll do that, Ben, promise me!"

"I promise," Ben lied.


A private investigator he had on the payroll showed Denton the feed from the security camera outside some flophouse Denton couldn't identify.

"That's your daughter entering the building, and here she is leaving."

He froze the screen on Victoria being supported by Max Younger, her boots turned inward, indicating her feet had been dragging. Another figure had advanced ahead of them, visible only from the rear. Denton couldn't identify him, but he could identify the SUV toward which the man appeared to be walking.

"You want me to handle this, sir?" the cop asked him, his droll monotone indicating that was nothing new for him.

"No," said Denton, rising from his chair set before the laptop the cop had set down before him, "I think I'll handle this one myself."


"He said he'd send me away if this happened again," Vicky told Max, rivulets of water from the bottle he'd given her dribbling out her lips, until she swiped a sleeve lightly across them.

"Rehab?"

"Worse. Boarding school."

"Hey, I hear those places have the best drugs. . . . Er, that was a joke."

"Ha-ha."

Max pushed the hair from his face and felt it drop back down over his brow. "He's not going to send you away."

"No? And why's that?"

"Because I'm not going to let him."

Vicky turned away atop Max's rumpled bedcovers. He'd been sitting adjacent to her on the bed's edge, but now he lay down next to her, looking up from the second pairing of pillows. Clasped his hands behind his head and fixed his gaze on the paint swirls on the ceiling.

"You don't know my father, Max. He's a *fucking* monster."

Max laughed.

"What's funny about that?"

"Nothing, but you swearing is."

"Fuck," Vicky said.

Max laughed.

And then they were cuddling, Max's face lost in her thick hair that was dampened at the edges by sweat, but still smelled of lilacs thanks to her floral-scented shampoo. Vicky ran her hand through his hair, the way she knew he liked.

"You look like a rock star."

"I get mistaken for one all the time."

"Which?"

"I forget now. It's not important."

Vicky sighed. "I wish I had your dad."

"I don't, because then we'd be brother and sister."

"We're already like twins. Born on the same day, same frigging blood type that, like, nobody else has, and practically raised together."

"But not related," Max reminded.

"Don't let my father send me away, Max. Please."

"I won't. My dad will help."

"Your dad's no match for him."

"And I am?"

Vicky slid from his grasp and propped herself up, the life back in her eyes. "I've got an idea."

Ben opened the door to find Dale Denton standing there, dwarfed by a trio of his private security guards, all ex-military. They barged past him before saying a word.

"Where is she?" Denton asked, sweeping his eyes about the foyer and penthouse great room beyond.

"Who?"

"You know damn well who. Vicky, my daughter. You and that hooligan son of yours were spotted picking her up outside a rat's nest of a hotel. I'm not sure if I should kick the shit out of you, or thank you for interrupting whatever they were up to."

"That's not what happened."

"Then what *did* happen?"

Ben wasn't about to say. "You'll have to ask Vicky about that." He watched Denton's three goons take up posts in the foyer, stopping just short of searching the penthouse without permission.

"Victoria," Denton corrected. "My daughter's name is Victoria."

"Not according to her."

Denton took a step closer, getting in Ben's face, glowering. "Listen, partner, you want to argue with me about business, that's your right. But when it comes to my daughter, keep the fuck away. Now, where is she?"

Ben shrugged. "Dale, look—"

"*Where* is she, Ben? Tell me how you'd be feeling right now, if the roles were reversed."

Ben nodded. Grudgingly.


He led the way along the back hall to Max's room. Only Denton accompanied him, his three goons remaining behind in the foyer.

"She needs help, Dale."

"We all need help." Denton started on again without him. "I'm getting my daughter and getting the fuck out of here. I don't want to hear another word from you."

"Suit yourself," Ben said.

But when he hurried to catch up with Denton, he felt suddenly weak and light-headed. He leaned against the wall for support, started to slump down it.

"Careful there, partner," Denton said, from in front of Max's door. "A man in your condition shouldn't be overexerting himself." Denton tried the door. "It's locked."

Ben pushed himself back to his feet and staggered to Max's room, knocking on the door.

"Max?"

No answer.

"Max!" Ben tried louder, banging on the door this time.

When Max still didn't answer, Denton threw a shoulder into it and shattered the door even with the knob. He surged inside, but froze with Ben just behind him.

Because the room was empty.

# FIFTY-SEVEN

### Siberia, Russia; 2008

T he private jet landed at Tolmachevo Airport, twenty miles from the city of Novosibirsk, an industrial and scientific center in Siberia and also Russia's third largest city. It wasn't the closest airport to the site of what Father Jimenez would be investigating on behalf of the Vatican's Miracle Commission, but it was the only one where they could obtain permission to land. A six-hour drive would follow to the site in question.

The town of Kusk here in West Siberia where something unimaginable had happened.

"Understand something, Pascal," Martenko had warned him back at the Vatican. "Not everything the Vatican investigates is the purported work of God. Much of what we do involves quite the opposite."

"Exorcisms, that sort of thing?"

"If by that sort of thing, you're referring to the devil, then yes. In some regions disproving his involvement in something is far more important than proving the involvement of the Almighty."

"I didn't think Siberia was one of them."

"It isn't, per se. This particular case warrants an exception."

"By which you mean . . ."

Jimenez let the thought dangle, expecting Martenko to complete it. Clouds had rolled in, covering the sun over the Vatican gardens, making for a much better fit for the look on Martenko's face.

"Politics, Pascal," Martenko said finally, "in this case coming in a formal request from the leader of the Russian Orthodox Church, Patriarch Aleksey II, himself responding to widespread panic and wild rumors spreading through the area. Superstition is winning out and, when that happens, the devil is winning too."

"Politics indeed, especially given the Russian Orthodox Church's rocky relationship with the Vatican."

"I'm glad you're a student of the world," Martenko nodded. "It inspires me to have even more faith in your ability to carry out this assignment. You're going to a town called Kusk in the Krasnoyarsk Krai area. Population until two days ago, nearly two thousand."

"What happened two days ago?" Jimenez asked, as if he really didn't want to hear the answer.

"They all died, violently and inexplicably, each and every resident. Women, children, the elderly—no one was spared. I tried to look at the pictures, Pascal, but I couldn't past the first couple, and yet what I saw will haunt me for the rest of my days. Any probing by the Russian press has been slowed, if not halted altogether, by the Kremlin, and the army has taken control of the area."

Jimenez knew the early postings of Martenko's career in the church, including Nigeria, had subjected him to all manner of atrocity. So for him to make such a statement carried a significant degree of portent on its own.

He waited for Cardinal Martenko to continue, looking suddenly small in his billowing robes. "They died by their own hands, Pascal. Killed each other. Families, friends, loved ones, neighbors, even infants . . . They were found torn apart. Literally."


The cardinal had gone on to explain how the town was served by the Russian Orthodox Church and how church officials had petitioned the Russian government to request Vatican involvement in the form of an investigation. While acceding reluctantly to those demands, that government had officially requested that the Vatican keep its involvement confidential. In spite of that, rampantly spreading rumors were flying, in lieu of any rational explanation for what had happened. Most of these involved superstition and the devil in some form, a wild myth that at this point could be debunked only at the highest levels of the Catholic Church to calm the local population. The Russian government, known for its penchant for controlling any situation, had proven utterly unable to control this one, and that made them even more concerned about containing it. Word had leaked out and was spreading fast, reaching the cities by now, even though the government had imposed a news blackout. But that blackout hadn't stopped the Russian people from fanning the rumors that extended well beyond Moscow's ability to contain them.

And yet forcing the Vatican jet to land so far away, when there must've been airfields closer to Kusk, represented a feeble attempt to create the illusion that the government still had a handle on the unprecedented tragedy. The deteriorating weather conditions, light snow expected to grow into a blizzard, provided a convenient excuse in this regard, as well as to keep the curious out of the area until the proper "sanitation" procedures were completed. Jimenez knew that, especially in a case like this, a priest who possessed his level of scientific acumen was in the best position possible to dispel the kind of myths and rumors likely to otherwise take on a life all their own, as had already been somewhat demonstrated by superstitious tales of a small town supposedly visited by the devil himself.

He was met at the airport by Father Alexi Sremski, an emissary dispatched by Patriarch Aleksey II himself to serve the Vatican's needs, as well as act as an intermediary with the Russian government and military. Sremski was a short, stout, bald man who dressed in full ceremonial robes in spite of the rigors of the journey and deteriorating weather that was confronting them.

"You've been to this town already?" Jimenez asked him, after greetings were exchanged.

Sremski nodded, the motion seeming to genuinely pain him. "And now I know what Hell looks like. You've heard the reports of a meteor strike somewhere in the area of the town?"

Jimenez felt a chill surge through him. "No, I hadn't."

"Among the last confirmed contacts with the people of Kusk were several calls received in the aftermath of the strike, forty-eight hours or so before all contact was lost. But there's no evidence of anything even resembling a crater anywhere in the area."

Jimenez nodded, trying to push the trepidation he was suddenly feeling as far back in his consciousness as he could. Mention of a potential asteroid strike in the area rekindled too many memories, stoked too many fears.

Their three-vehicle convoy, Jimenez and Sremski's sandwiched by two Russian military SUVs, encountered no less than three checkpoints on the roads leading to Kusk, the last of which was entirely closed to traffic. At each, they were required to present the same identification and clearances to steely-eyed sentries clearly on edge over the tales that had undoubtedly reached them as well. They wore heavy, woolen overcoats, the piles of snow on the roadsides seeming eternal, unaffected by the sunlight and moderating temperatures.

They were kept longer at the final checkpoint set up on the single artery leading into Kusk. Jimenez busied himself with studying what he could glimpse of the town through the trees. Judging by the number of mill-like buildings they'd passed along the way, he guessed this was an agricultural town, impoverished by a combination of the weak Siberian economy and shuttering of virtually all the surrounding industrial mills. Jimenez realized their parking lots had been empty and their gates locked. He could see any number of homes dotting the landscape on the town's perimeter, no signs whatsoever of the people who'd lived in them.

Army personnel, meanwhile, were everywhere, along with trailers from which government officials dressed in civilian garb came and went. There was also a parade of what he believed were unmarked ambulances, either waiting to enter the village of Kusk or having already been there and back.

Finally a major in the Russian army named Krilenko, who headed up Jimenez's escort party, walked briskly to his vehicle and leaned in toward the open window.

"I'm afraid there's no longer anything to see, Father," Krilenko reported. "The bodies have been removed to a secret location. I am to inform you that you have our apologies for coming all this way for nothing, and my orders are to escort you back to the airport immediately."

Sremski responded before Jimenez had a chance to. "The Vatican's involvement was requested, and approved, at the highest levels of the Russian government."

Krilenko shrugged. "But now the military is in charge, a special, secret branch that answers to no one but themselves. I'm sorry. To both of you for having wasted your time."

"You haven't wasted our time," Sremski said, settling back in his seat. "Because you're going to escort us on, Major."

"On whose authority?"

This time Jimenez chimed in first. "Pope Benedict. And God Himself, if you require an authority higher than that. I was sent here to do a job, and I'm not leaving until it is done."

"Father—"

"Or, if you prefer, I could report what happened in Kusk to the international media, stress with them that the Russian military is taking drastic measures to suppress the truth. And I'll be certain to mention your name, along with the existence of your special, secret branch to them, Major Krilenko."

Krilenko swallowed hard, rotated his gaze between the two priests. "Let me see what I can do."

The soldiers glared at Jimenez, as his vehicle was passed through the final checkpoint and entered the outskirts of Kusk. There was only an hour of light left, but he wanted to be gone from here before the storm intensified, potentially stranding him. Weather forecasting was spotty at best in this part of the world, but Jimenez knew a potential blizzard when he saw one.

The convoy rumbled on along the rut-strewn road, continuing into the town center, marred by abandoned cars strewn in all directions. Some of their windows were splattered with blood. Others were shattered. And there were what looked like dried pools of blood staining several spots in the streets they rolled over, Jimenez left to picture the horrific scene as it must have unfolded, until he went cold, trembling, and turned his thoughts elsewhere.

Back to the investigation.

It looked like a single accident had snarled the thin traffic. But what had happened to the people who climbed out of their cars, many of the doors still open? And now that the bodies had all been removed, how was he supposed to conduct his investigation?

Jimenez noticed a computer bag sitting on the front passenger seat floor between Krilenko's legs, giving him an idea, at least a notion.

"You supervised the removal process, Major," he said, after flashing Sremski a glance to signal him. "Of the bodies, I mean."

"I did," Krilenko said, as if proud of the status that implied.

Jimenez let the major see his gaze shift to the computer bag. "But you made a video record first, I trust, to share with the proper ministries once you return to Moscow."

Krilenko didn't respond.

"Because it occurs to me, Major, a man who holds both the Vatican and the Russian Orthodox Church in his debt is like a man holding the lion's share of the chips in a poker game. Isn't that right, Father Sremski?"

"It most certainly is, Father."

Jimenez leaned forward. "So, Major, what do you say we have a look?"

Thicker snow was collecting on the windshield, resisting the wipers' attempts to swipe it off. The wind had picked up as well, rocking their big SUV from side to side, as it moved slowly through Kusk toward a much larger government headquarters than a town this small seemed to need. But Kusk had once been a primary command and control site for the portion of the Soviet nuclear arsenal aimed at America's West Coast. As a result, the town boasted any number of missile silos and bunkers, now mothballed as a result of various disarmament treaties. Krilenko had commandeered the former headquarters as his command post, doubling as living quarters, given Kusk's remote Siberian location.

He escorted Jimenez and Sremski to a third-floor office he'd appropriated for himself, and set up his laptop for them to view.

"I don't know how long this is going to work," he explained. "The battery is low, and we're operating on generator power here. I haven't even watched it myself, since I uploaded the raw footage." He paused to look at both Jimenez and Sremski. "I hope you have strong stomachs, Fathers."

The first footage to appear looked to have been shot in a house, and he was instantly glad for the small size of the screen. There were blood and bodies and not much more. Jimenez counted six in all: two adults and four children. The children ranged in age from approximately four to fifteen or sixteen, the oldest being a boy with knives stuck through his throat and both his eyes. The mother was a blood-soaked mess that barely resembled a human being, except for what appeared to be the handle of a bathroom plunger wedged all the way down her throat. The youngest were a set of twins, at least Jimenez thought they were twins; it was hard to tell, since their bodies had been stitched together with baling wires before railroad spikes had been hammered through one into the other. The frozen agony on their faces indicated they'd been alive through much of the process.

Jimenez stopped long enough to cross himself. He started to pose a question to Krilenko, but no words emerged.

"It happened fast and it happened throughout the village at the same time," the major explained anyway, as if reading his mind. "The first of us to arrive entered the village in full biohazard gear, but we shed it once the air tested clean."

The other homes and buildings captured in the videos were the same as the first. People struck down violently by co-workers, loved ones, or strangers—it seemed not to matter.

A bus that had slammed into a building in the town square where they were parked was gone now, but the shattered façade remained. The inside of that bus turned Jimenez's stomach and almost made him gag. An even mix of men, women, and children, all returning home from work or school, the bus working its way on its daily route. The worst of the victims looking as if they'd been attacked by wolves or bears. The hands of all were covered in blood.

"Stop!" Sremski barked suddenly, pointing at the screen "Can you make that larger?"

Krilenko did, again reluctantly.

"Is that," Jimenez started.

"Yes," Sremski cut in, before he could continue. "That boy is holding one in each hand. He tore out his own eyes."

"A mass psychosis of some kind," Jimenez managed. "That's the only thing that could explain this." He looked toward Krilenko. "I need to see the inside of some of the homes firsthand. I need to see what's left for myself."

Krilenko gazed out the office window, as best he could, into the building storm. "Another hour and you'll be spending the night here. I don't think you want to do that, Father."

"Take me there," Jimenez said anyway, pointing to a house now filling the laptop's screen. "Take me there now."

They drove to the house Jimenez had selected, the three of them entering alone, leaving two of Krilenko's men inside the vehicle.

Inside, blood painted the walls. Blood painted everything; pieces of bones, flesh, and brain matter splattered everywhere as well. The bodies might have been removed, but not the residue of what had happened there.

Proceeding on thinking he hadn't shared with either Krilenko or

Sremski, Jimenez casually entered the kitchen where plates of uneaten food remained on the table, indicating whatever had happened had started here.

"My glasses," he said suddenly, pretending to feel about his pockets. "I must've left them in the car. Would you be so kind, Major?"

Krilenko nodded, wary but not looking too suspicious.

"Thank you, Major."

Jimenez figured he had mere seconds, fifteen or twenty at most. He quickly moved across the kitchen and scooped up an empty mixing beaker topped with an old-fashioned tight cork. Wasting no time, he used a ladle still sitting in what looked to be a now coagulated stew to scoop up some of the contents, drain them into the beaker, and then fit the cork back into place.

Jimenez heard the heavy steps of Krilenko's soldiers coming, as he tucked the beaker into Sremski's vestment pocket inside his robe.

"Get this to the Vatican," he whispered. "Now. Tell Cardinal Martenko it's from me. He'll know what to do with it."

The soldiers reached the doorway and stopped, standing rigid. Moments later, Krilenko returned with no glasses in hand.

Jimenez flashed his pair to the major. "I had them the whole time. Sorry to inconvenience you."

Krilenko brushed the snow from his heavy wool jacket, making a pile on the floor. "You need to get going, if you're going to get out of here tonight."

"I quite agree," Sremski said, his insistence only partially rooted in the mission now before him.

"But I need to stay," Jimenez said. "As I said before, Major, I came here to do a job and it's not finished yet."

Krilenko frowned, shook the last of the snow from his hat and the shoulder pads of his jacket. "Suit yourself." Then, to Father Sremski. "I'll see you get to the airport, Father, but you might end up staying the night as well."

"As God wills," Sremski said, turning to Father Jimenez.

The weather deteriorated in incredibly rapid fashion after Father Sremski's departure for the airport. Even for Siberia, the conditions were harsh, well before the heart of the blizzard had even arrived.

Jimenez insisted on visiting more houses to view the effects of the mass hysteria he believed had swept through the town. His tour of the third was cut short when Krilenko received word that his vehicles were no longer able to advance through the mounting snows, and the winds picked up to near monsoon force.

With all attention now turned toward making it through the long Siberian night safe and sound, Krilenko ordered his entire platoon to take refuge from the storm in one of the abandoned missile bunkers, shielded well underground. They brought kerosene-fueled space heaters with them, along with battery-operated lanterns that put out enough light to chase off at least a measure of the fear they all felt of the pounding blizzard they could hear raging above them.

The next morning, though, brought the passage of the storm and, with it, a return to the surface to find the day bathed in bright, unbroken sunlight blazing down from an utterly cloudless sky accompanied by a penetrating cold. But it wasn't just the cold; it felt as if everything that passed for life, from trees to plants to birds to even insects, was dying, freezing from its core outward. It was like nothing he'd ever experienced before, although the similarities he felt with Nigeria were striking. The weather there had been tropical, steamy, in stark contrast to this. But the feeling was the same, one that Jimenez hadn't felt since looking into the face of Cambridge on the verge of his own death. He knew what he had been looking at then, just as he knew what he was sensing now:

Evil.

Something you can feel and sense, but not see. Something *alive*. He could feel it watching him, as huge snowplows fought to clear the streets of Kusk, so Major Krilenko could evacuate his team.

"The storm seems limited mainly to this area," he heard Krilenko tell him, suddenly by his side. "It's twelve degrees warmer just twenty miles away."

"How long before we can leave?"

"It will take another hour, I suspect, to clear the roads. But there's something you need to see, Father, and you need to see it now."

# FIFTY-EIGHT

### The Adirondacks, New York; 2008

Years ago, Max and his father had occasionally spent weekends hiking and camping in the Adirondack Mountains of upstate New York. Though they never made use of one, the pair had often glimpsed hunting cabins abandoned for the season. That's where Max and Vicky decided to stop for the night, once exhaustion claimed them, planning to make the Canadian border the next day. After that, who knew? Neither Max nor Vicky had thought that far ahead.

Max didn't have a car. Living in New York City, what was the point? But his family had three and his mother hardly ever drove the Volvo wagon anymore, hardly ever left the penthouse period. Claimed she could see people's souls, how dirty and retched most of them were. The sight so revealing and repulsive that she couldn't stand to go out anymore.

"The world's an ugly place," she'd say to him over and over again. "Ugly and getting uglier by the day, by the minute. Don't be tempted by the devil, Max. Lilith told me the devil says you belong to him, so always stay away from the darkness, because the darkness belongs to him. You have to fight him, fight him and push him away, and keep pushing until he's gone for good. Pray, Max, pray to the Lord for forgiveness and He will listen, He will be there."

It got so he began avoiding her, detesting in advance the next crackpot shit sure to come out of her mouth.

He couldn't talk to his mom, but he'd bought a burner phone to call his dad, after ditching his and Vicky's cell phones, so no one could use the signal to track them.

"Where the hell are you, son?"

"I'd rather not say right now."

"Yeah? Then let's try another question: You know the penalty for kidnapping?"

"I didn't kidnap anybody. Vicky couldn't go home to her father, Dad, you heard her."

"She needs help, Max. She's an addict. You need to be headed to a rehab facility, not the Canadian border."

"Promise me you won't tell her father."

"Dale and I aren't exactly on the best of terms right now."

"Promise me."

"I promise." A heavy silence fell between them, broken only when Ben Younger resumed. "But I want you to come home."

"I can't."

"You're not thinking straight."

"Yes, I am, straighter than ever. You want to know why she does drugs? It's because she's got that piece of shit for a father. Best rehab for Vicky is getting away from him for good."

"That's not your call," Ben said, although he wished it was. "You need to think like an adult here and bring her back."

"That's Vicky's call, Dad. I've got to help her. I've got to . . ."

"What?" Ben prodded, when his son's voice trailed off.

"How'd you know that you were in love with mom?"

"I couldn't imagine my life without her. Is that how it is with you and Vicky?"

"I don't know, I don't know anything right now. Gotta go, Dad. I'll call you later."

And he'd hung up.

After leaving the city, they'd driven as far as they could until neither could keep their eyes open anymore. They'd stopped at a rest stop to buy gas and snacks, Max's gaze lingering on a display of something called mood rings right next to the register. Just before paying, he couldn't resist adding one of them to give Vicky as a gift, a souvenir of their escape from the city.

Midnight had come and gone, when Max steered the Volvo along a collection of backcountry roads on which theirs was the only car. He knew the general area most of the hunting cabins were clustered, all of them abandoned this time of year and suitable for borrowing.

He found one nestled back in the woods down a root-marred drive, hidden from the view of anyone—Vicky's father, included—intent on following them. The one-room cabin was furnished well enough, but abandoned for the season, as expected. The utilities were shut down.

And, although there might've been some juice left in the propane tank, Max figured it would be best to remain in the dark. Any light, other than the meager spill from a battery-operated lantern, would stand out and risk drawing attention to them.

They polished off all the snacks they'd bought at the rest stop in rapid fashion, washing them down with big bottles of water. Vicky was just draining the last of hers, when Max plucked the mood ring he'd purchased out of his pocket.

"Will you marry me?" he joked, handing it to her.

Her eyes gaped. "You're not going to believe this."

"What?"

She reached into a front pocket of her jeans and came out with the very same ring, smiling as she extended it toward him. "I couldn't resist."

Max smiled back. "Neither could I."

Vicky slid the ring she'd bought onto his finger; Max took the matching one he'd given her back and did the same.

"I now pronounce us," Max started, but stopped. "Pronounce us *what*?"

"How about 'To Be Determined'?"

"Works for me."

Then they lay down atop an old bare mattress, topped by a tattered woolen blanket, both utterly exhausted.

"Weird, isn't it?" Vicky asked Max.

"What?"

"Being together like this."

Max couldn't make her out clearly through the darkness, but he knew she was looking at him. They'd never slept together, never even kissed until recently.

But tonight felt different, tonight felt *right*.

It wasn't Max who made the first move; it wasn't Vicky either; it was both of them together in the same thought, the same mind. Lying next to each other one moment, then embracing and kissing in the next.

The rest was a blur, played out amid the soft glow of the lantern light from the floor. Time measured in the blips between shifting about atop the bare mattress beneath the ratty old blanket. Or maybe time had stopped, explaining why their lovemaking seemed to go on unbroken forever. There were moans and Max quickly gave up trying to figure out the source. He knew this was his body, but he was no longer in control of it. As if the two of them had merged into one.

They finished together, both of them heaving for breath and collapsing in each other's arms. Max fighting against sleep, so he could enjoy every moment of this. And then Vicky was taking him in hand, and they were going at it again, even better and longer than the first time, the second time ending with the expectation of a third, a fourth, as many as the night would allow. Max let himself fantasize about ditching their plans to go to Canada and staying right here. Make a home in the middle of nowhere where he could keep Vicky safe from her father, and the drugs, and temptations that had nearly destroyed her. Playing house. Making believe they were all grown up.

They fell asleep in each other's arms, Max's dreams the most pleasant he could ever remember, until a nightmare of the door to the hunting cabin being kicked in jolted him awake.

An instant before that door burst open behind a heavy boot.

### New York City, 2008

"I wasn't sure what to make of you asking to meet me so late at night like this," Ben told Franklin Kirsch.

Kirsch closed and relocked the service entrance to CyberGen behind him. "I need to share the results of your son's DNA tests immediately."

"Tests plural?"

Kirsch didn't nod. "I had it repeated. To be sure."

"Sure of what?"

Kirsch waited until they were inside his office with the door closed before responding. He didn't offer Ben a chair this time and Ben didn't take one.

"Your son's not sick," Kirsch started. "Whatever is afflicting you hasn't touched him."

"Well, that's something to be grateful for, anyway," Ben said, feeling a wave of relief sweep over him that was just as quickly replaced by a sense of foreboding. "But you didn't call me here to tell me that."

"The matching mark on Max's hand," Kirsch continued. "You recall what you told me about it, ever since he was an infant?"

"How we'd touch palms, press the marks against each other."

"Do you recall how it started?"

"With crystal clarity," Ben told him. "Max was in his crib, a month old or even less, when he raised his hand toward me, palm up. I pressed my palm against his. It was the first time he flashed a smile."

Kirsch nodded, as if that was exactly the answer he'd expected. "I didn't ask you to come here about Max, I asked you to come here about you. You see, Mr. Younger, I think I may know a bit more about your illness."

## The Adirondacks, 2008

Dale Denton entered the cabin last. Took a look at Vicky covered up to her neck by an old, worn blanket, Max standing against the far wall buck naked with three sets of former special operator eyes locked on him.

"Put your fucking clothes on, you piece of shit."

Max swallowed hard, continued holding his hands cupped around his dick. He smelled of musk, hair oil, and the stale lavender scent that clung to Vicky's hair.

"You look like a girl with that long hair," Denton continued, his words hissing out of his mouth. "A fucking faggot." He turned toward his daughter. "So which is it, Victoria? Are you fucking a girl or a faggot?"

She sat straighter up in bed, pulling the blanket in tighter against her, tears starting to stream down her cheeks, as embarrassed as she was upset. "Daddy . . ."

"You're still seventeen. Either way, he's a rapist. Either way, he's going to jail."

"Daddy!" Vicky wailed, shaking now.

"How'd you find us?" Max asked him, underwear in hand.

Denton aimed his answer at Vicky. "When I gave you your mother's locket for your thirteenth birthday, you swore you'd never take it off."

Vicky grasped the locket dangling from the end of the chain round her neck.

Denton smirked, looking back toward Max. "Before I gave the locket to her, I had a tracking chip implanted inside it. So I'd know where my daughter was at all times."

"Not anymore," Vicky snapped, stripping the chain from her neck and tossing it at her father. "You can have it back!" she screamed at him, and then practically jumped out of bed, ended up on her feet, with the raggedy blanket clutched around her. "This is bullshit, total bullshit!"

Denton jabbed an imposing finger her way. "Watch your mouth."

"He wasn't my first, you know," Vicky said, a biting edge to her voice all of a sudden. "More like my fiftieth. Guess the locket didn't help you find all the rest of the boys I screwed. Guess you missed out there."

That's when Denton lurched toward her.

### New York City, 2008

"What's killing me, you mean," Ben said, checking his phone again to make sure he hadn't missed a call or text from Max.

"I'm a scientist, Mr. Younger, a geneticist, a physician for over thirty years," Kirsch resumed. "I'm trained to evaluate facts and make clinical decisions, or help patients come to their own decisions. But I have to set aside facts for a time. That's what I've been doing for the whole day before I called you. Setting facts, knowledge, training, logic, science, and medicine aside."

Ben swallowed hard, didn't prod Kirsch to go on but he did so anyway.

"I have a theory that touching palms wasn't just a game for your son, Mr. Younger, or some infantile bonding ritual. I think, in theory, he was taking something from you, absorbing it."

"Taking, absorbing, *what*?"

"Your energy at the subatomic level. Remember, this isn't the scientist in me talking—I'm not really sure what it is. What I know, and as we've discussed already, your disease is due to a breakdown in the ability of your cells to reproduce. Oncologists looked at your test results and saw some non-primary form of lymphoma or blood cancer, decided that's what you had even though none of their testing produced a definitive diagnosis. Your disease was differentiated based on the process of elimination."

"I don't understand," Ben said, trying to even then.

"The results of both your son's DNA tests I ordered indicated his cellular reproduction, the primary building block of life itself, proceeds at a rate ten times that of a normal person's. How often has he been sick?"

"I never gave it much thought, traveling as much as I did. Not very, as I recall. Maybe never, now that you mention it."

"What about sports injuries, broken bones?"

"He's never been very interested in sports or had the discipline for them. He's never broken a bone either, never even gone to a doctor, other than for regular checkups. My wife and I figured he was just lucky. And . . ."

"And what, Mr. Younger?"

"Something I just remembered," Ben said, feeling distant all of a sudden, Kirsch's words beginning to truly sink in. "We set a goal years ago to climb the highest mountain on every continent. And on every climb I can't ever recall Max being short of breath, labored, in need of oxygen—anything like that. I just thought he was in good shape. And . . ."

"And what, Mr. Younger?"

"I've never told this to anyone. But we were hiking in Alaska this one time when a grizzly bear lurched out from the woods right in front of me. He would've torn me to shreds, and all I could think was to shove Max behind me so he wouldn't be killed too. But Max had already stepped out, between me and the bear, trying to protect me. He said something inside him made him do it, that he had to take a stand to stop the animal from attacking, that running would have angered the bear even more. Told me, in that moment, he'd been ready to die for me. Max just stood there, looking up at the animal, their gazes locking. The bear growled, whined, then, shockingly, dropped down from its hind legs and scampered off. And you know what? The bear looked scared, actually scared. Tell me how you'd explain that?"

"I can't, at least on a rational basis. But I can tell you about his test results. If I didn't know the testing was on the level, I'd figure myself to be the victim of a hoax, an elaborate fabrication. Because on the subatomic molecular level your son's cells aren't aging, reproducing, developing, or replicating the way human cells do. And part of the origins of this . . . condition, or whatever it is, lies in his ability to absorb the life force out of your cells and into his."

Kirsch stopped, started to compose himself with a deep breath, then just resumed.

"If you're dying, Mr. Younger, as crazy and unprofessional as this sounds, it's possibly because your son's been killing you for nearly eighteen years."

Ben's phone rang, the number of Max's burner phone lighting up in his caller ID.

### The Adirondacks

*Whap!*

That's what Denton's slap against Victoria's cheek sounded like to Max. He was pulling his jeans on at the time, had all the buttons done except the top one when . . .

*Whap!*

. . . the sound came and drew his attention across the room. Somehow the meager spill of the lantern captured Vicky's face in all its perfection and beauty. In that moment she looked more like a photograph than a person, leaving Max to wonder absurdly why he hadn't been head-over-heels in love with her for years already.

Because maybe he had been, the mood rings they were both wearing now a kind of testament to that.

And then Max was in motion. Before he could even think to move, he was halfway to Dale Denton, his face shiny with sweat in the spill of the lantern light he'd switched on.

"Hey!" a voice blared, Denton's three goons converging on Max in the shabby, dust-riddled single room that suddenly felt more like a closet.

Max knew what was coming from a place deep inside him, before it got there. He'd felt it plenty often over the years, always when he was angry, always when something inside him boiled, and this was the hottest yet.

*Whap!*

The sound of the slap resounding against Vicky's cheek resounded in his mind again, carved from his memory in the last moment before the three men were on him. Life blinked—that's what it felt like. A blip in which everything stopped like a frozen image on a television screen, only to restart with the missing moments lost forever.

*Blink . . .*

One of the men was holding his throat, gasping and coughing blood in huge plumes. Max's right hand was wet and sticky, coated in the blood residue of the impossible barehanded strike that must have pierced the man's throat like a knife.

*Blink . . .*

Hands tugging at his shoulders, pounding his head, while he pressed both his thumbs into a second man's eyes, a great indescribable euphoria rushing through him when he heard dual popping sounds and the thumbs sank into something squishy. Pushed and kept pushing until they disappeared to the bases of his sockets. The man shaking horribly, convulsing.

*Blink . . .*

The third man's body hit the plank floor with a hollow thud. Max looked down, saw he was holding the man's head in his hands, the eyes seeming to look back at him while the legs attached to the rest of him kicked and twitched.

Max heard a *plop* and realized he'd dropped the head that was a gory mess of blood, splintered bone, and gristle oozing from the jagged line where he must've twisted the man's head around 180 degrees. Then he turned toward Dale Denton, his cowering form slumped against a wall, face caught in the flickering light of the lantern, frozen in terror, Max wishing he could prolong that moment forever. Weak, reduced to nothing—Denton's true essence.

Max stood over Dale Denton's cowering form, pushed up into the corner, as if he was trying very hard to melt into the wood. Max felt the next *blink* coming, no idea what Denton might resemble when consciousness returned.

He felt himself almost smiling at the thought, a hot surge of absolute joy coursing through him because of the power he felt, the thick smell of blood he'd spilled only adding to it. Something was on fire inside him, a flame he couldn't, and didn't want to, extinguish. He wanted to feel this power, for it to be his, forever. The heat reduced to a simmer, only when a shape forced itself against him, washing the light back into his eyes.

"Max, *no*! Stop, *please*!"

Vicky pushed him away from her father, back across the room where the stench of blood was even stronger, his bare feet sloshing through the muck.

"You've got to get out of here, you've got to run!"

Max's gaze flitted back to Denton's shriveled form tucked into the corner, seeming to disappear a little at a time into the crack where two walls met.

"Max! Max, listen to me!"

His gaze met Vicky's.

She gasped. "Your eyes, Max, what's wrong with your eyes?"

He turned to the mirror mounted on the wall over the laminate wood bureau. The lantern light was enough to reveal his eyes had gone all black, impossible to distinguish the pupils from the inky patches that had leaked over the whites. Max squeezed them closed, then opened his eyes again to reveal the ink patches seeming to recede, the whites returning.

"Please, get out of here!" Vicky ranted at him, her voice ringing with heartache and desperation. "Get away from him, as far as you can!"

She separated from Max long enough to fetch his boots, the rest of his clothes.

"Now. Now, Max, go. Please. . . ."

Maybe Vicky had kept talking, and Max had stopped hearing. He couldn't remember whether her lips were moving or not. Denton was still there in the corner, but Max didn't register his presence anymore. Didn't give him another thought until he realized he was behind the wheel of the Volvo wagon, no idea where he was or how much time had passed in getting him there. A glance in the rearview mirror showed his face and hair to be mottled with black, scabby blood. The burner phone was tucked in the pocket of his jeans, the top button still undone.

Max threaded it closed as he dialed his father.

## New York City, 2008

"Dad," Ben heard Max say, his voice barely audible.

"Max, are you all right? Is everything okay?"

Of course, Ben already knew it wasn't, the only question being how bad.

"I killed these guys, Dad."

"What? *Who?*"

"Three of them. Denton's men, those goons he's got."

Ben felt his heart hammering his chest. He felt dizzy and short of breath, needed to lean up against the wall outside Dr. Kirsch's office for support.

"Slow down, son. Where are you? Is Vicky still with you?"

"Yes—I mean, no. She was."

"What happened, Max? Slow down and tell me what happened?"

Ben shouldn't have been surprised. He'd been in denial about this for too long, going on eighteen years now. Kirsch's claims had brought it all home to roost. All the times bad things happened to people who crossed Max Younger. It had started innocently enough with spills off bicycles, falls down stairs, one boy who was hit by a car, and another who lost two fingers in a wood shop saw after stealing Max's baseball cap.

Max was always so matter-of-fact about it all, that Ben was able to convince himself he'd had nothing to do with any of it, at least not consciously. Because opening his mind to the alternative meant facing the fact he had raised a monster, conceived somehow in the depths of a cave in the Yucatán.

And that, one way or another, it was his fault.

"What about Vicky, Max? Is she okay? Is she with you or not?"

"She's not with me. I ran. I don't know where I am. I just kept driving."

"These three men . . ."

"I killed them," Max said, his voice breaking. "They were alive and then they weren't. I killed them in what came in between."

Ben felt as if he'd been struck by a heavy, hot gush of wind. Had to press himself tighter against the wall to avoid being spilled over.

"What about Denton, Max?"

"Vicky stopped me before I could hurt him. I would've done it too. It would've been easy."

"All right," Ben said, through the chill fostered by the casual sureness of Max's assertion, "I want you to drive on until you reach someplace I can find you, somewhere with an address. Walk away. Hide. Leave the car but keep the phone and call me. I'll get there as soon as I can."

"Dad, those three guys . . ."

"Max—"

"I killed them all. They came at me and I killed them all. And . . ."

"And what?"

"I enjoyed it, Dad. I loved it. What's wrong with me, what's happening to me? Am I sick?"

Ben tried to swallow, couldn't. The rock, he thought, it had all started when he'd touched the rock. An impossible escape from the depths of the cave, an impossible oil strike, an impossible miracle conception.

Or maybe a curse.

"We'll get through this," Ben Younger resumed, trying to reassure his son. "It's not your fault."

"Bullshit."

"You need to trust me, son. Do you trust me?"

Silence.

"Do you trust me, Max?"

"Yes." Finally.

"Then do what I tell you, and we'll get through this. I'll meet you wherever you end up and we'll figure it all out. No choice with mountains left to climb. How many peaks left, Max, how many?"

"Three."

"Say it again."

"Three."

"That's right, and we're going to climb them all. Do you hear me? We're going to climb them all. I want you to think about that. I want you to think about that and nothing else until we're together. Do you hear me?"

"Yes," Max said, his voice barely audible.

"Good, son. Now, drive."

# FIFTY-NINE

## London, 2008

"Sit down, Pascal," Cardinal Martenko said, upon meeting Father Jimenez in London, in the lobby of the Savoy Hotel where he was attending a conference of Catholic bishops. "Are you sick? You look terrible."

Jimenez tried to collect himself, sort out his jumbled thoughts. "When I landed at the airport, the television monitors everywhere were covering news of an airplane crash. As soon as I saw footage of the wreckage, I feared it might be Father Sremski's plane. Then the announcement came that it was bound for Italy from Moscow, and I knew my fears were justified."

"Sit, please, Pascal. Because a Vatican emissary was traveling on board," Cardinal Martenko continued, after Jimenez finally took the chair next to his, "I was made privy to various details not shared with the public, including the last recording when the pilot called in the Mayday. Horrible, high-pitched screams, the pilot going on about the passengers killing each other, trying to break into the cockpit. Then nothing."

"Father Sremski was transporting a sample taken from the scene of the catastrophe. It must have gotten loose on the plane, just like it did in that village," Jimenez said, chilled by the lobby's recirculated air. He hadn't been able to rid himself of the chill since braving the storm in Kusk. "I was a fool to act so rashly, to put so many lives in jeopardy."

"This isn't your fault, Pascal. You were doing the Lord's work."

"And all the people on that plane are dead now, thanks to me. The fact remains, Your Eminence, that I never should've tried to secure a sample without proper safeguards and equipment."

"Which the Russians would have forbidden under any circumstances." Martenko stopped and studied Jimenez closer. "You don't look well, Pascal. I've read your preliminary report about Kusk, being trapped in the onslaught of a blizzard. . . ."

"It wasn't the storm, Your Eminence. There was something else in that town."

### The Vatican, 2008

Mohammed al-Qadir watched the scene unfolding in St. Peter's Square on Vatican television. On instructions from the Holy Father himself, the members of the Curia stood at the forefront of the multitudes gathered in St. Peter's Square for the papal address. According to reports, the pope had taken the criticism pointed at the church hierarchy to heart, choosing this as the first symbol of his desire to showcase the Vatican's most trusted cadre of cardinals out among the people. Just symbol, of course, but symbol could go a long way toward easing the perception of the church as elite and out of touch. Members of the Curia, more accustomed to the hallowed halls of the Vatican, mixing with common people that included three men in wheelchairs.

Al-Qadir focused on those men.

### London, 2008

"The morning the storm passed," Jimenez continued, "the Russian military resumed their search of the area surrounding Kusk, and unearthed something beneath a layer of ice: a crater, Your Eminence."

Martenko remained silent, his eyes urging Jimenez on.

"Though substantially smaller, it resembled another crater we're both familiar with, from the country where we met for the first time."

"Nigeria," Martenko realized.

### The Vatican, 2008

Al-Qadir watched the three men in wheelchairs disperse, and edge closer to the members of the Curia from different angles, no one paying them any heed at all. On the television before him, he thought he actually met the gaze of one fighter looking to him for one final blessing, one last affirmation of the holy mission with which they'd been entrusted.

Al-Qadir couldn't help but nod, in the last moment before all three of his fighters detonated their suicide vests from their positions, and the television screen erupted into a bright flash that gave way to smoke, flames, and screams.

Especially screams.

## London, 2008

"A crater carved out of the frozen ground instead of the tepid jungle, Your Eminence," Jimenez resumed. "There had been reports of a meteor strike in the area, forty-eight hours before contact was lost with the town, but nothing scientists and geologists could pin down."

"Making you first on the scene again, Pascal."

"And, again, I could find no trace of any meteorite, in spite of what had clearly been a moderate impact."

"Are you drawing a connection between Kusk and your unfortunate experiences in Nigeria? That doesn't sound like the wisdom of a scientist, Father."

"No, it's the wisdom of a priest." Jimenez groped hard for his next words. "Have you ever experienced true evil, Your Eminence, an evil that was as real and present as anything physical?"

Martenko's lips quivered. "You ask me that in an unprecedentedly dangerous time for the church, with radical Islam practically at war with Christianity. One of these groups I've never heard of before even threatened the sanctity of the Vatican itself, if you can believe that."

Before Martenko could respond, a young aide rushed over to him and handed the cardinal a cell phone in a trembling hand. Martenko took the phone, listening in silence for several moments, before handing the phone back to his aide. Trembling himself now, he struggled up from the chair, his legs suddenly wobbly.

"I'm sorry, Pascal. I must get back to Rome."

Jimenez rose with him. "Your Eminence?"

Martenko's face had gone deathly pale. "There's been a terrorist attack. In St. Peter's Square. I must get back there."

"Is there anything I can do?"

Martenko regarded Jimenez, as he walked away in the company of his aide, tears welling in his eyes. "Pray, pray for all of us."

# PART 6

# BLOOD OF THE LAMB

## The Present

Nature has no principles.
She makes no distinction between good and evil.

—Anatole France

# SIXTY

### *George H. W. Bush*

Father Pascal Jimenez had tossed and turned through the night, the face of Mohammed al-Qadir returning to haunt him every time he started to nod off. He'd nearly vomited right in front of Admiral Darby and the man named Red, his legs buckling and hands shaking so much he couldn't still them, after recognizing al-Qadir's piercing emerald-green eyes, remembering the last time he'd seen them. Staring up into the face of the man about to kill him in Nigeria.

*Your God is not here.*

Cambridge . . . Al-Qadir.

Jimenez saw one, saw the other. Transposed the face of one onto the other.

*The same man . . . Cambridge and al-Qadir, they were the same man!*

Jimenez had realized he couldn't breathe, found himself sitting in a chair with no memory of taking it.

"You okay there, Father?" Red had asked him.

Jimenez wiped the drool and stray flecks of vomit from the edges of his mouth. "Just a bit sea sick, that's all, and I haven't been sleeping much lately," he managed. "If I could just have some water . . ."

And he guzzled down the Styrofoam cup Red brought him between his trembling hands.

"I think we better get you settled," Red had offered, taking Jimenez by the arm and helping him up. "Everything else can wait until morning."


He'd brought Jimenez to his stateroom, but every time sleep tempted the priest, Cambridge's face filled his mind. The man who'd killed his own SAS team, along with the scientists who'd accompanied Jimenez to

Nigeria back in 1991. Killed them all with the ease of crushing a bug under his boot, and he'd had every intention of killing Jimenez as well.

*"I think we'll take your head, Professor. You won't be needing it anymore anyway."*

Those final moments in Nigeria had never lost their crystal clarity in his mind's eye.

*"Your God isn't here. If he is here, beg him to give me a sign and I'll spare your life."*

Cambridge had leaned over and plucked the gold pen that had belonged to Jimenez's father from his pocket moments before the eclipse that had led Cambridge to spare Jimenez's life struck. He'd never seen the man again, except in his dreams.

Until he'd looked into the eyes of Mohammed al-Qadir.


The stateroom they'd given Jimenez was tiny by hotel standards but comfortable and functional. The cot-sized bed was cramped, and Jimenez hadn't managed to sleep anyway. And the times he did nod off found him seated in the single chair squeezed under a small desk.

That's where he was, his mind trying to settle on a place in his consciousness where the memories would leave him alone, when a knock fell on the door, and Red entered without waiting to be invited.

"Feeling better, Father?"

"Quite a bit, thank you," Jimenez said, sitting up straight in his chair and stretching his arms. He noticed that Red was holding a tablet.

"Good, because there's something I need to show you," Red said, firing up the tablet and jogging it to a screen filled with images of tiny pages.

Jimenez watched him click on the first page and angle the tablet so the priest could see the screen.

"Look familiar?"

"Lord in heaven, it's the scientific journal I kept in Nigeria."

"Forty-six pages of notes. Sound about right, Father?"

"About, yes. But how . . ."

"Did we come by them?" Red completed. "We had a mole planted in a scientific research team linked to the New Islamic Front, a German Muslim named Gunther Brune. He infiltrated the group on the eve of the members taking up residence at a facility in southern Lebanon, and managed to get this to us just before something went terribly wrong. See, this scientific team was trying to develop a bio-superweapon for the terrorist group. Looks like they unexpectedly came up with something worse."

"The pathogen that's spreading through the Middle East," Jimenez realized, recalling that part of his conversation with Red during the course of the long flight from Brazil. "But what could this pathogen have to do with my notebook from Nigeria?"

"That's why you're here," Red told him, "to help us figure that out."

"There's something else I need to tell you," Jimenez said.

"The man you knew as Cambridge disappeared after Nigeria, fell off the face of the goddamn Earth," Red explained, returning to Jimenez's stateroom an hour later after learning everything he could glean from various intelligence files and sources. "The British government never stopped looking for him, and now we may know why all their efforts failed."

"Because, if I'm right, he became somebody else." Jimenez hesitated, his gaze drifting before returning to Red with new focus and intensity. "I've always looked at life as being full of uncertainties and, ever since I took this job, there have been fewer and fewer things I'm truly certain of. But I'm certain of this, because I've seen those eyes every night of my life for the past twenty-seven years in my dreams, and my nightmares."

Red nodded in noncommittal fashion. "'Cambridge,' as you knew him, was born in Chechnya and became part of a wave of orphans to reach the West in the mid-1970s in efforts led by the Catholic Church after a Soviet crackdown on anti-Communist movements. He was adopted by a minister and his wife in England. That couple later died in a mysterious fire, after which Cambridge lived on his own for a time before joining up with the British army and being selected to serve in the Special Air Service. After Nigeria, we know he was a high-ranking member of al-Qaeda in Iraq. His debut performance with the New Islamic Front that he personally founded came in 2008 when the NIF claimed credit for the suicide bombing in St. Peter's Square that wiped out a hefty portion of the Curia."

"So he joined the SAS to, what, hone his skills?"

"And bide his time."

"Until Nigeria," Jimenez said, trying to suppress the chill that had seized him. "Why then and there? What changed?"

"Nobody's got a clue. Opportunity, perhaps, and convenience, what with that country's first wave of Islamic radicals beginning to make their presence felt. The British government, for its part, has traced Cambridge's movements from the time he came to London as a boy. They developed a timeline that covers every day of his life until he disappeared. And there's nothing whatsoever in their reporting that links him to these Mai-tatsine rebels. That tells me Cambridge didn't know them until he went down there. So how exactly did he meet them? Who handled the intro-ductions?"

Jimenez stiffened, the memories returning with a force that hit him like an uppercut to the chin. "What was the New Islamic Front doing with my notebook?"

"Your 1991 report to the British Ministry of Defence indicated all the geological samples you took from the scene were destroyed. But you're not sure they were destroyed, are you, Father? The man you claim became Mohammed al-Qadir, leader of the New Islamic Front, could just as easily have taken possession of them, along with your notebook."

"Where are you going with this?" a suddenly curious Jimenez posed.

"That something you found at the site of that meteor strike in Nigeria became the basis for whatever Gunther Brune's research team was de-veloping in Lebanon, a pathogen they unwittingly created that ends up turning humans into monsters." Red checked his watch and rose from the cot set against the wall next to Jimenez's chair. "Let's go, Father."

Jimenez struggled to his feet, knees cracking. "Where?"

"To meet someone else who can tell us more."

# SIXTY-ONE

## The Middle East

Can you hear me clearly, Dr. Tanoury?"

"I can," Vicky said to Admiral Keene Darby, who was speaking to her from the aircraft carrier *George H. W. Bush*, currently on station in the Mediterranean Sea. "I can see you clearly too, sir."

"Hope the sight doesn't horrify you too much, Doctor. Not much sleep these past couple nights, if any. But, unfortunately, the crisis we're facing doesn't allow for a lot of down time."

"I haven't slept much either, Admiral."

In fact, she hadn't slept at all, since Major Musa and his Lebanese army forces rendezvoused with a similar Israeli force at the border, in the wake of barely escaping the facility in southern Lebanon with their lives. Normally, those two armies working together cooperatively would have been unthinkable, except these were anything but normal times.

The Israelis had driven Vicky south to a command and control bunker, on the outskirts of Tel Aviv, activated to monitor what had been deemed now to be a dire threat. She'd been collating her notes and reaching out to disease experts around the world ever since. None, though, had proven even remotely helpful and some went as far as to vigorously dispute what she'd witnessed firsthand, adding to Vicky's sense of unease.

She even found herself staring at the Apple Watch her late fiancé Thomas had given her in the hope of another message from him scrawling across the screen. All evidence of the first one was gone, further convincing her that she was dealing with something in the overall sense here that science and rational thought *couldn't* explain. Something was happening that stretched across borders far different than the ones she was used to crossing for the WHO.

Meanwhile, the data she continued to assemble indicated that exposure to the creatures she'd encountered in southern Lebanon effectively eliminated the apparent pupa stage, the victim transitioning directly in what appeared to be a matter of mere hours. Those exposed to the pathogen through traditional means, on the other hand, transitioned through phases, delineated by a rapid absorption of the host's cells and their wholesale replacement by cells consistent with Medusa's genetic makeup.

"None of us are sleeping much these days," Admiral Darby acknowledged, on the screen before her. "I've seen the drone and satellite footage of that facility in southern Lebanon, before Israeli F-16s hit it with bunker busters. Can't make out much of whatever was attacking you, but it was enough to steal the little sleep I tried to squeeze in."

"You caught a glimpse of the final stage of the pathogen that's spreading across the entire Middle East," Vicky told Darby.

"You're telling me it was a *disease* that turned those men into monsters?"

"Disease is more a layman's term than a scientific one. We haven't isolated the causation or origins yet, and I don't want to define what we're facing in anything more than the most general means. It could be a germ, a virus, a bacteria, or . . ."

"Or what, Doctor?"

"Something we can't quantify, something we've never seen before. What I saw in Lebanon certainly suggests that. We've labeled the pathogen 'Medusa,' because of the hardened condition of each patient's skin, more advanced in Lebanon than Jordan. Prior to that, the infected exhibited symptoms more consistent with traditionally virulent infections. Bleeding from the mouth, eyes, and ears, for example, followed by depressed breathing capacity and diminished heart rate, accompanied by palpitations."

"And what happens in the wake of these more traditional symptoms, Doctor?"

"A complete metamorphosis on the level of the stages through which butterflies, bees, flies, beetles, and other insects develop."

"Last time I checked, the patients covered in your reports weren't insects."

"Please bear with me, Admiral. Complete metamorphosis, or transformation, is composed of four stages," Vicky explained. "Egg, larva, pupa, and adult. What we're facing here, with Medusa, is another version, a modification of that staging, but the general principles are the same. The infection, the pathogen itself, plays the role of the egg and the body in its original form is the actual larva in which the egg can develop. The next stage in this scenario is the hardening of the dermis, or skin, creating a pupa in which the creatures can gestate unmolested by any environmental factors. And, once the gestation phase is complete, and the adult is fully developed, it emerges from the pupa which is then discarded."

"So are we talking about people here or not?" the admiral wondered.

"Not to any degree we're capable of understanding. They used to be human, yes, and certainly whatever they've become retains the base elements of life as we understand it. By the same token, though, I'd venture to say that a thorough examination of their remains would reveal strands of DNA we can't identify or place anywhere in human or animal development." Vicky stopped rattling on, composed herself with a deep breath, and continued. "Nothing about what I observed firsthand in Lebanon suggested a human being in any way we understand human beings to be. It'll take more data and analysis to fully explain the transformation, and until that point, I'm at a loss to offer anything more substantive at this point."

"I think I may be able to help you there, Doctor," Admiral Darby told her. "You see, we've found a witness."

# SIXTY-TWO

### Middle East

The Navy chopper had been waiting at Ercan International Airport in northern Cyprus to shuttle Max to the *George H. W. Bush,* still on station in the Mediterranean. The long series of flights from Vancouver had proved a maddening exercise in racing airports in the process of shutting down in view of a crisis involving the reported spread of a virulent pathogen through the Middle East. That pathogen, by all accounts, was forcing countries to wall themselves off from the rest of the world.

Max found himself stranded at London's Heathrow Airport for a stretch, during which time he studied television monitors in the terminal updating the situation that was growing more dire by the minute. Flights in and out of the region had been canceled altogether, and authorities were fighting to control unruly masses seeking to flee their countries at any cost. Riots were beginning to break out across cities attempting to enforce blockades, quarantines, and curfews, and widespread desertions from both military and police units were being reported.

The upshot of this was congestion at every level, since there was nowhere for those trying to escape the region to go and no way to get there, even if there had been. Borders throughout the region had been shut at every level—air, land, and sea—with armies setting heavy weaponry, even tanks, in place, their orders uniformly to take any measures necessary to stop any and all incursions or mass exoduses.

Max was finally able to board a small military jet bound for Cyprus out of London. Only because of his presence on board, along with other military personnel reporting for duty, was that plane allowed to land in Cyprus, after Athens had shuttered its gates as well. Walking across the stilled tarmac toward the chopper dispatched to retrieve him, he was struck by the sea of civilian faces of the stranded pressed against the terminal's windows, rapping futilely on the glass. The congestion reached three or four deep in places, and Max boarded the chopper, picturing comparable scenes unfolding at airports all across the Mideast, as well as all of Europe and Asia by now, with the United States, almost inevitably, certain to follow.

For Max, the first leg of his journey out of Vancouver had gotten only marginally better in the wake of his dream, vision, or whatever it had been. He tried to recall the room, the setting, but it was the beautiful woman in the mask that continued to consume him. He hadn't been able to get her out of his mind, an attraction, obsession even, he couldn't explain or quantify. Like so much else that had happened this past week, it made no rational sense. And yet he felt that room, and the woman in the mask, were somehow meaningful, foreshadowing something to come.

While aboard the chopper, his mind drifted a decade back. "Max Borgia" had been born the moment his father had come to get him at a shuttered backwoods bait store, both of them knowing Max Younger could never return after what he'd done to Dale Denton's thugs. So he'd escaped into another life made possible by his father's connections and money. A veritable fortune spent to turn Max Younger into Max Borgia with documents that would hold up anywhere, anytime. From that night on, he'd become a nomad, never even aware that his father was sick. Only Dale Denton had commented for the news reports, lamenting his best friend and business partner's untimely passing, while never mentioning that Ben Younger's son had been on the verge of killing him until Vicky intervened. Max's mother, the articles had said, could not be reached for comment.

Looking back on that night in the Adirondacks and tension-riddled days that followed, Max could tell something had indeed been wrong, that his father was in pain. But he passed it off to discomfort over Max having finally gone over the edge his parents had always feared he might. And his father knew full well that, had he told Max the truth, Max never would have left, remaining by his side until the inevitable happened.

He was a thousand miles away when Ben Younger jumped sixty stories to his death, in a shabby motel that took cash and didn't ask questions, unable to attend the funeral or be present to comfort his mother. In retrospect, Max figured his father's death had pushed her all the way around the bend. He'd later find out that she missed the funeral herself, hospitalized due to a fit of stress-induced delirium that had stolen her grasp of sanity, particularly place and time.

The scandal that had followed his father's death had both bankrupted his mother and led to her ultimate institutionalization. His reunion with her, on her birthday just a few days before, had proven discomforting, even before the killers appeared in the guise of orderlies. His mother's recitations of her conversations with the little blind girl she called Lilith had left Max distinctly unsettled, particularly Lilith's prediction of what was coming.

*"All the tribulations. She told me about them."*

And right now, as the chopper finally settled into its descent for the *George H. W. Bush*, Max was struck hard and fast by the realization that these tribulations weren't coming at all.

They were already here.

# SIXTY-THREE

## Cape Horn, Chile

D ale Denton and Orson Beekman landed at Malvinas Argentinas International Airport in Cape Horn aboard a Western Energy Technologies GS650, exactly twenty-four hours after the disastrous conclusion of their latest experiment. All eight personnel who'd been inexplicably and brutally stricken in the underground lab were dead. Only the fact that he and Beekman had been upstairs in his twentieth-floor office had spared them. Nor were they likely to face any legal recriminations at this point, although the disaster was sure to result in an investigation Denton would eventually have to buy his way clear of.

Making this the perfect time to lay low for a time, while still pursuing their experiments on the rock.

"We're going to Cape Horn," Denton had informed Beekman, even as they watched the constant stream of arriving ambulances and rescue wagons on the street below, in the aftermath of the sub-sea earthquake. "A setting far better equipped to handle our continued work, away from any scrutiny from the authorities we may face now. We can't risk losing that rock again."

Beekman couldn't believe what he was hearing. "After what just happened, what we just witnessed, you still want to . . ."

His voice had trailed off there, unable to finish his thought.

"Even more," Denton had told him, in the spill of the stream of flashing lights below. "Even more, *because* of what we just witnessed."

"What are you going to say to the authorities about the scientists and technicians found dead in our lab?"

Denton smirked. "You let me worry about that, Professor. It's just another mess, and I've been cleaning up messes my entire career. Part of being successful is knowing how to rectify mistakes, circumstances beyond your control. And I pay the proper professionals whatever it takes to deal with these type of problems."

"By deal, you mean covering them up."

"I mean, doing whatever has to be done. Coming clean, confessing culpability, won't bring those people back, Professor. And they knew the risks, just like you and I did. It wasn't like we caused this, or had any reason to anticipate it. I mean, can you really explain what happened?"

"I don't think anyone can explain what happened."

"All right," Denton nodded, "then how would you describe the level of energy the rock is capable of generating or amplifying?"

"I can't."

"Precisely why we need to go someplace you can. Cape Horn, Professor," Denton said, and studied him briefly. "That concerns you?"

"Doesn't bringing that rock anywhere near a supercollider concern you?"

"On the contrary, it excites me. And, correct me if I'm wrong, but the vacuum-sealed collider chamber might well be the best, the only safe way, to truly harness and quantify that resulting level of energy the rock produces."

"The only safe way is to abandon our efforts entirely."

"Something I'm not about to do, Professor. There's no need to pack anything. I'll have a change of clothes waiting for us in Cape Horn when we land. I've already called ahead to have the Gulfstream prepped."


Cape Horn was the southernmost headland of the Tierra del Fuego archipelago of southern Chile. Located on Hornos Island, it was best known for its strategic maritime location at the point where the Atlantic and Pacific Oceans intersect. Prior to the opening of the Panama Canal, it had represented one of the most heavily traveled points for sailors traversing the seas.

A multi-national consortium of foreign governments had built a smaller-scale supercollider beneath a rocky sprawl of land on Cape Horn, only to see their efforts go for naught when far larger facilities at CERN and elsewhere commanded all the world's attention and research dollars. That had allowed Denton to buy a stake in the facility for an absurdly low dollar amount compared to the original investment outlay. He'd kept the transactions hidden from authorities, thanks to WET's substantial cash reserves, generated by gas revenues from a massive strike nearby Tierra del Fuego. With the right people in the Chilean government on board, thanks to their own wallets being fattened, the venture became a win-win across the board, assuring the facility would remain open as a prime generator of employment in an otherwise depressed region.

"There's something else," Beekman said, as the Gulfstream streaked into its descent, looking up from the laptop that had commanded his attention through much of the flight. "I've been studying and analyzing all the data from our latest . . . experiment," he finished, wishing there was a better word to describe it.

"And?"

"We shouldn't have come here," Beekman said, gazing out the window at the island below enclosed by nothing but blue. "We shouldn't be doing this. What caused the sub-sea earthquake in the Gulf of Mexico boasted the energy equivalent of a single atomic bomb in the forty megaton range. Add a supercollider to the mix and we could be looking at measurable energy output in the range of ten million atomic bombs."

"Enough to power the entire world," Denton realized, barely able to restrain his smile.

"Or destroy it," added Beekman.

# SIXTY-FOUR

### *George H. W. Bush*

R ed led Father Jimenez to a bulkhead door deep in the bowels of the ship guarded by two marines. The door was outfitted with an optical scanner Red waved a blank white keycard before. A light flashed from red to green, as the heavy door clicked, and one of the marines pulled it open.

Jimenez followed Red inside, struck immediately by the cold, clammy air that felt different from any other part of the ship. Before them, personnel in white lab coats scurried about, working a variety of machines set against a glass wall. Beyond that wall, what looked like medical personnel, wearing helmeted isolation suits, hovered over a trio of beds holding a man, woman, and young child.

"They don't speak any English, but we've got more personnel who speak Arabic on this ship than salt shakers," Red explained. "Stand back and listen, Father. Let's see if we can learn something."

Jimenez aimed his focus through the glass at the man, woman, and child. "Who are they?"

"Refugees. Or, more accurately, survivors from a Sunni village in western Iraq under the control of the New Islamic Front." Red's expression flattened, empty even for him. "We believe that village to be the first one infected by whatever's spreading through the Middle East. They must've gotten out just in time. We're about to find out what happened."

The man's bed was rolled closer to the glass and one of the suited medical personnel inside the sealed chamber fitted a headset in place, compressing his thick hair and adjusting the microphone into the proper position. Jimenez turned to his right to see that Admiral Darby had entered the front room, trailed by an intelligence officer accompanied by a sailor wearing ensign's bars. The ensign looked nervous, uncomfortable in the intelligence officer's presence, as if he'd been enlisted with a task that brought more responsibility than he feared he could handle.

The translator, Jimenez assumed, as he watched the ensign step right up to the glass, waiting for the intelligence officer to nod before beginning.

"What's your name?" the ensign asked the man behind the glass in Arabic.

The man on the other side of the glass swallowed hard, Jimenez being fluent enough in Arabic to not need to listen to the ensign's translation into English. "Masul."

"And this is your wife and child, Masul?"

The man nodded.

"And the name of your village?"

Another swallow, Masul seeming to struggle through the motion this time. "El Mady."

"What happened in El Mady?"

"It all started with her, when she came."

"Who?"

"The little girl, a refugee, we thought."

Jimenez felt his insides seize up. His heart skipped a beat.

"Describe this little girl," Jimenez heard the translator say in Arabic.

"She was blind. Nobody knew where she came from. My son spotted her," Masul said, trying to cant his body to gaze back toward the boy, but the confines of the hospital bed wouldn't let him. "He said he saw her wandering through the village, but we couldn't find her. Then someone else spotted her too. And someone else. We all looked for her, believing her to be an orphan from a nearby besieged village, but she was nowhere to be found." Masul's eyes bulged. He looked suddenly terrified. "Our village was peaceful! We had done what we needed to do, made our deal with the devil. But still *she* came. Still, she . . . A demon, that's what she was, a demon sent by the devil to punish us, even though we'd done nothing wrong!"

Masul's voice choked up. He suddenly seemed to be short of breath, taking a few moments to settle himself.

"And then Assawi returned from Lebanon," the man continued.

Red stepped up close to the ensign, bristling as he pointed toward Masul. "Did he say Assawi? *Hanan* Assawi?"

The man on other side of the glass must've heard Red because he nod-ded. "Yes, Hanan Assawi."

"Operational commander of the New Islamic Front. One of al-Qadir's most trusted lieutenants," the intelligence officer said, addressing Red before returning his attention to the ensign. "Ask him about Lebanon."

The ensign did, Jimenez listening to him translate Masul's answer this time. "He says he doesn't know what Assawi was doing there. He said it was a mission for the Front, as he calls it. He said the Front chose their village as one of their bases, moved personnel in and displaced residents from their homes. Those who protested, he says, were beheaded or tor-tured. The rest, like him, became virtual slaves."

"Ask him what happened when Assawi returned," Red interjected.

Again, the ensign waited for the answer and then translated, panic spreading over Masul's expression, as his words moved a few beats ahead of the translated portion. "He says Assawi wasn't right when he returned, that he seemed ill and angry, more angry than usual. His eyes were red and he was bleeding from the nose, and looked very pale and sick. Masul says he saw him at the river, where Assawi came to collect his clothes the women of the village were washing for him. Then Masul no-ticed a figure standing on the other side of the river. It was that little girl they'd been looking for, he says, just standing there and watching. She looked at him, before turning to Assawi, and Masul says he felt a chill like nothing he'd ever felt before. He says it left him shaking from cold in the blazing hot sun. Assawi kept looking at her, and Masul says he could tell she was staring back at him. Then Assawi waded into the shal-lows, out toward her on the other side.

"The little girl was standing there, staring at him," the ensign continued, translating the words as quickly as he could, "no longer acknowledging anyone else. And he kept walking toward her through the water. As-sawi's nose was dripping blood. Masul says he remembers him wiping it with his sleeve; the flecks of it he cast into the air looked like mist. And then Assawi went under and never came back up. Masul said he didn't dive in to rescue him because he can't swim, but others plunged into the water and came up empty. They couldn't find his body, and by the time they gave up, the little girl was gone."

"Son of a bitch must've brought the infection back with him from the facility in Lebanon," Admiral Darby said, shaking his head. "They were concocting God knows what there, right under our goddamn noses. And whatever it is, Assawi must've contaminated this town of El Mady with it."

"Others in the village took sick soon after," Jimenez listened to Masul continue. "And then the sick got sicker and sicker. They began to bleed from everywhere, and then their skin turned gray, hardened to feel more like wood. And when the skin that felt like wood was gone, they turned into monsters that killed and killed and killed, and the ones they killed became like them, and, and—"

The man's voice dissolved into sobs that left his face soaked with tears, choking up. By that point, Jimenez's mind was back in Brazil, where he'd encountered the little blind girl himself.

*"Your God is not here."*

Spoken as if she knew those were virtually the same words spoken to him years before in Nigeria by Cambridge.

Because she had, she had known.

"Tell me more about the little girl," Jimenez said in Arabic, no longer able to contain himself, approaching the glass.

Both Red and the intelligence officer swung his way, but didn't intervene.

"We had never seen her before," Masul responded. "We don't know where she came from. Then she went away. After Assawi drowned, and our people began taking sick, she went away, and we never saw her again. I took my family and fled at the first sign, never able to get the little girl's stare out of my mind. She seemed to see right through me, even though she was blind."

"We need to communicate this to the WHO team in the field," Red said to Admiral Darby. "This village is where the spread began. It started with Assawi."

"I'm not sending civilians anywhere without protection," Darby told him. "I've got three SEAL units prepping now."

"How long before they can reach western Iraq, to whatever's left of El Mady?"

"Six hours, once the Team Six commander is aboard this ship."

The admiral's assistant hurried over and whispered something in his ear.

"Make that six hours period," Darby announced. "He just landed."

# SIXTY-FIVE

## Northern Israel

While awaiting the all clear for transport to Iraq from the Israeli military base where she was currently hunkered down, Vicky busied herself with what the latest report from the *George H. W. Bush* added to the picture she was already forming. Specifically, the fact that the infected facility in southern Lebanon, by all indications, had been set up and operated by someone fronting a ruthless terrorist operation. Clearly they'd been developing something that went horribly wrong, the infection just beginning to spread when one of the terrorist group's commanders paid a visit to the facility. He'd brought what Neal Van Royce had called Medusa back with him to a village in western Iraq.

The infected man had, by all accounts, drowned himself in the river that supplied the village with its water. Mere days later, the entire village was infected.

*Water . . .*

Vicky had already turned her attention to the means by which the pathogen spread, a task complicated by the apparent random assemblage of afflicted zones. And the notion of water as the potential means by which Medusa was spreading led to a series of calls, one after another, with civil engineers across the Middle East. As a result, a map of the region displayed on her laptop screen became a smorgasbord of random pinpricks, with no discernible linkages, at least not aboveground.

According to the various experts made available to her by governments throughout the region, there were two major types of aquifers supplying the vast majority of the Middle East's water supply. Along river valleys and beneath the plains, there were shallow alluvial aquifers. These were generally unconfined, small in area, and had water tables that responded rapidly to local precipitation conditions, as was the case in the village of

El Mady. The second type were deep rock aquifers of sedimentary origin, usually sandstone and limestone, containing water supplies that could be thousands of years old and extended over thousands of square miles.

Studying the map that had resulted from her collating all the data she'd accumulated from nine different water supply experts, Vicky could see that the Harh el Kabir aquifer supplied water to southern Lebanon, where the former bio-weapons facility had been located. The village in Jordan she visited first got its water from the Bazalt-Azraq aquifer, while the doomed village in Egypt's north Sinai was supplied by the Great Western aquifer. But these three aquifers were actually unified by a deeper underground alluvial pool so far beneath the surface that its very existence had remained under dispute, until the Saudis laid out plans to base a large-scale, deep sandstone aquifer development project on its huge untapped resources.

So if Medusa was a waterborne pathogen, as opposed to air, the mishmash of dots on Vicky's screen, representing infected areas, made perfect sense. Although she'd never encountered one on this level, there were ample precedents to support the possibility; typhoid, for example, or dysentery. There were even theories that the bubonic plague had spread that way, after the bodies of rats infected with the pestilence were dumped in the rivers.

Overwhelmed and frightened by the vast array of material she'd collected, Vicky imagined the pathogen feeding off the molecules of standard $H_2O$ to divide and replicate on the order of something like ten parts per million. That meant a single drop was capable of infecting every single person exposed to a defined water source.

Vicky hadn't had the opportunity to test the water supplies in any of the sites she'd visited so far. And that made a visit to El Mady, where Medusa had first migrated from its origins in southern Lebanon, all the more vital. She needed to test the water samples there. She needed to compare what she found in them to the meager data she'd managed to accumulate on Medusa from her analysis of the tissue harvested from the two patients she'd examined up close and personal.

Toward that end, Vicky was waiting for the Israeli officer in direct communication with the *George H. W. Bush* to give her the word it was time to depart for Iraq. She'd been told a protective force was being assembled for her and the CDC team she'd be rendezvousing with at a base in

Turkey, before moving on to the virtual wasteland controlled almost in total by Mohammed al-Qadir and his New Islamic Front.

Vicky heard a knock on the door, but didn't register it, until the door opened and an Israeli officer poked his head in.

"It's time," he said. "We have the Go."

# SIXTY-SIX

## Western Iraq

Mohammed al-Qadir walked the desert grounds layered over the New Islamic Front headquarters that had been serving as his base of operations, feeling the scorching sun bake his skin. He found something as simple as fresh air to be incredibly refreshing, given the subterranean hideout in which the recirculated air felt stale and dry. Climate controls could only do so much, and the air always felt damp and spoiled.

He was expecting a call any moment on the satellite phone tucked inside an inner pocket of his robes, currently billowing in the breeze. That breeze carried something else with it, not a smell so much as a feeling he couldn't describe in rational terms. As if something was happening in the world around him and this was residue of that. Because . . .

Al-Qadir's mind drifted briefly, then snapped back in tune.

Because *something* was coming.

Something that was beyond even his control, and yet capable of helping him fulfill his vision. So many others before him had sought this same destiny, only to fail, often miserably. Not him. Al-Qadir had realized the movement he'd unleashed had taken on a very real life of its own, after dispatching two of his most trusted lieutenants to look into the progress being made at the facility in southern Lebanon. The report they'd furnished had been routine, but not the fates they'd suffered in the wake of issuing it.

By all accounts, they'd taken sick around the same time. All contact had been lost with the village of El Mady, where his commander Assawi was based, while he'd had the other transported to the Front base in Syria, still alive for the time being. That man had been transformed into something most would see as monstrous, but that al-Qadir saw as blessed. Because in that transformation, he realized, a pathogen far different from what he'd intended to release was now spreading through the Middle

East. Maybe the air carried some vague hint of that pestilence and all the death it was destined to leave in its wake. Maybe that was what he was sensing.

*Because something is coming.*

As a boy, he'd witnessed the murder of his parents, at the hands of Soviet troops. They might have killed him as well, if he hadn't had the sense of mind to hide under their blood-soaked, bullet-riddled bodies. He'd stayed there for hours, until he was found by officials inspecting the countryside after the series of Soviet raids had crushed the country's spirit.

From that point, time became a blur. He'd just turned seven when he was taken to London to meet his new family, devout Catholics who'd tried to convert him to the ways of a different God, Jesus Christ. Going to church with them, squeezing their hands with a contented smile plastered over his face, was al-Qadir's first experience with wearing the mask he ultimately became very adept at donning. He'd learned in those early years the importance of appearances and how easy it was to manipulate the opinions of others.

He'd let them baptize him, made himself flourish in a school taught by priests and nuns. Then, years later, he'd burned down a church with his adoptive parents inside, among other worshippers to a false God. The Russian soldier who had raped his mother before killing her, after all, had worn a crucifix dangling from a chain round his neck. For years, until the day he watched that church burn, al-Qadir had visualized himself strangling that soldier with his own chain.

Strange that he honestly couldn't remember his Christian name from those days, any more than he could remember the Halloween costumes he'd worn as a child. The name too was nothing more than a costume, to be discarded and forgotten when the time was right. He'd entered the army and then Special Air Service under his real name, though he thought of that version of himself as "Cambridge," the name he used in missions.

Nigeria was the tipping point. Nigeria was when he'd tucked all the costumes away in a metaphorical closet to become the man he'd always been meant to be. He wasn't sure how or when he'd actually realized it. Something about the oddities surrounding a meteor strike that apparently wasn't, all the mumbo jumbo Professor Jimenez kept spouting about the unprecedented nature of what they were facing. Tribes indigenous to the area had been wiped out by whatever carved a crater out of the jungle. Animal carcasses sent floating down the rivers, birds falling out of the sky, fish washing up on shore.

To this day, al-Qadir still didn't fully comprehend the role being bitten by a snake had played in all this. He knew only that a fever had followed for days, the bite giving way to a festering sore that smelled of something worse than death. In his feverish state, he thought he felt something different about his blood, about the way it coursed through his veins. Even after the fever had passed, though, he continued to feel different than he ever had before, as if the man he'd been up until then was gone, and someone else had taken his place. And then fate had delivered unto al-Qadir the man who would become his partner in an effort to remake the world, each man with their own motives that could best be achieved mutually, the two of them serving each other's ends.

"Cambridge" had been nothing more than another costume, to be shed with all the others. So al-Qadir felt nothing when he killed the SAS troops with whom he served, because they were only an extension of the same costume. The Maitatsine rebels, who'd eventually evolve into Boko Haram, had helped open the door that was always destined to someday be before him, and the samples and notebook he'd taken from Jimenez held the means to realize his vision for the future.

But something had gone wrong or, more accurately, right.

And now *something* was coming.

The satellite phone rang and al-Qadir jerked it from his robes, the voice on the other end of the line coming in crystal clear without the layers of shale and limestone to impede it.

"God has smiled on us," the voice reported. " 'For, behold, I will send serpents, cockatrices, among you, which will not be charmed, and they shall bite you, saith the Lord.' "

His mention of serpents made al-Qadir think of the snake biting him at the outset of his becoming. The wound had festered for months, welcomed for the symbol of the great awakening he had experienced. That bite had left its permanent mark on him that remained to this day, never understood until these recent events had made al-Qadir see it as the harbinger it must've been, assuring his place in the new world that was dawning.

"The serpents have been unleashed by our hands with His guidance," the voice on the other end of the line continued. "The Middle East will soon be overrun, the entire world to follow. Just as we hoped from the beginning."

"We have His intervention and stern hand to thank for this," al-Qadir told him, "not our own measly efforts which had been intended to pro-duce something else entirely."

"But we never knew what those samples from Nigeria were really going to produce, did we? All the time we thought we were in control, doing God's true work, when we were no more than thoughtless ves-sels doing His bidding instead. And right now He bids us to impede any efforts undertaken by the World Health Organization to thwart our intentions. That's why I'm calling."

"Leave the World Health Organization to me," al-Qadir said, grasping his arm on the side where he'd been bitten all those years ago.

# SIXTY-SEVEN

### *George H. W. Bush*

Enjoying the view, Father?" Red said to Jimenez, after finding the priest pacing the aircraft carrier's main deck.

"I needed to get some fresh air." Jimenez snapped his gaze from the waters. "And I need to present my report to the Vatican."

"You going to tell them the Book of Revelation had things right all along, Father?"

"Is that what you believe?"

For a few moments, Red looked as if he had no intention of responding. As Jimenez regarded him, the bracing wind lifted his thick hair up and dropped it back down exactly in the same place. And when Red finally spoke, his voice was lower, as if buffeted by the wind, a man revealing himself for the first time to Jimenez as one might in the confessional.

"Let me tell you what I don't believe. I don't believe it's a coincidence that you, a Vatican investigator, was on the scene of three different meteor strikes that made no scientific sense."

"Then what is it?"

Red flashed his familiar smirk that Jimenez now realized was rooted in uncertainty more than anything else. "You're the miracle man, Father. That's your specialty. Speaking of which, I have that picture from Brazil you requested."

With that, Red removed a plain piece of paper from his pocket and unfolded it to reveal the picture of a young girl clutching the remnants of a toy bear in the portion of the Brazilian rainforest that had been inexplicably blighted.

"Looks like you were right, Father."

Jimenez crossed himself, refused to take the picture from Red's grasp.

"You want to call this paranormal," Red resumed, "go ahead. You want to call it supernatural, that's fine too. But I think both of us have finally met our match when it comes to dealing with the inexplicable. I showed this picture to that Iraqi we questioned who survived the infection in his village. He looked at it and lost his breath—literally. When he got his breath back, he claimed it was the same little blind girl who appeared in his village. You want to tell me how that's possible?"

"If you're looking for a rational explanation, you won't like what I have to say."

"Try me."

Jimenez looked away and spoke with his gaze drifting out over the sea. "She didn't speak English, when I met her in Brazil, but she told me, 'Your God is not here.' The same thing Cambridge said to me just before the eclipse that changed my life forever." He turned back toward Red. "How could she know that?"

"You tell me, Father."

"The Brazilian authorities said her name was Belinha, but she corrected them, and told me it was Bituah. I should have realized then. It was right in front of me. . . ."

"What was right in front of you?"

Jimenez held Red's stare for a moment before responding. "Bituah is one of several names across the world that the biblical Lilith goes by. According to the Old Testament Lilith was the mother of all demons."

"So you're saying this little blind girl is a *demon*? Is that it, Father?"

"No, not a demon," Jimenez corrected. "As crazy as it sounds, I believe this little girl may be the devil himself."

Red did a double take, waiting for Jimenez to recant his words, and responding only when he didn't. "Sounds like you've found religion again, Father."

Jimenez swung back toward him. "Religion has never been able to adequately explain the existence of good and evil."

"And that's what you believe we're in the midst of, some ultimate battle between them?"

"I'm not sure how much the good actually figures in. The dark is winning. That's why the little girl is here. She's a personification of everything that is dark, now in the process of shutting out the last vestiges of light."

"Pretty grim outlook for a man of God."

"I became a priest because I was convinced a miracle saved my life."

"There are no miracles, Father," said Red. "You know that as well as I. Instead, there's fate, and our particular place in it."

Jimenez squeezed the deck railing so tight the blood rushed from his hands. "Cambridge was bitten by a snake in the Nigerian jungle, a snake likely infected by this pathogen in its base form. Beyond these waters, the Middle East is being overrun by monsters. I believe Cambridge, Mohammed al-Qadir now, was the first monster the pathogen created."

Red nodded, studying Jimenez the whole time, rigid stare boring into him again. "Then let's assume whatever was in those samples Cambridge took from you at the site of the Nigerian strike ultimately became the basis for what the WHO has labeled Medusa. Any idea what might have been in those samples?"

"No, not even a clue."

"But they must've come from the meteor, right? Just like the meteor that wiped out the dinosaurs maybe, or the meteor that may have infected that town in Siberia you also investigated for the Vatican."

"Where are you going with this?"

"Oh, back about thirteen and a half billion years ago, when a massive collision of energy produced a vacuum in space, a Black Hole so to speak, that birthed physical matter out of intense gravitational pressure."

"The Big Bang theory," Jimenez nodded.

"I read your book on the subject, Professor," Red told him. "I especially enjoyed your theories on singularity, specifically that the Big Bang released an immeasurable degree of pressure so intense that finite matter was crushed into infinite destiny. A planet reduced to something no bigger than, say, the size of your fist."

"I'm glad I can count you as a fan."

Red ignored Jimenez's attempt at levity. "So what if the Big Bang produced a similarly infinite number of these singularities? Light matter gets left behind in droves and congeals the Universe. Dark matter sticks around only long enough for scientists today to realize it was there. It was isolated in CERN for a hundredth of a second a few years back in what was considered a major accomplishment."

"Where are you going with this?"

"You're a scientist too, Father. Why don't you tell me?"

In spite of his own reservations, Jimenez couldn't resist picking up on Red's question. "After the so-called Big Bang, light matter stuck around and formed planets holding at least the possibility of life. Dark matter got scattered light-years across space."

"You're getting warm, Father. Let me heat things up a bit more. The express train known as a black hole was taking passengers and that's where dark matter's ticket got punched. Thirteen and a half billion years ago, dark matter didn't just get scattered, it went into the black hole on one side and came out an immeasurable distance away on the other. And it's taken all this time for it to get back, starting sixty-five million years ago, drawn back to the light matter like one magnet to another."

"Then these meteor strikes without meteors, the fist-sized objects that actually left the craters, like the one that brought on the Ice Age . . . You're postulating they're comprised of dark matter, coming home to roost?"

"I'm not postulating anything, Father; you suggested as much in your book. The strikes are coming more frequently as dark matter finds its way home: Nigeria, Siberia, Brazil, and who knows how many more in total. You want to know about good and evil, God and the devil? Then look no further. Science explaining superstition. Hey, it was Einstein himself who said that imagination was more important than knowledge."

"We could use his help now," Jimenez said, trying for a smile that never came.

# SIXTY-EIGHT

### Cape Horn

D r. Ernst Stowell, the Swiss scientist Dale Denton lured away from a similar post at CERN to oversee operations for WET's supercollider, looked up in amazement from his third read of the report prepared by Orson Beekman.

"You're certain these figures are accurate?" he asked Denton, after clearing his throat.

"I was there, Doctor."

Stowell turned to the photos but stopped short of regarding them again. "And these pictures?"

"Like I said, I was there."

Stowell shook his head. "Amazing, incredible even, as well as terrifying."

"That's why we're here, Doctor."


A generation before, following the company's whirlwind initial string of successes, Denton had been part of a consortium that had pushed for the okay to build a supercollider in Waxahachie, Texas. Desertron, as the project became known, would have created the largest particle accelerator in the world, surpassing even the Large Hadron Collider at CERN, in Switzerland. But after half the four-billion-dollar budget was spent with too little to show for it, and estimates to complete construction grew to twelve billion dollars, the project was shelved.

Denton had given up on Desertron, but he had no intention of giving up on owning a piece of a particle accelerator. So when the opportunity arose to buy the whole of one constructed in Cape Horn, Denton pounced. The price was a mere seven hundred million dollars, a fraction of the original construction costs.

He'd sold the Western Energy Technologies board of directors on the investment by demonstrating how they'd make their money back by leasing the facility's vast capabilities out to any private concern or country that could afford them. In point of fact, little of that revenue had ever come to pass. Although his board was getting restless, Denton continued to assuage their reservations and misgivings, the whole time visualizing the day when the Cape Horn collider became his ticket to achieving his greatest dream of turning WET into the world's most dominant energy producer and supplier.

The particle accelerator here was buried two hundred feet beneath tons of shale and limestone that provided the island its structural integrity. It was tubular in design and had been constructed inside a spherical tunnel that boasted a circumference of nearly twenty miles, even larger than CERN. A dozen feet wide, the tunnel was constructed of the highest grade tungsten steel available, its walls reinforced with the strongest concrete imaginable.

The asking price had been so low, it was almost like Chilean officials were paying him to take the facility over. And why not, Denton mused, given the virtual exchange of Chilean currency for dollars, thanks to the auspices of Western Energy Technologies. A win-win situation that Denton could only hope was about to pay off in a big way for him now.


"You want to test the capacity of your stone with the supercollider," Stowell concluded, standing alongside Denton on a catwalk that overlooked the massive tunnel.

"That's right."

"In spite of your experiences back in Houston."

"*Because* of those experiences, Doctor."

"Have you ever heard of the Szilard Petition, Mr. Denton?"

"Can't say that I have."

"It was a letter crafted by Professor Leo Szilard in the wake of meetings held at the University of Chicago to discuss a post-nuclear world. The petition was signed by a large number of scientists involved with the Manhattan Project and delivered to your President Truman in July of 1945 urging him not to drop the bomb on Japan. The signees were concerned about the morality involved in using nuclear weapons, and a few even believed the use of one outside the confines of a test environment could set off a chain reaction that could destroy the world."

"The world was still standing the last time I checked."

"You're missing the point, Mr. Denton."

"What point is that?"

"That man's capacity for knowledge sometimes exceeds both his judgment and ability to control it."

"You believe that describes me?"

"I believe your . . . discovery is as advanced beyond the atom bomb, as the atom bomb was beyond the bullet. I believe the results of your initial testing in Houston indicates that testing was rushed, and that far more study needs to be done on this rock before subjecting it to further experiments of such a nature."

Denton broke Stowell's gaze and looked down again at what, from this angle, looked like an elaborate train tunnel, albeit one fitted with literally thousands of superconducting magnets.

"Maybe you're forgetting who's in charge here," Denton snapped, turning back toward Stowell so abruptly that the scientist recoiled.

"Me," Stowell said, without hesitation. "Last time I checked, anyway. I read my contract before I signed it."

"Then take a look at your paycheck and see who signs that. I've been paying you a fortune to operate this facility ever since my company took it over, and you have the balls to refuse a direct order?"

Stowell bristled, his slight, bony shoulders stiffening. "My grandparents were killed for resisting the Nazis."

"Here's the difference, Doctor: your grandparents didn't work for the Nazis. You work for me, and if you don't do what I tell you, you'll never work for anyone again." Denton paused to let his point sink in, but he wasn't finished yet. "By the way, your father learned from the experience of your grandparents, didn't he?"

Stowell tried to look away.

"Klaus Stowell joined the Nazi Party in his late teens and ended up a member of the Waffen SS. But he went by the name of Heinrich Strauss at the time. Managed to escape Nuremberg and build himself an entirely new identify after the war ended."

"How do you know all this?" Stowell asked, not bothering to deny Denton's assertion.

"You work for me, Doctor. I made it my business to know. And what do you think the world would make of such a revelation? What do you think it might do to that sterling reputation of yours?"

"Then at the very least, hear me out. You're correct in the assumption that the controlled environment provided by the particle accelerator is the ideal way to accurately measure your rock's capacity to generate energy through amplification."

"So we're finally on the same page."

"But a different book. The assumption only holds so long as the seals of the collider are intact. Should they rupture, should the collider implode, we would be talking about an energy burst millions of times more powerful than the one in Houston that caused a sub-sea earthquake."

"A risk I'm willing to take."

"Did you hear what I just said?"

"I didn't get where I am by sitting on my ass and watching others take the chances."

"This isn't like searching for oil, Mr. Denton," Stowell insisted, regaining his bravado.

"If you have something to say, Doctor, just say it."

"Imagine the world without gravity, Mr. Denton. Imagine the oxygen we breathe sucked into the atmosphere like air from a popped balloon. Because that could be what exposing the stone to the supercollider could yield. You want my advice? Go home. Give me some time to study your rock, come up with a definitive analysis and concrete strategy for containment. Six months, a year at most."

"I've waited too long already, and I can't wait any longer."

Stowell nodded. "Then perhaps I should contact your board of directors for approval. I wonder what they would make of all this, if they're even remotely aware of how much you've been keeping from them."

Denton nodded, remaining unflappable, as he took his cell phone from his pocket and extended it toward Stowell. "Call your son."

The man's lips quivered. He looked suddenly unsteady on his feet.

"Ask him where your grandchildren are," Denton continued, the appropriate precautions he'd ordered Spalding to take now justified. "He'll tell you they're late coming home from soccer practice. He'll tell you they're not answering their phones. He'll tell you he's beginning to get worried." Denton waited until Stowell met his stare again. "Do you want your grandchildren to ever come home again?"

"You're not just a criminal, you're a monster," Stowell hissed, his eyes welling with tears.

"A monster who made you rich, who will stop at nothing, absolutely *nothing*, to get what he wants. Control energy and you don't just control the world, Doctor, you own it. And now you're going to help me do that."

"You can't own something if you have to destroy it first, Mr. Denton."

"Just focus on your job, and think of your grandchildren," Denton told him, "and then tell me when you'll be ready to get started."

# SIXTY-NINE

### Western Iraq

**M**ax was mission commander for the three SEAL teams transported from the *George H. W. Bush* to Ayn al-Asad Airbase in the western Iraqi province of Al Anbar. From there, the SEALs would transfer onto a trio of Black Hawks for the sixty-mile trip over the desert to the village of El Mady, where they'd be rendezvousing with personnel attached to both the WHO and CDC, within territory that was as hostile as it got.

"Enjoy your vacation, Pope?" Griffon asked him, as they boarded the Black Hawks.

"New York is beautiful this time of year."

"New York? You mean you didn't visit your heavenly father on high?"

"That was my second choice."

The members of the three SEAL teams, amounting to thirty-six in total, were back in the air as soon as their equipment was loaded.

"So what do you make of this bug hunt?" Griffon asked him, settled in the back of their chopper while they waited for takeoff.

"That those things they showed us photos of make bug hunt an apt metaphor."

"Shoot for the head, right?"

"SOP for us, Grif. This is gonna be a cakewalk compared to what we faced in Yemen."

"You really believe that?"

"No," Max told him, "not even a little."


"Coast is clear according to intel," Admiral Darby reported through Max's earpiece, as the Black Hawk pilot finally settled into his seat. "No NIF fighters or any trace of those creatures in the area."

"So we're good to go," Max said, into his throat mic.

"We're a go, but there's nothing good about this I can see, son."

"You're smoking a cigar now, aren't you, Admiral?"

"I'm the one watching the live feed from the drones, son. How the fuck you know that?"

"Because you sound nervous, and you only smoke when you're nervous."

"You keep those scientists alive and kicking, maybe I won't have as much to be nervous about anymore. You hearing me?"

"Loud and clear, Admiral."

"Apaches are already staged at a forward operating base ten miles from your destination. We'll have F-16s airborne and circling, as soon as you touch down. Keep you as safe and snug as a good warm blanket."

"That's what I'm hoping, sir."

"I'm going to order the experts airborne now," Darby told him. "Give you the head start you need to secure the territory."


The increasing winds and diminished visibility at ground level had already kept the Apache gunships from taking off from their forward operating position to offer further protection. Those same winds could render moot the response capability of the F-16s already on station overhead, in the event a force was spotted advancing on El Mady. The best Max and his men could give the scientists, under such conditions, was ninety minutes from the time they landed.

His orders were to rendezvous with a Dr. Tanoury from the World Health Organization. But Max delegated that duty to Griffon and busied himself with erecting a strategic perimeter to secure the abandoned town that was more expansive than photo arrays indicated.

True to all available intel, and the testimony of a refugee aboard the *George H. W. Bush*, El Mady was, by all appearances, deserted. Motion scans by drones circling overhead before they set down had revealed no movement of any kind in the structures. Still, Max wouldn't feel satisfied until the SEALs completed their building-by-building search to make sure no harm befell the members of the scientific team soon to be landing.

Minutes later, he watched a single Sikorsky carrying that scientific team land uneasily in the buffeting winds on a flat patch of land adjacent to the SEALs' Black Hawks. The scientists had dispersed by the time he returned to the primary staging area, approaching a scientist garbed in a biohazard suit taking ground samples by plunging a collecting rod at various intervals.

"Excuse me," Max said, and raised the goggles that protected his eyes from the blowing sand. "I'm looking for Dr. Tanoury."

"I saw her heading toward the mosque," the man said, pointing toward a rectangular, flat-roofed building formed of sunbaked, sand-colored brick.

"She?" Max raised.

Vicky had left scrutiny of the local mosque to herself. The mosque was the village's largest building and central gathering point, the place to which villagers were most likely to flee in an emergency. Thus, it could provide a treasure trove of evidence that would help her determine the sequence of exactly what had transpired here after the infection began its spread. Even more to the point, the building featured a back room where water was stored in fifty-gallon drums, containing a wealth of anecdotal data that could prove crucial to her investigation.

This village had no running water, drawing their entire supply from either an adjoining river when the bed was full, or the storage drums in dry times when it rained. The plan was for CDC personnel to take samples from as many of the homes as possible to ascertain both the state of the victims' DNA and the state of any remaining water samples, toward isolating the Medusa strain which was the first step toward coming up with a vaccine or a cure.

Through the mosque windows, she spotted uniformed men, armed to the teeth, continuing to fan out through the village streets, but still made no move to greet them herself. The faces of the SEALs were camouflaged by goggles set over their eyes and kerchiefs strung round their mouths to protect from all the sand and dirt blowing about. So far she'd lifted samples from eight of the drums leaving around twenty left to go, hoping these troops would provide her the time she needed.

Max approached the mosque, rotating his gaze about the buildings and hills surrounding El Mady for any signs of movement or flashes of reflections off sniper sights. He could feel the tiny grains of sand peppering his face, leaving it tingly in some spots and painful in others. Then he real-ized his hand bearing the identical mark as his father was hurting again, unsure whether that was a bad omen or a good one. But the looming sand storm was definitely bad, certain to obscure view from above by drones and reconnaissance satellites.

Max was almost to the mosque when Grif's voice called out to him across the village square, instead of bothering with a walkie-talkie.

"Get back here, Pope!" he shouted, after Max had swung round. "On the double! We got ourselves a problem."

An eighth of a mile away, Mohammed al-Qadir stood with two hundred of his best fighters in the brushy cover provided by a thick grove. Experi-ence had shown that so long as they didn't move into the open en masse, their presence was effectively masked from the drones and satellites the Americans were certain to have in place overhead. At present, though, that was hardly a concern, given the thick swirls of dust forming minia-ture funnel clouds that whipped about the surface, strong enough in some instances to nearly topple his men from their feet.

Al-Qadir had already heard from his spotter that the American med-ical team had set down with somewhere around thirty American soldiers—Navy SEALs, by all indications. Formidable opposition to be sure, albeit severely reduced by the current conditions that precluded any close air support. He understood exactly how they operated because a long time ago, in his previous life in the guise of Cambridge, he'd been part of a comparable force.

Al-Qadir knew from his call with the man God had delivered unto him in Nigeria, that he was standing on the precipice of a great and blessed awakening. He believed the literal End of Days was being visited upon the world, due more to fortune than design, a fate set into motion by God Himself the moment al-Qadir, then Cambridge, had snatched up the samples taken from the meteor strike that had left no evidence of a meteor.

He scratched at his left arm through the flesh-colored sleeve that kept it hidden from even his closest associates. No point in showing them a mark that could be interpreted as weakness, when al-Qadir knew it to be a sign of strength, in fact, blessing the day all those years ago in Nige-ria when his final transformation had begun.

Al-Qadir checked the watch he'd taken from a Western journalist before having him beheaded, then returned to the NLF officers who would be commanding his two-hundred-fighter force to tell them it was time to move on El Mady.

After completing the task of drawing samples from the steel drums stored in the rear of the mosque, Vicky turned her attention to taking samples from the mosque floor, prayer rugs, and prayer books. Anything a worshipper might've come into contact with that might still hold their DNA. All across the village, CDC personnel were doing the very same thing, the collective goal being to gauge the spread and relative saturation of Medusa. There were still any number of variables that needed to be factored in to their final analysis from response to temperature, to the infection's life expectancy once isolated, to the pace of its ability to gestate and reproduce.

Listening to the winds picking up outside, Vicky set about collecting her next series of samples in the mosque proper.

Grif handed Max the handset of the radio currently strapped to another SEAL's back.

"This is Borgia."

"We got a change in plans, son," came the slightly garbled voice of Admiral Darby. "A sand storm bigger than the tornado that swept Dorothy to Oz sprang out of nowhere and is headed your way, and that's not the worst of it: We got ground intel assets reporting a New Islamic force less than a few klicks from your western flank when we lost sight of them in the muck."

"Shit!"

"That was my thought too, Commander. Mission parameters have changed. We're in full evac mode now. Get it done. Get everyone loaded and headed for home, while those birds can still fly."

"Roger that, Admiral," Max said, his hand really starting to throb now.

Max ordered the SEALs on patrol to round up the dozen members of the scientific team, while the remainder of the force would remain in place guarding the perimeter until the last possible moment. Max assigned himself to get the leader, Dr. Tanoury, in order to explain personally to her what was going on.

The mosque door was closed and stuck to its hinges when he tried to open it. So Max threw his shoulder into it and felt the wood crack slightly when it finally swung open.

Max froze, because he thought he recognized this place, but couldn't say from where. Just an illusion, he figured, until the lighting, layout, and size became suddenly familiar to him.

From the nightmare he'd had on the plane! Shadowy figures surrounding a beautiful woman, naked except for a black mask worn over her face. So clear in his mind and memory, that it felt exactly like he'd been here before.

And then, off to the side in the shadows, a woman, Dr. Tanoury, swung toward him, freezing as soon as their eyes met.

Vicky.

She couldn't believe her eyes, thought the dim lighting was playing a trick on her, a vision conjured up by the incredible stress she'd been under.

It couldn't be Max. Max had long hair, like some rock star he always got mistaken for. Max wore shapeless jeans under his boots and a motorcycle jacket he'd distressed all on his own. Max was always smiling, always holding a mischievous look in his eyes.

But this Navy SEAL's eyes were the same. Max's eyes.

Because it was him.

"Max," Vicky said, the clog in her throat blocking the rest of whatever she was going to say.

"We can't talk," Max said, finding his voice, wishing he were holding Vicky instead of his M4. "We're on the clock here. Full evac, as of right now. We need to move."

"But—"

"Save the buts; we got a storm and enemy fighters incoming at the same time." He moved forward, shrinking the gulf between them and taking her by the arm. "We need to move *now*!"

Vicky held her ground. "I can't leave yet. I need ten more minutes, five at least. It's vital."

Max looked at his watch, then at the padded sample case lying at her feet. "Ten minutes to load the rest of your team. I need you at the chopper then. Don't make me come back for you myself."

She forced a smile. "It's been ten years. I think I can wait a little longer to catch up."

The first chopper had just lifted off when Max reached the flat stretch of land adjacent to the village. The sand storm was picking up to a steady swirl in the air. No way any chopper would take off under such conditions in ordinary circumstances, but these were anything but that.

"You forget something, Pope?" Griffon asked him, raising his voice over the wind sounds and rotor wash.

And that's when an RPG took out the first chopper.

# SEVENTY

## *George H. W. Bush*

G oddammit!" Admiral Darby exclaimed, the fire burst still evident on
the reconnaissance drone's view of the scene below through the
swirling sand that clouded the picture. "What the hell's happening
down there?"

"The sand storm's playing hell with our communications, Admiral," a
com-tech called out from his monitoring station. "We've lost contact for
now."

"Get it back, son, 'cause now's all we've got."

### Western Iraq

The chopper turned onto its side in a ball of flame and then came crashing down a hundred feet away. The SEALs took the remaining scientists
down under them to avoid the spray of shrapnel from rotor blades turned
into deadly segmented shards. In the next instant, exchanges of gunfire
cut through the thick air, the enemy having reached the outskirts of the
village and the perimeter manned by the SEALs.

"Where are my eyes in the sky?" Max said out loud, trying to raise Admiral Darby. "We're blind down here!"

The gunfire intensified, Max's battle-seasoned ear telling him the
enemy force was attacking in overwhelming numbers.

Clearly, the initial wave of New Islamic Front fighters had been much
closer than available intelligence and recon had indicated. Now, under the
circumstances, even if the SEALs were able to somehow secure the area,
no other choppers would be leaving, the sand storm having now swallowed the world. Visibility reduced to the hand in front of your face. Max
had been on enough rough deployments in the Middle East to know his
way around battling the elements, along with the enemy. But he'd never

experienced anything like this, a sand storm that left no pockets or even slivers of sight to peer through. The sand caked up on his goggles and flooded his mouth, forcing him more and more to raise his kerchief to spit it out.

Max joined Grif behind the cover of a boulder at the edge of the flat stretch of land.

"We got hostiles everywhere, Pope, coming in from every angle of the village," he reported. He tried for a smile that didn't come. "Looks like we're gonna need some of that heavenly intervention of yours."

"I'm not sure it works in hell, Grif," Max said, clearing his goggles yet again.

Just in time to watch one of their Black Hawks perish in a huge fireball, followed almost immediately by the second.

### George H. W. Bush

"Get me something!" Admiral Darby ordered. "Anything! Try going to thermal!"

"Negative!" his chief com-tech reported. "Sensors can't penetrate the sand!"

"They were designed to penetrate any goddamn muck."

"Not muck this thick, sir."

Darby moved right behind the chief and grasped the back of his chair. "Son, I don't care if you've got to switch on the biggest pair of windshield wipers in the world, get me goddamn eyes on what's happening down there!"

### Western Iraq

Gunfire poured through the village in a now constant din, as the fighters' shots were matched by the SEALs left to guard El Mady's rear flank until the evacuation was complete.

That evacuation had ended when the first chopper had been hit, meaning they were stuck here with no help coming in these conditions. The best they could hope for was for enough improvement to allow the Apaches to stream in, but the sand sticking to the air seemed to be getting thicker, the storm showing no signs at all of abating.

"We got one stray still in the field," Max said into Grif's ear. "I'm going to make a pickup."

Vicky kept herself low and clear of the mosque's windows, the battle raging beyond like a fireworks show that never abated. The intensity of the sand storm that had sprung up without warning, stole view of anything through the glass anyway. And then much of that glass had been shattered by explosions that blazed orange in the sky beyond, bright enough to cut through the blowing sand. A pair of explosions that followed had rocked the building, seeming to tilt it one way, then back the other. She worked to secure the samples she'd already taken, while bullets peppered the building's walls, sending slivers of the storm inside through the holes and remnants of the windows.

Vicky pictured Max bursting through the mosque door, scooping her up in his arms and carrying her away. Realized in that crazed moment she was grateful for the danger and horror that had brought him back to her, that she'd never stopped loving him, even as she'd forced him from her memory, as she prepared to marry Thomas. For a brief moment, that brought all the baggage from the past back; how romantic it had been when she and Max had run away together, how much she hated her father, what a mess her life was at the time. Max had been the single constant, the only one who stood by her always, her one friend before he became much more than that on their night together in the Adirondacks.

Her gaze turned toward the door, certain he'd come bursting through it at any moment to save her.

Again.

The clamor of gunfire around Max was constant, and he could hear men screaming out instructions to each other in Arabic. Impossible to tell in these conditions how many fighters had invaded the village or where they were concentrated. But they were good, far more professional than he'd experienced before and far better equipped as well.

A fireball erupted just down the street, followed by an airburst and shock wave. Then a building exploded just fifty feet from him. Max could feel the center of the battle tugging at him like a magnet. He crouched lower to reduce his target, identifying enemy fighter after enemy fighter. He clacked off single shots, rotating with sprays of automatic fire, and three-shot bursts. The whole scene like one of those video training exercises where no matter how many you kill, more waves of gunmen keep coming.

And so they came, Max and the other SEALs dropping all they managed to claim in their sights without any hesitation whatsoever. But the hordes of enemy fighters stormed the village in overwhelming numbers, anything but the kind of hit-and-run tactics that was the normal terrorist strategy.

"We're taking casualties, Pope," he heard Griffon say in his earpiece. "More than a dozen men down and that's just for starters."

"Goddamnit!"

"Whoever heard of a gunfight in the middle of a sand storm? I swallowed what feels like the whole Jersey Shore already. If you ask me—"

A burst of static blared, so piercing Max wanted to strip out his earpiece. He thought he heard a wet, wheezing sound followed by the thud of a body hitting the ground, and now Griffon . . .

"Grif, do you read me? Grif, do you copy?"

. . . was gone.

Max continued to advance into the sandblasted air still thickening around him. He couldn't even see the tip of his M4's barrel anymore, but still didn't risk firing purely at shapes, at motion, since a measure of the surviving SEALs would've been forced into the streets at this point. Max swiped a sleeve across his goggles to clear them of the layer of pasty sand, but a fresh coat covered the lenses almost immediately. His mouth felt chalky, so much grit blowing into him that his kerchief was powerless to keep all of it out. It felt like he was chewing sand, fighting against the urge to retch, every time he reflexively tried to swallow it down.

A grenade blast shook him, and then he felt shards of exploded glass pepper the back of his flak jacket and prick his legs through the thick fabric. Another trio of blasts followed in rapid succession, screams trailing them until rapid bursts of fire silenced those too.

The fighters were killing his men. How many of the medical personnel had they found already, as well? How long before they found Vicky?

The last time he'd seen Vicky, ten years before, Max had wanted so badly to kill Dale Denton in order to save her from him. Now he had to save her from something else. As if the forces of the cosmos were conspiring to tear them apart yet again, after they'd finally found each other.

*Not this time*, he thought, as he pushed forward, *not again*.

The sand storm thickened around him, seeming to swirl about in concentric circles that further fed its power.

*I've got to find Grif.*

Max vividly recalled the area in which his second-in-command was posted, just as he could recall them for all the members of the team he was commanding. The problem was the sand storm had stolen his sense of direction from him, turned the world into a dark room where bearings were as valuable as gold.

"Grif, can you read me? Grif, do you copy?"

Only static greeted his call, and Max decided to let instinct guide him to Grif. Relinquish his conscious thought and let the more primal mechanisms at work inside him find the man he trusted more than anyone else in the world. Because Grif would do the same for him.

The swirling sand cleared in a pocket to his right, exposing a stream of fighters surging down the street, wearing goggles that made them look like giant insects. Max opened up with one spray and then another, none of the fighters even spotting him until he was halfway through the third burst that tore the legs out from two of the fighters and blew a third one into the air. All three wearing goggles comparable to his own, high-end models that were strictly military ordnance, meaning these fighters were exceptionally well-financed for a terrorist group.

Max ducked back into the thicker swirls of the storm, the cacophony of gunfire everywhere around him, realizing in that moment how badly his palm was aching now under his glove. And he could feel the warm soak of blood oozing out of the mark, starting to push its way through the neoprene material. Max tried to ignore it, but the stinging pain was like holding a cigarette lighter to his skin. The worst it had ever been, and it had been pretty bad as of late.

Then he heard a high-pitched scream, Vicky's scream, and the pain didn't matter anymore.

Inside the mosque, Vicky had stayed low through the battle, minutes stretching into what felt like hours, hunkered on the mosque floor low beneath any sightline from the windows when she heard the rear door crash open. She lurched back to her feet, just as a pair of fighters with faces like Halloween masks burst from a room in the rear.

They grabbed her before she could reach the front door, one on either side. Tugging, tearing, yanking, and finally dragging her toward the altar, their gleaming eyes all she could see beneath the black hoods draped over their heads.

Max felt something stirring deep inside him, like a surge of static electricity mixing with his blood. He felt a strength, a power, starting to rush through him, different from anything he'd felt before. He felt no fear, no trepidation, only certainty in the task before him. In the height of battle, there was never time to feel weak or vulnerable. But in this battle, somehow, there was time to feel supremely confident and, even, invincible. He was certain the scream he'd heard came from the mosque he recalled from his nightmare, was sure it was Vicky's.

Just like he was now sure she was the woman in the mask. It hadn't been a nightmare aboard the plane, it had been another vision, the meaning of the shadow figures, the altar, and the mask itself still unclear to him.

The surge he felt pulsing through him was eerily akin to the ones he'd experienced in the midst of so many of his experiences. Only what he felt today was different. More intense, more concentrated, more powerful. He felt as if he were floating, detached from his own body and gliding through the air instead of feeling his way over the ground.

He could still feel the sand peppering his face and clothes, could feel himself slogging through the increasingly powerful winds, but something was different. Because, suddenly, he could see through the swirling sand, as if the rage he felt bursting from inside him was acting as some kind of filter. The street was suddenly crystal clear before him, to the point where Max wondered if he'd lapsed into yet another vision.

He wanted them all dead, but not *just* dead. He wanted them to die in pain, in a lingering agony that visited upon them the wrath their actions demanded. By his hand. Pay the price for what they'd done, the pain he was about to inflict upon the sons of bitches worse than any they dispensed. That thought revived, recharged him.

Max didn't stop to consider the inelegance of his intentions. He thought only of killing the dozens of remaining fighters, every single one of them in as agonizing and gruesome a fashion as he could.

First, though, he needed to save Vicky, had just turned toward the mosque, when her piercing scream split the sandblasted air around him.

A quarter mile away, Mohammed al-Qadir stood in the company of his private guards, waiting for the battle to end and the American hostage to be delivered unto him. Up until that moment he'd felt celebratory, even joyous. Up until that moment, God's light was shining upon him even through the blessed storm that had engulfed the town of El Mady.

Then a blast of frigid air struck him. It was more like a wave, then a current, showing no signs of abating, even as it chilled him straight to the bone. When he went by another name, he'd thought nothing could be chillier than the dank air of Britain. But this burst of cold didn't feel like the product of nature at all, at least any nature al-Qadir knew or understood. It didn't just leave him trembling, it reached down to his core like icy tentacles that wrapped themselves around his very insides.

Before him, the swirling sands continued to hide any view of the world beyond, and al-Qadir was almost glad, having no desire to regard the source of the shrill cold that seemed to be freezing him where he stood.

Max burst through the mosque doors, spotting the two fighters holding Vicky down atop the altar, about to strip off her clothes. The hoods they wore, that were part and parcel of the New Islamic Front uniform, eerily resembled the hoods worn by the dark shapes that had surrounded the naked woman who obsessed him in a vision he now grasped in all its meaning and purpose. Max glided toward the altar, noticing they'd covered her face in black fabric to cloak her screams, making her appear masked, just like the woman in his vision.

The wind pushed through the breached entrance, a shrill dry gust of air Max recalled from his vision aboard the plane as well. He kept coming, approaching the altar, the fighters never once acknowledging his presence. Realized his M4 was now shouldered behind him, fourteen-inch tactical blade with customized rubber handle in his hand.

Max felt himself pounce. The men were holding Vicky and then they weren't, amid the swirls of sand blowing into the mosque from the street beyond. He felt the warm soak of blood, saw her unconscious frame covered in it, the bodies of the fighters lying in pieces around her.

Max scooped Vicky up and laid her over his left shoulder, unslinging his M4 from his right, as he moved back into the street. More fighters were coming, pouring into the square, converging on Max amid the already fallen bodies. He followed their motions with crystal clarity. Mohammed al-Qadir's fighters needed to pay for what they'd done here, each and every one of them. They'd taken out his team, his friends, the closest thing he had left of a family. The anger and rage in the face of that was hardly new, the lust he felt for blood something else again.

Max heard the constant clatter of gunshots, could feel the heat of the bullets singeing the air all around him. He didn't care about living or dying, the last moment or the next. There was only now, each moment elongated so it seemed to swallow the one that followed.

Max knew the sand was there, even though he could see through it. The world seemed to turn to slow motion all around him, he alone moving at regular speed. Suddenly, the view before him sharpened to crystal clarity. Suddenly, he was breathing normally, the sand no longer sifting into his mouth, Vicky feather light in his grasp, almost like she weighed nothing at all.

The last thought he formed before lurching into motion was that he felt . . . cold, freezing even.

Of all things.

# SEVENTY-ONE

### The Vatican

T hat's quite a story," Cardinal Josef Martenko said to Pascal Jimenez amid the breeze blowing through the Vatican gardens.

Jimenez watched him use a gold pen to jot some notes down on the small pad sitting on his lap, his gaze holding upon it.

"I've had this pen for a very long time," Martenko said when he noticed, holding the pen up for Jimenez to see closer, "through all the most daunting phases of my life."

Jimenez shook himself alert. "An excellent description of this past week, Your Eminence."

Martenko shook his head, expression still framed by disbelief. "Of course I've seen the reports of the infected rising from apparent death in these monstrous forms to infect and transform others into the same form." He shook his head again. "Horrifying, positively horrifying. To follow the media coverage of this scourge spreading through the Middle East is one thing, but to hear about it all firsthand . . ."

"There's more, Your Eminence," Jimenez told him.

"I don't want to hear it, Pascal. Your conclusions have ventured into a realm the church can have no part in. We are not in the business of passing off science as superstition, searching for the paranormal when logical explanations inevitably suffice. You of all people should know this."

Jimenez found his gaze straying to Martenko's gold pen again. "I did, Your Eminence. I don't anymore."

"So you would have your version of the battle between the forces of good and evil be reviewed by those Vatican officials certain to reject it out of hand. You'll destroy yourself in the process, Pascal, become a pariah in the only world you have left."

"I'm well aware of that."

Martenko twisted to better face Jimenez on the same park bench they'd shared many years before when the cardinal had convinced him to put his scientific knowledge to good use by debunking so-called miracles and providing rational explanations for the otherwise inexplicable. "I agreed to see you in my capacity as head of the Vatican Bank as a courtesy in view of our past relationship and my part in your becoming an investigator. In return for that courtesy, I ask that you rethink your intentions very carefully here, especially in such trying times for the church."

"I've heard the Holy Father is not well."

Martenko's expression crinkled in a mix of mourning and regret. "He was just given Last Rites, isn't expected to live through the day."

"I've also heard you are one of the favorites to replace him, in all probability *the* favorite, Your Eminence."

Martenko shrugged. "If that is to be my fate, then so be it."

"And what of the world's fate, Your Eminence? You would have us ignore the inescapable conclusions I just presented?"

"Yes, I would. First and foremost, you are a priest. You serve our Lord as I do, and everything we do must be with His best interests at heart. People are flocking back to churches in droves, Pascal. They are returning to God, because they feel He alone can save them. This report of yours would only confuse the issue, cast aspersions on the faith people have regained in His word and only His word. The last thing they need to hear is all this mumbo jumbo about stones and meteors and demonic children. Let us enjoy this moment and seek ways to keep the numbers of His flock strong."

"Did you just say *enjoy*?"

"Figure of speech."

Jimenez looked away, then back again. "There's something else, Your Eminence. The terrorist Mohammed al-Qadir—we both once knew him as Cambridge. In Nigeria."

Shock glazed Martenko's features. "How could that be?"

Jimenez held the cardinal's stare. "There is much I still don't understand. Only that everything has been connected. From the very beginning of this, it has all been connected."

"The beginning meaning Nigeria?"

"Long before that, Your Eminence," Jimenez said, shaking his head dismissively. "Billions and billions of years."

"Something else it is better to leave out of your report, Pascal," Martenko cautioned.

He pocketed his notepad, slid the gold pen back into his robe, and rose slowly from the bench.

"Go with God, Pascal," Martenko said, leaning over to bless Jimenez with the Holy Trinity.

Then he turned and walked off.

One of the cardinal's aids escorted Jimenez from the gardens, leaving him with only his thoughts until his phone rang. Jimenez answered, in spite of not recognizing the number on his caller ID.

"I catch you at a bad time, Father?" Red greeted, before he could say a word.

"No, not really."

"Wrong. It's a bad time, all right. You just don't know how bad yet. I've got some fresh intelligence to share on our friend Cambridge, aka Mohammed al-Qadir, from back when he originally immigrated to England as a young boy. Remember how the whole Chechnyan refugee program had been arranged by the Catholic churches?"

"Of course," Jimenez said, still trying to gather his bearings in the wake of his fruitless meeting with Cardinal Martenko. "What's it have to do with what we're facing now?"

"Only everything, Father," Red told him. "I hope you're sitting down. . . ."

# SEVENTY-TWO

**Western Iraq**

Max awoke in the central square of El Mady, the sand storm beginning to thin out around him. Grit and dirt clung to his clothes, a cooling ooze soaking through them.

Blood, Max thought, realizing what was pasting the muck to him. But not his blood.

He looked down to see an unconscious Vicky beneath him, his heart skipping a beat when he saw her covered in blood too.

*Oh God, please no . . .*

Swabbing his hand across her revealed the blood not to be hers either, and he recalled using his knife on the two fighters about to rape her in the mosque. Their blood, then, not hers.

What had happened, though, in the interim between this moment and what he last recalled?

Max remembered the rage boiling over in him, as he emerged from the mosque with Vicky slung over his shoulder. Mohammed al-Qadir's fighters needed to pay for what they'd done here, each and every one of them. The anger and rage in the face of that was hardly new, the lust he felt for blood something else again.

*And then . . .*

Nothing. He couldn't remember a thing, including the source of the blood drenching him everywhere, so much Max felt as if he'd dove into a river of it.

Around him, the sand storm continued to dissipate, the swirls becoming less concentrated and intense, allowing him to view the street through the blaring sunshine starting to burn through. The dozens and dozens of mounds unrecognizable at first, until Max stripped off his stained goggles to better view the aftermath of the battle.

### George H. W. Bush

The clearing of the sand storm finally allowed a drone to return to station over El Mady, the picture it revealed of the central square, streets, structures, and alleys below stealing the breath from both Red and Admiral Darby.

"Tell me I'm not seeing this," Darby managed.

"Oh, you're seeing it all right," said Red, a twinge of what sounded like excitement lacing his voice. "The bodies with the flashing Xs are ours, thanks to the locators each SEAL carried. The rest we can take to be the New Islamic Front fighters who were converging on the village."

"You seeing this the same way I am?"

"I think so, Admiral. The location and spacing of downed friendlies indicates they were taken out in pretty short order. Took as many bad guys with them as they could based on the spacing, but the enemy numbers and firepower were just too much to overcome. All those remaining bodies, all that carnage confined mostly to the central square, well, your guess is as good as mine."

"I'd like to hear yours."

Red zoomed in closer, the downed bodies easier to discern. They hadn't just been dropped by what would've been a nonstop torrent of heavy fire; their bodies had been shredded, mutilated. So much blood that, from the drone's perspective, it looked like a black blanket covering the square in an impressionistic pattern around the bodies, including a dozen or so that looked to have been impaled with their own rifles.

"Mine? If you really want to hear my thinking, right now I'm looking at the same thing you are: Left side of the screen lists thirty-five dead SEALS, identified by the codes on their locators keyed to their names. That leaves one missing. Care to take a guess as to which, Admiral?"

### Western Iraq

Max walked, Vicky's weight no more a burden now than it had been in the town square. He carried her on through the last of the afternoon sun. Besides a few moans and mutters, interspersed with a fluttering of her eyelids that always stopped short of opening, she hadn't shown any signs of regaining consciousness. As soon as they were clear of the village, Max laid Vicky down to check for wounds, the breath lodged in his throat. His heart felt firmly planted in his mouth, as he felt for an entry or exit bullet wound. But there was nothing, other than some bruises, his own dried blood, and scratches that likely came from her struggling with her two captors.

Max found a thick grove of brush and tucked himself inside it, protectively shielding Vicky. His plan was to wait out the sun here and move on, once darkness stole the sight lines of any possible pursuit through the flat ground that offered only meager cover.

He spent that time holding Vicky's head in his lap and softly rubbing her face and hair.

"We're quite the pair, aren't we?" he asked her, at one point. "I look at you and all I can remember is that final night in the Adirondacks. Not because of your father and what I . . . did, but because it was the only time we ever slept together, the moment I could no longer deny how much I loved you. The friendship thing was bullshit, Vick. We were fooling ourselves all along—growing up like brother and sister can do that. And the truth is I was afraid to love you, to let you know I did, because I couldn't live without you in my life in some, in any, capacity.

"I'm going to confess something to you that I'm damn glad you can't hear, because there hasn't been a day since that night where I haven't thought about you. Could never forget how much I loved you, no matter how hard I tried. I had no idea what you'd been doing over the years and I didn't want to, because then I'd have to contact you. Tell you I was no longer Max Younger, that I was a Navy SEAL commander on perpetual rotation because I've got nothing to go back to, because I don't have you. And thank God you're not hearing this."

But then Vicky's eyes opened, and she managed to flash a trace of a smile through lips cracked by the blowing sand. "I missed you too, Max."

### George H. W. Bush

"We can assume all the scientists from the CDC and WHO are dead too," Red added. "Won't know for sure, of course, until we can get a team on the ground, but it's a safe bet, Admiral."

Darby looked back at the monitor, the incredible carnage pictured in what was now a live feed in the building sunlight. Carrion birds already picking at the mutilated remains of the New Islamic Front fighters, including a dozen who'd been impaled with their own assault rifles, the barrels driven straight through their torsos into the ground below, leaving only the butts and trigger guards showing. Only the intermittently blurred picture, thanks to interference and transmission issues, made the scene even remotely watchable.

"He killed them, didn't he?" the admiral asked suddenly. "Max Borgia. He killed them all."

"I believe he did," Red affirmed. "Each and every one."

### Western Iraq

Vicky was able to walk, but not well. She refused Max's overtures to carry her again, another village finally appearing as flickering lights in the distance just after night fell. The village was mostly abandoned, just a few stubborn stragglers left to cower behind locked doors and shuttered windows.

Max found an old truck encased in dust between two burned-out buildings, and hot-wired it while Vicky fell off to sleep in the seat next to him. The truck was running on fumes within a few miles of setting off, its fuel finally drained just after reaching an extension of the Sinjār Mountains that cut across the western part of Iraq. The night had taken firm hold and brought a deep chill with it. But Max didn't dare stop to light a fire for the attention it could draw to them.

"Of course," he managed to quip to Vicky, "there's always body heat."

Max found a cave in which to hide out, shining the utility light from one of the cargo pockets of his fatigues toward the cave's far wall, so they wouldn't have to be in the dark. Then Max wrapped his arms around her and felt Vicky do the same to him.

"World Health Organization," he said softly.

"Navy SEAL."

"I'm impressed."

"Likewise."

"But your last name," Max started.

"Remember the Lebanese nanny who raised me? It was hers. I took it to avoid any connection with my father."

"I don't blame you there," Max said, wondering how Vicky's life might have been different, if she hadn't stopped him from killing Dale Denton in the Adirondacks all those years ago. "Wait, I have something to show you," he added, plucking the scratched, worn, and superglued mood ring she'd bought him at the rest stop from his pocket.

"You're kidding," she said, recognizing it immediately.

"You mean, you don't have yours anymore?"

She looked at him almost guiltily. "After you . . . left, it hurt too much to think about you, what we shared. I couldn't bear to even look at it. I was engaged, you know," Vicky added, after a pause.

"No, I didn't. What happened?"

"He died."

"Oh."

"Just before our wedding. Car accident. It's a miracle I survived. An off-duty cop happened to be just behind us when the accident happened. My fiancé had swerved to avoid a little girl nobody else saw."

Max tensed, eased Vicky slightly away from him. "Did you say a little girl?"

"Yes. Why?"

"Because I think I know her," Max managed, his voice cracking.

### George H. W. Bush

"You were right," Admiral Darby reported to Red. "Response team found no trace of Max Borgia anywhere."

Red remained silent, waiting for Darby to continue.

"And there's something else. By all accounts, the woman from the World Health Organization, Dr. Victoria Tanoury, is unaccounted for as well. All members of the group dispatched by the CDC have already been positively identified. No survivors."

"What about al-Qadir himself?"

"Checking what's left of all those bodies is going to take some time, Admiral, but I wouldn't get my hopes up. Now, it's your turn," Red continued, shifting gears. "What about the search for Borgia?"

Darby shook his head. "Nothing from intel or recon. It's a dangerous area for Search and Rescue teams to operate, but we've got them on the ground anyway. Screw precautions."

"Tell them they're looking for two people, not one. Tell them Dr. Tanoury is with Borgia."

"You can't know that."

"No, Admiral, I can't, but tell them anyway."

## Western Iraq

Max told Vicky about his mother's recalling her encounters with the little girl she called Lilith, both when he was a boy and then at Creedmoor, and the fact that Lilith had also been his imaginary childhood friend.

"That's ridiculous," Vicky challenged. "How could it be the same little girl, if she's imaginary?"

"Because she isn't. I don't know what she is, exactly. Just like I don't know what brought us together again, any more than I know what drove us apart. All I know is that what we're experiencing *can't* be explained, none of it."

The thought of doing anything more than talking hadn't even entered his mind, any more than when he'd lain down on the bed next to her in that hunting cabin a decade before. But he felt the heart trying to burst out of his chest. Same rapid breathing, same stirring down low where the sun hadn't shined since that very night. Because he'd felt nothing even approaching such a feeling since, as if that night had scared the ability to feel love out of him.

*That night . . .*

"You're bleeding," Vicky said, pulling out of his embrace, as she rubbed her fingers together.

"It's nothing."

"It needs to be stitched. Trust me—I'm a doctor, remember?"

"Right, an epidemiologist, an infectious disease specialist."

"I know my way around a needle and thread."

Max fished his first-aid pack from a lower pocket of his tactical pants. "I can do it myself."

"Not a wound on your back, you can't. Come on, it could get infected and I have no intention of losing you again. Give the kit to me. What have you got to lose?"

"More blood," Max said, handing the kit over, impressed by how quickly and confidently Vicky went to work.

"Turn around," she instructed, after she had everything ready.

Moments later, she was wiping an alcohol swab across what were most likely bullet grazes, one considerably deeper than the other.

"Ouch!"

"Hold still."

"It hurts."

"Don't be a baby." Threading a stitching needle through his skin now. "Too bad this isn't enough to make us even for you saving me yet again."

She continued work on the stitching, tying off both wounds.

"There, good as new."

Max started to put his shirt back on, then stopped, turning back toward Vicky instead. "Prove it."

Max realized they were kissing, had to open his eyes to see if it was real, and not the product of another vision, because it felt so much like the one he'd experienced on the flight from Vancouver. He couldn't say who had moved first, because they'd moved together, perfectly in sync; not just their minds linked, but also whatever it was they carried for souls.

After all these years, it nonetheless felt like they were picking up just where they left off. The last ten years erased, their lives rewinding to the point just before Dale Denton crashed the party. Teenagers bumbling through the act of lovemaking itself that produced a level of pleasure adults could only dream of.

Max wondered if he looked in the mirror, whether his teenage self would look back. Eyes still full of innocence and hope, at least in comparison to today's version. And Vicky was as beautiful as ever; didn't matter if she was eighteen or twenty-eight, she still looked the same to him. A sight he lived with every day of his life, knowing she'd never change in his view; knowing he loved her now as much as he always had, and maybe more.

Once again, it seemed to go on forever, Max fearing the dawn more than anything, since that was the only thing that could end their reverie. Vicky's moans told him she was close, and so was he. But that moment, when it arrived simultaneously for both of them, came with the colors of the rainbow bursting before his eyes like a Fourth of July fireworks show. A cascading explosion of beauty and perfection that left Vicky gasping beneath him and their embrace so tight their hearts hammered as one.

Max forced himself to stay awake, afraid to squander the moment by awakening to find it gone. He kept his eyes opened, resisted all attempts of the lids to close even after Vicky's rhythmic breathing told him she'd succumbed to slumber. He needed to protect her, be ready on the chance any New Islamic Front fighters tracked them here.

Suddenly, as he was fighting to keep his eyes open, a hand shook his shoulder from behind him, while he stroked Vicky's hair. Jarred, Max swung, sweeping his pistol around.

To find his father crouched over him.

"You don't need that," Ben Younger said. "You need to come with me."

# SEVENTY-THREE

## Western Iraq

*I* *must have fallen asleep.*

Max felt the breath bottleneck in his throat and squeezed his eyes closed, trying to force himself to wake up. When he opened his eyes again, though, he was standing with his father in a valley watched over by the lowest stretches of the Sinjār Mountains. The night still held to a darkness unbroken by the moon, but somehow Max could see the world around him plain as day, as if he were wearing a pair of invisible night vision goggles. The effect was oddly like that, neither darkness nor light but some vague mixture of the two. A strange dark light that revealed his scuffed-up boots to be wrapped in a thick coat of gravel and grime that told Max he'd walked a long distance from the cave he could no longer spot anywhere in the area.

"I'm not your father," the form of Ben Younger told him.

Max couldn't tell if this was reality, a vision, or some strange hybrid of the two.

"But your father's with me, Max," the form continued. "And he loves you very much. He doesn't want you to be afraid."

"I'm not afraid."

"You have a choice, Max."

"What do you mean?"

"You can be anything you want, harness as much power as you need to do what your mind wills. Abilities you've glimpsed within yourself, but never gained clear sight of. This was all meant to be from the beginning, but that beginning is long done. We're nearing the end now, but it doesn't have to be. That's up to you."

"*What's* up to me?" Max asked the form of his father, realizing that even in the lack of any ambient light, the form seemed to be glowing.

"The future, the direction in which the world will follow. Free will gives that choice to every man, but you alone have the ability to make the choice for all men, to determine the fate of all mankind."

"If you're not my father, then who are you?" Max asked, fearing the answer as much as welcoming it.

"I am your father, Max, because I'm everyone's father. I came to you in this form so you'd know that, so there'd be no question."

"I've got plenty of questions."

"I can't answer them. You need to find the answers on your own, by following the directions your heart lays out. That's my point. Because I don't know what you're going to choose to do next more than anyone else does, including you. I'm here because you need to know that all choices remain yours. Free will remains both man's greatest gift and the swiftest instrument of his demise. The rules were set billions of years ago, but the challenge continues. Man could never reject evil, if evil didn't exist, and that choice is what defines the very existence of humanity. Nothing is set. The world is sand, Max, not brick. You are your own master, and the true deceivers are those who'd have you believe you exist to serve them, when, in truth, you serve only yourself."

"I'm a Navy SEAL. My job is to serve plenty more than that."

"Of course you do, but you must focus on what's to come, not what has been. You can't change what has been and you can't control what's to come. You can only choose which direction to take."

"Why did you kill yourself?" Max snapped abruptly, a teenage boy's angst and frustration surging through him anew.

"Your father didn't kill himself."

"He jumped out a sixtieth-story window."

"Your father didn't kill himself, Max. You'll understand in time."

"Why have you come to me now?" Max asked, feeling like a boy again with all its accompanying uncertainty and flailing for answers.

"The blood of the lamb. You must remember the blood of the lamb."

"Why is that important?"

"You'll see. And once you see, you'll know what to do." The form of his father flashed a smile different from any smile Max remembered of Ben Younger. "I have faith in you, Max."

"Faith," Max repeated, feeling weak and stupid. He had so many more questions he wanted to ask, but couldn't find the words to pose even one in that moment.

"Between beginnings and ends, between then and now, between what has been and what will be, you alone can make the choice. And so long as you remember the blood of the lamb, you'll be ready when the time comes."

"Ready for what?"

"You're being tested, Max," the figure said, instead of responding. "Your entire life, from even before you were conceived, has been a test. A test that dates back to the beginning of time when everything we see was forged out of the nothingness. It's all been building toward this moment, because that's all it is in the great shape of things: a single moment that will determine the shape of all time to follow on Earth."

"Who are you? I need to know."

"You already do."

"I need to hear you say it."

The figure smiled, a placid, calming gesture, again entirely different from how Max's father smiled. "You need to have faith, you need to believe. Listen to your heart. You need to go forth without certainty, because there must be doubt, and the decision must be yours and yours alone, culled from that faith. That's why I came to you, Max, so you'd have it. So you'd know."

"I'm not even sure I believe in . . . God."

The form of his father flashed a smile that was happy and sad at the same time. "He believes in you, Max," his father said, then smiled warmly. "And it's okay not to believe in Him, so long as you believe that there is something greater, something more, both from the light and the dark. The decision as to which is yours, just as the decision whether to keep your eyes closed to darkness or open them to the light is yours. Everything has been building to this moment, nearly fourteen billion years all rising toward a singular instant in time. A darkness forged out of the light or a light forged out of the darkness. How to tell the difference. How to know which to choose. I've seen your heart and I know your soul. The blood of the lamb, Max, remember the blood of the lamb. You have a choice. You don't have to heed his call."

"*Whose* call?"

"He can take any form he chooses, forged from the darkness he inhabits, like the one he came to your mother in and also to you."

"I don't know what you mean."

"Yes, you do. He's been around you since you were a child, and has been watching you ever since, waiting for the same day I have. A day that is now before us. He wants you to do his bidding, wants you to serve him."

The form of his father suddenly stiffened and turned, Max following his gaze toward a short mound of rock and earth extending out from the Sinjār Mountains above them.

Lilith stood there, staring down at Max through the night from the hill, sneering at him and seeming to hiss, coming up just short of a growl. Her bared teeth were brown and rotting, the residue of meat and gristle clinging to them. Her scar-riddled skin was flaky and dry as parchment, pieces of her face shed in the stiffening wind, revealing—

*Wake up!* he heard his father, or whatever had taken the form of his father, tell him, *Wake up, Max!*


And Max did, recognizing where he was in the sunbaked shadow of the Sinjār Mountains well enough to rush back to the cave, no memory of when, or how, he'd left it. He ran for a solid mile, surging through the sunbaked morning air without struggling for breath, finally reaching the cave.

Vicky was gone.

He could see signs of a struggle, in the form of crisscrossing boot prints in the cave floor, his own steps pressed over their remnants.

Outside the cave, he found the impressions of tire treads in the breaking of the dawn light. Three trucks, maybe four, carrying several dozen fighters. He followed the route along which the New Islamic Front fighters had reversed, swung around, and drove off with Vicky as their captive.

He knew she was still alive, could feel her heart beating as clearly as his own. And he knew where the fighters were taking her, without needing to follow the tracks any further. That was the direction in which Max set out in a dead run, his pace settling with an ease that defied the heat and thickness of the air.

Max ran into the light dawning around him, a new day beyond which Vicky was waiting for him.

# SEVENTY-FOUR

## Cape Horn

I f everything's ready," Dale Denton said to Ernst Stowell in the particle accelerator's main control room, "why haven't we started?"

"We are required to seek clearances from the local government and insurance company, whenever experiments of a new nature are conducted," Stowell explained. "I'm waiting to hear back from both now."

"Who owns this facility, Doctor?"

"Western Energy Technologies."

"And who controls WET?"

"You do, of course."

"That's right, I do," Denton said, stealing a glance at Orson Beekman who continued to yield the floor to Stowell, further infuriating Denton. "And I'm ordering you to start the process now. I don't think you want to disappoint me, do you?" he continued, not needing to elaborate on that point further.

Stowell swallowed hard, his thin neck suddenly looking like a bird's. He looked to Beekman for support, hoping he'd side with a fellow scientist against this layman's crass approach to an undertaking so fraught with risk. But Beekman offered him nothing as well.

"Professor Beekman's theories about testing the capabilities of your rock within the collider's confines are well-founded," he expounded calmly. "Indeed, particle accelerators use electrical fields to speed up and increase the energy of a beam of particles, which are steered and focused by those fields, generated by electromagnets, through a vacuum-sealed environment.

"That's how we're going to get an accurate measurement of the rock's ability to amplify energy waves," Stowell continued, not caring if Denton understood or not. "And by conducting the experiment within a vacuum-sealed chamber, we should theoretically be able to contain the rock's drastically increased output, as it amplifies the energy it draws in from the supercollider."

"How much longer is this mumbo jumbo going to continue?" Denton snapped, losing his patience.

"A disaster nearly resulted in Houston when you exposed the power of a mere lightbulb to the rock, Mr. Denton. Down here, inside a particle accelerator, the rock will be subjected to a power stretching close to the level of infinity by comparison."

"That's the point, isn't it?" Denton smirked. "And you've already warned me about all this. It didn't change my mind then and it won't now."

"I hoped you'd come to your senses."

"I have, Doctor: About powering the planet for the next millennium and beyond. To eliminating the need for fossil fuels, coal, nuclear power, and all that green energy bullshit. OPEC proved that monopolies work when it comes to energy, and I'm talking about the ultimate monopoly here, once we harness the power of this rock."

Stowell checked the wall clock and let out a deep sigh. "Thirty minutes," he said, finally relenting. "That's how long the final prep will take."

Denton gazed down at the segment of the tunnel visible through the observation glass. "Twenty-nine minutes, forty-five seconds now, Doctor, and the clock's ticking."

# SEVENTY-FIVE

### Syria

Max continued to run, following the path left by the tire tracks of the New Islamic Front's vehicles, until he reached the area where he'd concealed the truck that had gotten him and Vicky to this point yesterday. He climbed behind the wheel of the old relic, as much as anything to get out of the blazing morning sunlight, only to find the fuel gauge registering near the FULL line. Had he somehow read it wrong the night before or . . .

Max left his thought there, focused instead on the clear direction in which the New Islamic Front fighters were headed:

Syria . . .

The original headquarters of the New Islamic Front, after they'd risen as an even more lethal, and far better financed, group than ISIS. A headquarters built as well in al-Raqqah, after absorbing the last vestiges of the dwindling Caliphate, its remnants cowering in their path.

Al-Qadir's fighters had returned in modest measure to al-Raqqah with a multitude of civilians already loyal to their cause and willing to help the New Islamic Front hide in plain sight. By all indications, that was where the trucks were headed, and those indications included the sense that Vicky was still alive. Max couldn't be more certain of that than if she were sitting alongside him in the truck now. Something from the vision he'd just experienced had left its mark inside him, an ability to see not so much into the future, as a deeper, broader view of the present.

*The blood of the lamb, Max*, the form inside his father had said, *remember the blood of the lamb.*

It would be the blood of others, though, that would be spilled soon.

### Al-Raqqah

Mohammed al-Qadir's two guards, culled from his best and most seasoned fighters, stood on either side of the woman's chair. A third adjusted the tripod-mounted camera directly before her.

"You are going to die," al-Qadir told her. "You're going to die on live television for all the world to see. Millions of people bearing witness to your leaving this word ahead of the rest of the infidels who will be following you."

The woman swallowed hard. "I'm not scared."

"Then you're stupid."

"No, I'm not. I just know he's coming."

"Who?"

"You know who: the man who wiped out your entire force in the village of El Mady."

"A single man? You expect me to believe that?"

"You want my head?" the woman challenged him, instead of answering. "You'll have to take his first. Because he's coming."

Al-Qadir found himself grinning "Your head? Who said anything about taking your head?" he asked the woman, turning toward a chamber built into the back of the room, located several stories underground, and outfitted with a heavy door something was banging on from the inside even now.

He couldn't wait for what was about to happen, thinking of nothing else until one of his commanders entered with concern, even fear, plastered over his features.

"We've spotted someone coming."

"How many?"

"It appears to be a single man," the commander said, as if not believing it himself.

Al-Qadir glanced back toward the woman from the WHO, before returning his attention to his commander. "Make sure all the men are in position. When this single man arrives, order them to shoot and keep shooting."

### Cape Horn

A faint hum.

That's all Denton heard when the particle accelerator first fired up. Lights had already snapped on, illuminating the exterior of the tube that circled through the tons of shale and limestone layered deep beneath the island's surface.

He could see the lights, see the tube, but the rock itself was tucked inside the multi-billion-dollar machine, resting on the floor where in normal circumstances someone might kick it aside and not know any better.

These were not normal circumstances, and Denton studied the LED readouts indicating the slow, gradual increase in power inside the tunnel. All the atoms and molecules soon to be sent smashing up against each other, generating massive electromagnetic waves. This time, whatever energy the rock sucked up would remain trapped by a chamber capable of generating dark matter for a fraction of a second and even simulating an actual black hole.

Perfect, Denton thought, feeling the hairs on his arms and the back of his neck stand up at attention, chills pulsing through him. His breath slowed, and then there didn't seem to be as much air to suck in, making him feel a bit light-headed, like an oxygen-deprived scuba diver.

*Something* was happening.

### Al-Raqqah

Max had abandoned the old truck a mile back, and continued on foot to the outskirts of al-Raqqah, the remains of the once thriving city reminding him today of the bombed-out shells in World War II photos. Buildings reduced to jagged clumps amid piles of crumbled refuse. No structure seemed entirely whole and the air looked perpetually stained by the dust rising with the wind from all the debris.

Max felt no excitement, no anxiety, no fear. Only certainty in what lay before him. He knew this was real, knew his boots were leaving real marks in the ground, not just figurative ones. And yet it felt more like one of the visions he'd been experiencing. As if his two worlds, his dual selves, had merged. As if life and death themselves had merged too, the distinctions blurred, impossible to tell where one ended and the other began.

In that moment, dark clouds rolled over a sky that had been crystal clear just moments before, day turning to virtual night as the heavens seemed to open, unleashing a violent rainstorm. Max felt it soak him, washing him clean of grime and muck, but not of the hatred and rage simmering inside him. He felt those too about to flood outward, just as the torrents were now dropping from the sky.

## Cape Horn

Denton tried to focus on the LED readouts that measured the power being generated by the particle accelerator. Another screen showed a different readout and bar grid associated with the total power output, as calibrated in electromagnetic waves and having been amplified by the stone. The screen was flashing, that particular hard drive having crashed.

Meanwhile, he thought he detected the accelerator tube quaking, pulsing.

Wrong.

Because it was everything else in the complex that was quivering, as if the whole of Cape Horn was being struck by an earthquake. The hairs on his arms and neck were no longer standing on end, but he felt something in the pit of his stomach; an unsettled feeling akin to the jolt of an aircraft smacking down and racing across the tarmac until the brakes engaged.

Only no brakes engaged here. And the pulsing was increasing, some of the personnel grabbing for their water bottles before they spilled over. The air suddenly seemed drained of oxygen, more rapid heaves required to take enough in. Denton visualized millions and millions of hairline cracks appearing on the Earth's surface; crisscrossing, spreading, and widening. The whole planet losing its structural integrity.

"All right," he said to Ernst Stowell, keeping his voice calm. "I've seen enough, Doctor. Shut it down."

What little color Stowell had drained from his face. "We can't. I already tried," he said, as an alarm began to screech. "I warned you! For God's sake, I warned you!"

## Al-Raqqah

Vicky heard another impact from inside the door leading into the chamber beyond, rattling it this time.

"You've got one of them in there," she said to al-Qadir. "One of the infected that's been transformed."

"You'll meet it soon enough," he told her, "as the entire world watches.

I'll let it take your head, and anything else it wants. Let the world see it in action, introduce the upshot of Allah's vision for the End of Days to those who have destroyed His vision for the way the world must be. Let them see you transform too after it's done with you."

The heavy door rattled again. What had once been a hand slapped the glass plate even with eye level. A face pressed up against it, appearing even less human than what Vicky recalled from Lebanon, looking like the skin had turned inside out. Narrow, almost feline eyes set more forward than they should've been over an elongated mouth with so many dagger-like teeth that the jaws hung open.

"The infidels will see what's coming," al-Qadir continued. "They will see what's headed their way and know their time is coming too, that hell has opened to take them, and that you will be waiting when they get there."

## Al-Raqqah

Max kept walking, even when he spotted the first gunmen mounted atop the highest remaining rooftops. Others were poised behind street-level windows or positions of cover. Dozens of gunmen, hundreds maybe, all waiting for him, all packing a variety of weapons.

Max didn't stop. Kept walking, impervious to the fire they would rain down, and secure in the notion that it paled by comparison with what he was about to unleash.

Because they were his to control, to exert his will over. Clay to mold in his grasp, subject to his whim. Weak-willed and spineless killers who preyed upon the weak and frightened about to face their reckoning.

## Cape Horn

Men were talking, screaming, but they couldn't hear each other, a few on the floor or leaning against a wall with their hands cupping their ears to shut out a sound Denton couldn't hear, blood slipping through their fingers. He understood all too well the incredible force and power of a tornado, and right now he felt as if he, all of those in the control room, were being sucked up into the vortex of one beyond an EF5, beyond measure. He looked down, half expecting to see his feet rising into the air.

Denton reminded himself to breathe, but wasn't sure if any of the air actually reached his lungs, wasn't even sure he was alive anymore. Pinched himself, actually pinched himself, but felt nothing. Looked toward Stowell, who was still frantically trying to shut the collider down. The world all jumbled around him, Denton no longer able to keep his thoughts straight or be sure he was thinking anything at all.

## Al-Raqqah

Al-Qadir felt something too, felt *something* in the pit of his stomach he could liken to the initial sensation of a high-altitude parachute drop back when he was still Cambridge. The sense of weightlessness and being tossed about at the whims of the wind. Helpless.

Then he realized it wasn't a feeling at all, so much as a sound. More accurately, a sequence of sounds that peppered his ears with a constant ratcheting din like fireworks heard from a distance.

*Gunfire!*

Al-Qadir snatched a walkie-talkie from a nearby table and depressed the communicator button. "All sector commanders, report in."

Nothing.

"Repeat, all sector commanders report in with your status."

Still nothing. Just more of what sounded like random clicks and clacks from the streets above. Al-Qadir didn't bother trying to hail his commanders a third time, because he knew; somehow he *knew*.

His great, fated enemy was here. Whoever, or whatever, had massacred his fighters amid a sandstorm in El Mady had arrived, true to the woman's word.

Al-Qadir swung toward his personal bodyguards. "Arm yourselves!"

The men looked down at the assault rifles they were holding.

"With more!" al-Qadir elaborated, gesturing toward the table lined with weapons, and moving to grab some for himself. "As many as you can hold!"

## Al-Raqqah

Max neared the central avenue that sliced through the city, one of the few passable roads left in the city. He could feel all the guns, so many, trained on him, ready to erupt in a torrent of fire.

Max stopped and froze, at which point the men should have opened fire.

They didn't.

He should be dead.

He wasn't.

The hatred and rage had peaked inside him, turning him hypersensitive to the world around him. He heard everything, saw everything. Felt the same surreal sense of transcendence familiar from his visions. His dual worlds, his dueling, twin consciousness having finally merged into one, filling him with not just a sense of what was to come, but a certainty in his capacity to create it.

Max looked up, peering through the sheets of rain at the gunmen above him. Then he tightened his right hand into a fist, feeling the blood leaking out from the mark on his palm, dribbling through his fingers to fall in steady drops to the puddles pooling at his feet. He kept his gaze focused on the fighters above, their guns starting to move, aiming, steadying, ready to fire.

Not at him . . . but at each other, as the air crackled and the world moved in jump cuts through the curtains of rain being dumped from the sky.

The barrage of gunfire that followed was like nothing Max had ever experienced in combat before. As many as two hundred men hitting their triggers at the exact same moment. The echoes of the shots drowned out the screams, as the New Islamic Front fighters obliterated their own number. Those left standing turned their weapons on themselves, Max certain he glimpsed a fighter through a street-level window continuing to pull the trigger, firing into himself even after he was dead.

Others on the rooftops looking over him, had abandoned their weapons and were tearing each other apart with their bare hands. Knives flashed too, blood spraying in all directions. Still more fighters were hammering each other with their rifles as if they were clubs.

Max walked through what had effectively become a tunnel of carnage, a spray of blood catching him like mist as he steered toward a building at the end of the block.


### Cape Horn

The particle accelerator itself was now shaking, Denton realized, threatening to tear itself apart at the points where hinges joined sections together, and releasing an energy equivalent to ten thousand atomic bombs.

Or worse.

The closed circuit monitors picturing the supercollider's tunnel showed something glowing, as bright as the sun and forcing Denton to turn away. Then, suddenly, Stowell was at his side, grabbing hold of him, his eyes bulging.

"The readouts are upside down, everything reversed!" And, when Denton gave no response, "We've unleashed dark matter in there! Somehow we've unleashed dark matter and it's colliding with the oppositely charged particles faster and faster. If we can't stop it . . ."

Stowell was still talking, but Denton couldn't hear him anymore.

### Al-Raqqah

The man who'd once been one of al-Qadir's most trusted confidants had been chained up inside the chamber before his final transformation was complete. Al-Qadir first feared the sickness the man had brought back with him from southern Lebanon. Then he'd rejoiced, realizing the man was still a soldier, albeit one serving in the army of God's final war against the infidels who'd besmirched His name and His word for so long.

Al-Qadir had decided to keep the creature alive for a purpose God had not shared with him. He had no real sense of that purpose, until his fighters had tracked the woman from the WHO to a cave in the Sinjār Mountains and brought her here. Only then did truly divine inspiration of what he must do strike him.

The pathogen soon to spread across the world might've been based upon samples recovered from the meteor strike in Nigeria all those years before, but it had taken on a life all its own, in accordance with God's will. The fact that it had escaped the laboratory to wreak havoc no one had expected only reinforced al-Qadir's commitment to the cause. For what, other than the direct intervention of Allah, could possibly have caused that?

Al-Qadir shouldered one Kalashnikov and readied another before him.

"Put her in the room," he ordered his guards, the din of gunfire that had ratcheted through his eardrums, down now to a sporadic rattle. "Let's introduce her to the future of man."

# SEVENTY-SIX

### Al-Raqqah

Rain poured from the sky in blinding sheets, precluding Max's view of the carnage swirling around him. He walked through it untouched, didn't even feel the rain drenching him, as he continued to steer toward Vicky.

Max wished he'd felt nothing, instead of a flit of joy that followed each shot, each scream, each death around him. He felt the hot surge of a near primal exuberance, continuing to increase every time he thought it had peaked. He'd never felt so fulfilled, so triumphant, so *alive*, the feeling one he wished he could cling to forever. He wanted the killing to go on, and on, and on. Go on forever, with him at its center, as its instrument.

*What's happening to me?*

It didn't matter; Vicky was all that mattered. She was *everything*, the rest of the world paling by comparison. Let it burn, so long as she lived. Max tried not to think what he'd do if he found her dead at al-Qadir's hands, the purpose in life he had found with her last night stripped away again. Max realized Vicky *was* his life, his love, and always had been.

*If she's dead* . . .

Again, Max failed to complete the thought, afraid to this time, afraid to consider what his unleashed rage and energy could do, afraid the carnage here in the central square was just a microcosm of it. He felt an indescribable power surging through him, a race car engine running in the red while somehow holding to the track. Max's track brought him to the left, toward a square building, featuring a bombed-out façade.

Max waded through the refuse, a pair of fighters spinning out from behind crumbled walls. They tried to pull their triggers, but their fingers refused to complete the task. Max stared at them intensely, watched as their arms trembled horribly, their weapons angling upward against their determined efforts to hold them down, muzzles ending up flush under their chins and . . .

*BANG! BANG!*

. . . Max was showered with blood and brain matter, after their fingers finally squeezed inward. He spotted a staircase on his right and steered toward it.

### Cape Horn

Having lost total control of the energy building in the particle accelerator, Ernst Stowell had ordered a total evacuation of the facility, Denton not bothering to protest.

Outside, the air pulsed with the same irregular jostling he'd first felt a mere half hour before. If that air had been solid, Denton would've said it was tearing itself apart. Meanwhile, the entire structure built over WET's supercollider was quaking, its structural integrity compromised, cracks and fissures spreading across its exterior, as it began to break apart. It seemed to lift in the air, only to drop down again, the massive burst of energy still contained in the particle accelerator soon to be unleashed onto the world.

Denton's thinking froze there, because a dull hum lacing the air had built into a banshee-like screech played on a constant loop, stealing his thoughts from him and numbing his mind.

Beekman had been right all along, and so had Ben Younger. Fuck them both, men unwilling to take the risks he had in an attempt to change the world forever.

As Denton heaved for breath amid the oxygen-depleted air, he thought he heard the laughter of a young child through all the screeching, a little girl.

### Al-Raqqah

"If you are watching me now," Mohammed al-Qadir spoke into the camera positioned before him, "it is because you are following God's will, just as I am. I come before you today charged with an awesome responsibility as both maker and messenger. To inform you of what I have wrought on God's behalf. That would be my God, not yours, because your God has let the world reach the point of its own destruction, so mine can preserve the little that's worthy to survive.

"And I come before you today to state it isn't too late for you to join the survivors. All you must do is renounce your material lives and worship of your false gods, and turn to the one true God in their place. Embrace Allah and the word of the prophet Mohammed and you can be saved to live on after the End of Days fully dawns. That dawn is beginning to shine even now. You can't escape it, or the army the West's own insolence and disregard has bequeathed on the world.

"I would like to reveal a soldier in that army to you now," al-Qadir continued, toward the camera. "I would like to show you the fate that awaits all infidels."

The camera followed al-Qadir as he moved to an old-fashioned lever built into a wall of the ancient police station that had once occupied this building. Yanking that lever down would release the tension on the chain holding the creature back inside the adjoining chamber, so it could reach the woman whose excruciating death would be replayed over and over again, the instrument of the End of Days revealed to the world.

"Now," al-Qadir told his audience, "behold."


Inside the chamber, Vicky noted the positioning of cameras on the walls, as she clung to the farthest one to stay out of range of the creature stretching the bonds of its chains to reach her. Snapping and clawing at her, no longer seeming even remotely human.

It moved in a stoop, hunched over to exaggerate the knobs of vertebrae pressed out to the limits of its skin's bonds. Not human skin, but something that looked more like rubber, folds and folds of it wrapped around each other, which accounted for the ridges and depressions that dominated the creature's face and body. Its eyes peeked out from behind mere slits, colored entirely black and never blinking. Its teeth kept clacking together, blood leaking between its lips, as if it were chewing on the tissue inside its mouth.

The creature reared back and flung itself at her, the chain holding it just inches from Vicky's throat. Dying terrified her, but the thought of being bitten, and transforming into one of these things, was even more unthinkable.

*Max*, she thought, *Max, where are you?*

. . .

Max heard Vicky calling his name, as he exploded through the heavy se-curity door like it wasn't even there. A pair of New Islamic Front fighters trained their weapons upon him, only to freeze up briefly as he poured fire into them, streams of bullets holding them up until Max eased back on the trigger.

They fell, leaving Max face-to-face with Mohammed al-Qadir, his hand just about to yank down on a lever built into the wall, a camera recording all that transpired within a separate chamber equipped with a bulkhead-style door. Max steadied his M4, al-Qadir regarding him with a mix of fear and uncertainty.

"Don't move!"

Al-Qadir froze, but left his hand on the lever. He'd shed one of his assault rifles to manage the task before him, but now flirted with the notion of twisting the Kalashnikov from his shoulder. Meeting the eyes of the man before him, though utterly black without any trace of white, filled him with a sense of fear and foreboding he hadn't felt in a very long time.

"*Shaitan*," he muttered, shaking his head in disbelief, as something made him switch to English. "You are Satan, he whom I've been chosen to defeat."

"Close enough," Max told him, just short of pulling back on the trigger.

*Shoot! Kill him!*

But Max didn't, couldn't for some reason lost to his consciousness.

"No," al-Qadir raged, "you must see, you must *know*!"

With that, al-Qadir moved his right hand across to his left arm, and peeled off a tight, flesh-colored sleeve to reveal an arm that looked as if it had turned to stone above a pulsing, oozing, raised reddish fleshy patch where his wrist should've been.

"Behold the mark," al-Qadir ranted. "I was sure I was going to die, but Allah saved me for this purpose, for this day. So I may open the gates of heaven in His stead."

"Only gates you're going to see are the gates of hell," Max said, and pulled his M4's trigger.

*Click.*

It was empty, even though he'd just changed magazines . . . or had he? The memory eluding him, as al-Qadir worked his hand back over a lever.

"Behold the future!" al-Qadir ranted, and jerked it downward.

The creature came at Vicky, plenty of slack in the chain now to reach her. She managed to duck beneath its initial charge, grabbing the chain and yanking to tip its balance briefly.

"*Max!*" she cried out, as it lurched at her again.

Max twisted away from al-Qadir, as soon as he heard Vicky's voice scream his name. And by the time he swung back, al-Qadir was gone, having disappeared through a secret panel carved out of the wall that was swinging closed again.

*Vicky!*

It was either save her or pursue al-Qadir, not much of a choice in Max's mind. This was his chance, maybe the last one he'd ever get.

He rushed to the entrance to the inner chamber from which he'd heard Vicky scream his name, spilling over the camera that shattered on impact with the floor. He threw back the lock and thrust it open with such fury that it split from its hinges.

The creature inside twisted its face away from a jagged bite carved through Vicky's thigh, and lunged with snapping teeth bared toward her throat. Max's gaze locked on the chain. Pictured it retracting, and then watched it retract, snapping back toward the wall and jerking the creature with it. The thing fought futilely to reach Vicky again, but the slack had all been taken up.

Max formed a fresh picture in his head, and the length of the chain still extending from the wall wrapped around the creature's throat.

And tightened.

Then tightened some more.

Until the creature's head was torn off, the chain left dangling now, as the rest of the creature that had once been a man seemed to seize up and topple straight over forward to the floor.

Max rushed to Vicky.

"Better late than never," she managed, failing to muster the smile he saw her try for.

"Don't move," he said, crouched over her with eyes on the gaping wound in her thigh that was gushing blood.

Vicky looked at him, puzzled. "Your eyes . . ."

"Stay still."

". . . They looked all . . . black, but they're not now. Am I losing my mind?"

"No, just blood, but I can stop it."

"Don't bother," she said, eyes misting up, voice sounding heavy. "I'm infected. I'm going to transform. Leave me, please, just leave me."

Max tore off his shirt, applying pressure to the wound as he turned the fabric into a tourniquet wrapped tightly over the sucking wound.

"Max," Vicky started.

"I'm busy."

"It's no use."

"We'll see about that," he said, lifting her into his arms.

## Cape Horn

"A black hole!" Beekman cried out. "That was a black hole! I think we may have just witnessed a miniature re-creation of the Big Bang."

Dale Denton was continuing to drag him along, when a prickly ripple in the air left Denton swinging back toward the complex housing the supercollider. He could swear it was wavering, blowing like a piece of notebook paper slung in a binder, in the last moment before a single bright flash flared. He watched the earth open up into a spreading pit of empty darkness that seemed to swallow the entire facility in a single gulp. A vast torrent of water gushed out moments later, from the gaping hole left behind that must've extended down through the entire substructure of the island.

The geyser climbed for the sky in a manner that reminded Denton of that first oil strike in the Yucatán, courtesy of the same rock that had sewn the seeds of what he'd just witnessed. The facility not falling into the sea or exploding, so much as sucked out of the world.

A vast circular pit remained, filling rapidly with churning water that swirled in blinding fashion. Denton felt a tug, something like a gust of wind angling him back toward the low ground. He fought against the pull, more like a rope's now, fighting it to a stalemate long enough to allow him to reclaim his footing and slog on.

Others were not so lucky.

Denton turned to the sight of dozens of people being drawn violently toward the spinning whirlpool, as if being sucked in by a vacuum cleaner. Uprooted trees obliterated those in their path to the sucking vortex that continued to swallow vehicles, the remnants of structures decimated by the loosed wave of energy, and more people who flapped and flailed the whole way down into the gaping chasm.

*Wop-wop-wop-wop* . . .

The sound drew Denton's gaze upward, toward the helicopter angling for a flat stretch of high ground that would serve as its landing pad. He'd summoned it at the first sign of trouble calling for potential evacuation. Almost to the clearing, Denton heard, and felt, an earthquake-like rumbling that shook the world to its very core. Swinging again toward the remnants of the supercollider, he spotted a tsunami-like wall of water burst from the crater, climbing toward the higher ground from the massive hole drilled out of the ground. Denton tried to catch his breath, running again as the ground seemed to shift under the force of the flood, and the wall of water darkened the day.

He crested the ridge where his helicopter waited, warm and ready, a trio of guards armed with assault rifles standing between it and the surging hordes, holding back the throngs who would've otherwise stormed it in their desperation. Denton pushed his way through them, Beekman becoming a lead weight behind him.

"You're a murderer!" he rasped, terrified. "This was all your fault, every bit of it! All these deaths!"

Denton stopped long enough to kick the man's legs out from under him, and he dropped like a felled tree.

"So what's one more? Fuck you, Beekman. I hope you can swim."

He rushed the rest of the way to the chopper, past the three gunmen there to keep anyone else from following. The last gunman slid the door closed behind him, the chopper lifting off, just as the massive wall of water swallowed the world below.

# SEVENTY-SEVEN

## *George H. W. Bush*

You want to give that to me again?" Red said to Admiral Darby.

"You heard what I said, son. That firefight in al-Raqqah was one-sided, New Islamic Front fighters shooting each other. Another inexplicable massacre, in other words."

"And that's confirmed?"

"You bet your ass; from intel assets on the ground. You want to lie to me and tell me you're surprised, go ahead."

Before Red could, the intercom flared from the carrier's communications center.

"Admiral, we have incoming traffic from Syria heading straight for al-Asad Airbase in western Iraq."

"Specify."

"An MH-6 Little Bird."

"One of ours?"

"Transponder designation indicates it was delivered to the Iraqi military, one of those seized by the New Islamic Front."

"Well, god-fucking-damn."

"Hold on, sir," the voice blared over the intercom. "Whoever's flying it is communicating via the base's exclusive frequency."

"Put it on speaker."

And a moment later Max Borgia's voice boomed through the room.

". . . Repeat, this is Commander Borgia, SEAL Team 6. I am incoming with wounded. Please have a medical team standing by. I say again, Mayday, Mayday!"

Darby and Red just looked at each other.

### Ayn al-Asad Airbase, Iraq

An armed phalanx of troops was waiting when Max touched down in the Little Bird. He was ordered to stand down and eased himself from the pilot's seat. He reached back for Vicky and lifted her out as gingerly as he could, the troops before him making no move to part.

"There's no time! She's *dying*!" he yelled at them.

The captain in charge nodded slowly and signaled his men to break formation, before falling into step behind Max as he hustled Vicky toward the base hospital.

"I'm a mess, Max," she said, the blood dribbling out her mouth now, bubbling with froth.

"I'll give you that much."

Her eyes widened, through the blood leaking out of them, and bore into his. "Promise me you won't let me change. Promise me."

Max noticed drops of blood were seeping out of Vicky's ears now too. "No need. You're not going to die."

Vicky was placed in isolation at the base's medical center, the trauma team seeming to take forever to get their heavy biohazard suits on. Max stayed with her the whole time, refusing a suit for himself, the doctor reporting the results of his initial examination while Max was still poised over her.

"She's lost a lot of blood," he said, his voice sounding like it was being channeled through a cheese grater. "We need to get her transfused before we even address the bite. But there's a problem."

"What?"

"She's AB negative, rarest blood type there is and not compatible with the universal brand of—"

"I'm AB negative, just like her," Max told him. "Use my blood to transfuse her. As much as she needs, that's how much you'll take."

"She needs more than you can give her, not without dying yourself."

"A chance I'm willing to take, so do it. Do it now!"

· · ·

The process began mere minutes later, Max laid out on a gurney that had been positioned alongside Vicky's. Her fading eyes regained their life, the color returning to her skin almost as soon as Max's blood began to flow into her. The first of the flow hit her with a jolt that almost caused the doctor and his trauma team to panic, until Vicky settled back down, her gaze placid and calm.

Max realized she was squeezing his hand and squeezed hers back. He felt weaker by the moment, as his blood continued to drain into Vicky.

"Commander," he thought he heard the doctor say.

He tried to squeeze Vicky's hand tighter but could feel the strength ebbing from his grasp.

"*Commander . . .*"

He managed to hold Vicky's gaze, but his eyelids began to flutter and his vision blurred.

"This is as far as we go," the doctor said, reaching to switch off the machine that was transferring Max's blood into Vicky.

He latched a hand onto the doctor's wrist, freezing it in midair. "No" was all he could manage.

The doctor tried futilely to wrench free of his grasp, shocked by the show of strength. "You'll die."

"There are worse things."

A few moments later, Max's eyes finally closed, even as Vicky's continued to brighten.

Two hours later, the doctor led Red and the phalanx of heavily armed soldiers who'd accompanied him to al-Asad Airbase down the hall to the base's makeshift morgue.

"I'm sorry you wasted a trip. After his heart stopped, we tried CPR for over twenty minutes, exhausted every measure available to us to get him going again. I just wanted you to know we did everything we could."

"I'm sure you did," Red said, matter-of-factly. "Now I need you to release the body to me. All the authorizations should be in order."

The doctor reviewed the documents in cursory fashion again. "They seem to be."

"Did you put guards on the door, as I ordered?" Red asked.

They reached the morgue's double doors. "He's dead, sir. There's nothing to guard."

The doctor pushed open the doors, Red entering the morgue ahead of him to find a single black body bag lying on one of the steel gurneys.

Red moved up to the bag, the heavy DOD model, unzipped it and peeled back the material to reveal the face of the corpse.

"This look like Max Borgia to you?" Red said, tilting the unfamiliar face toward the doctor.

The doctor's mouth dropped, his eyes bulging. "I, er, I don't know what to . . . That's a private who was killed in a training accident."

"Then where's Max Borgia?"

The doctor didn't offer an answer, and Red didn't really need one. He already knew Max Borgia was gone. Somehow. Just like he'd survived in Yemen, and then against even greater forces of fighters in El Mady and Syria. Somehow. And now he had transfused a fatal amount of blood, only to survive again. Somehow.

"I warned you," Red said.

"There's something else," the doctor muttered, through his own shock.


"I've never seen anything like it," the doctor said, peeling back the bandages wrapped around the heavily sedated Dr. Victoria Tanoury's leg. "The healing process seems to have started almost once the transfusion was completed."

He eased back the last of the bandage to reveal that the portion of her leg that had been shredded by the creature's deadly bite clearly showed improvement, the swelling down and much less discharge leaking through the stitches.

"Any idea how I should explain this in my report?" the doctor asked Red. "What I should say when they ask me what the hell happened here?"

"Yeah, Doc," he said, finally. "Tell them we're hopeful that we've found the basis for a vaccine."

# AFTER

## The Present

God judged it better to bring good out of evil
than to suffer no evil to exist.

—St. Augustine

# SEVENTY-EIGHT

### The Vatican

Pope Anthony I, formerly Cardinal Josef Martenko, continued signing the vast array of formal letters to churches all over the world. Using the pen that had brought him luck since the figurative start of his ascendancy, a souvenir from the very moment it actually began, he continued to scratch out his signature, until the large phone atop his desk buzzed.

"Your guest has arrived, Your Holiness."

"Send him in."

A few moments later, he greeted Father Pascal Jimenez at the door. The priest immediately dropped to his knees and kissed the papal ring.

"Your Holiness," he said solemnly.

"Rise, my son," Pope Anthony said, and led Jimenez to the chair set immediately before the desk that had been used by papal predecessors for more than three centuries.

Jimenez took the chair, bowing slightly as the pope sat back down behind his desk. "Thank you for seeing me, Your Holiness."

"The least I can do for an old friend." Pope Anthony took his gold pen and twirled it about in his hand, as he leaned forward. "And you said it was important."

"Vital. I didn't realize how much so, until the last time we met, just before I completed my report on the recent activities I was assigned to investigate."

Pope Anthony smiled tightly. "I appreciate the rather sanitized version you presented to the Curia, by the way."

"A gesture well earned, after all you've done for me, Your Holiness. But I didn't realize how closely we were truly connected until that last meeting, when you were making notes."

Pope Anthony I stopped twirling the pen and held it still.

"Because it was mine, Your Holiness," Jimenez continued, staring at it in the new pope's grasp. "My father gave that gold pen you're holding to me, just as his father passed it to him. It's a one-of-a-kind and I should have recognized it before. It was taken from me in Nigeria by the man we both knew then as Cambridge." Jimenez canted his frame closer to the massive desk before him. "And I'm afraid there's only one possible way you could have come to possess it."

Pope Anthony's features flared. "Absurd! A complete and utter fantasy! You have no proof to support such an absurd conclusion," Pope Anthony said tersely. "A simple gold pen, Pascal, really?"

"Monogrammed with T for *Tomosel*," Jimenez said, staring straight at the letter etched into the gold. "My father's name. I'd recognize it anywhere. The man we both knew as Cambridge took it from me in Nigeria. He must have given it to you at some point. And that's not all: You were in London with me when the terrorist attack in St. Peter's Square wiped out much of the Curia. I'm convinced that's how you became head of the Vatican Bank, a position from which you secretly financed the terrorist ambitions of Mohammed al-Qadir, the man we both knew as Cambridge, whom you met in Nigeria. After all, we both know the immense resources the Vatican Bank wields across the globe on the church's behalf, with its ability to move huge amounts of funds inconspicuously and undetected through the many charities operating in Third World countries. That's how you bankrolled the New Islamic Front."

"That's insane, Pascal. Have you lost your mind, coming into this office to show me such disrespect?" the former Josef Martenko said. "I guess I shouldn't be surprised; you don't look well at all. I promise we'll get you the best help available, the best."

"I don't need it. Your first posting upon joining the priesthood was to run a resettlement program for Chechen orphan refugees, displaced when the Soviet government crushed a resistance movement to Communist rule in the mid-1970s. One of those orphans grew up to be the man we knew as Cambridge. His father was one of the movement's leaders."

Jimenez stopped to let his point sink in. Pope Anthony made no move to dispute or disparage his assertions, just stared at him smugly from behind the large ornate desk.

"That's quite a story," he said finally. "Good luck getting anyone to listen."

"I don't expect they will," Jimenez conceded. "You kept watch on Cambridge all that time, maybe even encouraged him as a boy, didn't you? So, tell me, was Nigeria just a coincidence, or a setup to bring the two of you together at long last? Then you financed a madman from your position as head of the Vatican Bank, a position you assumed only after Cambridge wiped out a large measure of the Curia. Thanks to you, he's brought the world to the brink of the Apocalypse. What better way to realize your grand plan to bring people back to the church?" Jimenez shook his head in obvious disgust. "But it's not fear that turns people toward God, Your Holiness, it's love. And you're no more than a run-of-the-mill fanatic who murders innocents and kills in the name of God. You're even worse than al-Qadir."

Pope Anthony grinned, then rose slowly from his chair. "You would have the world believe I orchestrated my way onto the papal chair, that I planned and plotted these many years toward that end, with no evidence to support your claims at all? Your word against mine, Pascal. No one will believe you."

Jimenez remained seated. "I'm aware of that, Your Holiness. And I'm also aware that you serve another power, one not named God, but one with an equal stake in what the world is facing. In delivering your version of the word of God, Your Holiness, you've made a deal with the devil."

The newly coronated pope smiled smugly. "I've only become what He wanted me to be. I am His vessel on earth who alone has heard and heeded His word to visit His wrath upon a world that has turned away from Him. God isn't dead, Pascal; it's the world that's been dead these many years, and I seek only to bury its remains before the decadent and debauched devour what's left of its rotting corpse. And now I will achieve that from the papal chair. The whims of fate again, Pascal, or the work of God?"

A pair of plainclothes papal guards entered the office, summoned, no doubt, by a press of some hidden button. They moved to either side of Father Jimenez, who felt them take him by either arm, as he rose.

"Now," Pope Anthony said, stepping out from behind his desk, "go with God, Father. Oh, and I believe this belongs to you."

And with that he handed Jimenez the gold pen.

# SEVENTY-NINE

## Brandenburg Air Force Base, Germany

After ten days at the American military hospital in Brandenburg, Germany, Vicky had continued to make remarkable progress, as did the world. Not only had Max's blood miraculously cured Vicky, preliminary computer models and lab testing confirmed it, now combined with hers, could act as a vaccine capable of eradicating Medusa and stopping the pathogen's spread in its track. Toward that end, production on an unprecedented scale was set to begin in a matter of mere days now, subject only to Vicky's health continuing to improve to validate the potential vaccine's efficacy.

Vicky had already been briefed on the armada of C-130s, packed with nothing but bottled water, that were making regular flights to the Middle East. The plan was to hold Medusa in check, until the vaccine was ready for distribution. The initial supplies would be allocated to the Mideast, before the West, Asia, Russia, China, and beyond received their allotments, mostly on a precautionary basis. Meanwhile, countries large and small had sealed their borders to retard any potential further spread of the infection, no country about to take any chances. The only planes flying to and from the affected areas were military, WHO, or CDC, one of which had gotten her to Brandenburg.

Those already infected who'd been transformed, meanwhile, were being tracked down and eliminated by an alliance of armies through the Middle East and the West, with the United States taking charge of the response in cooperation with NATO forces. The operation, involving the entire Sixth and Seventh Fleets, was being staged off the *George H. W. Bush* and progress had been slow but sure. It was a war, yes, but a distinctly one-sided one. For those patients in the midst of the transformation, and too far gone for any hope, a humanitarian drug cocktail was given to ease their passage to peace—very much under the radar, of course.

All data and analysis gathered so far by both the WHO and CDC had confirmed the pathogen to be waterborne. That meant the West, America particularly, should be spared any outbreaks so long as anyone who'd traveled to or through the Middle East within the last month was denied entry to the country, or temporarily quarantined if they were already there.

Vicky hadn't heard from or spoken to Max since he'd disappeared from the al-Asad Airbase morgue in Iraq, nor did she expect to; it was too dangerous for both of them. As much as that reality had regularly moved her to tears, Vicky knew that something was happening here that stretched well beyond her comprehension, that science could in no way explain with regards to Max. It went all the way back to the fact that they had been born on the same day at virtually the same time, both miracle babies of sorts who shared the same rare blood type. The odds of that were fifty million to one, the first sign, she was now convinced, that they both had a mysterious destiny to fulfill. Together, as it turned out.

Knowing Max was still alive filled her with an indescribable joy, along with the fervent hope that destiny had further plans for them. Regardless, she knew her love for him was eternal, just as she was certain his was for her.

Vicky was imagining what she'd say to Max if she ever saw him again, when the door to her hospital room opened all the way. A man she'd never seen before entered and closed the door behind him.

"Is there something I can do for you?" she asked, sitting up straighter in bed.

"Oh, I fully expect you can," the man told her. "Call me Red."

The man who called himself Red moved to the foot of Vicky's bed.

"I'm here about Max Younger," he continued. "I've been doing nothing else but look into him, since his 'body' disappeared in Iraq, and I was already looking into him before, though not close enough clearly."

"And what is it you think you've figured out?"

"The fact that he joined the Navy under a very well-constructed alias and ended up breaking every record in his initial SEAL training put him on my radar. What's kept him there is that even his secrets have secrets and none of them make any rational sense."

"So what do you want from me?"

Red smirked. "First and foremost, to keep you safe. I might be the first to figure out your close connection to Max Younger, but I won't be the last. Far from it. You're about to become very popular on the world stage, Doctor, and not from the kind of people you want on your tail. I can take care of that. I can keep them off your back."

"Why?"

"It's what I do."

"For who exactly?" Vicky asked him.

"I don't carry a badge or an ID, because the group I work for doesn't exist, at least not officially. If I told you our name, you wouldn't recognize it anyway. Suffice it to say we serve State, Defense, the military, and intelligence agencies in equal measure."

"And now you want to help me."

"That's why I'm here," Red told her.

"And what do you want in return?"

"To know where I can find your lover boy."

"He's not my *lover boy*, and I can't help you."

"Do I need to say this is a matter of national security? Do I need to issue the usual threat that we can do this the easy way or the hard way?"

"It won't change the fact that I've got no idea where Max is."

"Maybe not now," Red said, after a taut pause. "But sooner or later, he'll contact you. Help us and your life stays your own. Refuse my polite request and we'll be watching you every minute of every day until we find Max Younger. And that also means exhausting every United States government resource imaginable, no matter the expense or how long it takes."

"Which would be a complete waste of time and money," Vicky told him.

"Why don't we try this a different way," Red said, the cadence of his tone moderating. "Thanks to Max's blood, you're sitting here talking to me, instead of being dead, or much worse."

"Why bother stating the obvious?"

"Because his blood type was the same as yours, but that's where the similarity ends."

"I don't know what you mean."

Red leaned his upper body further over the table. "Yes, you do. The transfusion of his blood saved you because it contained antibodies that killed the infection in you. That allowed your blood to serve as the basis for the vaccine that's going to save the world. So what we have is a young man who was walking around for twenty-eight years with the means to save the world swimming through his veins, once it was mixed with yours. You want to explain that to me?"

Vicky shook her head. "I can't, because I don't know."

"And what about that mark on his palm, inherited from his father who got his while drilling for oil in the Yucatán?"

"Let me ask you a question," Vicky said, sitting up straighter. "What exactly do you want from Max? What is it you think he can do for you?"

Red hedged for the first time since he'd entered the room. "Answering that question would be a violation of protocol, because Max Younger is an asset, an incredible asset that could prove crucial to the national security of the United States. I don't pretend to know everything, or even much beyond anything. But I do know, from what I've seen and managed to string together, that he's someone who needs to be kept safe and on our side. I don't claim to know about how he acquired the . . . well, let's call them skills he's got. All I know is that he's got them. And if there's a rational explanation for the things Max can do, things you've witnessed firsthand, what happened back in Iraq and Syria, I'd love to hear it."

"The world was saved."

"That's not an explanation."

"No, it's a fact. Hate lost."

"To what?"

"Love," Vicky said, with no hesitation at all. "Think about it."

"I have," Red said, scowling in derision, clearly not buying into Vicky's conviction. "And you're not leaving me a lot of choices here, Doctor. First priority for the United States government is to find Max Younger. Our second priority is to make sure the Russian or Chinese don't. If I don't have you helping with Priority one, I'll have no choice but to go with Priority two," Red said, not leaving much doubt as to his true intensions.

"Right," Vicky said, flashing a smirk equal to Red's, "good luck with that."

"Think about what you're doing here, think very hard. Our global enemies won't be nearly as hospitable, if they find him before I do. I don't pretend to have all the details here, but I've got enough to know Max Younger isn't like the rest of us. He's got powers and abilities that defy explanation and, in the wrong hands, could inflict terrible damage."

"That would make you the right hands?"

"Everything's relative, Doctor. I know you want to find him as much as I do. I've got the resources but I'm missing what it will take to draw him out." With that, Red leaned forward over the foot of the bed again, interlacing his fingers before his face. "This is the best way to keep him safe, keep both of you safe, believe me. He needs to be among friends."

"You're not his friend, and Max can take care of himself."

Red moved around to the side of the bed, drawing as close to her as the rail allowed, letting his anger peak through the thin veil disguising it. "When you're talking to me, you're talking to the whole U.S. government. You don't want that as your enemy, you don't want me as your enemy. Trust me on that, Doctor."

"I know my rights," Vicky said, refusing to break his stare. "I can't help you and I don't have to help you. Trust *me* on that."

Red nodded stiffly, and backed away from the bed. "We're not going to stop looking for him, Doctor. And we'll be watching you, listening to you, following you. Welcome to your new life, Doctor. Get used to having company around you all the time."

Vicky lay all the way back down in the tangle of bedcovers. "I'll make sure to add them to my Christmas card list."

# EIGHTY

### The Vatican

Pope Anthony I rode through St. Peter's Square in an open-air vehicle, offering blessings for the multitude of worshippers who'd gathered to celebrate his installation. Hands stretched out, straining toward him. Cameras and cell phones clacked away, taking pictures under the watchful eye of the papal security force that operated in comparable fashion to the American Secret Service. The white vehicle, embossed with the papal crest, crawled on, through cheers so loud that when the gunshots came, few heard them.

Father Pascal Jimenez, dressed in civilian clothes, had met the gaze of the former Josef Martenko an instant before opening fire with his 9mm Beretta, certain enough that his bullets had found their mark, even as a barrage of shots fired by the papal guards punched into him. Jimenez fell to the pavement, dying in a pool of his own blood, but not before glimpsing the new pope's brains splattered over some of the guards whose gunfire had struck him.

"Go with God," Jimenez whispered, facedown on the pavement, as the world turned dark around him, clutching the gold pen that had belonged to his father. "Go with God."

# EIGHTY-ONE

### Rome

Mohammed al-Qadir enjoyed thinking of himself as Cambridge again, especially after so many years of denying himself all the pleasures and luxuries he was free again to partake in. That included staying at the elegant Hotel Michelangelo just a few minutes away from the Vatican. His luxurious room offered a beautiful view of St. Peter's dome and, after so many years spent living like an animal in the desert, he had come to rejoice in the simple joys of things like air-conditioning and room service.

Being fluent in Russian, thanks to his Chechen background, allowed him to slip effortlessly into the identity of a Russian businessman, an identity he'd created just for this eventuality, although he still had to memorize the name imprinted on his new passport. He'd shaved his beard and cut his hair back to the length it had been when he was still known as Cambridge, back to a disguise that had served him well for so many years, until he'd met the man now known as Pope Anthony for the first time back in Nigeria more than a generation before.

They'd both come a long way and had plenty further to go. Together. It would take time to fashion a new plan out of the refuse of the old. The former Father Martenko's new position afforded a far greater platform for them to realize their mutual goals. So al-Qadir was here in Rome, awaiting word of where and when to meet the new pope.

He heard a sudden hail of sirens screaming from the streets beyond, and moved to the window. Staring out through the French doors leading onto the balcony, he spotted what looked like an armada of police and rescue vehicles tearing down the streets in his view, converging, it seemed, on the Vatican.

A deep-seated sense of unease had struck al-Qadir at his very core, when a knock fell on the door, signaling delivery of the room service meal he'd ordered. The blare of sirens and feeling of foreboding had stolen his appetite from him, but al-Qadir still went to the door.

The room service cart crashed into him, as soon as he yanked it open, propelling him backward. Stealing his breath as it slammed him into a wall and pinned him there. He slumped all the way to the carpet when the waiter jerked the cart backward, rattling its contents further. Then al-Qadir looked up and saw the same dark, empty eyes he'd glimpsed in al-Raqqah, before managing to escape. And the man attached to them was holding a silenced pistol against his forehead.

"Get on your knees," Max ordered, holding his pistol in place.

He sneered, refused to break Max's stare.

Max yanked him up to his knees. Then he aimed his pistol downward, straight for al-Qadir's face.

"Now close your eyes."

Al-Qadir shut them, with a smirk, as if still seeking the upper hand. Max moved behind him, withdrawing a knife he pressed against al-Qadir's throat.

"Looks like your God isn't here," Max continued, into his left ear. "Or maybe he's taking the day off. If he is here, ask him to give us a sign and I'll let you live." He stopped to let the words sink in. "Sound familiar?"

"You've caused so much pain, so much suffering," Max resumed. "And now you're going to experience what your victims have experienced. All their humiliation, pain, terror, heartache . . ."

With that, from behind Max laid his palm bearing the same mark as his father upon al-Qadir's forehead. The skin reddened under Max's touch, then spread downward across his face, onto his arms and torso.

Al-Qadir started to rock back and forth, then tremble, his mouth gaping for a scream that never came, the breath seeming to catch in his throat. His eyes snapped open, rolling back in his head to reveal only the whites. His expression stretched into a mask of twisted agony, shaking violently under Max's touch. Then his eyes started bleeding, followed by his nose, mouth, and ears.

Max left his hand in place. "Death won't end the pain either. Welcome to your eternity, every bit of suffering you've ever visited upon the innocent, visited back upon you. What you feel now is just the beginning, death for you is just the beginning of the horror you're going to experience in your blessed afterlife."

Frothy blood began spilling out of al-Qadir's mouth, as he twitched and shuddered. Finally, he keeled over, racked by writhing spasms.

"Because, for you anyway, it turns out hell is real," Max said, as al-Qadir gasped for a final breath.

# EIGHTY-TWO

### Newark, New Jersey

Max knew something was wrong, as soon as the jet stopped short of the Jetway and remained on the tarmac. Moments later, commandos stormed the plane from the rear.

"Nobody move! Nobody move!" Max heard so many voices shout at once, that they melted into each other.

He could tell they were pros, wearing the uniforms of the New York City SWAT team, their spacing and the way they held their weapons showcasing their prowess.

The passengers, including Max, tucked low in their seats, forcing the commandos to check row by row. One of the SWAT team members jerked a teenage boy seated behind him brutally into the aisle, foot pressed against the back of his neck, when Max rose with hands in the air.

"It's me you want," he said, and then they were on him.


"We've got him, sir," Max heard the man he took to be the leader say into a throat mic. "Acknowledged. ETA forty minutes, depending on traffic."

The man looked up, Max's gaze following his to a helicopter circling overhead before he was rousted into the back of a black truck and chained to the floor by both his hands and feet. Six of the commandos joined him in the rear, all with M4 assault rifles trained on him.

Then the double doors were slammed closed and the truck pulled away, led by one SUV and trailed by another.


### New York City

The last thing Dale Denton wanted to do was return to Houston after all that had befallen him and Western Energy Technologies in Cape Horn.

That disaster had not only destroyed the multi-billion-dollar facility, the flooding he'd narrowly escaped had done incredible damage to the island itself. At best, being investigated for his part in an international catastrophe would keep him in court for the next ten years, complicated all the more by criminal charges he was potentially facing at the hands of the Chilean government. At worst, WET would have to file bankruptcy well before that.

Denton had been holed up in the Park Avenue penthouse apartment he'd never sold for almost two weeks now under heavy security. But he'd only shared the possibility that Max Younger might be coming for him with Spalding, and he wouldn't feel safe until the lone child of his late business partner was dead or in custody.

Today his heavy security accompanied Denton to the building WET also still owned and his office on the sixtieth floor, where he'd be meeting with a team of lawyers this afternoon. The press was after him, WET's board of directors was after him, his top investors were after him. And, worst of all, Max Younger might be after him.

The stories coming out of the Middle East were as explosive as they were confounding, impossible to tell where the line between real and tabloid journalism was. One thing they all agreed on was that Navy SEALs had saved the day. And, as soon as he heard that, Denton felt Max Younger had most likely played a big role in that and had managed to survive.

Something had long been afoot that defied any rational explanation. Denton hadn't cared about that when it served his needs, starting all those years ago down in the Yucatán. Now that it didn't, though, he found himself wishing he hadn't tried to tame nature in the form of the rock he remained convinced was behind all of this.

That rock was gone now, either sucked into the late Professor Orson Beekman's black hole, or lying at the bottom of the ocean. Never to be seen again, either way. Pursuing that object had defined Denton's life, his ambitions, for almost thirty years now. In the ultimate irony, those same ambitions, behind all his wealth and achievements, had conspired to destroy him.

But he wasn't done yet.


The man who called himself Red followed the convoy the whole way from a police helicopter tracking it from above, never taking his eyes off the black truck sandwiched between the pair of SUVs, led by a parade of New York City squad cars with lights flashing and sirens blaring.

Then again, nothing about Max Younger was simple. Red had exhausted every intelligence research he'd developed over the years in tracing Younger to an Alitalia flight from Rome that connected in London before continuing on to Newark. Maybe it had been a bit too easy, but he figured Younger was desperate, finally showing his hand.

Either way, Red had him, planning his next move when the convoy disappeared into the Holland Tunnel. He felt his pilot slow the chopper to a hover, waiting for the three vehicles to emerge on the Manhattan side.

But they never did, Red watching the cars that had entered the tunnel after his convoy emerge first, no flashing lights to be seen.

"Shuttle One, come in," he said, into his headset, continuing when there was no response. "Shuttle One, Shuttle One, do you copy?"

Still nothing.

"Shuttle One, report," Red resumed, his voice quickening. "Shuttle One, do you read me."

Dead air.

"Set us down!" Red ordered his pilot. "Set us down!"

There was a cleared, fenced lot not far from the tunnel exit that made for a decent landing pad, and Red leaped out of the chopper just as it touched down. He sprinted through traffic, to the screech of brakes and blare of horns, followed into the tunnel by the two former Force Recon Marines who were his best, and most ruthless, operatives.

Good thing, because he was about to need them.

Red found the convoy an eighth of a mile into the tunnel, the three vehicles squeezed into a construction zone, along with the six police cars escorting them with lights still flashing. As Red approached, palming his own pistol, he could see the patrol cops seated stiffly in their squad cars and the SWAT team members looking out blank-faced from the SUVs.

None of the men acknowledged Red, when he moved straight for the black truck and threw open the double doors, thrusting his pistol into the breach.

The first thing he saw was the chains that had bound Max Younger lying on the floor. Next, he saw the six SWAT team commandos, plus the driver, with flex cuffs lacing all their hands behind their backs. None of them were gagged and they looked at Red in confusion, like they'd just woken up from a deep sleep and had no idea where they were or what they were there for.

"What happened?" Red demanded, already knowing no answers would be coming. *"What the fuck happened here?"*

And he really didn't need to ask, not anymore.

*Maybe it had been a bit too easy . . .*

Of course it was, because Max Younger had used him to get into New York City.

Dale Denton arrived under armed guard to the office tower that had served as WET's original headquarters, and from which Ben Younger had plunged to his death through Denton's own office window. That office had been under constant guard both inside and out. No one had come or gone, as confirmed by Spalding who personally ushered Denton inside an hour ahead of his upcoming meeting.

The giant closed and locked the door behind him, leaving a dozen former special operators armed with assault rifles and submachine guns in the reception area beyond. Denton settled behind his desk in the spray of the sun streaming through the windows to prepare for the coming meeting.

Max entered the lobby of Western Energy Technologies' original headquarters to the accompaniment of canned classical music playing in the background, not a single one of the veritable army of armed guards paying him any heed whatsoever. Neither did the men standing on either side of the elevator that had opened on the sixtieth floor before what looked like a SEAL team in civilian tactical clothing.

Max looked at them, holding their stares as they briefly seemed to note his presence, reaching for their guns, before their gazes went blank, and they looked away, as if he wasn't there at all. He walked right through them, drawing not a motion, a gesture, or even a blink, Max continuing to stare into eyes that did not stare back.

Max glided toward the big double doors ahead with a piece of classical music just reaching its crescendo. It felt as if he was moving through time, slipping through some folded-over flap of it that allowed him to slip through time and space, without actually being there in the physical sense.

The entrance to Dale Denton's office was locked, but the knobs twisted easily in Max's hands, and he pushed through the double doors, feeling them close behind him.

"Shoot him!" he heard Denton cry out. "Kill him!"

And a big, bald man drew his pistol, aimed straight for Max, but he couldn't make his finger pull the trigger. Sweat pouring off his face bent in desperate determination, as Max approached calmly. Max stripped the gun from the big man's grasp and hammered him in the skull with it. Once, twice, three times, until he felt something crack, and the big man crumpled to the floor unconscious.

"It's been a long time, Dale," Max greeted the man behind a big desk with a clear top.

Denton looked toward Spalding, sprawled between his desk and the door. "What . . . How did you . . ."

"It's complicated," Max responded.

Denton reached beneath the sill of his desk to trigger the panic alarm. "I still have photos from that night in the cabin. I'm still a witness to you murdering three men in cold blood. There's no statute of limitations on murder."

Max took a step closer to Denton's desk. "I should have killed you too. But that wasn't the way this was supposed to go, didn't match the plan."

"What plan? *Whose* plan?"

"Think about it."

Denton looked Max up and down, as if trying to make sense of what he was seeing. "What the hell are you?" he asked again.

"The end of days, Dale, yours anyway." Max hesitated. "Go ahead, push your panic button."

Denton did, but nothing happened. His security team didn't appear.

"Guess they're not coming," Max told him. "Maybe there's a short in the wiring somewhere."

Denton jerked a 9mm pistol from beneath the clutter atop his desk and aimed it at Max.

"Go ahead," Max said. "Pull the trigger."

Denton's finger wouldn't move, started to quiver inside the trigger guard.

"Come on, kill me."

Then the gun was heating up in his hand, scalding his flesh. He let go of it, and the pistol rattled atop his desk, his hand scarlet and blistering through the palm where he'd been holding it.

Denton looked down. Steam continued to lift off the searing-hot pistol, its finish peeling off atop the Lucite.

Max took another step forward. "Guess I'm not as easy to kill as my father was. You did it. I know you did."

Denton shook his head. "That's crazy, fucking nuts. He was my best friend. We built this company together. He jumped out that window over there, because he was sick. I don't know, maybe the cancer was eating away at his brain."

Max started around Denton's desk, looming over him "It wasn't cancer."

With that, Max laid a hand on Denton's shoulder and closed his eyes.

# EIGHTY-THREE

### New York City, 2008

'll have him arrested!" Dale Denton raged, in his first meeting with Ben Younger since the Adirondacks. "I'll make sure he never sees the outside of a prison. Hell, do they have the death penalty in New York?"

"He's gone, Dale. You'll never find him, neither will the police."

"Don't test me, Ben."

"I don't have to, because you've already failed. You want to go after my son, ruin me, go ahead. But do that, and the board will learn how you've spent millions off the books on a series of fool's errands. I believe in New York that's called embezzlement."

"I built this goddamn company!"

Ben shook his head, calmly. "*We* built it, in spite of you."

Denton came out from behind the desk. "But there's not going to be a 'we' much longer, is there? You think I don't know how sick you are, that you're dying? And here's some breaking news. I also know your kid's a genetic mess. You want the rest of the world to learn he's a murderer, a psycho, a circus freak, then keep talking. I won't even need the police to find him—his picture will be splashed across airwaves and newspapers from one side of the world to the other. The Internet will have a field day with the story. But go ahead, keep threatening me."

Ben lurched around the desk and jerked Denton out of his chair. "You leave my son alone! This is between you and me!"

Denton barely resisted him. "But he's a part of us now, partner. And he's a monster. You didn't see what he did in that cabin. The world would be better off with him locked away and so would you."

Ben tried to tighten his hold on Denton's shirt, but couldn't find the strength. Felt it draining out of him like a leaky faucet, knew he couldn't hold the grasp much longer.

"Always looking out for my best interests, aren't you, Dale."

Denton brushed him off and away. Effortlessly. "I'm sorry, partner, I truly am. This never would've happened if you hadn't gone down in that cave. It could just as easily have been me."

"Except you didn't have the balls then, and you don't now."

Denton smirked, the bravado-full braggart as always. "But I was always stronger, Ben. Even more so now."

And then Denton grasped him by the lapels, mimicking Ben Younger's own earlier action as he drove him backward, toward the office's biggest window.

The mounts of which he'd loosened, in expectation of this moment, the inevitable upshot of all that had transpired.

Denton gave a final, brutal shove at the last. Ben Younger slammed backward into the window, his weight enough to tear the frame from its loosened mounts and project him out into the air. He'd hit the sidewalk by the time Denton gazed down, nothing of him left recognizable from sixty stories up.

"Nice knowing you, partner."

# EIGHTY-FOUR

### New York City

By then, Denton was shaking so violently he looked to be in the throes of some kind of seizure. Beads of sweat pooled on his face, dripped down into his lap, his clothes already soaked through. His eyes snapped open, regarding Max with a terror that turned his features milk white.

"Care to comment?" Max said calmly, taking his hand from Denton's shoulder and backing away.

Denton's mouth gaped, but only a gurgling sound emerged.

"But the story doesn't end there, does it, Dale? I saw the rest of it too. How even killing my father wasn't enough for you. How you cooked the books so the crooked numbers, your embezzlement, got blamed on my father. You bankrupted my family and sentenced my mother to life in that psychiatric hospital, because she could no longer afford proper care."

Denton tried to speak, this time managing only a guttural gasp.

"You should have left well enough alone, but you couldn't, could you? So you came after me at Creedmoor, and then again in Canada. Would you like me to tell you exactly what I did to your goons up there?"

Denton wheezed.

"You destroyed my family," Max continued, "and now you're going to pay for your sins."

"Did I, did I really?" Denton managed to rasp, the words oozing, leaking, out of his mouth. "Or was it you? Apple of your father's eyes." Denton shook his head, Max seeming to be moving away from him. "Know something? You're just like . . ."

"What's the matter, Dale, cat got your tongue? Hey, where you going?"

• • •

At first, Denton thought it was Max Younger who was moving, realizing quickly it was actually him, as if yanked along by an invisible force, its tether too tight to fight.

Toward the window. The same window he'd pushed Ben Younger through a decade before.

As his legs continued to take him toward the window, picking up speed, Denton gathered all the air he could and screamed at the top of his lungs.

*"Help me! HELLLLLLLLLLP ME!"*

"Your guards can't hear you, Dale, they can't hear anything. Scream all you want, if it makes you feel better."

Denton fought with all his strength to resist the invisible force tugging him. He tried to dig his feet into the priceless Persian carpet, but the force dragged him on across it, his heels buckling, until he finally smacked hard into the window.

"You're the real monster, Dale, and you murdered my father."

"He was already dead," Denton said, shaking horribly as the force pressed him tight against the glass, his words barely intelligible.

"But you destroyed his legacy, his reputation, sentenced my mother to live out her life in the same place you're going now."

Denton screamed again, but the pressure against the window swallowed his cry, even as the glass cracked along neat fracture lines.

"Hell, Dale. Fitting, don't you think?"

The cracks crisscrossed, deepened. And then Denton felt the force yank him one last time, the glass giving way and the swirling winds beyond greeting him. And then he crashed through the window, following Ben Younger into oblivion.

# EPILOGUE

### The Tropics, three weeks later

They were making love on the beach under the spill of a sky full of twinkling stars that shimmered off the placid sea, and made the grains of white sand look like miniature pearls. Their bodies were cushioned by the soft breeze blowing over the currents that lapped over their feet. Vicky never wanted to leave Max's arms, wanted to feel him inside her, feel his breath upon her. She wanted this night to last forever, and it would because they would be together forever, the stars forever shining over them.

The pleasure, the ecstasy, felt eternal, like nothing she'd ever experienced before, just as her love for Max was. There was him, the sand, the stars, and nothing else. That was all she needed, all she wanted. Ever. For time immemorial. If there was more to her life, she didn't know it now and didn't want to.

"I love you, Max. Promise me you'll never leave me again, promise!" Vicky said, feeling sand in her hair and her feet still wet from the gentle currents lapping over them in the last minute before . . .

She woke up, bolting upright in the dark of her bedroom, to the realization it had all been a dream.

And yet, and yet . . . it was so real. . . .

"I love you, Max," she repeated, fully awake this time. "And I miss you so much."

### Paraguay

I miss you too, Vicky, Max thought playfully, as he lay on the roll mattress, shielded by the canopy of the jungle that swayed softly overhead. "And I love you too."

Vicky's thoughts were as real as words, sounding in his mind instead of his ears. It had been hard for him to leave her this time; it was getting harder *every* time. But this was all they had for now, and it would have to suffice.

He lay back again and cupped his hands behind his head, staring up at the bright stars and wondering if real sleep would come to him tonight. Sleep without visions or nightmares, pictures of things yet to be or that had already come; it was difficult to tell, and Max wasn't sure he wanted to. Wasn't sure he wanted anything in his life to tempt him back to the world he had abandoned.

Being alone here, in the middle of nowhere, made him feel safe, made him feel . . . normal. Alone, but connected to Vicky, which meant he wasn't alone, not really. Here, in the middle of nowhere, he was safe from the world and the world was safe from him.

The wind rustled through the trees, the chirp of night birds and the clacking of insects forming his lullaby.

Max closed his eyes and drifted off to sleep.

### The Mariana Trench

The specially designed, robotic submersible had just passed the point of the deepest depth ever recorded, when its aft-mounted camera caught something on the bottom of the sea, more than five miles beneath the surface.

"Is that a . . . light?" wondered oceanographer Frank Tull, of the research vessel *Mariner*, as he huddled with other personnel behind the submersible's pilot.

"Let's take a closer look," the pilot said, maneuvering the submersible, affectionately known as *Mariana*, after the trench that represented the deepest depth of any in the sea, around and lowering it toward the strange glow that had emerged from the darkness.

"What is *that*?" Tull asked, a shape growing before the tight cluster of marine scientists watching the screen.

"If I didn't know better . . ."

"Go on," Tull prodded the submersible pilot.

The pilot started to extend the submersible's robotic arm, manipulating the joystick to ease it toward the light that, closer up, seemed to emanate from a core of jet-black darkness. That effect created a strange hue that could best be described as neither light, nor darkness.

More like, a dark light.

"Where's that light originating from at such a depth?" Tull asked.

"Beats me," the pilot told him, clearly mystified.

Tull moved closer to the screen, hoping to get a better look at the object. "If I didn't know better . . ."

"It looks like, well, a rock of some kind," the pilot finished for him, working the joystick to capture the object in the robotic arm's pincer-like extension.

"Careful."

The pilot snared the rock between the pincers. "Got it!"

Tull patted him on the shoulder. "Good work. Now, let's bring it up and take a closer look."

*Mariana* had barely begun her ascent back to the surface, when Tull heard the captain's voice over the loudspeaker from the bridge. "Attention all personnel, attention all personnel! Radar shows a big storm coming in fast. Damn thing sprang up out of nowhere! Prepare for heavy weather. Repeat, prepare for heavy weather."

Tull grabbed a handhold to steady himself, continuing to follow *Mariana*'s view of the black depths, as the submersible rose toward the surface. "Looks like we're in for a rocky ride."